WANTED & WIRED

VIVIEN JACKSON

sourcebooks
casablanca

Published by Sourcebooks Casablanca, an imprint of Sourcebooks, Inc.
P.O. Box 4410, Naperville, Illinois 60567-4410
(630) 961-3900
Fax: (630) 961-2168
www.sourcebooks.com

Printed and bound in Canada.
MBP 10 9 8 7 6 5 4 3 2 1

To Jen DeLuca, for talking me off that ledge so damn many times.

# CHAPTER

1

Mari adjusted the rifle butt against her shoulder and thumbed the bolt, chambering a custom wildcat. She had nine more rounds in a box magazine, but she wouldn't need them. Mari didn't miss.

Correction: she wasn't *used* to missing. If there was one thing she could count on in this whole fucked-up universe, it was her own aim on the squeeze. Steady. Fearless. Badass. That was her. She wasn't some shaking, wibbly mess of a thing.

And yet, a ribbon of sweat tickled her eyebrow, and her trigger finger burned to move. *The fuck?*

Her elbows squished in cool mud, but it didn't soften the concrete beneath them. She lay prone two stories up in a half-finished shell of a building, waiting out her target. Folks said that once upon a time, southern California was pretty, crammed full of gorgeous weather and gorgeouser people. Hard to believe that description these days, though. Now, an ocean of filthy water gave way to a dirtier sea of concrete, butted up tight against the mountains and stark, baked desert beyond. But ugly didn't bother Mari. Dirty didn't either. She was used to both.

In fact, nothing about this setup struck her as odd. Not the stark, posturban downtown encased in fat black clouds that pissed stagnant drizzle over everything. Not the chill of cement dust turned to mud. Not even the miasma of mildew and petrichor.

So if it wasn't the place making her batshit crazy, it must be the thing. The job. The mech-clone.

Mech-clone. N series. Indistinguishable from a human person. Oh God, why'd it have to be one of those? A tremble rolled up from her belly, and she gnawed it into her bubble gum.

"Mari?" The voice in her earpiece cushioned her panic somewhat.

"Yeah, I'm in position," she mouthed into her com rig. A receiver embedded in her throat picked up the vibration of her subwhisper and transmitted it to her remote partner, Heron. She didn't even need to speak. He was right there in her head, or at least his voice was.

"I can see that," he said evenly. "Read me in on the rest of it."

Mari laid her gaze down the sightline and took a couple of long, steady breaths. "Uh, I got a bead on the building. No movement so far, which really isn't that unexpected, given we're peeking at a holoporn suite at midday. Fancy-pants one, too. Don't you figure patrons at a place like this would have day jobs?"

"I try not to think about the proclivities of our targets," he said witheringly. Except the words didn't wither, not when he said them. He had a way of making his voice sound like exactly what she needed to hear. In another man, she'd call it magic. In Heron, it was probably wetware calibration. "But I was asking about neither the building nor the mech-clone, querida. What is *your* status?"

For instance, he said *your* exactly as if he gave a shit. Not just about the job, but about her. And that warmed her up far more than it should have.

Logically, Mari knew where she stood with him. He might call her querida from time to time, but in the same offhand way bar rats back home had called her ma'am. They hadn't meant it as a mark of respect. Just like Heron didn't mean to imply she was dear to him.

They were working partners, sharing a contract but not much else. On this particular job, she functioned as shooter to his operations planner, but he had lots of other assets in play: drones, cameras, software bots, you name it. More dependable assets, too. Of the lot, she was the only one who had to get talked down from having the shakes.

Which, weirdly enough, had lessened. They hadn't gone away entirely, but at least her hands were steady, dogs to the Pavlov of his voice. She could do this.

"Oh, you know me." She flattened the gum behind her incisors. "Always itching to kill something." Which wasn't true at all, but it sounded appropriately badass.

"Not kill. The contract is to capture or destroy a stolen mech-clone. It isn't living and never was. It's just a machine."

"It's a pretty fucking special machine, though. There are, what, ten known N series mech-clones in the whole world? This contract is big balls, at least for me. I gotta get it right." Heron might have pulled bigger, more high-profile contracts, but most of Mari's work was small-time property destruction and softkill intercepts. She could bring down a drone like nobody's business. But then, most drones didn't look like people.

She shouldn't have taken this job. Everything about it stank to high heaven. Heron had been against it from the start. But then, on the flip side, there was that payout she'd been promised. The thing that would make it all worthwhile. The thing she hadn't told her partner about yet.

Heron didn't say anything for a long while. Silence roared where his voice should be. Then, "If it's really bothering you, we can call this off right now. You know I'd rather capture the mech-clone and return it intact. I believe I know who it belongs to."

Mari forced breath through her gum, popping a quiet bubble. "Nah, let's take this fucker out. Less messy, no loose ends, and we don't have to pack it up and ship it afterward. Just get your drone ready to vid the kill confirmation."

"The bounty would be higher on a capture," he reminded her. "And we could sell it to somebody other than Texas."

The way he said *Texas* got her hackles up, but she bit back a defensive reply. Depending on who you talked to, postsecession Texas was either a geopolitical object lesson in what not to do or else a deep hick land of lawless gun-toters, enviro-containment zones, barbed wire, and whacked-out technocrats.

"What was it you said about the proclivities of our clients? That we don't need to like them?"

"My reservations have nothing to do with our client's hobbies or fetishes. Quite simply, I don't trust the Texas Provisional Authority."

Heron's voice on the com was as carefully modulated as ever, so maybe Mari was imagining the criticism. Maybe she was just too sensitive about where she came from.

"They got money same as anybody, maybe more if those power grid rumors are true."

"I'm not talking about the payout, querida. I'm talking about you. I don't trust them with you." He paused. "I can get you other contracts. ZaneCorp is looking to take out the group that hacked them last month. Their data center is off the coast of Belize. Easy job, nice payout, white sand beaches nearby. You could wear a bikini *and* use explosives."

Her mouth relaxed into a half grin. Regardless of the fact that they didn't socialize outside of work, this man knew her far too well. "Nah, we've been over this. I got a job to do here." She pushed the gum against her soft palate. "Anyhow, don't you got something better to do than chat me up while I'm working?"

"Your bios spiked." She could almost see his articulated shrug, a movement that was too smooth, too deliberate. And also god-awful sexy. "You *are* my mission priority."

So hard not to sigh. Mission. Job. That's all she was to him. Getting her in and out of jobs was the beginning and end of his care for her.

No matter that she had a thing for skinny, dark-haired smart-asses—even biomechanically enhanced ones. No matter that sometimes she thought of him as her guardian angel out here when things got hairy. No matter that she wished sometimes—okay, lots of times—that she could take him with her on a downtime, one of those booze-hazy interstices between jobs. Her usual contracts—thieving, demolition, corporate data smuggling—paid well enough that she could hie off for a few weeks after, blank her mind, and abuse her body in all the best ways.

She tried to picture Heron with her in one of those downtimes. Sand, still warm from the sun, now splashed with bonfire and moonlight, music so loud her bones throbbed, and Heron lounging beside her, ass naked and relaxed, swirling a margarita. With his tongue.

Whoa. Well, if she was looking to settle herself, that mental image sure wasn't gonna do it.

Except it had.

Or maybe just talking to him had. Regardless of the cause, sometime during all that salacious thinking and silent chitchat, the quavers in her knuckles had eased. Gone was the overwhelming need to twitch, to run, to scrub the burnt-rain smell out of her sinuses. Just that easily, Mari found her groove and settled in a half inch of mud.

She didn't move after that, not even when the stolen mech-clone exited the building two blocks down, look-ing dapper in its vat-grown skin and tasseled couture waistcoat. And also looking exactly like the recon vid Heron had taken. Stolen, high-end, whoa-expensive little shit. And slagging it was going to buy her a trea-sure in information.

The gun rested cool and perfect in her sense-gloved hands, a high-caliber extension of her will.

A novice would pull the trigger now, but Mari was far

too veteran for that. She trusted Heron to let her know when her angle was best, when she'd be clear of drone interference. She was pretty damned accurate, maybe the best human shooter around, but Heron's post-human brain could still parse inputs more efficiently than hers.

Now she waited for his sign, and it came nine chews into her bubble gum: an aural ping in her earpiece. Mari moved her thumb atop the barrel and painted her target.

"Got your big red dot," Heron said. "Stand by for the microwave blast. In three."

She stretched her gaze through the scope—

"Two."

—braced her feet against two construction-tarp spikes—

"One."

—and eased the trigger back. It gave under pressure like a milk-sopped cookie, and it was just as sweet.

Four hundred meters away, the microwave burst from Heron's drone and the wildcat slug from Mari's gun hit simultaneously. Mari slammed her eyes shut at the moment of impact.

Heron's blast would blind security direction sensors and simple electronics, bringing down personal shields, leaving the target naked. Mari's bullet would slip in, finish the job. It would. Her angle had been perfect. She didn't need to watch. Couldn't, in fact. She had a habit of not looking death in the face, not even machine death. So long as she turned her head the other way, she wouldn't catch it looking back.

She waited for Heron's subvocal kill confirmation, but it didn't come right away. Odd. Her hands tensed, ready for the second tap.

"We good?" she mouthed into the com.

With her eyes still closed, she played these seconds in her mind, what her target would look like going down. Her custom bullets would fragment on impact, dispersing chemicals cooked up specially to ruin electronics, such as the crud in a mech-clone's skull. Couldn't have anybody vulturing the corpse afterward and trying to reverse engineer it. Her contract instructions were pretty specific on that point.

When the brain-like innards were goo, the mech-clone would twitch, slow, and then tip over, gears whirring. No matter how much they resembled human beings, all mech-clones reverted to their true nature when they got slagged. Junk heaps. Scrap metal with fake skin.

Mari tentatively opened her eyes and stared down the scope. This target sure didn't look right. There was blood everywhere, and its head lolled out to the side, hanging on by a red noodle of tissue. Mech-clones usually took high-caliber clean, as if they were armored all over. She'd expected a throat shot to incapacitate but not tear her target apart like that.

She swallowed.

"We got it." Heron's voice sounded tight.

A jolt of wrongness zinged up her spine, but she didn't have time to analyze it. Right now, she needed to get her shit together. Her com had initiated a countdown at the squeeze, giving her twenty-eight minutes to break down her weapon, toss some clothes on over her muddy tank and leggings, and meet Heron at the street-level bodega for extraction. She had the bipod folded, the dust cover popped, and the recoil assembly and barrel tucked safely in a snazzy floral-print duffel before she peeked through the detached scope again. She shouldn't have taken the time, but she couldn't help herself. She had to *know*.

Traffic had tangled around the scene. Even the commuter pods had stopped. As she watched, some guy skidded his Ducati right to the curb and lined up his wristplant to record the whole thing, probably so he could post it on his channel later and get an IWasThere achievement. Sick fucking bastard. No way that dude could've guessed the corpse on the concrete was a mech-clone. For all he knew, he'd just seen a whole-organic murdered.

He should be horrified, and instead, he'd swooped like a vulture to the gore. Clearly, there were several ways a girl could define *inhuman*.

"Mari?"

She tore her gaze away from the scene. Stuffed the scope into the duffel. Zipped up. "Yeah?"

"Slight change of plans. I need you to cut through the alley, heading eastward. Reclamation crews framed in enough of that building that you should have some cover. Just keep tight to the wall in case security has drones up. There's an autobus stop on Sixth, right in front of a taco cart. I'll be behind the number 13."

"Which is arriving in"—Mari consulted her countdown—"twenty-three minutes?"

"No. More like seven. Move."

●　●　●

For Heron, keeping to a speed limit was like wearing a monk's collar three sizes too small. A car like this wasn't meant to be penned, and *he* certainly wasn't. He crept up behind the fat city bus, trying very hard not to ram it just to vent some of his frustration.

He'd failed. After all these years looking out for her, protecting her, he'd failed. The job was a disaster.

He'd watched that microwave burst from his drone take down all electronics within a ten-meter diameter. The bodyguards had wilted like wet tissue. But not the target. He had been willing to allow for some resilience in this target, some extra shielding, given that it was an advanced model, but then Mari's bullet had hit. It should have slagged the mech-clone within seconds. Should have.

With the last of its power, his drone had transmitted kill confirmation images. Startlingly clear. Horrifyingly clear. That blood. All that blood. Whole-organic blood, not process Red No. 72.

The contract hadn't named names, but Heron had run the target through the United North American Nations facial recognition.

He knew whose blood that was.

They were being paid to slag the mech-clone, vat-grown, machine-hearted imposter of Daniel Neko. Not the real Neko. Mari wouldn't have taken a whole-organic assassination contract, not even if the fucking Texas Provisional Authority had promised to wrap her missing dad up in Christmas paper and deliver him to her postbox.

At least he didn't think she would.

But what if they *had* made such a promise? An unspoken agreement he wasn't privy to. She would have told him. Right? They were partners. Of course she would have told him. But once the suspicion niggled into his brain, Heron couldn't make it go away. He hated doubting her like this, but...*shit*.

And after all he'd done to keep her insulated from the chaos.

He inhaled deliberately and connected to a mirror. He wouldn't log into the cloud, not in real time. Couldn't trust himself there. Last time he'd connected directly to the cloud with no firewalls or buffers, things had gone...badly.

When his mirror connection was set, the augments at his temples projected a heads-up display, showing him data streams from the crime. Alert systems from the traffic cameras in that area notified local police, who notified regional paramilitary, blip blip blip...and there went the North American counterterrorism command.

Now Mari was flagged as an enemy of the United North American Nations. A Texas rebel. A public danger. Shoot on sight.

Not good.

It was just a matter of time before the UNAN offered a bounty, and then a whole horde of vigilante, anti-Texas continentalists would also be aiming for her. Mari. His partner. His responsibility. His...*damn it*. Heron's hands gripped the steering wheel so tightly, it cracked.

For a second, all he could do was look at the break. Technically, he didn't need the steering wheel, not in this car. Steering and gear progression went through his neural, but he liked the connection, having his hands on the car, driving it. At the moment, though, fracturing the steering wheel hurt. A physical pang, like a broken tooth.

He blinked again, logged off the mirror, and scrubbed

the connection, then smoothed his fingers over the leather wrap, testing the fissure beneath. It throbbed.

He needed to order his thoughts. He needed to plan. He needed control.

The autobus in front of him whirred atonally, shredding his calm. All-electrics were required by city ordinance to emit sounds to alert pedestrians and other vehicles of their approach. But nothing in the law said they had to sound like intoxicated crickets. Heron extended his wireless bubble outward from the car, touching it to the back of the bus. He caught the synthetic audio wave on wireless, deconstructed it to its base musical components. Gave it melody. Overlaid it with some John Williams. Bounced it back through the bus's onboard speakers. Now that ugly behemoth farted something approximating "The Imperial March." Ahhh, control. He was back in charge of this extraction, a realization that soothed him almost as much as speeding.

But not nearly as much as catching sight of *her* at the bus stop, exactly where he'd told her to wait. Mari. Safe. Looking like springtime in a pink sweater and holding that pretty really-her-converted-rifle-barrel parasol against one shoulder. She'd taken off the sense gloves she used for shooting—he could feel them wadded up in her duffel, still transmitting—so he scanned her com instead, counting her pulse, measuring her pupil dilation and blood chemical levels. Not an adrenaline spike in her whole body.

She popped her bubble gum and leaned against a Plexiglas route map. Cool as a daiquiri was Mari.

He waited for the bus to pull away from the stop and then rolled his car to the curb, about a meter from her mud-caked wellies. Green ones, with tiny sunflowers on the pull loops. He moved one hand off the steering wheel, signed a command, and her door shished open.

She leaned in, twirling the parasol, flinging errant raindrops all over his contrast-piped leather interior. Cool sprinkles, like cupcake dusting. A dimple tucked itself next to her flirty smile. "Hey, stranger. Goin' my way?"

Heron pressed his lips into a line. "No funning, please. Get in. Quickly."

"No kiddin' no fun," she muttered under her breath, probably forgetting that her com was subvocal. Although she was sharp as a shiv when her hands were on a gun, she could forget crucial things on planning and extraction. Or she deliberately relied on him to keep all that sorted.

Either way, Heron didn't mind. He reached through the wireless and shut down her com.

She furled the umbrella, tossed it to the floorboard, and folded herself into the passenger seat. Heron had the door down as soon as her skirt was clear of the seals.

He'd examined this sector extensively in planning and had every escape route timed down to the second. He hadn't counted on the law enforcement response being so fast, though, almost instantaneous. Road blocks and drones were popping up like dandelions every time he polled the mirror, and he had no defenses set up to counter them.

He knew precisely the speed at which information flowed, and there was no way within normal parameters the authorities could know her identity and location this quickly. Clearly, Mari had been set up. He even had a good idea who'd done it. The cloud, with its delicious glut of information, hovered just beyond his vision, tempting. He could see her doom erupting, 33.3 milliseconds behind real time, and he couldn't do a damn thing to stop it.

No, that wasn't true. He had a range of options, but the only one he allowed himself, the only one that made sense, was to get her away from here. Get her somewhere safe. Hide her.

Traffic became a torment, not just because his escape was slowed or capture crept closer with each passing second, but also because…she was here. Close. Too close. Within touching distance close. He could practically feel her vibrating with postjob adrenaline. Just eight blocks to the expressway entrance ramp. He endured them. Every bloody inch. Every stroke of her naked hands on the cushion. Every drip of skin-warmed rainwater from her ponytail, teasing its way down between her shoulder blades and along the seatback. Every push of her breath against damp synthetic cashmere. Every distant siren, every rolling update from his mirror… Interpol had her bios now, but he suspected the UNAN agents would find her first.

No. Over his goddamned corpse they would.

He hit the entrance ramp at 120 and blew into the cruise lane. The wireless exchange with the bus earlier had reminded him of another closed system, off-cloud. A bigger one. Private. Safe.

"Thought our exit vector was south. Cabana down in Cabo San Lucas and an endless tab of mojitos? This ringing a bell, partner?" Mari craned to see a road sign too blurry to read with naked eyes.

Heron cataloged the sign, crossed three lanes, and

slung the car onto a flyover, taking them decidedly not south.

"I told you our plans had changed. No cabana this time, but don't worry. I'm taking you someplace safe."

"What place? *Your* place?" She waggled her eyebrows.

He inhaled deliberately. *She doesn't mean it the way it sounds. It is not an invitation. You know how she is.* Bald come-hithers and poor timing were typical of her postjob process. Everybody had a different way of ramping up and down for jobs like this, and hers was invariable. A peek at her biometrics showed elevated hormone levels in her blood. Flight or fight or fuck, and Mari had an unnatural ability to suppress the first.

Any other job, he'd have her on a plane by now and off to the hired harem of cabana boys she needed to seduce to prove she was still alive. But this wasn't any other job. This was a botch. On a contract held by Texas. She was in danger, and he didn't have time to wrestle with her attempts to make him into another of her temporary playthings.

Temporary, because the only time she'd be able to stomach fucking a post-human would be right after a job. And then she'd hate herself after. He knew what she thought about people with implanted tech. Cyborgs. No better than machines.

And he sported a metric shitload of implanted tech.

So he'd kept their relationship purely professional, and there had never been a reason to alter that structure. Until today. Now, to keep her safe, he was willing to suffer a lot more than her derision. He was willing to lay bare his most deeply held secrets and hope she didn't heckle. Or worse, send him away.

He accelerated through fourth gear, and the car lowered, uncomplaining, hugging the asphalt.

Fuck it all—he was taking her home.

*　*　*

Mari hadn't completely come off the postjob high, but even in her present jitterbug state, she could tell something was wrong. Like, flat-out, fucked-up wrong. And dollars to doughnuts it had something to do with that bloody mess on the sidewalk downtown.

She'd brought down mech-clones before. A whole shipping container full of them once. Man, that thing had burned. But every time she slagged one of those fuckers, they fought it, gears whirring, electrics sparking, machines till the end. They didn't bleed like her target had today. They didn't just fall down, give up.

She swallowed, but her throat was dust-dry, and it hurt.

But more painful was the stark truth: she'd just offed a whole-organic. She closed her eyes tight and swallowed past the burn.

Some of her work was illegal, stuff governments and corporations needed done but didn't want on their transparency-touting newsfeeds. Convenient, inexpensive plausible deniability with a gun: that was Mari. But she was fairly low on the food chain of freelance chaos wreakers, and the jobs she ran, while legally iffy and dangerous, generally didn't draw law enforcement notice. Who cared about a missing vat of nanos or a stolen pallet of vanadium batteries or a slagged mech-clone? Even a pricey limited-run mech like that one today was likely to go down without too much trouble. The authorities had bigger fish to fry.

Murder of a whole-organic, though…that was a whole different thing. High stakes. Felony. Thirty to life.

Murder hadn't been part of this contract. And even besides the legal shitstorm it brought down on her head, having done something *that* wrong…hurt. Hollowed her out, filled the new empty space with guilt and dark and yuck.

And memories. Wispy scraps of memory, sneaking up on her like flies when she had lived the last eight years perfectly happy without them. They were looking to swarm her. Soon. She could already feel them pressing around her, cutting off her air.

She squashed them mercilessly. Couldn't wig out now. Not in front of him. *Keep it together, girl. Just a little longer.*

She pinched the com unit at her throat and pulled, disconnecting the embeds.

"You okay?" Heron didn't look at her when he spoke, just stared straight ahead at the highway, unreadable but using that voice. The velvet, wubby, hot-toddy delicious one.

She snuck a glance at him, wondering if he got an alert or something when she removed the com. A muscle might have flexed just below his jaw. Or it might not've.

Mari's control over her aim was laser precise, perfect, but Heron exerted that kind of control over *everything*. His job, his environment, his drones. His body. Every movement was deliberate, every scowl of his narrow mouth, every crick of those long fingers. When ink-dark hair fell over his eyebrows—and it did that a lot—he never brushed it aside. He acted like he wanted it there, untidy. His odd mix of self-possession and mystery was a cocktail Mari had a damn hard time resisting.

A year ago, when they'd first met, she wouldn't have given a second thought to somebody so obviously post-human. Folk with that much metal in them weren't really people—or so she'd been raised to believe. But since they'd partnered up, she'd come to rely on his immutable self-control. And his care. Yeah, that too.

"No worries. I'm just cold," she said. "From the rain."

He didn't move, but the vent in the dash angled and breathed heat over her knees. Sweet-smelling heat: almond, neroli, leather. Mari rolled up her skirt a few inches and let the air lick her leggings, warming the mud. Humidity built up in the galoshes, and she kicked them off, stretching her toes under the machine heaters. *Ahhhhh*.

She dropped her head against the seatback and settled into the leather, but relaxation wouldn't come. Instead, a claw of panic scratched the inside of her skull. She shoved it down. Hard. *Later, darkthing. Lemme keep it together just a little bit longer, at least while he's here. I'll let you wreck me as much as you want when it's just me and you. Deal?*

She sucked in a breath, concentrated on how baby-butt-soft that leather was. Concentrated on Heron's classic aquiline profile, his steady hands on the steering wheel, the sweet heat enveloping her body.

"So, partner, when are you planning on telling me how badly I just fucked up?"

Definitely a muscle twitch that time. She caught it.

"When we're clear," he said. "Patience."

He dipped the car into a trash alley between two multistories. About forty feet this side of the corner, a ramp led to a parking garage, and Heron turned down it without decelerating.

Mari grabbed the oh-shit handle above her door and dug her bare toes into the plush carpet. She had to remind herself that he wasn't depending on vision like she was. He had eye implants; he could drive blind. Theoretically.

Two levels down, he angled the car past a rusted-out delivery truck with naked wheels. Behind it yawned a hole in the wall, about eight feet square and beetle black.

The tension roiling off him eased down here, now they were hidden a bit, and she let some of that calm rub off on her. She recognized where they were headed but was kind of surprised. Originally built by the drug-smuggling cartels back when borders other than Texas existed on the continent, sin tunnels didn't show up on maps, not even the anomalous-gravity spreads, which made them perfect transit lanes for criminals and other off-grid folk. Going deep into one made total sense now.

She just hadn't expected a guy like Heron to know about the sin tunnels, much less ferret out the entrance to one. She'd never pegged him as hard-core into illegal shit, despite the contracts they'd worked together. Far as she knew, she was his only team for shady jobs. He seemed more like a byte jockey who'd gotten mixed up with the wrong crowd.

Mari being the wrongest possible crowd, of course. But maybe he hadn't needed her to connect him with illegality after all. If he knew about tunnels, what other seedy underground stuff was he involved in? Suddenly, his trademark reticence and calm weren't prissy at all. Suddenly, they were mysterious, maybe even…wicked. Bad. And Mari was just girl enough to breathe a little harder at that.

Clearly unaware of the salacious turn her thoughts

had taken, Heron shoved the car into the space with centimeters to spare, and it was like going down a drain. Everything went black. Silence roared in. The car's engine cut off, too, though they still hurtled forward.

"I can't run a combustion engine without good ventilation, so we're switching to the electric," he explained. "And we're safe, relatively speaking. So here."

Something landed in her lap. Plastic, cool, rounded edges. Mari stuck a ragged fingernail in the seam, unfolded the vintage phone, and thumb-navved to the messages. Most folks had gone over to implanted coms, but Mari was determined to sidestep the biohacking fad for as long as possible. She was proud of her all-human self, most times, despite her flaws. Besides, she liked the heft of an old-time phone in her hand. Felt a teensy bit like a grenade.

"Well? Did they pay what we asked?" He could have peeked, but he didn't. He just sat there not looking at her, not looking at the phone in her hand. Waiting.

She hunted for the funds transfer message…and maybe something else.

Come on.

"Nothing about our money, but…" She swiped through a stream of law enforcement bulletins featuring crackly overhead vids of her handiwork today and… *shit.* Now, *that* pic wasn't from today.

Darkthing panic squeezed the base of her throat. "How'd they…?"

"The police knew it was you right away. I have no idea how they found out, but one must assume somebody set you up."

Mari opened her mouth, closed it, swallowed…or tried to. "Texas?"

Their contract had been through the Texas Provisional Authority, the pseudogovernment that had been set up after secession, or at least the faction that seemed to be in charge at the moment. And "in charge" basically meant the group with the best plan for getting the nascent government's economy out of the shitter.

These particular dudes were technocrats, folks who thought that the smartest people ought to be the ones in charge. According to Mari's Aunt Boo, who still lived in Lampasas, the technocrats were about as useless as the last faction that had assumed control, but at least she'd had electricity to run her air-conditioning last summer, which was something of an improvement.

Plus, the TPA had won some goodwill recently by capturing a UNAN detention facility and releasing political prisoners, folks who had been rounded up as Texas sympathizers during the Austin riots and the crazy months that followed. Mari had watched vid of the prisoners coming out of their cages, haggard and squinting against the sunlight. People detained against their will held a soft spot in her chest to begin with, and she couldn't help scanning those vids for something else besides. One face. She didn't find it.

When her contact had messaged her details on a job sponsored by this new technocrat-run TPA, a job that seemed right up her alley and paid well besides, she hadn't been thinking with her cautious brain. She'd been thinking with her heart. *Dad*.

They'd told her they had her father, that the TPA had taken him after the Austin riots and was keeping him safe. They'd promised to tell her where he was, or at least let her speak to him.

She hadn't been able to say no to that. No matter what they'd asked, she would have done it.

To give him his due, Heron had warned her taking this contract wasn't a good idea. He'd said something seemed off about their initial info packet. And she'd still jumped in with both feet, dragging him along with her.

She stared hard at the pic. It was about six years old, taken back when she'd been in the habit of coloring her hair about as often as she changed her mind. She no longer worried so much about her looks. The price of fixing them was too high, both in aggravation and in money.

She couldn't recall having this photo taken, but that wasn't anything new. Her memories could get slinky, especially the bits from before the south Texas prison, before Nathan and the deep hole she'd had to claw out of afterward. In the image, she was smirking at the photographer.

In Austin. She could see the lake in the distance and the Pennybacker Bridge. The bridge no longer existed. Sometimes, she felt like the girl didn't either.

She swiped a thumb over the pic, leaving a smear of damp on the screen, and navved back to the list of messages.

"Look, I'm monitoring law enforcement," Heron told her. "It might seem bad now, but, Mari, it's going to be all right. You will be safe."

As if his just saying it rendered it so. Still, his voice was as dark and cozy as the tunnel blurring past the window, and Mari longed to pull it all around her like a blanket and snuggle deep. So deep she didn't have to think.

"The chatter on the cloud is that we just disappeared, and now the various departments are blaming each other.

Plus, I have red herring drones up all over. Tracking those things should occupy the authorities until our backup extraction team arrives."

She should have known he'd have a contingency plan, even for a major fuckup like this. "How long have we got?"

He made a sound that might have been a groan, only lots shorter and kind of strangled. "Two hours."

Two hours. In a tunnel. Mari slid a glance over to the driver's seat. In the meager light of the phone, she could make out his profile. He wasn't looking at her. Normally she'd be thinking ten thousand things she could do to him in two hours in the dark. And to be honest, even with death on her heels and panic in her gut, she could have gotten up for a few of those things.

"So we just hunker down for a bit? I can do that." But she couldn't, and she knew it. Her pulse thudded like a lit grenade chain behind her ribs. She imagined sirens beneath the faint vibration of the electric engine. Her body hummed.

And then Heron looked at her. She had no idea how he managed it, but despite the too-precise posture and carefully articulated movement, when that man turned the full force of his attention on her, the humming stopped. The guilt stopped. Time itself stopped. All that pause filled up with warmth.

The blue light of the LED outlined the sharp angles of his face, severity easing to care as she watched. Because of her? Was he more human when he looked at her, or was she just seeing it more clearly?

He pulled the phone from her nerveless hand. His gloves were butter soft and warm, cradling her cold knuckles.

She bit the inside of her cheek, then let it slide out from between her teeth. "I should tell you some stuff about me," she said. "I got this… I need to… Oh lord, this is hard to say. Look, it's hard enough for me to come off a job in any case, but this job was such a fuckup, and it's so much worse, and I might…"

"Wig out?" He smiled.

He looked different when he smiled, less intimidating, less machine. Of course, Mari, being the girl she was, only wanted to kiss that mouth more. She wondered if she ought to warn him what his smiling did to her.

"Heh. Yeah. What I really need right now is sleep, to force myself to step down, y'know?" *And also to keep my grabby hands off your bod when clearly you have no interest in hitting this.* "You don't happen to have an injector of happiness you're willing to share?"

He opened his mouth, and she waited for the reprimand, but he closed it again after a moment. "Not exactly, but I can help you rest. I just didn't want to alter the air mix in here without your permission."

"Go right on ahead." Now, how come she could trust him to put her down, but she couldn't bring herself to tell him about that damned contract? Guilt was sure to kill her if the feds didn't get her first.

The heaters eased up, not so hot on her toes, but the source of warmth shifted, radiated through the seat instead. It infused her, comforted her. The sweetness in the air deepened, putting her in mind of hot chocolate. Winter cedar. Fires at her Aunt Boo's hunting camp, back when she was a kid.

Her hand dropped to the side of the seat in search of controls. She tipped back even before she pressed the button. A yawn clawed its way up from her throat, and she let it out.

Her eyelids were way too heavy to prop open. All the panic and pressure of this day sloughed off, washed away by whatever he'd cooked up in the car's environmental controls. All that bad stuff would come back painful, sure, but right now, she was content to let it slip away.

"Rest, querida. I've got you," he might have said. But Mari wouldn't put hard money on that.

●   ●   ●

When the car stopped, she didn't open her eyes right away. Metal scraped—Heron disconnecting from his rig console, switching to mobile. His gloved hand brushed her hair. Tentatively. She would've missed it if she hadn't been waiting for that touch. She shifted, drawing his thumb to her ear. She'd purr like a kitten if it'd keep him petting her.

"Hey? You awake? We're, uh, home." He moved, and she missed the weight of his hand even before she opened her eyes. He got out of the car on his side and then came around to hers.

Mari shook the chemically induced sleep off. After the machine warmth inside, the dank chill of an underground parking garage slapped her awake in a hurry, and her calf muscles contracted against the cold. Her rain boots waited on the floorboard, but when she thought about shoving her feet in there, into the cool rubber and the scuff of blisters, she just couldn't.

Weird how she could endure discomfort for long stretches when she was working, but the moment the

job was done, boom, she hauled in every shred of comfort she could get her hands on and hugged it close.
Putting the galoshes on right now would be a step back,
back into the shooter's blind, back into the squeeze.
Back into the darkthing spiral of guilt, horror, and
oh-God-what-had-she-done.

Screw that. The boots were staying. Snagging her duffel
from the floorboard, she climbed out of the car barefoot.

Wobbled. Heron set a hand beneath her elbow, and
once she was steady, that hand slid down to her wrist.
Mari looked up at him, blinking against the smoky, off-
code halogens.

Lace scraps of a dream caught on the edges of
her brain, and she had an overpowering need to tell
him…something. He needed to know it. Whatever it
was. But it floated off, and realization moved in like
a loud neighbor.

She was awake and…where at, exactly? They hadn't
stopped in a generic parking garage as she'd first
assumed. This underground was littered with bulk storage containers, arranged like a labyrinth, but she could
make out a bright sign at the far end, self-illuminated
deco-style letters spelling out the structure's name:
Pentarc Hyperstructure.

If Heron was going for anonymity, he'd kind of failed
bringing her here.

Pentarc was the inverse of the sin tunnels: everybody
knew about it. When somebody mentioned it, most folks
shrugged their shoulders and had something pithy to say
about megacorps and their big fat egos.

About a decade ago, give or take, a handful of West
Coast megacorp builders had gotten together and, with

a whole bunch of public grant money, constructed this gigantic, looming monstrosity of an arcology, a high-density, self-sustaining mini city. It was supposed to be home, school, work, shopping, entertainment, the whole shebang for forty-thousand-plus souls, complete with the most advanced automation and haptic remote reality, so no one would ever have to leave. Advertisements promised it would rekindle a sense of community, relieve stresses on the coastal power grid, save millions in unnecessary transportation.

But then Black November hit, and most average folks could barely afford to rent a sleeping bag in a FEMA tent. Leasing posh digs here had been unthinkable. And the massive almost-complete structure had been closed even before it opened.

Mari had sort of assumed it was abandoned like most superstructures these days, a shell too expensive to light and heat and cool. But clearly, it wasn't abandoned. The homey smells of axle grease and burnt tortilla indicated somebody at least lived here. Heron?

He twined his gloved fingers with hers and squeezed, drawing her away from the side of the car so the wing-like door could whisper shut. He didn't break the clasp of their hands, though, not even after locking the car. Not even when connection was completely unnecessary.

She sucked in her bottom lip to keep from saying something boneheadedly obvious like, *Hey, you're holding my hand*. Because then he'd stop, and she so didn't want him to.

Comfort, right? She was hoarding that stuff. And he was made of it.

Still some distance away, he gestured with his

free hand toward an unmarked metal door—service entrance? Inside, a heavy lock rolled over.

He tugged, luring her toward the door. "This way."

CHAPTER

2

HE WISHED SHE HADN'T TAKEN OFF HER WELLIES. AND HE wished he didn't care that her bare feet were quiet as kitten paws on the concrete — vulnerable, small enough to fit in his hands. Or that they peeked at him from under her skirt.

Distracting.

He was used to being distracted by his partner, though. He'd set up a whole partition in his neural just for watching her, thinking about her. Every time his thoughts got a little too graphic, he could tuck them all behind that partition, regulate the surface temperature of his skin, and slow his heart rate.

Redirect blood flow from his groin.

These simple processes were necessary when Mari was close. Holding his hand. Yawning and rubbing her eyes with the back of her wrist and flashing bare toes every time she took a step.

He couldn't take her up via the lifts in the center of the spire. Too many sense ports there would identify him, and probably her as well. If the authorities polled the Pentarc thereafter, they'd find Mari right away. He knew several other ways into the structure, of course, but any of those routes would reveal things to Mari. Things about him.

He sucked in a breath. Well, he'd brought her here, hadn't he? If he couldn't handle a few questions, he should have gone elsewhere.

The unmarked service entrance gave way to an HVAC control room. He led her over to a vertical vent and reached up inside it until he could feel the first of the welded-on ribs. A makeshift ladder.

"Here." He took her hand and placed it on the first rung. "Climb up."

She shot him a look as she wiggled past him, trailing hints of government-issue soap, petrichor, and WD-40. No doubt the sexiest combination of smells on the planet.

He mounted the ladder behind her, not even bothering to pretend he wasn't ogling her ass. She couldn't see him anyway. He could indulge, this once.

"You gonna tell me where we're going, or is it a big secret?" Her voice echoed in the narrow space, curled around him.

He blinked, realized that the disc of light from the HVAC room was getting smaller and smaller below them, and switched the tiny hornlike augments at either side of his forehead to extrude light rather than his usual holoprojected heads-up display. The implants themselves were too small to throw much light, and to make them useful at all as a torch lighting the way ahead, he would have to look past her gorgeous behind rather than directly at it. Oh well. The ogle had been good while it lasted. He let it go without too much fuss. This wasn't the first time he'd deliberately tucked away his feelings for her. It wouldn't be the last.

"Not secret. Pentarc is a closed system, off the cloud. We should be safe here. I have a unit on eleven," he said.

"We're climbing ladders for ten floors? Ugh."

"Something wrong with your stamina?"

She paused, one foot on the bar above his face, the other already on the next step. He could see directly up her floofy pink skirt. He'd never at the same time cursed and blessed combat leggings so desperately.

"Partner, I am very loose right now," she flung down at him, "job-high and humming with whatever was in your car's ventilation. You keep teasing like that, you just might have to fight me off."

Briefly, he entertained the idea of not. Not fighting her off. Letting her lay him on a bed somewhere and use him as her postjob catharsis. He knew she did that, typically, with men, though she never had with him. Again, both a curse and a blessing. Intimacy with Mari was only the most tantalizing and dangerous fantasy he could imagine. Dangerous because it would lay bare certain secrets he had no wish to share. And tantalizing because, well, yeah. Always that.

"Point taken." Deep breath. "But in answer to your question, the ladder's only for one more floor. We have ramps and more graded steps after. Patience."

"You say that a lot," she grumped.

Even more frequently to himself.

"You never answered my question before, you know," she said.

"What question do you mean?"

Something like a tsk floated down, but her ascent

remained steady. "You were going to tell me exactly how much I just fucked up."

"We, querida. *We* fucked up. We're a team, remember?"

"Duh. Now, how bad?"

He swallowed, grasping the rungs maybe a bit too tightly. His hands felt humid inside the driving gloves. "You saw the law enforcement bulletins. Murder, whole-organic."

Her footing faltered. He caught a breath in echo, but she didn't say anything.

"But you also received some message from Texas, if I am correct," he went on, "so at least you should have gotten the payout you were expecting." He modulated his voice just so, excising the censure from it. Like he hadn't accused her of betraying their partnership. Like he wasn't on fire with a toxic mix of love and lust and anger. Like he had zero emotional investment in her reaction. Sometimes the extent of his physiomechanical control surprised even him.

She stopped climbing. "Nope, not a whisper of that four point two…"

Oh well. Said physiomechanical control was utter bullshit anyhow. "Stop it, Mari. We both know that's not the price you negotiated."

She turned, looked down at him. In the brilliance of his light augments, her face shone like wet metal. Her eyes were huge. "You *know*?"

"Yes." No modulator on the planet could disguise his tone this time, and he wouldn't have wanted it to. If she couldn't hear the forgiveness there, the understanding and the fear, she didn't know him at all. Which, after all their time together and all he'd done for her behind the scenes, would cut pretty deep. "What I don't comprehend is why. Why would you risk dealing with Texas after what happened on your last job for them, in Corpus Christi?"

He searched her face for clues.

She'd taken the Corpus contract before they'd started working together, and she'd only mentioned it to him a couple of times and in a deliberately offhand manner. How much of that job did she remember? He had complete files, of course, but he didn't want to tell her anything that would spark memories she'd rather not walk through. She couldn't go forever without talking about it, though. Human psyches weren't meant to suppress like that.

Or maybe she just didn't want to talk about it with *him*.

He waited the space of two heartbeats, hoping.

She didn't say anything else. Her mouth formed an oval, and her brows ticked up in the center, and after a moment, she tucked her bottom lip between her teeth and turned, resuming the climb.

He carefully removed the sharp emotional hook in his chest. *Patience. She'll get used to me. She'll trust me, and then we'll talk through all of it. Like friends. Just have to give her time.*

But how much time did they have, after what they'd just done? The worst-case scenario—which he always sketched out and planned for, even while he fought against it—saw them both captured and imprisoned without ever unraveling all the history and tension that had balled up in angry knots between them.

He had to prevent that scenario, keep her physically

safe. Focus on the goal. And after, well, if he did his job well, they'd have plenty of time to sort the rest of it.

Two floors up from HVAC, he focused his light augments on the manual latch, and Mari popped a trapdoor open. He let her go through first. No dangers in here. Not of the physical kind, at any rate. But he still held his breath as he came into the room behind her.

He replaced the trapdoor, then looked around. A couple of free-fae lights illuminated a far corner, but most of the room was lit just by him. He boosted power so Mari could see better, and then he stood stiffly and waited for her reaction.

Crates were stacked floor to ceiling, some labeled and others open and emptied. Right next to her was a pallet of boxed heirloom seeds. A horticulturist had painstakingly drawn sketches of the mature plants onto the plastic boxes and noted the source county.

She'd recognize some of those counties. He waited for it.

But Mari didn't say anything. She sniffed like she was about to sneeze, swiped the back of her hand against her nose, and then turned back to him. "Where to now?"

"Mari?" he nudged.

She blazed a look at him, fierce, intense. "Okay, *yes*, I negotiated for info on my dad. Of-fucking-course I did. And I'm sorry I didn't tell you, but you would have argued against taking the contract. You would have told me it was a trap."

"I did tell you it was a trap."

She huffed out a breath. "Well, duh. But the TPA *has* him, Heron. They have my dad."

She wasn't telling him anything new. He waited some more.

Her eyes glittered in the high-contrast light. "He's an ass, I know. Everybody knows. And no, we don't much like each other. He never made a secret of choosing his…his *work* over me, but damn it, he's family. Mine. My own. What kind of daughter would I be if I didn't try and save him?"

He gazed into the face of pure loyalty, and something lurched inside him. Fierce Mari, courageous Mari, vulnerable Mari: these facets he knew. He hadn't seen her loyalty on display like this before. Granted, she had precious few people in her life deserving of such care.

All the gods knew *he* didn't deserve it. But if she could forgive the father who'd scandalized the scientific community with his lack of concern for unintended consequences, who had abandoned Mari not once but often and cruelly, perhaps she could forgive Heron his sins. Maybe? He'd never let himself have that hope before. Not the least because he wasn't anywhere close to forgiving himself.

"You are a good daughter," he allowed at last. "Too good."

But that didn't dry the sheen from her eyes. "And a shitty partner," she said in a small voice. "I should have told you."

His fingers flexed. He longed to touch her, but to reassure her…or himself?

"Probably," he forced past the constriction in his throat. "Now, if you've no other questions…"

Her eyes bored into him, pools of dark energy, and then the intensity shifted. One eyebrow climbed up her forehead. "You brought me here, to your treasure vault, and you don't expect a shitload of questions? Seriously?"

He blinked, lowered the intensity of the light. "Okay then. Ask away."

But she didn't. Not immediately. He showed her the way to a set of circular wrought-iron stairs. They creaked when she stepped up, and the center pole wobbled. He reassured her that it was safe, and she went right up. He wasn't sure if that indicated that she trusted him or that she didn't give two shits about her own safety.

He hoped for the former. Suspected the latter.

They went through other rooms with stores of stuff. Silks from Xi'an, vintage machine parts, bootleg French wine.

She paused beside an open-topped box crammed with what looked like old textiles. Gilt leaf glittered through lace and dust. A corner had fallen aside, revealing the delicate craftsmanship beneath. The 1902 Kelch Rocaille was a new arrival, one he hadn't logged and sorted yet. He needed to get right on that. A piece like this deserved to be crated more securely, stowed in the vault until he could find a good home for it.

"What?"

She shook her head. "Nothing. Just reminded me of this house outside Houston, back when. Some big-haired gal had taken over her grandad's petrochem company and invited my father over to talk about something sciency. Don't know what, but it wasn't the mech-clones, or he sure as hell wouldn't have brought me along. Anyhow, that gal, she had a whole shitload of eggs like this one."

"Fabergé. The McFerrin family of Kingwood used to own the largest private collection."

His team had braved the ruins of north Houston to retrieve McFerrin's collection. Some things he had no qualms trading on the black market, but these were unsellable, legacies of not one but two eras on their way out. Besides, he had a line on the owner, or heir, and would see these objects safely home. Heron wasn't a thief.

Her finger hovered centimeters above the egg, but she didn't touch it. "You know folks who've been to Texas since secession? How…?"

He gestured at the crates. "This is what I do, for the most part, when I'm not working with you."

"You're a treasure hunter?" She said it like it was something impossibly noble.

He ducked his head, pulling the light beams off her face. "I take care of precious things."

He expected more questions from her, but she didn't ask anything after that. Reticence was odd for her, but he would have been more surprised if she'd exhibited no human reaction to this day's events. She'd been through the wringer. He just hoped it was over, or nearly so.

At the eighth floor, he established a connection with the Pentarc system, and by the ninth floor, he dared log on to his mirror to check the status of law enforcement. So far, Pentarc seemed to be off their radar. Thankfully. He pinged his extraction team, and Garrett, his copilot, responded: weather delay made them still eighty-six minutes out.

And the bad news just kept coming.

At the tenth floor, he opened a half door into a closet, handed Mari through it, and then led her out onto a balcony off an uninhabited, west-spire living unit. They took the fire escape up to the eleventh floor without speaking.

His room in this spire was 1121, and he passkeyed them in, then reset the box, digitally wiping traces of his presence. And hers.

With only a slight hesitation, he let her precede him into the unit. His home. Ish. Well, one of his homes, one of the several places he could stow away, meld into the walls. Relax. He'd lived in a total of seven countries before age ten; he had a fluid definition of home.

The lights were motion activated, and they flared when Mari stepped in past the kitchenette, taking it all in with a glance. She turned, pierced him with a hot-whiskey gaze, and nodded toward the glass-brick shower tucked in a corner behind the refrigerator.

"So, now we got all the bad stuff out in the open, you mind if I get naked?"

It took pretty much every micron of control for him to say simply, "Be my guest."

●　　●　　●

Mari showered alone, alas, though she could see Heron's shadow through the glass-block wall the whole time. He'd told her she was safe enough here in the Pentarc, and she believed him. They hadn't seen another living soul the whole way up, probably because of their twisty secret-passagey way of getting here. They were as good as alone. She could shower, get cleaned up, take a breath. He'd plan out her next move, something that definitely wasn't in their contract, though she wasn't complaining.

She felt wobbly about being on her own right now, like the first moment she was alone, the darkthing made of guilt would eat her bone-bare and chase her wounds with lemon. Heron soothed that a bit. Not with hot toddies or kisses but with gestures that seemed second nature to him.

Like showing her his stuff. She hadn't expected that. Funny, she hadn't been aware for the last year that she was thinking up a nonwork life for Heron, populating it with things she thought he might be into. The fantasy Heron mostly spent his time in dark rooms, eating takeaway and coding on one of those giant, vintage supercomputers. She'd never thought he might be Indiana Jonesing all over the war-ravaged globe, handling priceless Russian eggs like they belonged in his big hands. The new info changed her view of him some. But she liked it. It fit.

She located his shape again as she squeezed lather through the sponge bristles, letting foam globs drip down her belly.

Some of her job-related tension was sloughing off with the decadent warm water, but he was still smackdab in the zone. Focused, palms flat against the smartsurface countertop, tension evident in his stillness.

She watched his blurry outline through the shower wall. If she'd had her com in, she might have listened in to see if he was speaking out loud. She wished she could see his face clearly.

What she wouldn't do, what she shouldn't do—and what she out-of-her-gourd desperately *wanted* to do—was slither out of the shower stark naked and dripping, lean back on that narrow bed, and sling him a come-hither he couldn't possibly resist. She knew ways to work tension from a man's body—and from her own.

True, Heron shied away from her flirting generally, and she had some good guesses why. Professionalism, for one. Also, he didn't understand her process. And how could he, really? How could anyone get it if they hadn't swirled death and sex until the whole thing blended into a desperate right the hell now?

Take advantage of the now, because the later, the alone, was going to hurt. A lot. And it was going to be equally bad whether she was in a cell somewhere or a cabana in Cabo. He was all about saving her from the authorities, but that wasn't where her worst threats came from.

She needed connection, touch, to chase away the darkthing. She was the pin on a teeter-totter, one end bringing death, one bringing joy, and they were badly out of balance. She needed to see orgasm break over somebody's face—orgasm because of her, because she could create something *not* horrible and guilt-making.

She needed that. From him. And apparently, it was the one thing he didn't put on offer.

As it was, about all she could do was swirl the sponge and *hope* he was spying on her half as much as she was spying on him. But she doubted it.

"Look at me," she whispered, pressing index fingers behind her ears where he might if he held her head for a kiss. "See me. Damn you, there's a naked woman right *here*."

He didn't look. Of course he didn't.

Hot with disappointment, she ducked her head under the rush of water, pushing her fingers back into her hair and squeezing the soap from it. Water couldn't clean her completely, though. She knew what she was, what she'd done. Shame marked her.

She closed her eyes, thankful this time that he hadn't looked. That he didn't realize.

Steam surrounded her. That subtle neroli scent wasn't just in the car. It was in his soap, too. This lather didn't suck the moisture out of her skin like that sulfate-ridden crap she usually used. Expensive. Another one of his "precious things"?

God, what was she even doing here? She didn't deserve this...care.

Outside the shower, Heron still looked tense. He must have read something bad on the smartsurface, because he stood and stalked to the far end of the living unit, over by the bed. Something in his posture made her nervous. Or nervouser.

She reached back and palmed the cracked ceramic knob. It slid back into the wall, and the stream of water trickled to a stop.

"Everything okay?" she called, leaning head and shoulders out of the stall.

He turned his face toward her—damp and naked and just-out-of-the-shower her—then slid it right past without so much as a hitch. A lesser man might have made a comment. Or pushed her ass-first up against the glass-block wall.

Heron, on the other hand, was the picture of professionalism. "Law enforcement still hasn't found us, if that's what you're asking."

Mentally sighing, Mari snagged a thin towel from the post by the commode niche and wrapped it around her body as she stepped out of the shower cube. "Good thinkin', then, bringing us here. Thanks, partner."

He didn't reply, but his eyes tracked her movements

like she was a radar target, the subject of intense interest for a fraction of a moment but not much longer. No
emotion there, no clue to his thoughts.

She bent to dry her legs. She had fresh clothes
folded neatly in her duffel by the door, but her just-
scrubbed skin felt raw, hot. Instead of reaching for
her clothes, she donned a cheap terry bathrobe that
had been hanging on a peg by the towel rack. Big
one. Its hem dragged the floor, and the sleeves more
than covered her hands, but Mari didn't mind. There
was something yummy about wearing his clothes.
She tied the sash and wrapped her hair in the already-
damp towel.

When she looked up, he was still at the far end of the
apartment, paying attention to anything but her. Dangit.

She wrung her hair with the towel and watched him
fiddle around in the kitchenette. Tea. He was making
tea. She reached for her com and held it against her
throat, counting her pulse. The pinch of the embeds
flared along her skin.

"Hey," she said, heading to his end of the narrow
apartment. She plopped down on the bed, within touching distance. "I probably ought to let Aunt Boo know
I'm still breathing, in case she sees vid saying otherwise.
You got a security code to log in?"

This close, it was everything she could manage not
to grab him and pull him down here with her. Her hand
might have even moved in his general direction, but the
floppy sleeve disguised it.

"Um, no." Frowning slightly, he went back to the
kitchenette.

Maybe the sight of a mostly naked her sitting on his

bed was just too much for him. Nah, not likely. Though a girl could hope.

The conk of ceramic and the scuff of his boots on linoleum: things that were supposed to settle and comfort. But Mari knew nothing was going to settle her right now. At least, nothing short of an orgasm so intense she passed out.

"I don't log in to the cloud here, not directly," he said. "The Pentarc system is closed and only interfaces with the world outside at intervals. It's inconvenient sometimes but provides a buffer between the cloud and…me." As if one were a danger to the other, though between the two, Mari would put her money on Heron. "But you can give me your message, and I will send it along to your aunt."

He put the tea things aside, and Mari told him her Aunt Boo's handle and dictated a short note: "Am fine. Did a bad thing, though. Running. Like it or not, you're connected to me, so it's probably a good idea for you to hide out a while. Sorry, Auntie B. Love you."

Heron removed his gloves and pressed his palms against the kitchen counter. Casual, like he was just leaning there. Nothing lit beneath his hands, no navigation display, and his posture looked more like meditation than a brain-machine interface. It occurred to her right then that this interaction might not be. Human, that is.

Heron wasn't a mech-clone; he had been born a whole-organic and lived at least part of his life without implants. But he'd been altered along the way so much that she might well have been watching one machine brainspeak to another, straight through that kitchen counter.

Straight through his hands. Sharp knuckles, long, tapered fingers with a glint of sense-tips on the ends. Wires probably augmented his reflexes, aided in the transmission of instructions from neural to muscles, and sensory inputs ran back up to command and control. That was all pretty standard. But most post-human alterations included comprehensive rebuilds, which covered over the metal and obvious bits. He must have kept the sensors on the ends of his fingers bare for a reason. Either that or he hadn't gone through a government-licensed clinic.

Like so much of him, though, the things that she would have once considered off-putting or creepifying were just...him. Confident, capable, badass him. Her partner. She ached to feel those long hands, tipped in quicksilver, on her skin, every contour and crease. She wanted to kiss them and look at them and tell him they were beautiful. That *he* was. To her.

She didn't move.

"All right." He lifted his hands, flexed his fingers, and retrieved his teacup and hers. "Your message is queued in the Pentarc and should upload shortly. I insulated it so it can't be tracked back here, just in case authorities are monitoring your aunt's communications, which, let's face it, they probably are." He skirted the counter's edge and reached one cup toward her. Chamomile wafted off the top.

"Thanks." Mari breathed in the steam, trying to recapture the threads of their conversation, which kept slipping away through the film of yearning she fought. "But really, you *never* log on to the cloud?"

He didn't reply and wouldn't meet her gaze. Just

retreated back to the counter and sipped his tea. And that was answer enough.

"Dang, how do you do anything? All that monitoring and job prepping and… I mean, you have to connect somehow."

Heron blinked slowly and blew the steam from his cup. "This is really what you want to discuss, querida?"

No. She'd rather discuss getting him out of those clothes and over here on this bed. She shrugged, trying for casual. "Nah, I guess not. Thank you for sending my note."

"You're welcome." He pinned her with a look over the rim of his cup.

She swallowed. Her skin hummed like high voltage needing ground. That shower hadn't relaxed her one bit, and at this point, she wasn't sure if the nervous energy sparking all over her was guilt or regret or lust. Most likely a combination of all three. "So now what?"

"I have someone coming to fetch you, once you get dressed and have something to eat. There's a helipad on the south half spire, level ten. If you still want to go to Cabo San Lucas, they'll take you."

Would you go with me? "Who's they?"

"My crew."

"This the same crew that does the treasure-hunting stuff with you?" She dropped her gaze to the duvet, picked at a piece of embroidery fuzz, and tried not to sound too needy when she added, "Y'all have something lined up for after you deal with me?" She imagined he planned artifact extractions sort of the way he did shooter extractions like hers. Couldn't be too terribly different, right, braving danger to fetch a barrel of rare wine or a girl with a gun?

He'd gone still. She couldn't read those dark eyes, but something in his posture had changed. He seemed... confused? Embarrassed? Definitely out of his comfort zone, but still too in-control of his face and body for her to get a clue what he was thinking.

"You're all I'm concerned with right now, Mari."

Wait. What?

A thought sliced through all her confusion and guilt. *She* was one of the precious things he took care of? Like a Fabergé egg or a bolt of raw Chinese silk. Her? Was that what he'd been implying? No way. No way. And yet...

An anchor dropped deep in her chest.

She had never been a precious thing. Not to anybody. She'd been an angry-making burden to Aunt Boo, a disappointment to Dad, a fun career move to Nathan.

Was this what it felt like to be wanted, just for herself?

● ● ●

Heron had to look away from her. Mari. On the bed. Mostly naked. Twenty-seven degrees warmer than ambient temperature and dew-damp from her shower. She would taste like salt and hot cinnamon, and his mouth filled with want of her.

She had no idea how cruel this teasing was. Nor how much control it took not to shove her down into the cheap arco bed and fuck her raw when what he really needed to concentrate on was getting her out of here, keeping her whole. Keeping her safe. Keeping her asshole father as far away from her as possible.

He put the counter between his body and hers, flexed his fingers against the cool surface, and opened the data flow in through his palm sensors. Flash log. Info flood.

Surge. Steady. This was the sort of input he understood, could interpret and handle.

Not the temptation reclining on his bed. Couldn't handle *that* one bloody second longer.

He breathed, regulated his pulse, parsed incoming data. Beyond these walls, out in the information cloud, law enforcement was still scrambling. Good.

But...no, something wasn't right. Something with the elevator. Something out of balance. Hoist cables flinched; knurled rollers groaned. A sense-tipped finger pressed the button for this floor. A finger with no ID informatics embedded. Not a resident, not a citizen, not a member of law enforcement. But coming this way just the same.

Someone off-grid coming to his floor precisely when Mari was here and her image and vital statistics were flashing all over law enforcement bulletins? Statistically not coincidental.

Enemies had found them. Here. In the Pentarc. In his sanctuary. *His*. Fury sliced up his veins, but he settled it instantly. Soothed it. Shhh.

With a swipe of his thumb on the counter, he accessed security camera footage from the landing. Two nonresidents exited the spire lift. Big, rough-looking, and with lumps beneath their clothes that could indicate weapons. They headed left, toward his unit.

Heron ran counterweight logs from the elevator car. These weren't unaltered humans, and weight indicated metal alterations, not on-trend cosmetic biohacks. These intruders weren't meant to be pretty; they were meant to break things. Mercenaries, then. Trouble.

The kind of trouble that wouldn't waste time arresting Mari if they found her.

"Oh, fuck that. Not here you don't." Heron straightened, detached his palms from the info stream, and held out a hand. "We need to go. Right now."

In an instant, she slipped into her professional mode. Gone was the lazy, languorous glint, the come-hither half grin and deliberate peek up her thigh. Her feet hit the floor, and she blew past him, retrieving her duffel by the door, putting her body between him and the danger outside.

She didn't need to. But she did.

And he loved her for that. For a long time had.

Heron stopped her with one hand on the door. He knew what she had in that bag, and it wouldn't be enough.

He leaned into the galley-style kitchenette and slid a drawer out. Raised it up from its rails and felt for the clip on the back wall. Yes. Right there. He withdrew the petite hunk of metal and death and slid the drawer back.

He handed the gun to Mari. She looked down at it, then back up at him. Her grin was savage. Hot. God, even in danger, even on the run—hot. He regulated blood flow, blocked vasodilation and tumescence. She wouldn't see her effect on him. Ever.

Her eyebrows perked. "You keep a Taurus .38 snubby in your oven mitt drawer? Isn't that kind of…pussy?"

He didn't want to think about what hearing that word in her voice was doing to his autonomic suppression. "You're the muscle, querida."

"Right on." The grin slipped to serious. "What kind of load you…"

But she didn't get to finish that sentence. The passkey box fired, fried, and intruders pushed the door aside, wrenching the dead bolt as if it were made of butter.

Heron knew what was coming but didn't quite have

time to pull Mari back before the door crashed in. It hit her behind the left temple with enough force to knock her off her feet.

She didn't fall down, though. Heron caught her below her arms, holding her up. The sensors in his palms flared, searching for data transfer points. But there weren't any, of course.

Without looking down, he saw the gun disappear into the sleeve of the bathrobe, and he swallowed a grin.

That's my girl.

CHAPTER 3

THEY WERE GOOD AND CORNERED, BUT IT CERTAINLY wasn't the worst situation Mari had ever faced. What worried her more was Heron. He didn't get in scrapes like this for a living. He wouldn't have much experience fending off attackers. She needed to keep him calm, assess the threat, and get them both outta this.

Inside the wide robe sleeve, she rubbed the grip on his pistol. No slot in the bottom, no ceramic appliqué on the side. Probably no biometric identity controls. Off the registers, then. Nice. Cute little thing, Heron's gun. Bitty, yeah, but she could make do.

With her left hand, the empty one, she detached wet hair from her face and touched the throbbing spot behind her ear. It didn't sting the way an open cut would, so probably just a bruise. And no dizzies or any other symptom of concussion. So, not a big deal. She was good to go.

The two thugs who loomed between her and the door didn't come right at her. They didn't draw weapons or look like they were about to bust anybody up. One dude, pale skinned, with a belly grown big from too much homebrew and a bar code tattooed on his forehead, walked back to the yawning door and tried to close it. Didn't work too well—he'd probably ruined the passkey on the way in. But that didn't keep him from fiddling with it a few seconds while Mari checked out his partner.

Taller, leaner, with one shitty, cheap eye-alt that kept swerving off-center as it ran data on her, this dude was probably the brains of the operation. Such as he was. Neither thug wore insignia, just plain denim and leather. Not law enforcement, then. Freelancers, like her? Or run-of-the-mill home invaders? She didn't see any weapons, but that didn't mean they weren't armed.

"Y'all lookin' for gold, check the bag right there by the door. Bracelet in the inside pocket ought to trade high." She slung a tremble in her voice, and Heron tensed behind her. She waited for both dudes to glance at the bag, and she mouthed into the subvocal com, "Easy, partner. I got this."

"Not gold," said the wobble-eyed thug. "Lookin' for the legal resident of this unit and also, uh, some gal named"—he checked his wristplant—"Marisa Vallejo. That you, sweetheart?"

Her name—her whole name—whumped her in the chest. Home invader thieves wouldn't know her name. She hadn't used her full name in years. Heron didn't even know it. "I don't know who you…"

He angled his wrist, pointed it at her face, and a red flash made her blink. Faceprint targeter. He had her in his system now. Fuck.

Bigbelly gave up on the door, shoved her heavy duffel up against it, and straightened. He moved twitchy, too fast but not controlled. Most likely had wire augments, but they clearly hadn't gone through UNAN-licensed clinics.

Which would make sense if they'd gotten altered in Texas.

A thrill wiggled up her spine. Even though the TPA had most likely just betrayed her, she couldn't help hoping that they'd still tell her what she wanted to know. Needed to know. Whatever his sins, Dad was hers. Her family, her home, her past. She needed to know where he was and if he was okay. She opened her mouth but felt her partner, warm and tense and probably scared shitless, behind her.

Heron.

She'd put him at risk, taking this contract. Keeping her side payment secret. She wouldn't do that again.

She scooted back, pressing closer, covering him. Nobody was shoving them together right now, yet his hands were still at her waist, twin vises. He held her tight against his body. Weird thing was, knowing he was there, at her back, holding her like she was something precious, well, that made Mari invincible.

She swallowed her curiosity and cocked the gun as quietly as she could.

Heron didn't relax, but he didn't do anything stupid either, which impressed Mari. Tech guys like him parsed information for a living and usually logged zero training for these sorts of up close and personal things. Her first two tech partners had haired out completely on the job. Of course, she hadn't been much better. Those early contracts had been more oops than win, everybody just learning the ropes. And of course Nathan…now that had been a spectacularly shitty experiment in partnering.

Not Heron, though. He had never done anything but save her ass. She leaned against him a smidge more, to let him know that she was relaxed despite whatever she said.

That shit-eating grin on Wobble's face just got wider when he looked up from the wristplant readout.

"Evenin', Miss Vallejo. Sorry 'bout the rough entry, but we needed surprise on our side. Says here that you're armed and dangerous." He waggled his eyebrows as if *dangerous* wasn't the word he was thinking. He glanced pointedly to her chest.

Scumbag. During the scuffle, the robe had fallen open enough that half a boob hung out, bare for anybody to see. Mari's first instinct was to right her clothing, put herself together, but honestly, naked tits were likely to be more distracting to her attackers than they were to her. So a net advantage. She nudged her shoulders back and tried not to think about how Heron saw all this.

Wobble's good eye glazed over a bit, and his mouth opened. He seemed incapable of looking away from the show. Mari reached back with her free hand, letting the robe fall open even more and thinking of how much force she'd need to push Heron behind the foot of the bed, shielded. He was pretty big and had the balance of a cat, and he was still holding on to her hips. It would take a lot of shove to move him.

But she waited too long in planning.

Before she even realized he was moving, Bigbelly had pushed past his slack-jawed partner, grabbed Mari by the upper arm, and wrenched her away from Heron. His augments packed more of a punch than she expected, moved her fast. Her thigh hit the nightstand with a crack. The nightstand took the worst of it.

She yelped, but not in pain. He'd grabbed the wrong arm, and in the brief scuffle, she'd dropped the snubby. Dadgummit. She thought it might have fallen near the foot of the bed, but she couldn't get a good line of sight on that floor space, and besides, she wasn't doing all that well holding up against Bigbelly's kung fu.

It'd been some years since she'd certified in hand-to-hand, and her muscle memory was toast. Not to mention her reflexes were still a jumble from the emotional wringer she'd endured today. And it wasn't easy fighting in a flippin' bathrobe either. She blocked, but her position was wrong. She found herself on the defensive and knew she was physically outmatched.

She tried to get beneath her attacker's hold, but even as she went to her knees, the thug secured her arms behind her back, hyperextending her elbows and shoving a beefy biceps between her body and upper arms. Pain arced between her shoulders, the pulling, grinding pain of something horribly not right. Even breathing yanked her joints.

Mari went still.

Uncomfortable as her position was, she could endure what they were doing to her body. But what she was seeing sucked the breath clean out of her chest.

While she'd been scuffling with Bigbelly, Wobble had *done something* to Heron. Hit him? Drugged him? Whatever, he now sat in a metal folding chair, his head slumped to one side, resting temple to shoulder. He wasn't bound, wasn't struggling, and blood soaked the dark collar of his shirt.

Oh no. No, no.

"Heron? Can you hear me?"

When he didn't respond, Mari's extremities went numb, then hot.

"What you waiting for? Plug him in already." Bigbelly kept Mari's arms pinned tight, but he quivered, impatient as a pinched spring. Wobble ignored him, just shoved Heron's head to the other side, seeking the input.

Mari knew where it was. She'd watched her partner insert jacks and data spikes into that port, but he didn't use it all that often. He ran mobile most of the time and only needed to physically plug in to older machines, like the car.

But the mercs didn't know that. The guy at the back of Heron's head grunted, apparently finding the input. "He ain't got a SIP. Just some fucking obsolete fly-jack."

"Well, wire around it, man. Come on."

Mari suspected that these guys knew as much about tech as she did, but it didn't look like ignorance was holding them back any. What they couldn't connect cleanly, they were determined to force.

God, what if they broke him?

"Leave him alone," Mari said. *Heron, please answer me*.

Not unexpectedly, the thugs ignored her. Wobble shoved Heron's head forward so hard, he was facing down toward her, but his eyes didn't move.

They were open, unblinking, sightless.

As if he were dead.

Mari maneuvered herself just a little closer to the foot of the bed. She didn't feel the bite of the painted cement floor against her bare knees as she skidded forward. She didn't wince at the strain on her joints as the thug behind her resettled his hold.

She couldn't look away from Heron. *Hang in there, partner.*

Wobble stuck a wire into the back of Heron's skull, threading it with something near the port. An arc must have caught, because all at once, Heron's limbs jerked, and his head lurched up.

He stared at Mari with those dead-seeming eyes, forced a ghastly smile, and spoke. "There you are. I know your face."

Heron's mouth, Heron's voice. But that wasn't him. Ice clamped her spine. His creepy eyes scanned her. She wanted to shiver. Or scream. Or shoot something.

"Excellent work, boys. Yes, that's…her. Marisa Vallejo."

She'd heard rumors of com units that could do this kind of shit, get one person totally inside somebody else's head, essentially taking them over, making them into puppets. Underground carvers called it marionetting, and it creeped Mari out.

But not so much that she was without resources. She stilled against Bigbelly's hold and aimed a laser death glare at the other thug. "That is *it*. You fucking monsters are gonna tell me, real slow, what you've done to my boyfriend and how to fix it. Else I swear, I'll beat the shit out of you."

To his credit, Wobble didn't reply. He opened his mouth but left it that way. Come to think of it, he left his mouth open a lot.

"Don't this bitch know I got her pinned?" Bigbelly asked exactly nobody.

Not-Heron raised a finger and cricked it in the general direction of Wobble, the wire-poking mouth breather.

"I did warn you two she was dangerous. Check her for weapons, please."

It wasn't true what the kiddie vids said. Saying please didn't make a damn thing better. The lie of politeness was in Wobble's rough hands as he obeyed and searched her. He didn't so much as pause at her growl when he brushed her hair back, scanning her skull with his wristplant.

Looking for ports or other alterations. He wouldn't find any, of course.

Fuck you. I ain't some helpless whole-organic girl, here. I'm the girl who's going to put a bullet between your teeth. You can take that to the bank.

The puppeteer must have misinterpreted her growl and tension as signs of fear, because he went on in a soothing voice, as if to distract her from the grubby paws all over her body. "Nice shooting today, by the way. Of course, you realize I saw it. Everyone saw it. Security drones got up-close footage of the whole thing and back-tracked the trajectory. Full color, chulita: you're a star."

Mari remembered the guy with the wristplant, back on the sidewalk. That security drone had been awful quick to intercept. If the phone guy hadn't been so close to the scene, would the drone have come for her instead?

"But that isn't the only reason the feds are after you," the puppeteer went on. "You've done bad things before, but this was notable. Whole-organic murder in broad daylight, and the contracted spouse of a very important person to boot. Oh, you've drawn a lot of attention."

Including his? Who the hell was he anyway? No matter how it hurt, Mari pulled again at Bigbelly's hold. It didn't budge. Wobble reached behind and squeezed her forearms beneath the robe, probably hunting for wristplants or retractable claws, and for maybe the first time in her life, Mari regretted not having any alts. Sure would be slick to spring them suckers on him right now.

The move brought his body in close to hers. He smelled like cumin and sweat. Ugh. She would never eat a street taco again. Didn't want to think where else he might search on her person, and she closed her eyes tight as his hands slipped down, outlining her hips and then patting down her calves.

This was probably where they expected her to go all wilty and victim. Fuck that. "Whole-organic, my ass," she spat over the thug's bent head. "I slagged a mech-clone."

Wobble finished his pat down and stepped back, transmitting whatever info he'd gotten from the scan.

The puppeteer—*not Heron*—leaned forward in his chair, piercing Mari with those cold, beautiful eyes. "Would that make it better, in your estimation? Does your ethical calculus allow you to murder clones but not whole-organics? What about altered humans, like Heron, your, uh, *boyfriend*? He is no longer completely human, is he? Would you be able to kill him with no conscience?" He tsked but didn't look away. "Who is really the monster in this room?"

The darkthing made of guilt rose so unexpectedly from her gullet that Mari couldn't breathe for a split second. She hung there, held up purely by the puppeteer's gaze and Bigbelly's massive arms, and her chest ballooned with horror. Because what he said was true. She had made deals with her conscience. She'd done plenty of bad things.

But never, never in ever would she hurt Heron. She

was physically incapable of hurting him. He wasn't just a thing, like the N series target. He was...a precious thing. Precious to her. And right now, she was gonna do one better than not killing him. She was gonna fucking save him.

In front of her, the marionette—her *partner*—smiled, sleek and horrible. "Not to worry, though, little monster. These gentlemen will bring you both to a safe place, a place where none of those pesky police officers can find you. We can talk more then."

"You're arresting me? Fine. But you can back the hell out of Heron's skull first. You do that, and I'll come quiet."

The puppeteer laughed, and all Mari could think was that wasn't Heron's laugh. She'd heard him laugh a few times, and it never sounded like that: tinny and crazed. The difference comforted her some. She only hoped that he was still in there, and that she could get him back.

After she killed these assholes.

Her fingers flexed as if they attempted telekinesis. As if the snubby would just magically zip across the floor and leap into her grasp.

"I'm afraid I can't do that. His alterations are as extensive as I had suspected, so I'll need both of you. Oh, don't worry, though. My associates will be gentle."

But Mari was only half listening. She'd found what she'd been looking for: a metallic glint beneath the hem of the duvet. Sweet, sweet little snubby.

She'd no more spotted the gun than Wobble put his hands beneath Heron's arms, as if to pull him to his feet. Heron half rose but then fell into his chair. His expression twisted, and he reared back, knocking his mangled head against the thug's reinforced forearm. The crack of skull on flesh-covered metal was loud, like an egg cracking into a skillet. Heron didn't move after that, though Wobble still tried to haul him up.

Get your fucking hands off him, she screamed silently, but she kept her body still. When Bigbelly shifted, presumably to retrieve whatever he was planning to use to incapacitate or bind her, she tightened her core, pressed hard with her right thigh, and threw her weight sideways.

The thug fell against her, shoving her to the floor with his gigantic bulk. Her breath huffed out, and she couldn't suck it back in right away, but she didn't let herself panic over that. Instead, she yanked, and her left arm came free. Blocking the pain, she shoved her fist beneath the bed and grabbed the snubby.

Her first shot took Heron's assailant above the left eye.

"What th—bitch!" Bigbelly reached for Mari's hand and the gun, but he was still holding her right arm, trapped between their bodies. His leather vest had ridden up, and her knuckles were jammed against the flaccid warmth of bare skin. She felt for the fleshiest part—and there was plenty to choose from—and sank her ragged fingernails deep, twisting at the wrist.

Her captor howled and reared reflexively away from her grasp. Mari rolled, coming to her back halfway beneath the bed. She fired twice without a clear view and the third time steady. Was the third shot took him down.

In the quiet that followed, white feathers fluffed into the air all around her. Those bullets had torn Heron's duvet apart, but Mari didn't even wipe the feathers from her face. She scrambled to her feet, confirmed that both the mercs were dead, and popped the cylinder on her gun. One bullet left. Mari just hoped that would be enough to get them out of there.

"Hold on, Heron. I'm coming for you."

Mari's heel slipped in blood as she hauled one of the attackers aside, and when she got behind Heron's chair, the gore got only uglier. That wobbly-eyed asshole had made two trenches on either side of the port in his head, finding wires and splicing them with whatever com they'd jury-rigged. Mari used gentle fingers to unlace the wires. She cleaned up the blood with her robe and sash, dabbing away already stickifying bits and muttering all sorts of nonsense to him under her breath. God, she wished she knew more about biomachines. *Please, please, please.*

Finally, when she couldn't stand it anymore, she reached down, below his jaw, and pressed her fingers to his throat.

A pulse pushed back against her finger pads.

"I'm still here," he said, looking down as if he were getting his bearings. "How are you holding up?"

Mari laughed, but it cracked on the way out. Kind of like a sob, if she were a sobbin' kind of girl. "Nice of you to check in, partner. Yeah, I'm good. Can you move? I just made a lot of noise, and even shitholes like the Pentarc gotta have security. I need to get you out of here before they come lookin' for us."

"I can move." Heron tilted his head slightly from side to side, as if he were sighting in his eyes, even though he didn't have discernible cyber augments there. He palmed the chair arms and leaned forward, and Mari rushed around to his side, just in case he lost his balance. He looked up at her and grinned.

That familiar grin bloomed comfort all through her innards, and she let herself hope they were going to get through this.

"They didn't hurt me, querida. Just jacked me for a little while. You needn't worry over me."

Mari raised a hand, thought about touching him again, and then dropped it. She'd only be doing it to reassure herself, to gain that point of contact. And considering how violated he must be feeling, she couldn't subject him to another unwanted touch. Not even a caress.

"You don't even know what all they did to you."

He stood, a lithe, uncoiling movement that brought his body, warm and solid, within breathing distance of hers. A tang of blood whiffed below his usual scent. "I'll let you know the details once I've completed my diagnostic."

"That should be any minute now, though, right? It takes you, like, five hot seconds to check out my bios."

"That's because I have you loaded in active memory."

"Eh?" What she wouldn't have given for some plain speaking from her partner. For once.

But he got her frustration, or must have, 'cause his half smile looked a little sheepish. "Guess you could say you're always on my mind."

This time, her laughter barked, a full-out, tension-killing cackle. Considering the crappy situation they were in at the moment and the danger they still had to navigate through, letting loose a laugh like that was nothing short of a miracle. And it felt so good. Almost but not quite as good as a quick fuck in his shower, though she was willing to let go of that plan. With some regret.

"Thank you for pulling the wires, by the way. That disconnected my invader." He bent and retrieved the wad of metal doodad they'd rigged him with. After taking a quick look at the device, Heron cracked the case, exposing a rainbow of circuitry. He ripped out a couple of transistors and some other trash, replaced a couple of the wires, and then held it out to Mari. "Can you plug it back in?"

"Um, no."

"It'll help us get out of here faster." He crouched in front of her, pivoting so that the back of his head was even with her waist. She'd envisioned so many scenarios that had Heron kneeling in front of her, right at hip level, but this particular situation had never come up.

"I don't get why you want to do this," she said, even as she obeyed. She wanted to know *why* and what would happen now. If he was going to shut down again and start hosting other personalities, for instance, she would toss this little bit o' Frankenstein gadgetry into the wall disposal right now.

"They bypassed my wireless circuits and damaged a lot of hardware in the process, but if you stick this device back in, exactly where it was, I can get our coms up again." He reached back, framing her hands with his, guiding her placement of the tech. "Don't worry. I have repaired it."

At his direction, Mari pinched two wire ends together and twisted. Two more twists, and his fingers eased atop hers, stopped directing. He folded the skin flaps back over his skull, which did little to repair the gouge of ugly.

She was mildly surprised when Heron, instead of shrugging her off and standing up, grabbed her hands tighter.

He smiled up at her, triumphant and vicious. "I'm in."

"You're in where? The cloud?"

"Ah, no. The arcology." He rubbed the pads of his thumbs over her knuckles, and Mari contained a full-body quiver. "Logged in like this, for all intents and purposes, I *am* the Pentarc."

Oh. Probably why he kept a room here. Hugantic processor core that he could log into without touching the cloud, without being tracked or tagged? For a post-human with a neural as expansive as Heron's, that must be a little like stretching after a long, cramped, depressing sleep.

But before Mari could ask another question—and yes, she had one primed—Heron put one hand under her elbow and mouthed a word she didn't catch, and then the lights went out.

All of 'em.

Interior-facing units like this had no windows, and Heron wasn't the type to keep a free-fae nightlight on his shelf, so no lights meant zero visibility. Mari needed a second to get her bearings. His grasp steadied her.

"There," said Heron. "This spire is in lockdown, so our exit down the corridor should be unimpeded. No innocents will get caught in any crossfire. I've also shut down the vertical lifts."

"But we have to get down to the tenth floor of the other spire, right? Meaning we'll have to take the fire escape. Can do, partner."

"No. Meaning you have a coil of static rope and some descenders in your clothes duffel, beneath those, er, ruffled bloomers. I presume you know how to use them. The lines, not the underpants."

It was a testament to the remaining danger in their situation—and her lingering concern for him—that Mari did not follow up on his mention of her lacy underthings. Instead, she stowed that nugget for later.

"Fire escape would be safer," she observed.

"Rappelling is quicker."

"We on a timeline I don't know about?"

He squeezed her hand. "Law enforcement entered the underground before I could shut them out. Four vans, and their drones are covering the fire escapes. They currently believe that they have us cornered and all exits blocked."

"But they don't?"

"Querida." She could hear the grin in his voice, and it made her just a little wet in the nethers.

And boy howdy, was she glad she hadn't mouthed anything indicating *that* under her breath. She'd forgotten for a moment that she was wearing the subvocal rig. Thing could get a girl into a heap of trouble.

Heron guided her through the doorway and out into the hallway beyond. On the way, she bent and retrieved the duffel she'd dropped when the door had come crashing in. Heron was right: she had some random equipment in the bag, including some pitons, harnesses, and line. No useful weaponry, though, just the sniper kit in pieces and very little in the way of bomb-making stuffs. Even if she put the H&K together, it wouldn't be as effective as Heron's snubby in close-in combat. Alas. The single bullet was a craptastic last line of defense, but Mari had survived worse.

She knew the lockdown had cleared folks out of the main corridor, whatever few folks actually called this dump home, but Mari still picked her way along, not wanting to trip or step on anything prickly with bare feet.

"Hey," she subvocaled, "you know that head-augment light-lampy thing you did on the way up? Mind doing it again?"

"Not a good idea. Feds have visual recon, and a team is on its way up the maintenance stairs. They're currently two floors down, but their drones will be sweeping in advance."

She heard his response just inside her ear, like it moved along the bone. Clearly, he was using some kind of subvoc, too, but she hadn't seen him equip anything, and she hadn't noticed a rig like hers when she was fiddling with all those wires inside his skull.

"You know I have visual-only targeting, too, right?" If Mari had been using her out-loud voice, it would've been wry.

"When you need them, the sights will be there. Promise."

The further they went on, the more Mari thought that either Heron had memorized the Pentarc blueprints or his augments enabled him to see in the dark, even without lighting things up, maybe with some kind of back-of-the-eyelids heads-up? Or did he have a built-in GPS? There was so much tech in him, so much sparking her curiosity.

There was a time, back when they'd first met, when Mari would have been weirded to know this little tidbit about him, this further evidence of his post-human freakishness. Dad had worked in cybernetics, first in AI and then in mech-clones, and Mari had grown up knowing that machines weren't people, couldn't be trusted. Sure as shit couldn't love you back. She'd been careful to keep her distance from anybody who'd let themselves get biohacked. Her targets on the range back in Lampasas had all worn laser eyes and grafted armor.

But a full year of working side by side with this particular post-human had sure changed her mind. She was long past being anything but thankful for Heron's built-in nav, however it worked, leading them through the dark.

"Twenty meters to the cabling vent."

"That where we're jumping?"

"Yes."

To this point, Heron's stride had been sure, steady, but just then, it stuttered. The hand at her elbow clenched fractionally, but Mari felt it. Her first thought was of his wounds, that he was fixing to pass out on her, and she knew she couldn't drag him to safety here. He was too big. She reached along his forearm, grasping his hand.

"Heron?"

"Drone is thermo sweeping for us."

"Shit. What do we do?"

She heard a click to her right, a lock drawing back, and then Heron was pushing her gently. Her hip bumped a knob as she went through, but the door closed soft as tissue behind her.

Mari's world, already dark, now went silent and still as well. Her own breath sounded orchestral, and she became keenly aware of what sensory input remained. Heron had come through the door with her. She still held his hand, but that wasn't their only point of contact. He hadn't moved all the way into the entryway, and he was still near enough that Mari was squished between him and the door.

Close enough that she could feel the heat off his body, roiling in the space between them. His skin smelled like that fancy soap and car leather, and if she moved her head even a bit, her mouth would brush south of his collar.

Her nipples tightened, but she silently talked herself down. How sick was she to be lusting over her *injured* partner right in the middle of a getaway? She needed to think of something else. Anything.

Which made her wonder what *he* was thinking.

"You seeing all this somehow?" When she moved her mouth, her chin rubbed his knit shirt. Mari considered moistening her lips, but she couldn't be responsible for what her tongue did after that.

"I'm watching them on sixty-four cameras and the sat uplink. We have the advantage. Relax."

Not likely, but it was nice of him to try and reassure her like that.

Past the black outline of Heron's biceps, Mari could see a sliver of light along the floor. Soft and blue that light, probably a free-fae light box, like those freebies the technoreligious kooks passed out on street corners. She focused on the shape of the light: rectangular and low near the floor. A door, then. She and Heron must have ducked into a multiroom unit, and she was willing to bet that whoever lived here didn't realize they had company.

She didn't want to think what would happen if that

person, the one with the light on in the next room over, wandered into the foyer where she and Heron were hiding.

With her free hand, she slipped the gun into her robe pocket and dangled the duffel from her fingertips, ready to drop it if she needed to move fast to subdue someone. Out of practice didn't mean she couldn't do it, and quietly. She doubted the average Pentarc denizen was juiced and wired like those mercenaries she'd just shot.

Killed.

Shot and killed.

And she'd known the whole time they weren't mech-clones. That they were in fact organic, despite their biohacks. People. Murdered. By her.

Bile rose in Mari's throat, and the darkthing roiled, but she forced it back down, along with the keening: *Murderer. Monster.* Despite all her forays on the dangerous side of life, all her jobs wreaking chaos, she still hated killing whole-organics. Didn't mean she couldn't or hadn't, but she tried to make it rare. Today she'd offed three. Three.

Couldn't think about this right now. Had more urgent issues. But still: *Murderer. Monster.* The blood had clotted, sticky between her bare toes, though she'd walked it off her soles. In her mind's eye, she replayed the crumple of the body back on the street, the feeling that something wasn't right.

And yet, she'd finished out the job, like always. She'd let instinct and training take over and had excused herself afterward, blaming her emotional calluses.

But here was the kicker: she didn't regret taking out those two thugs back in Heron's room. They hadn't been a job. They hadn't been clones or mechs or even free-fae projections.

And she didn't give even the tiniest fuck about murdering them. Her conscience was easy. Just like the puppeteer had said.

Shit, am I really such a cold-blooded freak of nature?

"No guilt, querida," Heron subvoc'd. "Don't you dare beat up on the most amazing woman I have ever met."

Mari froze. Her breath paused.

Wait.

She hadn't said that out loud. Hadn't even mouthed it.

CHAPTER 4

"HERON? CAN YOU READ MY MIND?"

He pressed his lips tight together but otherwise stayed as still as he could. Which was not easy this close. To her. In the dark. He could feel her breath on his throat, and every part of him ached to close even the slight space between them.

Yes, technically, he'd been hearing her thoughts ever since he'd logged in to the Pentarc wireless. He hadn't meant to let on, though. Blood and heat rose in his face, and he was glad of the dark.

He was somewhat less thrilled that he didn't immediately compensate, though. What the hell was wrong with his internal systems? He regulated surface temperature and blood flow, but he still felt hot. No, not merely hot. His body was a wildfire, and he wielded an eyedropper trying to put out sparks. Clearly, harnessing all this extra power from the Pentarc was putting pressure on his control systems. He was holding steady, but just.

Mari waited, still and tense, for his answer. Finally,

he huffed a breath against her hair, tasting her shampoo. His shampoo. Her body lathered in his smell.

He knew he ought to put some more space between them. Ought to step away. But he didn't. He hardly moved at all, besides breathing. "The processing core of a hyperstructure like Pentarc is big, and I've appropriated a good portion of it, as much as I can on wireless. Imagine aiming a gun barrel the size of North America. All that firepower, and it's all mine. The increased capacity enables me to access your thoughts."

As if they behaved independently of his will, his hands sought her waist. The right one slipped beneath the burred terry of her robe, splayed against sweet, hot skin. The sense-tips in his fingers hummed with input, and there was no way he could process it all. Not with a thousand Pentarc cores at his disposal.

He couldn't make himself step away. He wanted to hold her closer, closest. Never let go. He wanted to loose his questing thoughts into her brain, make her think whatever he pleased, or simply make her pleased. His body tightened, ached for her. God.

He was running a full four degrees hotter than normal. Not enough to fry electricals, but definitely in the danger zone. And no matter how much power he sucked from the arcology's reactor, he couldn't douse the flames in his body.

Her thoughts smothered him.

He could see her desire in vivid imagery, hear it in her voice, spoken and unspoken. Her mind was a garden, lush and golden and gorgeous, and he wanted to stretch out naked in it, let it grow over him and encase him. He wanted to be tangled in her.

Oh, hell, as if he hadn't been for a long time now. The power surge was just making the partition of such thoughts harder than usual.

Hard. Thoughts. Fuck.

Mari leaned into his touch. "How long?"

He knew what she meant. She meant how long had he been reading her thoughts, if he'd been able to do it only since jacking into the Pentarc or if he'd had the capability before. But on the other hand, it sounded sordid, too, and she didn't clarify out loud. Hell, knowing Mari, she probably meant the double entendre.

The air didn't have enough oxygen. They might be hiding out in a multiroomed unit, but the foyer was damned cramped. Tiny. Stifling. Intimate. His thumb swept up, skirting the underside of her breast. Her breath hitched.

"Not long enough. But please, if you will, ponder something else."

"Come again?"

Supremely unwise choice of words.

He could have darkened the cameras, could have cut the communication with his evacuation team. So many sacrifices he could have made to focus power to his autonomics. To take control of his body. He chose not to jeopardize their safety. Instead, he sliced open the partition and loosed some of that roiling desire.

More came through than he intended. Rather a lot more.

It tore a gash, rushed out in a torrent. His hands clasped her, pulled her closer. "You can be so fucking provoking, you know that?"

And before Mari could formulate any more chatty

thoughts, his other hand came up, tipping her chin back, and his mouth descended, pouring some of that torrent down her throat, into her body.

He didn't spend the time to test her willingness or worry what this would do to their partnership. He couldn't. All he could do was feel. Press. Breathe. Feel. And kiss her, kiss her, touch her, wrap his hand behind, cupping her bare ass and pushing her hot against the swell of his dick.

Mari, slick and trembling beneath his mouth, his hands, his cock. God, he'd wanted this. He wanted her. In the dark, against the door, in danger of discovery or worse. Fuck it all, he wanted her. Right now.

He slid his left hand up her ribs and rolled a ripe nipple between his thumb and forefinger. His nipple or hers? Inputs had merged, and he was getting thoughts, hot and dark and roaring, from both their minds.

They danced, coalesced, fused. His will and hers. Theirs. One.

● ● ●

Fuck yeah. The flame-retardant metal door pressed up tight and cold against Mari's shoulder blades, but the heat radiating off this kiss, off his hands, was hot enough, it might just set the whole Pentarc on fire anyhow. The coarse terry of her robe scuffed against the one nipple he wasn't pinching, and she longed for a similar friction between her legs. A rub. His fingers. His cock.

She was wet for him. It would be so easy.

Her index finger straightened, and she let the duffel slip to the floor with as controlled a shush as she could manage, but really, her mind was elsewhere. In that moment, she wasn't thinking about the security drone outside or the feds or the job or even the poor schmuck in the next room. All she wanted right then was for Heron to pin her to that goddamned metal door and fuck her until they both hollered like banshees.

Between their bodies, she struggled with the robe's knot. He'd already delved in one side, but she wanted more. She needed to be completely open, full of him.

Dammit. He replied with fingers far too patient. Even his hand on her ass applied only the necessary pressure. She wanted him to squeeze, to grasp her so hard, he left bruises. She wanted him to rip open his fly and ram his cock into her.

The knot loosed, and Mari shoved her robe wide. She moved her feet apart on the tile floor and tipped her pelvis, inviting.

His patient hand cushioned her ass against the door, but the metal hinges groaned. Mari went up on her toes, moving her hand lower and matching her body to his, pressing her mouth deeper into his kiss.

His cock swelled against her knuckles, and she turned her hand sideways, sinking her thumb hard against her clit and her fingers firm against the bulge in his pants.

Come on, partner. Right here.

And then he did the unthinkable.

He stilled.

"God, Heron, don't you dare stop now."

But he had already, and it took Mari a couple of breathless seconds to realize that, in all her urgency, she had spoken.

Um, out loud.

The light beyond Heron's body expanded. Mari

strained to see around him, but his hands retreated to her hips and clamped like vises. He rested his forehead against hers, and she thought she heard the scruff of a *shhh* in her earpiece.

"Heron? Is that you, sweetling?"

Ack! The person who lived here, whose entryway they'd appropriated. A person who would be scared, probably, and...wait.

Sweetling? The voice from the doorway was scratchy, like someone who still inhaled her chems in direct defiance of the FedHealth air-quality regs. *Her* chems, too. Yep, definitely a female voice.

"It is. I'm sorry we've bothered you. We were trying to be quiet."

Lord, how could he sound so calm?

The bearer of that crackly voice might have snorted. "Of the three of us, I suspect I'm the one least bothered right now. And normally, I wouldn't have interrupted, believe me. Normally, I'd be thrilled you brought a friend around for drinksies. But it seems we're in lockdown, and I have a pretty good idea why that might be. You lot probably want to come in further, in case the intruders—federales?—do a door-to-door."

Heron still didn't let her move. Was like he was trying to settle himself down, and Mari knew she ought to do the same. But she didn't have to like it.

"You know the person who lives here?" Mari mouthed.

He held her, forehead to forehead. Their breathing matched, slowed. "Of course I know her." He switched to voice but still didn't turn. "Mari, meet Mrs. Adele Weathering. I wouldn't have barged into just anybody's home. That would have been rude."

Mari didn't turn either, and she didn't speak out loud. Not yet. The way he'd gotten her worked up, he deserved a piece of her mind first. "Now, you wait one dadblamed second. To recap: you're bleeding out the back of your skull, I'm mostly naked, we're hiding out from the law in some strange woman's vestibule, and we just damned near…well, seems like you could let some of them manners slide a bit."

He paused. Lord, what was he thinking? Didn't seem fair he could know her thoughts but everything in his head was still a mystery to her.

His face was in shadow so she couldn't see clearly, but he might have smiled. "I see no problem with the way you're dressed."

She considered tweaking his nipple through the shirt but somehow managed to resist. "Missing the point."

Heron turned finally, straightening Mari's robe in the process so that she was semidecently covered. Couldn't get her blush to cool down, though, and the kicker of it all was that she wasn't sure whether she was blushing because she'd just gotten caught feeling up her partner, or because she'd just gotten caught sneaking uninvited into a stranger's living unit, or because she wished-wished-wished that this Mrs. Adele Weathering person had waited maybe ten more goddamned minutes to butt in.

Mari's skin was still tingling where he'd touched her. Her mouth still throbbed from the pressure of his kiss. And if she hadn't been in the process of evading capture for her other sins, she would sure enough have sought seclusion and a hum-buddy to ease this storm between her legs. But she got control of herself, more or less, squared her shoulders, and followed Heron toward the next room.

He was all polite smiles, greeting Mrs. Weathering with a hug. She had to admit it: it did gall her somewhat that he took the whole transition so easily. Her own body, for contrast, was having serious trouble pretending all that by the door had never happened. She squeezed the rolled collar of her robe tight, but she squeezed her thighs tighter, dialing down the friction, and wondered what she could offer fate for a time warp back to a few seconds ago. So close.

It wasn't until Heron had already ducked through the doorway that Mari caught a clear look at Mrs. Weathering. Like Mari, this woman appeared to have sidestepped the cosmetic reconstruction fad of the last decade. Her face had deep lines around the mouth and at the corners of her heavily mascaraed eyes. Old-fashioned mascara, the kind that smeared. It filled a few wrinkles, spidering out at the edges and crumbling in spots. Same with her scarlet lipstick. She had a home-rolled chemstick pinched between her forefinger and thumb, Russian-style, and her mouth bore purse marks, like she used it to suck a lot.

Mari couldn't tell whether Mrs. Weathering had endured any other cosmetic alts: her whole body from shoulders to fuzzy-slippered feet was draped in a cheery, printed muumuu. Synthsilk charmeuse, true, but still a muumuu.

A curl from the chemstick wafted near Mari: patchouli, cannabis, and something sort of like cinnamon.

And also, Mari wasn't the only one doing a bit of inspecting. Faded blue eyes assessed her as if she were a pastry in a case, about to be consumed. Mrs. Weathering met Mari's gaze and cracked a grin.

"Oh, and speaking of manners," Heron went on, even though the previous discussion hadn't included Mrs. Weathering. "Adele, meet Mari Vallejo."

"Vallejo?" Mrs. Weathering's tatted-on brows marched up her creased forehead.

Mari caught her bottom lip between her teeth. Did the name mean something to her? Had she seen the news alerts? But the tiny frown on Mrs. Weathering's face slipped off, and Mari let her expectation go right along with it. False alarm.

"Well, aren't you a pretty thing? Taller than I imagined. Boy, you can bring her here any time."

Heron grinned and reached back, grasping Mari's hand and pulling her along in his wake. Mari almost snatched her hand away out of pique. Almost. But damn it, she couldn't bring herself to withdraw from his touch completely. Oh, she had it bad, she did.

Also, she found it oddly flattering that he'd mentioned her to his neighbors. That implied that he talked about her when they weren't working. Had to be a good sign, right?

"We'll see," Heron said. "I didn't really expect you to be here. Is Fanaida home, too?"

The pressure of his hand indicated that she should scoot on into the parlor, but Mari didn't much like being ordered around. She paused.

"Not at the moment. She should be coming back north any day, probably with new friends or pets in tow. I can't wait to tell her I got to meet your girl and she didn't. Ha."

When Mrs. Weathering cackled, Mari finally put a

guess on her age: she cackled just like Aunt Boo, and Auntie B had to be near eighty. For a whole-organic without any visible mods, Adele Weathering had held up spectacularly well.

"You kids come in here for a drink. Looks like you might need one."

"Actually," Mari said, disentangling her hand from Heron's and stepping back toward the front door and her duffel, "I'd like to get my clothes on. You got a niche where I can…"

"Oh certainly, cupcake, right over there around the corner. There's a free-fae on the shelf." Mrs. Weathering pointed toward a hallway.

When Mari moved away from him, Heron's fingers stretched long, trailing along the back of her robe, like they were still hoping she'd come back and hold his hand again. But he didn't look at her, and Mari counted that as a blessing. Her body was a jumble of hot-ended nerves, confusing and overwhelming and damn near incapacitating. And it wasn't just because of her legal trouble or the folk out in the hallway hunting her.

It was because of him.

She needed to get away from Heron for just a second, gut-check herself. Then she'd be okay. She'd be able to think. Just not while she was touching him.

Mari snagged the duffel and paused, letting Heron into the lounge first. Not touching. See how she was not touching him? She gave her self-control a mental cookie.

He ducked his head to fit under a low arch, and when he did, Mrs. Weathering gasped and pushed a fist against her mouth. "What happened?"

"Little head wound, and you know how those bleed.

It looks much worse than it is. Kellen'll patch me up shortly. I just need to get Mari out of h—"

Mrs. Weathering tsked behind her coffee-yellowed teeth. Two manicured fingertips reached up and moved his hair aside. "Ick. It's still seeping. You need a coagulator shot at least, and probably something for the pain. Come here."

"You really needn't…"

"Boy"—her tone sharpened—"you *will* let me bandage you."

Mari smiled. Heron totally deserved the talkin' to. The concern. The soft coo and gentle hands leading him to a settee with ball-fringe cushions covering cigarette burns. He deserved clean cotton rounds and tenderness. Love. Yeah, that's what he deserved.

Her own smile faded to shame.

She'd offered him none of those things, and especially not the last. Mari was danger, drama, baggage, sin, and soulless, right-the-hell-now sex when she could get it.

And it didn't matter one bit that she wished she could be what he needed.

She grabbed her duffel with both hands and ducked down the half corridor to change.

Her clothes. To change her clothes.

●　●　●

Back during the riots, when he had been trying to escape Austin, Heron had sustained several injuries that should have been fatal. The queen had been with him, though she wasn't a queen back then, just a thing, priceless and broken and scared. Disconnected from the university supercomputer for the first time in her short existence and flailing without her usual succor of information, she hadn't been much help in navigating through the chaos. They'd forced a path through a tangle of looters, National Guard militia, and rabble-rousers shouting about liberty and taxes, and he'd kept his head down and hauled her along in his wake.

A homemade bomb a block south of the capitol had turned his world red, had melted the skin and nerves and other tissues, laying bare the bone along the left side of his body, all in less than a second. He didn't feel the pain, not right then, but it would come soon enough, and it would incapacitate him. The queen knew this.

Behind a still-burning food cart near Third Street, they had hunkered together, the stolen thing and him, and waited for death. Or he had. The queen had lacked a human's capacity to lose hope. She had bent, unrolled a silicon-wrapped bundle, and drawn out an electrostatic containment vial.

"Eyes open. Be still," she had said in her raspy metallic voice. "You have a venous access port on your right arm. This vat will invade, replicate, repair, and you will have no pain. The nanos are programmed for me, though, and you will change. Everything will change, but you will live."

He stayed still while she ripped his sleeve off at the shoulder, exposing the port. After all that had been done to him over the years, her probe hurt least but dehumanized him more. He had known exactly what he was accepting with that injection, but he hadn't stopped her. Instead, he had focused his gaze on the blue-light dance of downed live wires in the street, the klaxon sounds of his city falling to chaos. Everything *had* changed that night, just as she'd promised. And he hadn't so much as blinked.

That was kind of how he felt now. His universe had shifted inexorably.

Mari had kissed him. Or he'd kissed her. Skin to skin, dark and hot and wet and within microns and moments of fusing. And he hadn't had a scrap of control, no resistance. Against her mouth, he'd become an electric pulse of raw and mortal and ignorant and wild and elated. Out of control but too terrified to stop the wild hurtle. His body had responded as if touching her, consuming her, fucking her, were the most logical and inevitable things in the universe.

Always before, he had damped those reactions. Repaired them. And he absolutely should not have failed to do so this time. What was wrong with him?

Through the vague pressure on the back of his skull, sensation pricked bright and white. It should not have. But it did. He made an inarticulate sound and stiffened, and the fingers gentled.

"Sorry, sweetling. Whoever did this really made a mess." Adele leaned back, drew a syringe from her sewing box, and filled it with something from a milk-glass bottle. "You already called Kellen?"

"Yeah. They will be here in forty minutes, give or take. I was going to use the helo pad over on South, but the police will have that covered."

"Mmmmhmmm." Dabbing antiseptic against the wound, but gently, as if he were an infant. "So what's your plan?"

"We can use the false floor in your closet. I'll take

her down to ten, across the skywalk to the east spire, and then down to the carpark. Main exits will be covered, but we can use the tunnels. The car's fast and has some stealth buffering, which will work better now it's dark out. We'll be okay."

And all the people in the Pentarc would be safe then, too. He was counting on that.

On wireless, he pinged the arcology's evacuation protocol, searching for the switches to open the escape tunnels. Nothing. Did it again. On the second try, it responded. Weird. Digital systems, unlike people, always replied predictably.

Always, except for right now.

He no longer had injector ports on his body, but when Adele stuck him, he didn't feel the needle's prick. He deliberately searched for the chemical bolus, routed it to the pain receptors at the wound in his head, dispersed it. His circulatory system wobbled. He blinked, resetting internal pathways, pulling more power from the arcology.

Something was seriously wrong with his body. It wasn't just the surge of being so close to Mari, of touching her. Kissing her. That had been so intense that he'd ascribed his bizarre loss of control to her. But there was more to it. Something else was fucking with him. He could run a better diagnostic if he had access to the cloud, of course, but even a closed system like the Pentarc would be more effective if he established a physical link. Not that he particularly wanted to plug anything into his head at the moment.

The deep, pulling discomfort at the wound site faded, chased off by the drugs. Adele decontaminated her needle, wrapped it in a wad of flower-print flannel, and tucked it back into her sewing kit.

Heron licked his teeth, tasted metal. Anxiety. "I need a port."

Adele gave him a one-eyebrow-up look. "*Cash Cow* is on in about ten minutes, and I always play, even during lockdown. Nobody would know any different if you were to piggyback on the wire."

He reached up and grabbed her hand. Her lacquered nails felt sturdy, but the rest of her was paper light. Thin. Almost insubstantial.

Adele was getting old. He knew it but didn't want to think of her as frail. He needed her to be his touchstone, his haven. His world was spinning, and he needed her stillness. He just wasn't any good on his own.

"I'm sorry about coming in here. I didn't know you'd be in your room and sort of hoped you wouldn't."

She patted his hand. "No worries, sweet boy. I'm always happy to see you, even when you're in mortal danger." She stepped away, humming as she made for a burled wood buffet littered with decanters. "Chocolate? I got it eighty proof."

"Driving shortly." Usually, he would have no trouble metabolizing alcohol, but today? Best not chance it.

Adele shot him a look as she poured herself a drink. Even from across the room, that stuff smelled like turpentine. "There you go resisting temptation. Eventually, you'll have to get over your guilt and start living again. I thought for a moment when you introduced her that you'd turned a corner. Forgiven yourself. Don't you think it's about time?"

Heron sank against the back of the antique settee. It

was too short for him, as were most of Adele's furnishings. He couldn't drop his head back. Couldn't close his
eyes and pretend he was home and a kid and innocent.
Couldn't relax.

And really, *really* couldn't have this conversation
right now.

Instead, he touched the needle mark on his arm, just
one more flaw on a canvas of scars, and rolled his sleeve
down. "Thank you."

Adele breezed past him, headed for the entertainment
unit on the far wall. *Cash Cow* in ten. Right.

On the way, she bent and dropped a kiss on his
antiseptic-damp hair. "Always, boy. Always."

●　　●　　●

In an alcove with a commode along the far wall, Mari
swung the saloon doors closed behind her and shucked
the torn, bloody robe.

Low voices drifted in from the other room. She followed Heron's half of the conversation through the com
and Mrs. Weathering's half through plain old earpower.
Walls here in Pentarc, when you could get 'em, were
awfully thin.

The cramped alcove was lit by a free-fae box, and
Mari took a moment to thank the thing. True, program-
mers shoved nanos together all the time, made them do
things. The nanos themselves weren't supposed to have
will. But sometimes, they did. Sometimes, they snuck
away and formed shit of their own volition, mostly
these boxes, which somehow produced light without a
discernible power source. Gray-market nutjobs hocked
them, and street-corner priests worshipped them. Damn

useful things all around. Mari knew they were just machines, but it still made her feel good to offer a thank-you here and there.

But she still didn't feel any embarrassment when she kicked the robe aside and stood there bare-ass naked. Wasn't like the free-fae was watching or anything.

Right?

She slipped on snug pants riddled with utility pockets. She usually wore skirts and petticoats, knockoffs of the West Coast fashionistas, but for jobs, she stuck with combat longstockings or pants. Girl needed to move fast sometimes, and those pockets came in handy for ammo.

She did wonder what it'd be like to doll up for Heron. He might not even recognize her if she was painted and primped, but her ego sure could sure use a little jaw droppage.

In the other room, Mrs. Weathering said something about guilt, and Mari paused for a second with her hands on the zipper.

No way would he tell her what they were up against, what she'd done this morning. She trusted him. Of course she did.

But she still paused and listened, waiting for his reply in her com.

"Thank you."

Now, why was it she thought he was talking to her when he said that? He wasn't even in the same room, but she could feel him all in her head. In her chest. It tingled, tickled. She shook herself, took a deep breath, and tried to regain focus.

She sausaged a stretchy, long-sleeved number over her head and reached back into the bag. Her hands skimmed the H&K's barrel, and she bit her lip. Put it together, just in case? But the custom stock, molded to fit against her cheek when she was prone, combined with the length of the weapon when it was all fitted together, made it unwieldy for tight spaces. No, the snubby would have to do.

After some hesitation, she dug deeper, pulled out an aramid-core button-up, and slung it over top of her shirt. From the interchange she'd spied on between Heron and Mrs. Weathering, it didn't look like Mari was going to take them down the cabling vent after all, but that didn't mean there weren't other, more ballistic dangers looking to catch her before this day was done.

More mumbling from Mrs. Weathering and the melodic trill of an entertainment console fizzing to life.

Mari secured her still-damp hair with an elastic and tucked the snubby into her waistband. She'd forgotten to pack socks and missed them when she shoved her feet into rubber-soled boots and snapped up. The humidity in there made the mostly dried blood between her toes sort of gooey, a gross reminder of what she'd done.

There was a mirror with another fae light above the commode, but Mari didn't so much as glance. No purpose to it. She knew what she looked like: cold-blooded killer. Monster.

"Hey, poppet," Mrs. Weathering called from the other room, and Mari started. "*Cash Cow*'s on in six, and I'm about to log on."

"What she means," Heron subvocaled, "is that you can stop skulking and join us."

Mari scowled but didn't deny she'd been skulking.

She repacked her duffel, shoving the blood-stained robe deep and laying the rope and descenders out on top, untangled, just in case she needed to get at them quick.

She was a little wigged to note, when she started zipping up the bag, that her hands were shaking. Never a good sign for a shooter. She stared hard until the tremors stopped, and then she grabbed the bag handle and made her way back to the main room.

She ducked in, reflexively scanning the room for exits and changes since she'd seen it last. The console was booting, Mrs. Weathering was drinking something brown and foul-smelling, and Heron was kneeling at the far side of the entertainment set, out of the monitor's sightline. He was also wearing driving gloves, covering the sense-tips. Because he was planning on driving? Or because he wanted a line of defense in case he had to touch her again?

Ha. Maybe that grope in the foyer had been harder on him than he let on. Mari plopped down next to him on the rug—too close, of course.

Gloves also offered another clue about his relationship with Mrs. Weathering. Neighbors didn't usually keep clothes for each other on hand, and she *had* called him *sweetling*.

Mrs. Weathering fiddled with some jacks, talking to herself the whole time. Something about trying to figure out which was the new socket connector on this bloody new upgrade hardware—she hoped it hadn't all gone over to hands-free because everyone knew first-to-market tech was rubbish anyhow. All the while, her grumbles covered up the fact that Heron had jacked into the console.

Mari flashed a glance at Heron and saw that he was looking right back at her. And frowning.

"What?"

He reached over and plucked something from her still-damp ponytail. Even though his hands were safe and gloved again, energy spiked at the point of contact, and Mari had an urge to lean into it and make him touch her, damn it.

"Feather." A pause and then, soundlessly, "Pity. I rather liked you naked."

Something like lightning forked all through Mari's body, and she bit back the words that bubbled up, afraid they'd seem too enthusiastic if she let 'em out. No question about it, though: he'd been flat-out obviously flirting with her that time.

It took considerable control for Mari not to climb onto Heron's lap right then. She felt very good about herself for resisting. And very bad for continuing to indulge naughty thoughts that she was sure he could read perfectly well.

Mrs. Weathering plugged in two connectors, and the ancient holo adapter crackled to life. She tuned the socket behind her ear. The room filled with the campy sounds of *Cash Cow* intro music. She settled in right in front of the unit and grabbed her brew-filled tumbler.

"Um, ma'am? I just wanted to say…" Mari began, but she heard an unmistakable *shhh* in her head.

Heron's hand snaked out along the loud paisley rug. He grabbed her wrist.

"They're scanning the whole structure for residents," he mouthed. "Note how she's positioned herself right in front of the holo unit? If they scan the signals and peek in, they'll only see her. We should be quiet just in case."

"Can't you just fuzz out their reception or something?"

Mrs. Weathering cackled and took a swig of her drink. The chemstick pinched between her fingers really needed to have the ash flicked off, but she didn't seem to notice.

"The agents in this building aren't the decision makers. They're just grunts following orders. I am giving them a chance to work through their protocols, hoping they'll give up and go home."

"And what if they don't?"

Heron's mouth twitched, and his thumb brushed the top of her hand. He didn't answer her, not out loud and certainly not in her mind. Instead, his thumb figure-eighted her first two knuckles, dipping along that sensitive skin between her fingers.

Soft leather, but damn, she missed the contact with his skin.

They sat in tense silence for about four minutes. On the holo, *Cash Cow* blared on, trilling its signature moo music. Right before the interval, Mari thought she saw a flicker, a miniflash from the entertainment console.

The tumbler slipped from Mrs. Weathering's grasp. It hit the floor before Mari realized that Mrs. Weathering's face had gone slack, too. But Mari didn't get a chance to register that properly, because in the same instant, Heron gripped her hand. Hard.

And then he let go.

CHAPTER
5

ONE MINUTE, HERON WAS CROUCHED ON THE FLOOR, and the next, he was over by the floral-print settee, kneeling beside Adele. He'd felt the electrical surge, had traced it real time through the tower wires.

The surge had come through the moment he'd used the Pentarc closed system to poll the cloud. Bots must have been lurking there, waiting. And now he'd confirmed that he was here. Worse, that Mari was here.

Ten thousand thoughts birthed like stars in his brain, and he sorted them instantly. Drones on every floor. Lifts covered. Reinforcements arriving.

He'd planned to take Mari down through the other spire, sneak her out. But now, as he looked at Adele crumpled on the rug, he shifted plans on the fly.

He walked right past the viewfinder on the holo, but he didn't give a fuck. They already knew he was here. He drew a sign in the air, cutting transmission. The display went dark. "No more peeking."

Tenderly, he bent over Adele, checking her pulse. Steady. No flutters. Thank God. She was okay.

He'd measured the voltage on the flash, and he knew it wasn't strong enough to knock her out for long. Still, it pissed him off that she'd taken another hit for him. He'd gone to a lot of trouble to make Pentarc safe, to make it *his*, and Adele was one of the people he'd tried to insulate most.

The worst part of this fucked-up day was not that the job had gone wrong or that he'd gotten jacked. It was that he'd brought Adele here to keep her safe, and he'd brought Mari here for the same reason, and now both were in danger.

Heron wasn't used to having his plans upset like this. It made him…angry. No, more than that. Furious.

"She gonna be okay?" Mari asked. She'd gotten to her feet and retrieved her duffel.

In the dim blue glow of the free-fae light, her eyes looked big as desert marigolds. Somebody who didn't know about her love of all things deadly might end their assessment right at those eyes. Delicate, they'd think. Delicate and precious.

Heron agreed, to a point. But he also knew what Mari was capable of. Delicate, precious, and…completely badass. The perfect mix.

"Yeah." He pinched a sliver of metal from behind Adele's ear. Careful, so it wouldn't ache when she woke. "The electrical surge fried her com, but it wasn't a permanent implant, just a surface rig like yours. She'll wake up and smell burnt silicon for a couple of days."

"You know, I bet they didn't do that to everybody on this floor, or not even to everybody watching *Cash Cow*, though considering that moo music, maybe they should. I'm thinking those feds were looking for *us*."

Mari's fist tightened on her duffel strap. Her mouth was stern. "How'd they know we were here?"

"I don't know yet. Maybe they had tracers in the mercs, and they projected our position from the time of those kills."

"Maybe they knew you were friends with Mrs. Weathering."

Heron pulled a ball-fringe pillow down from the recliner and tucked it beneath Adele's head. "Family. And let us hope not. Then they would know altogether too much about me."

He'd spent most of his adult life shielding his identity and those of the people closest to him. If somehow the authorities tracking Mari also knew who he was, what he was—worse, what he'd done—well, that changed the equation.

Changed a lot of things.

Heron loosed a signal and threaded it around the Pentarc, counting the threats. Three drones were on this floor now, and the actual feds would be coming up the stairwell shortly. Heron accessed the Pentarc broadcast to fuzz their com channel, so the drones wouldn't be able to talk to the officers.

With the subroutines already set up in the Pentarc architecture, this should be easy. No big deal.

And yet. A blip from the drone down the hall slipped through his net. Fuck.

Mari still stood there, perched like a bird on a lightning rod. Heron didn't even have to concentrate to hear her thoughts: *One bullet left. Of course, if Mrs. Weathering has some hydrogen peroxide around, I'm pretty sure I packed that canister of shaved magnesium dioxide.*

Could whip up a bomb pretty easy, blast our way out of here if necessary. Do so enjoy blowing shit up.

"I can still hear you, you know," Heron said, rising to his feet. He tapped his temple to emphasize the point.

"And what?" she sassed. "You want me to be all sweet just because you're in my head? Information: this *is* the sweet me. Any sweeter and you can brace yourself for a replay of that whole thing by the door, so don't push it, partner."

Oh, that was it. He moved past her, way closer than he had to, and, on a breath, murmured, "I believe the correct phrase here is 'Bring it.'"

● ● ●

Mari was still processing the innuendo—no, that was some balls-out flirting right there—when she noticed that he was ahead of her, already turning the door handle and leading them back into the corridor.

"Whoa, cowboy, I thought I was the muscle."

The free-fae light bleeding in from the parlor was low, granted, but she could still see the flare of his eyebrows, the tightness around his mouth, when he turned back to her.

"We don't need muscle anymore. They came here, invaded my home, attacked my family. Fuck that. They aren't playing nice, so neither am I."

He didn't explain further, but Mari felt a thrill at his words. She fisted her bag straps in one hand and steadied the little pistol in her other. Which left no hands to hold on to Heron in the dark.

Not that she needed to, as it turned out. "Don't need muscle" apparently also meant "don't necd the cover of darkness." The corridor emergency lighting was on, but the air had thinned, like they were at high altitude.

"I am altering the atmospheric controls throughout the Pentarc, remixing the O_2 balance in specific locations. Not enough to slow us down in the hallway but enough to incapacitate the feds in the access wells. Adele and the other residents are still locked in, at least until we're clear. You and me? We can just walk out."

Mari trusted this man—this machine—implicitly, and she followed him through Mrs. Weathering's door, back out into the west-spire corridor. But she still felt off her feed, uncomfortable. In her experience, going face-to-face, preferably with a firearm in her fist, was the best way to handle confrontations with folks who wanted to kill her. They almost always backed down.

Or they had until today. The grim reminder settled cold and yucky in her gut, and she wasn't smiling anymore.

As she and Heron approached the elevator, Mari caught a flash of stainless steel and raised her weapon reflexively. Just off to the right, she spied a floater drone, hovering between Heron and the shiny metal doors.

"Get down." She aimed without pausing her stride, making the calculations on the fly, knowing that she'd have a split second between her max range and the machine's. Though she had no idea what the snubby's dinky load would do against carbon fiber, she wasn't just going to let a robot take her out. Not today.

Heron put a calming hand on her forearm.

"Relax, querida. It's inert."

Mari didn't shoot, but she wasn't comfortable skirting around that thing. She could fucking see its anesthetic-tipped mini-A10s bobbing like doc's needles, ready to fang her as she walked by. Ready to hurt *him*. But they didn't. The drone's green light panel cycled, and its rotors hummed, but its metal hull didn't budge.

She and Heron passed without so much as a whimper from the robot.

She joined her partner on the platform and worked on calming herself down. But was she really to blame for being just a mite freaked out? She had a wild urge to stick her tongue out at the drone as the platform started to move.

They descended so quickly that Mari's ears popped. She swallowed. Seemed to her that maybe this elevator went a little slower when Heron *wasn't* controlling things, and she recalled how much he liked fast. She wondered if that applied to all things, and for a full couple of moments there, her serious slipped. Hard.

She wanted to ask him what they could expect when they reached the arcade deck, but a sidelong glance at him kept her quiet. He was processing, running a zillion things in that wired-out head of his. She could tell by the set to his jaw, his game face.

His gloved hands flexed, opening and closing long fingers, drawing glyphs in the air. It looked half geek, half mystical, and so perfectly *him*. She wondered what he was signing to the ether.

She wondered a lot of things about him.

He'd implied that the feds were just after her, and that could very well be the case, but she wasn't the one those assholes had taken apart upstairs. She wasn't the one who'd been violated and invaded. She also wasn't the one with clearly nonstandard, whoa-illegal tech in her body. It had never occurred to her before today, but he would be worth a lot on the black market. Tech vultures would pick him apart. And the mercs had said they were looking for the legal resident of that unit, hadn't they? That would be Heron.

A mental image of that merc with his grubby hands inside of Heron's head blasted into her thoughts.

A need for vengeance rose up black and horrible from Mari's gut, and she wished she'd looted that hydrogen peroxide back at Mrs. Weathering's. Nothing short of a brilliant explosion—or sheet-scorching sex—was likely to ease this fury.

"Easy." Heron echoed her words from earlier. "I got this."

And then the elevator stopped.

Mari looked around, getting her bearings. The arcade was lit, just as if this were a typical Saturday night. Signs had switched from daytime, kid-friendly fare to blinking and blurring come-here-and-get-chemmed lures. Mari stepped out first, placing her body between the creepily empty stretch and her partner.

The need to wreck something hadn't left her, and her trigger finger was twitchier than she'd've liked. When she passed a boarded-up crèche with a holo of a crino-lined schoolteacher out front, it was everything Mari could manage not to blow the light bank away.

One bullet. Make it count.

But there was nothing impeding their progress. They stepped onto the conveyor walk, and it surged forward. Typically, the outer rings of conveyors went slower, and if somebody was trying to get all the way to the far side of the Pentarc, they'd want to merge into the inner ring. But Heron, apparently, wasn't into merging. The outer ring sped them so fast that Mari couldn't even see the empty government storefront sector as they zipped by. She'd been thinking that the feds would be hanging out there, if they were capable of any blockade presence right now. But Mari's best chance at getting to beat the shit out of somebody had just swept past.

It wasn't that she was getting used to the feeling of being an actual killer. It was more that she had realized, right there against the door at Mrs. Weathering's arco unit, that killing, even whole-organics, wasn't such a bad thing. Heron was alive. She'd do a helluva lot more to keep him that way.

Murder, then, was a matter of priority. And the way Mari's priorities were situated right at that minute, those feds had better get the hell out of her way.

The conveyor downshifted and paused finally on the far end of the arco's version of a community college campus. The interior wall was glass, open to the funnel of sunlight that would be pouring in here during the day. At night, it just loomed. Mari didn't want to think about all the mechanical eyes that could be looking at her through that ten-story, impact-glass plate.

She felt pretty calm now that she'd decided to shoot first and ask questions later.

"Immediately past the money transfer station is an access gate to the carpark. That's where we're headed," Heron said. He touched her elbow just long enough to guide her.

Uni campuses the whole world over smelled like stale corn chips and burnt silicon, Mari thought as she passed through the abandoned miniature quad. Even the artificial on-sites like this one. Did they pipe the stench in or what? Regardless, that smell reminded her of some shit from her uni days, things that she'd thought tidily repressed.

And something else, an image, a memory…but it slid off her brain like a buttered noodle.

'Cause she had a lot more important stuff to pay attention to right now.

"Halt. Palms out. You are surrounded."

Shit. Mari, for all her rage and determination, had been caught off guard. She extended one arm across Heron's chest, raising her weapon with the other. Her shooter brain backtracked the voice and found the general direction of her threat, but she couldn't confirm visual. If she'd had a whole magazine, she would have started shooting, hoping to hit something. If she'd had a mag of frangibles, she would have laid into the taco cart ahead and to the right, which she was willing to bet concealed a whole slew of feds.

But even as she paused infinitesimally to set up her sightlines, Heron just kept moving, his long strides eating up the rubber pavement. He didn't pull her along this time, just went on right in front of her. Unarmed, unruffled. Serene. As if he were daring them to shoot.

"Keep up, querida."

Mari opened her mouth, about to say something, but then she forgot what it was she was going to say and just left her mouth open. Because even as she watched, even as her feet hurried to obey him, Heron moved his hands away from both sides of his body, turning them palms up. He drew twin glyphs in the air, and Mari heard a sound like a flock of migrating birds, big suckers, descending in a whoosh.

She looked up in time to see a fleet of maybe two dozen drones, just like the one she'd passed by upstairs, moving in on either side of her and Heron, circling them.

But all their nasty needle guns were pointed away from Mari this time. Behind her, the glass wall glowed, chemlit to simulate day. It warmed, maybe too warm.

Over the Pentarc communication system came Heron's voice. "Stand down, officers. Nobody needs to die today."

"Nobody else," Mari clarified subvocally.

"You need to be literal right at this minute?" he asked in his normal voice, and though he didn't turn to her when he said it, Mari thought there might have been some smiling going on.

"You mean like I'm *literally* freaked out of my mind right now?" She did not verbalize her physical reaction to this flex of his technological muscles. If he dug deep enough into her psyche, he'd see how fucking hard she wanted him right now. Not even that deep, the want. Felt like it was burning all over her skin, in fact, like the chemlight in the glass wall, easy for anybody to see.

"Getting there myself," she heard him in her mind, and she burned even hotter.

The drones moved in closer, forming an outward-facing circle with her and Heron at the center. He didn't walk any faster than normal, but Mari hurried to keep up. She wasn't really worried that those drones would sneak up on her from behind, but she inherently distrusted them. Even though Heron was controlling them.

Machine controlling machine. How could she trust one so completely, but not the others, his minions?

He passed into the gate, and the vanguard of drones stopped there, waiting for her. His partner. His team. She followed him without looking back.

CHAPTER

6

MARI DIDN'T SAY MUCH ON THE WAY DOWN TO THE underground, and Heron counted that as a rarity and a blessing. His brain was still buzzing, a thousand inputs screaming through his data streams—organic and mech—but the main thing he wanted to know, needed to ascertain, was this: could he get her out? Could he keep her safe?

Once upon a time, his goals in life had been lofty. Once, he'd thought that he might change the world, create something that would fundamentally alter how human beings lived on this planet, and above it. Now, though, a good day meant everyone who depended on him was safe, his secrets were still secret, and he could reach through one of his mirrors, count Mari's pulse, and know that wherever she was, she slept easy.

He no longer wondered how or when his universe had shrunk to this. All he knew was that as long as he could control the variables, he could affect outcomes. Could change the future and bury the past.

But he couldn't sustain this balance indefinitely.

Adele was right; the guilt was eating him up, and he needed to expunge it. Grow past it. He needed to tell Mari everything. That he'd been following her career for years, that he'd hired on as her partner to lead her away from Texas contracts, to keep her out of the state. To keep her safe.

And why.

Not the chest-pulling, desperate infatuation part. He didn't need to tell her that. But he did need to explain the guilt, and soon. She might already have started remembering, and though that would be bad enough on its own, he didn't want anyone else to tell her.

And he sure as hell didn't want anyone dragging her back to Texas.

A monster of emotion lurked close beneath his surface where she was concerned, and leashing it usually wasn't a problem. Until someone tried to harm her. It was a mercy those feds hadn't started shooting up there in the miniquad. He would have had no compunction about shooting back, and with the whole Pentarc core at his disposal, the resultant mess would have been ugly. His surges of anger had spiraled to catastrophe before, and he was thankful that such hadn't been the case today. Yet.

What would she do if she knew how little humanity was left in him? If she knew how easily he could set aside his conscience and focus on the task at hand, push the guilt and fury into a tidy aside to be dealt with later? Her thoughts from earlier echoed in his memory: *murderer, monster*.

If he told her the truth, she would run. And he couldn't bear that.

He needed to get her to safety, tamp down these dark thoughts. Cool his systems, center himself. *One heartbeat every 0.24 seconds. One breath every 2.2 seconds. One blink every 4 seconds.* There. He could do this.

Pressure plates in the garage shifted, and Heron transmitted a command that would block any new vehicles from entering. He sent a query up eleven floors, adjusting the chems in Adele's unit, so she'd wake up without a headache. In the same transmission, he downloaded location tags for his crew and the Chiba Space Station. Planning. Calm. In control.

He checked the evacuation protocol and was pleased that his instructions to the escape tunnels had finally gone through. He sent a signal to his car that would give them access to the exit. The Pentarc system didn't show the tube as blocked, and if he could get out that way, he had just enough charge in the fuel cells to get her out to the desert. Flat would be good for what he had in mind.

But even as he planned their next dozen moves, he couldn't tamp the fury entirely. What had happened this morning should not have happened. Mari's contract had been to either retrieve or slag the Daniel Neko mechclone. All systems had checked in, giving the green light. All of them.

Including Daniel Neko's wife.

Now Heron was wondering if Angela Neko had been complicit in the deception. Had she meant to send her flesh-and-blood husband to his death? Did she have enemies in the UNAN government who'd called in the hit just to hurt her? Or had those fuckers from Texas played her, too?

Or was the TPA after something else entirely? Like him.

Heron shook his head, ignoring the flash of pain between his ears. *Stop it. Think present, think future. Yesterday never happened. Later on, you can plan a suitable revenge for whoever is responsible for this morning.*

"You okay?" Mari touched his arm, and he almost jumped out of his boots.

"Always." He controlled the wince that his face wanted to make. His first priority, of course, was getting her to a haven, preferably one off-grid. Pentarc should have been that. How had those mercs gotten in here without him knowing?

The tube lift stopped. Curved doors opened. Heron knew that no one other than the two of them was on this level of the underground, but he scanned just the same. After all these years looking out for Mari, caution was a reflex.

The Pentarc processor core certainly sped things up, in addition to letting him peek in on her thoughts. That was a bonus he could get used to. Which, of course, meant he needed to disconnect soon. He had no desire to become dependent on the extended processing capacity. Too dangerous.

He reached behind his head, felt for the metal insert, and nudged it off of its connectors. *So long, Pentarc.*

The connection broke. He fell.

Hit.

Hard.

Whoa.

Retreating back into his own neural was the sudden stop at the end of freefall. It crushed his consciousness for a half second, cramming it into an itty-bitty space. And oh, he had enjoyed the stretch. He gritted his teeth against the squeeze, but fuck, it still hurt.

This fit was tighter than he expected. A lot tighter. He flailed, searching for threads of awareness, catching them and plugging them together, making connections. Ends still floated, frayed. He couldn't see the tapestry whole, and those loose ends throbbed like exposed nerve endings.

The mercs had fucked him up worse than he thought.

Biting back bile, Heron concentrated on presenting a composed exterior for Mari's benefit. People with regular organic brains did not implode when they disconnected. He couldn't let her see how much this affected him.

He tucked the skin flap back over his ruined port, feeling the wet stickiness of blood still matting his hair despite Adele's best efforts to clean him up. Lord, what must he look like to Mari? But he couldn't just reach in and ask now.

A machine, his logical brain answered. *A thing*.

Probably a pretty fucking terrifying thing, after what he'd just pulled in the Pentarc, too. And he knew it could have been so much worse.

He growled in the back of his throat, and three shipping containers over, the car growled back. Good car. Now *that* was a thing, and if it could haul ass fast enough to get Mari beyond the reach of the feds and the TPA and whoever else wanted her to pay for someone else's fuckup, Heron figured he could spare plenty of love for that thing.

He had his doubts about Mari's ability to do the same for him.

●　●　●

When the V12 roared to life from three stalls over, Mari felt it in the soles of her feet.

She's so hot. Well, that was the first thought that popped into her brain, and if Heron was still peeking in on her, he could just suck on that. She wasn't going to self-censor for his benefit. If he hadn't figured out by now that most of her thoughts had to do with the job, her family, and sex, he didn't know her all that well.

Her fingertips stroked the curved hood on her way to the passenger side. She dipped her hand to where a handle ought to be and spent a couple seconds stroking nothing but fiberglass before she looked down. No handle. How had she never realized before? Even as she watched, though, the door hissed open on hydraulic hinges.

She climbed inside and dropped her duffel by her feet.

"You might want to fasten your seat harness," Heron suggested. Metal scraped metal, a sharp sound with a slip of something wet that might have been blood, and she knew he was plugging in. Once the human-vehicle connection had set, the car shifted into reverse, and they backed out of the shipping container.

"In a bit." Mari leaned forward and unzipped the duffel, hunting down the various pieces of her weapon, and started fitting them together with sure fingers.

"And you don't need your rifle."

"Listen, I ain't about to…"

"Here."

And Mari did drop her rifle bits then, because Heron reached down, grabbed her hand, and settled it over something long and firm and so phallic, her mouth watered.

Gearshift. Oh, right.

"The switch at the base readies the weapon. Use the thumb button to shoot. Aim with your fist, and hold on tight. It's a gun, not a launcher or a laser, and I haven't upgraded yet, so no vents. The kick will sling us around some. We can put the top down if you need better visuals, but frankly, it might be better to keep the armor up and run for it. The cannon is really just for...fun."

She gripped the stick. Hydraulics behind the firewall in front of her feet hummed and slipped. A seam down the center of the hood parted, and a heavy-weapon gyroscopic mount pushed through. He wasn't kidding: sitting right there where most cars like this would have a trunk was a precious-huge snub-barrel cannon. She flashed Heron a glance. Looking to upgrade the guns on this car? Seriously? If he was making fun of her, she was going to...

But he wasn't. He was looking right at her, and there wasn't even a hint of smile on that mouth. It was everything she could do in that moment not to climb right over that gearshift and onto his lap, kiss his mouth to smiling, and pour a little bit of hells-yes right down his throat. She squeezed the gearshift, fighting the urges.

"Some fun." Her voice huffed through a suddenly dry mouth.

"Tell me about it."

And that, she thought later, was the moment she fell in love.

● ● ●

Nothing shot at them right away when they broke the surface and roared away from the Pentarc. Night had fallen on the desert, and the clear watchfulness of it bothered Mari more than she wanted to admit. She kept her hand fisted on the gearshift and couldn't calm down, but she was no longer certain whether she was worked up because the feds were after her, because she'd done some seriously guilt-making things this day, or because her libido was firing like all get out.

"Really, you can sit down and buckle up. We're safe."

"Uh-huh." She stroked the gearshift with the side of her thumb, and he…tensed? In response? Nah. She was imagining things. He had a lot more on his mind than watching her hands right now.

"Quarter panels, hood, and the soft top are reinforced with 60-carbon fullerene," he said. "We're as safe as we're likely to get from bullets, shrapnel, lasers, EMP attacks, fire—you name it. About the only thing that can damage this car is the hand of God. Now, Mari, relax."

The heater was going again: negative ionization and serotonin-exciting aerosol, soothing the burn of body and mind.

Mari's grip eased, but she didn't sit down. She glanced at him in her periphery. "I know what you were trying to do."

Heron didn't reply. His gloved hands tightened on the steering wheel.

Mari went on, "Back at Mrs. Weathering's, when you kissed me, you were trying to distract me, focus me, keep me from freaking out. I needed that. Thank you."

Heron still didn't say anything, and Mari swallowed a lump of regret. If he'd meant it, if he burned for her anything like she burned for him, she'd left the door wide open for him to say so.

The car shifted to fifth, soft in transition like a lover nuzzling in sleep.

"It seemed like you needed the distraction. You aren't a murderer," Heron said at last. "Never think of yourself that way. You defended yourself…"

"Yeah, but at what cost? I mean…"

"…when I could not."

Mari opened her mouth to say something, but she caught a glance at the dash. The lipstick-red speedometer needle hugged the right end of the arc. It didn't even quiver back down to the max speed, 220. They were flying over the desert.

Her gaze drifted up to his face, illuminated only by the dash lights. He looked perfectly at ease, focused on the road and unreadable, but Mari saw the little tells: minute furrow between his eyebrows, lips pressed together a smidge tighter than usual.

This was more than just him worried for her safety. Something else was freaking him out.

"Don't think I'm stewing now, partner. I'm glad I killed those guys." She watched the muscle near the hinge of his jaw. "If it'd kept their filthy fingers outta your head, I would've slagged the whole fed ops corps, and their pet kittens, too."

He cracked the faintest grin, more a hint of one really, and the needle still pegged 220, but it was enough. "No, you would not have. Broad-scale devastation isn't your game."

It isn't yours either. She watched, but he didn't so much as twitch. Apparently, without the Pentarc amping his neural, he couldn't read her thoughts. She kind of missed that intimate connection, even if it had been frustratingly one-sided.

After a while, Mari shrugged and settled down into the leather seat, facing forward. "Well, I'll work on the bloodthirsty, but it'd be a damn shame if I reformed completely, 'specially before I get to test out your cannon here." She nodded to the gearshift, still unwilling to let it go.

Out the wing-shaped windows, the desert stretched endless and black with no feds in sight, but she knew they were out there, looking for her. Hunting her. Being prey didn't feel so stark as long as she had a weapon in her hands.

Especially *this* weapon. She cricked her index finger, and the emplacement shifted, responding perfectly to her touch. The barrel was way too short for a conventional load at this caliber. Might be electromagnetic. Whatever its inner workings, she was pretty sure it was fully integrated with the car.

And so, she suspected, was Heron.

Mari firmed her fist on the gearshift, slipping her palm down to the base. A corresponding twitch fluttered over his jaw.

Holy crapfire. He *felt* it.

Felt her grip on the stick, felt her shifting the cannon. Felt her palm tracing in metal the shapes she would like to be making over his body. The certainty bloomed simultaneously in her mind and between her legs.

"You'll have your chance in about seven minutes." His voice was tight, clipped.

No way could they be thinking about the same thing. She bit her lip to keep from smiling. "Eh?"

"We don't have any live targets right now, but we will shortly. My inputs are showing a roadblock up ahead. Their lasers are hot, but our shielding will hold. We will be in range within six minutes."

She panned her gaze across the desert. She couldn't see anything yet, which wasn't surprising considering how fast they were going. But she did discern a shift in the pattern of the black sand horizon, a shudder of shapes. She leaned forward until her forehead mashed against the windshield and turned her head to look up.

She had to let loose of the gearshift when she moved, and she thought she heard Heron sigh. Regret or relief?

But she didn't have much time to ponder, because right up there, smack-dab in front of them but up in the air, the sky looked a whole lot darker than it had any right to be. No stars, just black, a giant black, and headed right for them.

"Um, Heron? Remember when you said that we were safe from everything but the hand of God?"

"Yes."

"Don't look up."

"Excellent advice. Five minutes now, querida. Be ready in case we can't get out of their range before they have targeting locks."

"Ready for what? To shoot our way through? Tell me you aren't fixing to ram this pretty car into a roadblock. And what *is* that thing in the sky?"

"Ready to hold on. Of course not. And that's our extraction team."

Four minutes and closing. Mari heard the countdown in her com, ticking backward. She tried to establish a visual along the road in front of them, but darkened headlights and a new moon sure weren't helping. And neither was the thing—*extraction team*—swooping in on the horizon.

"Okay, here's what we're going to do. I can't get our exit vector lined up before we're in range of those federal guns. We need to make them think twice about firing. You're going to get a go on that cannon, Mari, but probably just one shot. You don't even need to hit them necessarily. Just make them duck. But you'll want to hang on tight with the other hand, okay? Tight as you can."

Mari thought of a few things she could say, but she settled for a quick squeeze on the gearshift instead.

Heron shifted in his seat. Huh. Had she gotten to him at last? Even with all this tension, with feds ahead and allies above and speed making her soles vibrate, Mari could still spare plenty of brain space for innuendo. She only wondered if she'd stoked Heron to that point as well. He'd said some things back in the arco that had made her think he wouldn't mind fucking her blind, but then he'd also sidestepped her conversation thread about the kissing. Why the hell couldn't he just play nice and tell her what he wanted?

She checked the rear, shifted the barrel on her cannon slightly, but when she turned back, she saw the first of the flashing lights from the roadblock up ahead. Even as she zoned in on them, the dash display lit up with a ticker message, first in English, then in Spanish and French: This is UNAN regional police. Power down and exit the vehicle. Repeat: Power down and exit the vehicle.

If their communications system was in range, chances were their guns would be shortly. Mari armed the cannon with the switch on the base, and then, keeping her eyes on target and her whole body aware of Heron beside her, she slid the pad of her thumb over the brushed chrome button on top.

He jumped like he'd been pinched. His hands gripped the steering wheel, so hard he nearly wrenched the whole thing off. Mari contained a grin. No, he wasn't immune to her.

And yes, he was getting direct sensory input through the car. Hot *damn*.

"Fucking hell, Mari."

"What?" she said in her most I-have-no-idea-what-you-mean tone. Oh, this was fun.

"Never mind. Remember: hold on."

No, she hadn't forgotten. She peered hard out the front windshield, found the flashing lights in the distance, and lined the roadblock up with the digital sights that blipped along the top edge of the safety glass.

She remembered the way he'd projected light back in the arco and later how he'd navigated them through the dark. That boy almost certainly had a heads-up wired in, either holographic or tatted on the backs of his eyelids. The dash sights were unnecessary. Which meant he'd put them there for somebody else. Her? But no. She wasn't even close to letting herself believe he thought about her that much when they were off a job.

That would mean he *liked* her.

I take care of precious things, he'd said.

She eased her thumb down, bracing for the kick, but nothing happened right away. A keen from deep inside the emplacement made the small hairs on her forearms stand up, and then the cannon rumbled. She saw a flash in the distance full seconds before the recoil slammed into the car.

Collision, full impact and hard. Her back wrenched, and she wished for a half second that she'd put on the harness like Heron had told her. She tightened all her muscles, concentrated on her core, and gripped the harness strap with one hand and the gearshift with the other.

The stability control thunked, tires screeched against the blacktop, and then the car was spinning. Spinning like a teacup in a carnival ride. The holler those tires put up as they fought for purchase nearly popped her ear drums.

Mari heard the impact of her one shot at the same time that the car straightened out. She opened her eyes, stared straight ahead, but she could no longer see the flash of lights in the distance.

Had she hit them?

The engine revved, and then they were moving again. Twelve cylinders roared, and the car shot forward like it'd been launched. Mari's breath tore from her lips. She tried to sight in for another shot, but all her vectors were off. She didn't even know which direction she was facing, though it sure as shit didn't seem to be the same one she'd started out in.

And then their headlights came on, splashing the desert ahead with white, and Mari flinched back against her seat, instinctively covering her head.

That something, that thing that she'd seen as a giant black blot above them, their hand of God extraction team, was now directly in front of the car. Shit. They were going to ram right into…whatever it was. Plane or airship of some sort, obviously, but flying impossibly low, matching its speed to theirs. Low enough to...

It dipped, or at least part of it did. A cargo ramp extruded out the butt end of that plane. Heron gunned the engine.

Gravity gave for one hot second, and then the tires clutched the cargo ramp. He downshifted so fast the gears screamed. He slammed the brakes, and Mari heard the screech of tires on metal, felt a whump against her door, something padded but still too hard, grasping and lifting the car.

And then everything went quiet. All Mari could hear was the frenetic drum of her heart.

"Wha...?" She didn't have brain space for a whole word.

"We've docked. The plane is climbing. We probably ought to stay put for a few minutes, until we hit altitude. Then the cargo vent should pressurize, and believe me, this plane has weapons that roadblock wouldn't dare go against. They're prepared for asymmetrical threats, and we just evened the playing field. Breathe, Mari. You did well." Heron calmly unhasped his own harness and tilted his head, popping the kinks out of his neck. He laced his fingers, bent the bridge back, and cracked the tension from his knuckles, too. Exhaled deliberately.

"So we're not dead?"

He grinned, quick and wolfish. "Not even close. I am sorry about the wild ride back there, though."

Wild ride. Mari turned those words over and over in her mind, blurring her most recent memories with the fantasies of rides she'd like to take with him. Or on him.

The postjob high coalesced around all that tension, all that adrenaline, and she smashed her eyelids closed.

Settle, girl. Today's been a doozy, but it ain't over. Not by a long shot. And she didn't need to be molesting her partner while her self-control was down either.

"Querida? Mari? You okay? I didn't mean..." He'd turned in his seat and leaned toward her, his gloved hands clasping her wrists and sliding upward. Likely to check her bios again or to make sure she wasn't sobbing like a wee baby after the day she'd just endured, but it didn't matter, the whys and wherefores. All she could process right then was that he was touching her, and she had never in her whole life wanted something as much as she wanted to touch him back.

Touch him? Hell. She wanted to put her mouth all over him and swallow him whole.

She lurched toward him, burying her face against his neck and wrapping her arms around his body. The gearshift poked hard against her thigh, but she was too far gone to care if the cannon was armed.

His arms came around her like it was their cosmic purpose to hold her. She couldn't stop her lips from pressing hot against his collar, his throat, the divot beneath his ear, behind his jaw.

His mouth.

God, it wasn't even a kiss, not a real one, a brush of tongue against his closed lips, but her whole body hummed at the connection. Female to male, direct current, a closed circuit.

Electricity surged.

He tasted like mint and metal, a certain reminder of what he was, not that Mari gave two shits about his alterations anymore. No unaltered whole-organic man could have rigged that dock, could have matched speeds on two vehicles that perfectly, especially not coming out of a 360-degree skid and a cannon shot to boot. No man could have taken over the security bots for the Pentarc just to get *her* out safely or plotted a capture-or-kill job down to the second.

Nope, Heron wasn't a man. But he wasn't a machine either. No machine could make her insides roil like this, could make her writhe in frustrated lust equal to her terror and exhaustion.

Slowly, patiently—*frustratingly*—he splayed one gloved hand between her shoulder blades, holding her steady, and the other slid up, fighting with the ponytail elastic. The band snapped before he could unwind it, and Mari groaned when he skidded his fingertips along her scalp, spreading them through the mess of hair. The waft of expensive shampoo settled around her, knocking that ball of tension around her insides, setting off klaxons of awareness.

He hadn't returned her kisses, but he didn't push her away either. Instead, he just sat there and took it, endured her desperation, and gave back...what? Comfort. Kindness. All the stuff there was no way he could have known she craved. No way. He stroked her hair and murmured, "That's it, querida. You just let it all out. I've got you."

She rested her forehead against his jaw and closed her eyes. The kicker of it all was that yes, she wanted him so hard, her teeth hurt, but she also didn't want this moment to end. The pause, the sweet of it. It had been a long time since Mari had felt this safe, this treasured.

She was used to running, to fighting and slipping out of danger by the skin of her teeth. That kind of tension wasn't anything new. But what she wasn't used to was having somebody offer her comfort on the pause. These sorts of moments usually felt so goddamn bleak and lonely. Not here, though. Not now. Not with him.

She sniffed, fighting back the bulb of emotion in her throat.

And smelled blood.

His blood.

All he'd been through this day, and *he* had *her*? Um, no. Partnerships didn't work that way, not in Mari's world. She pressed one more kiss against his jaw and then drew back, moving her hands between them and smoothing his rumpled shirt.

"Nah. We're good, partner." She could control herself, could fight off the darkthing and lust combined. She could. She met his dark-eyed gaze and didn't look away.

"Mari, we should probably talk about…"

"Yeah, I know. You're not a natural at killin' folks or being chased, but you've clearly been in this kind of pinch before. It shows. The experience. Color me impressed."

One brow kicked up.

She barreled on. "Also, even though you didn't say as much, I 'spect I've just been taken home to meet the parents. Mrs. Weathering? I like her, your mom. She's pretty badass, despite that weird game show addiction. Well then. That about cover it?" She thought about the gearshift. "Oh, wait, one more: I know you're hiding other things from me. Technological things." Tension corded his arms, and oh man, she wanted to get his shirt off and inspect those tense areas up close, but she had a few more things to cover first. "I deserve it, though, since I kept secrets back, too, and anyhow, I can't worry about it too much, 'cause I got a bigger problem right now."

"What's that?"

"My partner has a hole in his head and probably needs a shitload of rewrap and rebuild, and I don't know anything about fixing mech. What can I do to help you?"

A corner of his mouth quirked, and he settled one hand at her nape. His thumb teased the fine hairs behind her ear, a thing that made it real hard for her to keep her shit together. She sucked in a breath, held it, and sterned her features. *Best get a hold on them sexy thoughts. This isn't about me. It's about him. Heron. Taking good care of him.*

It felt weird to care about somebody else's comfort this much, after so long living only for herself. She hadn't even visited Auntie Boo in years, just kept up via com. All those weekend flings with postjob hook-ups merged into a faceless blur of memory. Those folks didn't need her, she didn't need them, and it stunned her to think that, once upon a time, she had considered such relationships liberating. Once upon a time wasn't even so long ago.

Feeling was coming back into her long-numbed empathy, seeking a connection other than sex. She wanted to heal him, hold him, care for him.

Okay, there were other things she wanted to do to this man, no use lying to herself. But the other wants, the deeper wants, surprised her. Made her feel ridiculously human.

"It doesn't hurt, querida," he said, referring to his head wound.

"It looks like hell, though."

"You can't even see it right now."

"But I *know* what it looks like."

"My alterations have dulled the nerve endings in some areas and affect the way I feel pain." His gaze met hers, and that spark she'd tasted on his mouth arced between them. "Besides, I deeply suspect you're just searching for an excuse to play doctor."

So. Busted.

"And you're assuming I'm playing," she volleyed.

"Aren't you?" His face was dead serious when he said that. No teasing, no expression at all. Machine still, that face, but she could feel the tension in his arms, his neck. His lips were parted, and his leashed breath came quick and warm.

With a suitably salacious reply on the tip of her tongue, Mari hooked his gaze on hers, braced her left hand against his seatback, and reared up onto her knee. In the process, she dragged that gearshift the full length of her thigh.

He slammed his eyes shut. The fingers at the back of her head cricked, catching hair and tugging. The deep groan that escaped his mouth was seismic.

Ohhhhh, right.

Mari promptly forgot whatever flirty thing she'd been about to say. She blanked on where they were, the TPA's betrayal, Heron's not-hurty wounds, and all manner of other things. Damn near forgot her own name, because right then, she recalled what she'd figured out earlier. About the car.

"Wait." She looked down at him, her knee pressing painfully into the leather base of the gearshift. "So the alts just dull pain, right?"

"What do you mean?" He was made of strain.

Mari rocked forward, bringing the other leg across, settling her right knee in the center of the driver's seat. Which meant she now straddled both his right thigh and the shifter.

When she arched her body over him, bringing her face closer to his and nudging the shifter knob with her inner thigh, his face lit up in bright agony.

"Can you feel, you know, other things?" She turned her hand, pushing her palm against the leather seatback. Her fingers bent, raking nails over the leather, digging her knuckles into the sleek muscle beside his spine.

Heron shuddered and murmured something she couldn't understand, not even with the com. In a rough voice she hardly recognized—where were all his careful modulations now, hmm?—he said, "Mari, are you asking me whether I am so hard right now that I could fuck you through three layers of clothes?"

Her mouth went dry. Damn straight that's what she was asking.

And then, in a surge of motion and an inarticulate groan, his hands were on her hips, bringing her snug against him. Well, *he* wasn't playing, that was for damn sure. His cock was at least as hard as the shifter, even confined as it was in his pants. She had a hankering to set it free and check for sure. God, she ached to see him naked. From what she felt of this topography, ass-bare Heron would be a sight for sore eyes.

"Mari…"

Dangit, her hardpoints were situated all wrong. She needed to adjust, center herself over his lap better, for better aim. And how was she gonna get herself out of these pants? In a multiutility or a fully automated vehicle, maybe. In this car, though, no way. Too cramped. They hardly had enough room to breathe, no less get suitably nekkid. Argh. She adjusted her weight, nearly fell over, and braced one hand against the cool impact side window.

"Feel this, then." She caught his bottom lip with her teeth, tugged until he opened for her, and tongued a fire kiss along his hard palate, heedless of his will or breath.

This time he did kiss her back. Hell yes, he did. Hot, lip-bruising, breath and teeth and tongue and vibration— ooh, was that a growl? And in the midst of this all-the-way-to-the-toes kiss, he circled her waist with his long hands, slid them up her torso and over her shoulders, and wrenched the reinforced buttons on her armored shirt. They came off. Every single one of the suckers. He shoved the shirt down her arms, yanking her hands from their supporting positions at the seatback and window, but couldn't snag it all the way off, 'cause she was still wrapped around him.

He caught her before she could fall backward, one hand solid between her shoulder blades and the other further down her spine, but her arms were essentially trapped in the mess that used to be her shirt.

No matter. Heron dipped his chin and bit the neckline of her stretchy undershirt. He pulled. It tore. Not all the way, but enough. He traced the ripped edges with kisses. His breath was hot on her collarbone, silky and delicious and chased by the lightning-hot swipe of his tongue.

She wasn't in control of this encounter anymore. How'd he do that, turn the tables on her? Didn't matter. She wasn't particularly in control of her body either. She was shaking, not thinking properly, not anythinging anymore. Just wrapped up in a bigger tangle of passion.

She gave up, closed her eyes, and let his hands cradle her, his body warm her, his breath and kisses and soft words bathe her. The rest of her senses took over. All she could do was writhe and feel and roil and burn.

"Do you have any idea how hard it was not to do this back at the Pentarc?" he asked, clearly unaware she was way past making coherent words. "Or last summer, when we were staking out that skin trafficker in Miami? What is it about you and me and cramped spaces?"

If she had to say, probably balls-out lust. That was what was between them in cramped spaces. And in other spaces. That and…oh, holy *yes*. His mouth had sussed out the best sensitive spot low and in between her breasts, and he was nipping it. Good lord, if he didn't watch it, she was going to come right here with her pants still on.

He was still talking, in between all the other oral athletics, but Mari was having a real hard time caring what he was saying. His voice pebbled her skin like Jacuzzi bubbles on naked flesh: bubble, bubble, hot mutter, fuck yeah.

"I lied," he was saying. "I can't let you go on another downtime without me. I don't care if you *are* playing. I don't care if you despise what I am. This time, I can't…"

Even as he murmured on about things that she really ought to be paying better attention to, the corner of his mouth found her nipple. His teeth followed, and with a howl, she arched back hard against the steering wheel.

It never even crossed her mind that there might be a horn in it.

Loud fucker, too.

CHAPTER 7

"OH, HEY THERE. SORRY FOR THE DELAY! WE HAVE reached cruising altitude, and no one is currently shooting at us. Win! I was going to let you know, but Kellen told me to leave you two alone." The voice coming in through the GPS speaker on the dash sounded unholy chipper.

Mari *had* wondered who was flying this plane, but other things had needed her attention more urgently. Now that somebody was actually talking to them from the plane proper, she figured she would have been fine with a few more minutes of happy ignorance. Wasn't like they were falling out of the sky or anything.

"Good on you, Kellen," Heron muttered. Then louder, "Chloe, if we're pressurized, I guess you can unlock the hatch and let us in."

"Sure thing!"

The chirrup fuzzed out, and Mari opened her eyes.

"Finish this later?" she managed.

"Count on it."

It physically hurt to disconnect herself from Heron.

True, a lot of that was residual ache, bruising from the job, and rough treatment at the hands of those mercenaries, but still, it hurt. She retreated to her own side of the car, shrugging the armored shirt back on her shoulders and running a hand through her wild hair. She could only imagine what she looked like.

"Gorgeous," Heron said, and the stare he leveled at her might have been made of lightning.

"You reading my mind again, partner?" Mari grinned.

"Actually, no. Merely making an observation."

"Observe all you want, then. You messed me up plenty." Mari didn't look away from Heron, but she saw a circular door, like a port hatch, open in the wall toward the front of the cargo vent. She guessed that was the way to the body of the plane.

"Not half as much as I wanted to."

Oh yes, that hurt, too. But the good kind of hurt: he didn't even have to touch her to get that throb going between her legs.

"Got one more question before we head on in," Mari said, reaching back and twisting her hair into an impromptu braid. It'd slip out of its confines shortly, but right now, it cooled her superheated skin. "You said you're integrated with the car and stuff, but how deep? I mean, I touch this here gearshift, for instance, and you feel…"

Heron raised one brow and leaned over her, not touching. Her door hissed open.

"When you're doing it? I feel everything."

Well then. Mari put some extra wiggle into her ass as she turned on the seat, swung her feet out the yawning door, and stood up on shaky legs.

• • •

There wasn't a door to hold, but Heron paused beside the opening and gestured for Mari to go in first anyway. She about laughed out loud: look at him, getting his manners on even after what'd just happened in that car. She went through, holding the sides of her now-buttonless shirt. The undershirt was ruined completely, and unless she wanted the crew's first impression of her to be "Hey, tatas!" she figured she'd make an effort to keep herself covered.

The hatch retracted, spinning inward and receding into a reinforced track on the edges. Judging by the double-cylinder baffling and big-ass seals, Mari figured this plane could probably make it to ultrahigh altitude, maybe to full orbit. Though probably not while Heron's car was in its cargo clamp.

Mari looked up at a whooshing sound, only to realize that it wasn't a whoosh at all: it was the sound of a whole flock of folks swarming her and Heron. Well, a flock of three.

One was perky, blond, and with boobs that defied every natural law. It didn't take Mari long to figure out which of the crew was Chloe. Her pixie-adorable face tilted in cartoon concern. "Dr. Farad, are you bleeding?"

"Here, let me help you…"

"Tell me nothing's broken…"

And on.

Mari flexed her achy hands, rubbed them against the scraps of her armored shirt, and took in this fluttering. *Dr. Farad*, eh? The name rubbed on her mind. Had he put that name on their contract? She thought maybe he hadn't, but her memory, as always, was for shit. Nothing new about that, but it did annoy her, missing this detail about her partner.

One of the crew guys, lean and lanky and making those Wranglers look fine, yanked a scanner out of his back pocket and circled around Heron, getting a good look at that bloody port.

The other guy hung back, shrugging dark hair out of his face and shoving his skinny fists deep into the pockets of his black utility pants. He had an ash-gray smear on his chin and smelled like axle grease. He wore his nerves right out in the open, practically vibrating with anxiety, and somehow, that comforted Mari. Everything honest with this guy, no secrets.

Heron submitted the back of his skull to the cowboy's laser scan but kept talking. "I need an uplink to Chiba, a high dock on the tether, and a sterile med unit, preferably one with a crash cart and LOM module." Without turning his head, he looked around, pegging each of them with some sort of unspoken command. "And, everybody, this is Mari. She will need a coffee and rum and a soft place to rest. Querida, meet the crew: Kellen, Chloe, and Garrett."

Or, as Mari sorted them: cowboy, perky blond, and squirrel-nervous mechanic. She nodded to them all in turn. To their credit, nobody said anything about the sad state of her clothing.

"Erm, Dr. Farad? I really don't think we should mention Chiba in front of her." Garrett jammed a thumb in Mari's direction.

"You can trust her."

"Trust," Garrett said in a voice that made the word

sound just terrible. "You know they are tracking her. I can prove it. She's..."

"My partner," Heron said evenly. "Settle, G."

"They?" Mari repeated, her attention snagged on that eep-inducing word *tracking*. He was referring to the feds, presumably. How would they be tracking her? Hadn't Heron scanned her for bugs and signals? Their drones typically didn't go this high. Satellites?

"Yeah, they." Garrett nodded enthusiastically. "Our illuminati overlords."

Mari had no idea what to say to that.

"Oh good grief," Cowboy Kellen muttered, not even looking up from his data scanner. "Y'all will be lucky this gal don't run screaming to all the vid channels about nutcases in spaceplanes. Don't you mind him, Miss Mari."

"This is not an abduction scenario," Garrett shot back. He turned to Chloe. "We need to scan her."

"Hey," Chloe said, petting down Garrett's anxiety without having to so much as touch him. "I can do that, after the coffee and rum and soft places finding. Let me take care of it, okay? And in the meantime, I bet the car could use some petting and love, what with all it has been through."

His agitation wilted, and her soft murmurs followed him out of the cramped hatch space, back into the cargo hold.

Kellen was frowning at the data pad, analyzing whatever info he'd scanned off Heron. Mari had a half moment of privacy with her partner.

"I could use some clothes, too," she said in a voice meant just for him. "Again. Does it seem to you like I'm spending half my time changing clothes?"

He towered over her, up this close, and he raked a gaze down her body, lingering on the frayed, buttonless edge of her overshirt. It wasn't like he reached out or anything, or even that he moved at all, but Mari could feel a tsunami of heat surge right off him. "Thank you for a scintillating visual."

She swallowed and tried real hard not to dissolve into a puddle right there. She flexed her fingers and then tucked them in tight.

"So, a LOM module. That's lights-out management, right? You shutting down somebody's system, *Dr.* Farad?"

He cracked a smile, dispersing the tension as if he could order it around like another member of his crew. Frustratingly, it appeared to obey. "Sort of. I'll be the subject on this one."

Mari flared a look up at him. "It *does* hurt, doesn't it?" She made a gesture toward the back of her own head, but of course, she meant his.

Heron's smile was patient. "Not really. I told you before. But I need Kellen to take a look at the damaged area anyway."

Mari swallowed. "Why?"

His mouth tightened, but he didn't meet her eyes. "Because I'm transmitting. And I can't seem to make it stop."

●　　●　　●

Heron's airship-plane-thingy had a cockpit up front, more like a cubby really, and Mari followed Heron and Kellen that way. It didn't take too long for those two to sink into some techspeak sublanguage with bits of English interspersed. Mostly expletives.

Mari was right there with them on the shit-fuck-goddamn assessment of the situation. Heron was transmitting? What was he sending? And who was listening? A big part of her recognized that Heron had his big brain engaged in solving this problem already, and pretty cowboy Kellen was on the job as well. She couldn't add much in terms of brain power, so she stayed quiet.

When they swept into the cockpit, still chattering about containment units and surgical processes, Mari hung back by the hatch, watching Heron.

He was in his element, completely in command. Hot.

He peeled his gloves off and slid into a high-backed chair, thick with impact wadding. Pilot's chair? Or captain's? What was the correct terminology? Mari operated on the outside of proper military rank and prided herself in having no clue, but this time, she might have enjoyed knowing.

Before today, she'd never thought of Heron as part of something other than their little partnership. The two of them against the world. Had a romantic ring to it, yeah, but it wasn't true. He also had a Mama Weathering and a whole crew. Probably others out there, too. He and Mrs. Weathering sure hadn't brought all that contraband into the Pentarc by themselves.

Networks, relationships. Context. It all fit, and Mari could've thunked herself upside the head for not imagining all this for him, for not even asking. For assuming that his life during downtimes was as bare and isolated as hers. It made sense a guy like him wouldn't be alone. Made sense people would love him.

The moment he sat down, he sank into the digital morass the way a fish sinks into ocean after spending too long a time on dry land. Surfaces all around him lit up with images and numbers and weird punctuation. Code, probably.

Mari made one half-assed effort to get a sense of it before her eyeballs started to ache. Heron didn't even seem to notice how confusing this place was or how she was standing there with nothing to do and her clothes barely hanging on. Nope, his hands were going on those glyphs, and the plane responded like a kitten being petted. It purred now its master was home.

No. Wait. That wasn't the ship. Unless the ship was wee and furry and nuzzling her shin. Mari looked down. A cat looked up.

A cat. On a plane. For reals.

Well, mostly for reals. On second look, it was kind of a wrong cat. It was tiger-striped maroon and white, on the small side, but with visible alterations, including a set of horns to project a holographic user interface. It stared straight back at her. Curiously? Mari couldn't figure out whether the little fluffball was offended that a stranger was on its ship or was scoping Mari out as a potential food dispenser. Either way, it was clutching the rubberized floor with its claws but clearly wasn't freaked out. Probably this critter had logged more hours in the air than Mari had.

She reached down, and it nuzzled her hand, pushing the biohacked skull knobs into her palm. She wondered if its tactile sensors were dulled by all those alterations. Like Heron, unable to feel pain.

"Her name's Yoink." Even in a near-whisper, Chloe couldn't quite disguise that chirrup to her voice as she snuck up behind Mari. "She's Kellen's. He keeps most of the rescues back at the Pentarc while he's treating them, but Yoink's a ballsy little gal, has no problem flying. He used to be a veterinarian, back before secession. Um, Kellen, not the cat."

Mari looked at the cowboy. He'd cracked open that metal case and was yanking stuff out of it. Medical-looking stuff. Vet stuff. He lined up gauze and injectors and anesthetics on a tray near Heron's chair. Lordy hell, was he going to dig around in Heron's head *here*, while the plane was up and everything? What if they hit turbulence? Boy had balls, or else his hands were steadier than hers.

Which wasn't even possible, of course.

Last thing out of the case was a plastic bag full of kitty biscuits. Without looking over, he gave that bag a shake.

Yoink twitched one ear and looked up at Mari like, "Sorry, lady, but you ain't edible," and she was off like a prom dress.

Ditched. First by Heron, then by a weird little bio-hacked cat.

But Chloe was still hovering. Smiling. Great. She held out a squeeze thermobottle, hot to the touch and emanating the unmistakable whiff of coffee and rum. "We have some clothes back in the racks. Want to see?"

Mari took a long pull on the bottle, shuddering as the go-juice jolted through her system, at once padding the ragged ends of her nerves and soothing her to clarity. She looked out through the high-impact glass. This time of night, she couldn't see the cloud deck, and really, she had no idea what she was looking at anyway. Heron was busy, Kellen and Garrett were busy, and Mari suddenly felt bone tired. "Racks?"

"Places for people to sleep. Bunks?"

"Oh." Maximum distance on this plane must be pretty long if people were sleeping en route. But then, everything here felt off, out of her usual.

She followed Chloe back through the access tunnel, which was made even narrower by stacks of shipping crates like the ones she'd seen in the Pentarc. Contraband. Smuggled goods. One smelled mouthwateringly like tea. Her stomach grumbled, but a barebones plane like this wasn't likely to have a stocked kitchen. Galley? Feh. Terminology again.

Although Mari had to duck a couple of places, Chloe didn't. Wasn't often that Mari felt tall or gangly. Wasn't often she even thought about what she looked like, but tiny doll-like Chloe probably made most women insecure.

Navigating the length of this ship wasn't anything like walking the aisle on a 787 or a land jet. This one had been designed for purposes other than the comfort of paying passengers, and Mari was careful to keep her hands tight to her sides as she picked her way along. Some of the bulging pipes looked like they'd burn her if she touched them. Even the machines, the ones with blips and buttons that she passed, snerked at her, seemed to ask her what the hell she was doing here.

She was starting to wonder the same.

She'd grown up in the last vestiges of wilderness, new-rural Texas. She was used to scraggly trees and dirt and burnt sky, fences and guns and campfires. Tech had always mystified her. When she was a kid and Auntie Boo had told her all about her scientist father, Mari had ascribed holy powers to the kinds of technology he worked, and even as she'd grown older, she'd been a little in awe. Okay, a lot.

Heron had been trying to cure her of that for the last year, showing her pieces of tech that weren't magical at all, that were things she could wrap her hand around and control. But here in the labyrinthine passageways of his plane, some of that old distrust grabbed at her. The tech here was too big, too mysterious, too confining.

She crossed her arms over her chest and hugged the drink bottle close, careful not to touch the machines.

Chloe passed her wrist over a scanner, and the doorway leading to the back of the plane opened. She stepped through.

Four bunks, each with a plastic footlocker at the end, dominated the narrow space. It might be cramped and utilitarian, but it was also tidy and smelled no different from the rest of the plane: equal parts metal, machine cleaner, and tea.

Chloe arced her wrist over one of the plastic boxes, unlatching a shin-high footlocker chased all over with purple nano-ink fairies. The lid rose, and with its movement, the soft color changed to blue and glowed: free-fae.

But something about the way that particular blue reflected off Chloe hit Mari in the gut, and she stopped cold in the doorway.

Chloe didn't reflect the light. At all. She ate it up, like a perky blond, mini black hole. The physics in the space surrounding Chloe were not just fucked up. They were impossible.

Mari peered closely at Chloe in the faintly blue light, and…yeah, now she could see it. Textures were off. Her flight suit shouldn't have been that smooth, almost plastene. A certain amount of translucence, Mari could wrap her mind around, but the deeper she looked at Chloe, the deeper her gaze went. If she went on looking, she'd keep on sinking.

She reached out to touch Chloe's shoulder and wasn't really surprised when her hand passed right through. Cool space, thick like fog but insubstantial.

Holographic.

"So, what's a free-fae collective doing with a locker full of clothes?" Mari made her voice as kind as she could. Didn't want to scare Chloe off, didn't want to sound threatening at all. A free-fae collective probably spent her whole life in fear.

Chloe didn't turn. She hunched a perfectly rounded shoulder and shook her head. "Oh, you know what they say about folks always wanting the thing they need least." Her parametrically curved chin angled toward the fae-lit footlocker. "But technically, none of these things are mine."

Mari looked and saw a riot of color in that box: wine red, sunset orange, heaven blue. Every color she could imagine, in fact, and in a variety of textures, from neoprene to bubbles to velvet.

"You'd look pretty in the orange," Chloe said, doubtlessly trying to turn the conversation.

Free-fae. Lord. Heron was harboring a free-fae collective on his ship. Not just a little, light-box, middle-finger-to-the-nanovats collective either. These nanos had gotten together and made a *person*. That had to be at least sixty kinds of illegal. And here Mari'd been worked up over a little capital murder.

She drew her hand back, but not before she stroked the

holographic shoulder. It rippled like the disturbed surface of a pond. Chloe turned, looked back, smiled tentatively.

"I guess he knows."

"Dr. Farad?" Chloe's brow made a pretty dent of concern, but then it melted back to pixie cheerful. "Oh yeah. He knows everything about me. I'm his, or, I mean, from his original nanovat, back when he was a postdoc. You know, in Texas? But we're *good* now. He's helping me with autogenesis and self-awareness. Also Spanish. But shh. I'm secret."

Whoa. "Um, you probably shouldn't say that out loud to strangers."

Chloe's laugh tinkled like a china wind chime. "You aren't a stranger, Mari. We know all about you, too."

Yeah, that didn't creep a girl out. Except when it so did. The look Chloe was laying on her right then felt warm. Too warm.

"So, the dress? Tell me you love it." Chloe practically bounced. Or the holographic equivalent. "You are going to put it on?"

As in strip down right here? But Chloe just kept on looking, and Mari guessed that yep, that's exactly what she was expected to do. And it wasn't that big of a deal.

She figured most humans—whole-organic, post-human, whatever—worried about their bodies once in a while. Hell, even she had fallen into that trap when she was younger. How many hair colors had she gone through, trying to find the right one God had missed? She'd gone down the same rabbit hole her mother had, for a while, trying to improve upon whatever physical mess she'd started out with. Trying to become better, best, perfect.

But after Corpus, after skirting so near death and getting a second chance, she'd quit self-alteration cold turkey. This was the body, the one with the bubble butt and tree-trunk thighs, the one with weird, overlong toes and a resistance to nice-looking abs no matter how hard she worked, this was the body that brought her back. The one that had saved her, that kept her ticking against all odds. Girl had to love a body like that, beautiful or not.

But Chloe's covetous holographic eyes, tracking her every movement, sort of did make her feel admired. And what was that Heron had called her, back in the cargo vent?

Gorgeous.

Mari set her bottle down, shrugged out of her armored shirt, and yanked the ruined tank over her head. She unfastened her pants and kicked them and the boots off her feet, stripping down until she was ass-bare in the bunk room. Even when Chloe perched on the edge of her bunk, her pale-blue eyes literally glowing, Mari didn't feel embarrassed of her plain, unaltered, whole-organic body. It was clearly a thing that Chloe envied, and that made Mari more sad than shamed.

Chloe could look like anything she wanted—her whole existence was just a loose confederation of nanites and light particles held together with digital will—but she wasn't real, couldn't know smells and tastes and touches. Sure, she could be programmed for a variety of inputs, but those inputs weren't the same thing as human senses. Chloe would never stroke that sweet kitty down the corridor, never smell flowers or sex or ghost peppers. Never taste Jamaican rum or her own tears.

And if the continental government had its way, every fae in the country would be sent back to the vats, jumbled together into a messload of nanites to be reprogrammed and reconditioned and set to work the way they were intended.

Chloe should never have existed, the scientists said and the courts agreed. She wasn't a real, living person. But Chloe's attention was pretty rapt, and pretty damned *alive*, when Mari drew the orange silk free of that footlocker.

She passed the fabric over her head. Cool and indulgent, like skinny-dipping. She pushed her hands through the short, snug sleeves, pressed the closure seam along her side, and looked over.

Chloe's eyes were big as Gatling barrels. "I bet it feels like whispers."

Mari cracked a grin. "Nah. Whispers would tickle more."

Chloe laughed. Mari supposed Chloe could modulate her voice just as easily as she could change her appearance. She wondered why Chloe had chosen this face, this voice.

"Dr. Farad traded for that dress in Xi'an." Chloe's fingers cricked, as if she longed to touch. "And he held on to it, even though he could have traded it for a fortune. Real silk, no polys in it at all."

"Heron bought this?"

Chloe nodded. "Oh sure. For you."

"No, that can't be right." Mari said it without thinking, the reaction trained into her by years and years of disappointment. *Never assume they mean the compliments. Never assume that smile is for you.* Her world wasn't populated by people who gave a shit what she wore. Or even, sometimes, that she existed.

What if he did give a shit, though?

"But I am right," Chloe said. "I have a complete recording of the conversation the day he acquired this piece. Shall I recite it for you?"

"No, no, you don't need to do that." Mari brushed the silk with a hesitant finger and had to bite her lip to quell a bizarre surge of emotion. A need to grin like a crazy person. Or maybe cry. Was it physically possible to do both at once?

She hugged the information to her, this unexpected insight into her partner's life. Back when she was wondering what Heron did on his downtimes, she had assumed that he, like so many other folks who worked on the fringe of legality, raked in his earnings and used them to indulge. For a freelance jobber, that's what downtimes were for: celebrating the fact that another contract was complete and all team members were still alive.

Somebody with Heron's résumé could have bought a lot of stuff to show for it: a fabricated island or a cloud node or at least a garage full of fast cars just like the one clamped down in the cargo vent.

But not Heron. He spent his downtime plucking treasures out of ruined places, harboring a collective of free-fae in direct violation of UNAN executive order, and keeping tabs on a crew of regular folks who appeared to depend on him.

And thinking of her.

She pinched the silk between her thumb and forefinger and met Chloe's glowing gaze. "There's got to be a way for you to feel this. It's the fingers version of delicious."

Chloe laughed. Mari thought maybe that sound, the sound of a fae laughing, was what got them their name. It was like tiny bells chiming, that laugh. Fairy giggles. Made a body want to laugh right back.

"That's exactly what he said." Chloe effervesced again, floating around Mari and through the hatch. "He's been working on figuring out an integration protocol. I've donated some samples, and I think he's close to a live trial. But I'll warn you, if you mention it, he'll go on about it for hours. Things he considers obligations, like caring for me and the rest of the crew, he takes way too seriously. Which, of course, is why we all love him so much."

Yeah, thought Mari. *Yeah.*

HERON KEPT HIS EYES CLOSED LEST HE
inadvertently watch her. But he still felt her. Inside his
plane. Inside him. He wasn't used to having her so close,
so connected, especially for an extended time. It was
almost more than he could stand, the rush of pure processed sugar jammed between tongue and soft palate,
soaking into his system.

If he kept at this, he'd orgasm by osmosis.

He needed distraction, something decidedly not-her
to sink his attention into. He stretched along the metal
and cabling sinews of the plane, inhabiting the familiar.
Chloe hummed Bach in the galley, shimmering in and
out of visibility, a bright bit of digital fuzz and not in
any way distracting for Heron. His neural was full of
such things.

In the ward room, Kellen was reading a newsfeed and
scratching Yoink between the ears. Garrett was stretched
out on the deck in the cargo vent, only his legs visible,
sticking out from beneath the car's left quarter panel. He
had a rag jammed into his pocket, but he wasn't cleaning

sand out of the wheel wells. Not yet. Likely, he'd wait till Heron was off the plane and detached. Not feeling every touch on the metal.

They were considerate, his crew. Chloe melded into the digital white noise more often than not. Kellen, Garrett, and the cat had predictable movements and weight distribution, and more important, they knew better than to stroke anything they needn't. They knew their captain was rigged in tight with this ship and that if they so much as thumped a bulkhead, he would feel it.

Mari, however, had no idea.

Or did she? She had guessed as much about the car.

But she certainly wasn't acting like she was aware of any such thing at the moment. Understandable, of course: she was sleeping. Restlessly. Excruciatingly. The pinpoint of sensation, the rack she lay on, was lit up like a chandelier in his sensory array. On her back, legs and arms splayed, fingers clenched to fists. Her neck arched, the crown of her head slipping beyond the top of her thin pillow. She snored.

Heron gripped the arms of his pilot's chair. He shouldn't watch. He shouldn't listen or want. So much.

Did she shift on purpose in sleep, rubbing, kneading?

He huffed out a breath, shook his head to clear it. Yoink, done with her scratch, stretched and jumped down from the metal table. Deliberately, Heron followed her. Seven pounds, quadruped. Clambering toward the narrow galley. Probably hunting for a snack. Bottomless pit, that cat, but Kellen loved her, and Heron found her a useful experiment.

When his crew needed alone time, privacy, he could tuck them away from his input feed, focus on Yoink's biohacked transmitters, follow her through the ship. She became his eyes and ears, a warm, furry tickle on his awareness. And she didn't mind when he tagged along. Sometimes, he thought she even welcomed the company.

But she wasn't particularly helpful today. In the doorway to the galley, she unkinked her spine, digging her reinforced claws into the rubber floor, and then her ears pricked. She turned. Her padding steps led her unerringly to the racks. Exactly the place he had hoped to avoid.

Chloe had left the door open, and Yoink slunk inside. She leaped up, snuggled in the crook beneath Mari's ear, and wrapped her furry self up in Mari's cinnamon hair. Purred.

Heron yanked his sensors. *Disengage.* Only…they didn't. The sensors clung to Mari like Yoink's claws on the deck. He tried to set up a privacy partition, as he'd done countless times, but even after he placed the block, he was still *there*.

Beside her, above her, all around her.

Weight distribution on the rack shifted under the press of her shoulder blades, her silk-draped rear, as she inhaled. She nuzzled the kitty in sleep, and it pushed back against her neck. Her eyelids crinkled, her brows came down, and she whimpered. Nightmare? He longed to stop the dream, to stop himself, but he couldn't.

He couldn't.

Transmission commencing. *Not now, damn it!*

A chunk of his resources shifted to deal with the transmission burst, to block it, and all the while, his id indulged itself. Damn him, it did. He wrapped his senses around Mari, seeing with Yoink's machine eyes, touching her warmth through the deck temperature sensors, inhaling the tang and soap on her skin through the air reclamation controls feeding into his olfactory perception. He drowned in her, soaked in her, fell into her.

He did manage to shut down the transmission, cut the fucker off. But he knew this respite was temporary. He needed to get this shit out of his head. Now. This encroaching lack of control was going to drive him barking.

He didn't even notice when Kellen leaned into the cockpit.

"Chiba's comin' up soon. We're clear for dock eight. How's that for near the top?"

Heron started. Opened his eyes. Blinked. "Yeah. Right. I'll hook us in."

●   ●   ●

Mari hovered between awake and asleep. The orange silk made her want to cry it felt so good. Reminded her of other times, back before she went hard, back when luxury was more than a cheap lay and a jug of hooch. Back before she became a murderer for hire.

Murderer. Monster.

Claws scratched on the window of her conscience. Darkthing. *Coming to eat you, Mari-chulita. Take it, girl. You deserve this, what you done.*

She pushed her shoulders back against the thin mattress, fisted her hands, and squeezed her eyelids until she saw bright stains behind them. She hitched up her breathing and opened her soul. The darkthing would come at her now. It would ravage her, cut her up in strips, leave her in a heap, and she'd let it. So long as she picked herself up after, she'd let it do its thing. 'Cause it was right. She deserved it.

Strung taut, braced for impact. *Come on, monster*.

And out of the pure black came exactly the opposite of what she expected. Possibly something even worse. In his fingers-rubbing-velvet voice: *No guilt, querida. Don't you dare beat up on the most amazing woman I have ever met.* And his hands on her waist when she'd faced off against the mercenaries. His palpable calm, his halo of drones escorting her to safety in the Pentarc arcade. Wrapping her, insulating her.

Absolving her.

The darkthing fizzled. Sputtered and died like a campfire in a hurricane. In its place, that insulation settled, white and fine and warm as Italian sand. Her crunched-up face eased, her fists released. Something soft came up to her neck and nuzzled against her ear, and she turned her face into it. She painted Yoink's fur with disbelieving tears. Relieved ones, though.

Never had a downtime like this. Never.

And it was because of him, this peace.

She lay there, on a plane zipping through the night sky, rubbing Yoink behind the ears, and swimming in unexpected peace, until Chloe peered around the door, aglow with excitement. Literally.

"Hey, you awake yet?"

"Am now," said Mari, peeling Yoink off her neck. It wasn't just the snuggle that had relaxed her so completely. She sniffed and, yes indeed, there did seem to be an odd odor on the air. Almond neroli. Somebody was fucking with the chemical mix in the air again. Somebody who knew her sins and still thought highly of her. Somebody who was trying real hard to take good care of her. And all that made her warm in a way that had nothing to do with the ambient temperature controls.

Chloe perched on the end of her bunk, hugging her knees to her chest and watching Mari with bright, steady eyes. Trying to squeeze in some girl time? Did a thing like Chloe even know what that was?

"We're closing in on Chiba Station," she chirped. "If you head over to the cockpit, you can watch us come in to dock."

There it was again, that word. *Chiba*. Heron had mentioned it earlier, when they first came on board. Mari had a feeling they weren't talking about a postindustrial town in Japan. "Closing in on what?"

Chloe tilted her head and blinked, accessing an internal file. The movement was too robotic, totally gave her away. She'd need to work on things like that if she was ever gonna go out into the world and mingle. "Chiba Station is a privately owned space station, not allied with any government entity, and run by an entity who calls herself the queen of Chiba. It maintains a low orbit and a solar net that collects energy. Selling the surplus is probably how it sustains itself economically."

"Wait, we're far enough up to dock with a space station?"

"No, silly," said Chloe. "The station connects to the ground using a space elevator. Planes like this one can dock with it up near the top, and then we can ride up to the station. We call it the tether."

The *tether*. Now that term, Mari knew. Hell, everybody in her line of work had heard about it, but she'd never actually seen it, and she'd never heard that it was associated with just one space station. But that wasn't surprising. She wasn't high enough on the food chain to know when and where these power downloads would happen, and she sure as shit had never been on a plane that could make it high enough to dock with the thing.

Leave it to Heron to know all about the ins and outs of the best clean-energy racket running. Mari wondered just how high he was connected. Had to be pretty high. And why was somebody with contacts like that even running jobs with a peon like her?

Given her history, she ought to be wondering when he'd ditch her. But she didn't get the feeling that he meant to. And that unsettled her plenty, but not in the same hunted-and-wary way she was used to. She'd made out like a bandit on this partnership, and she wasn't going to fuck it up. So long as he wanted her around, she'd do her best to pay him back.

"So…you wanna?" Chloe bounced on the end of the rack and grinned. The rack didn't so much as tremble with her movement.

Mari flashed a grin and righted the butterfly-clasp straps on the orange silk. "Sure. And thanks again, for the heads-up and for the rack. Haven't rested so deep for a long time."

"It's the engine hum, I bet. Garrett says white noise produced by these engines elicits theta waves in a human brain, which prepares us for the sudden and inevitable mind-control apocalypse that's coming." Her eyes glowed somewhat brighter than usual when she mentioned the grumpy mechanic, whether she knew it or not. "Of course, he says my voice does the same thing, so it could be all bullshit."

Probably not bullshit, or not entirely. Probably Garrett had it bad for the free-fae, to the point that all kinds of waves spiked for him when she was nearby. Mari couldn't reckon which of the two was more pitiable, the phantom girl or the boy who wanted her.

Except…she was coming to realize that touch wasn't the only way two people could connect. Spiritually, or whatever.

She remembered the way back to the command cockpit, so she didn't have to wait for Chloe to lead her this time. On the way, she ran a hand through her hair and wondered what a girl would have to give for a brush around here. She checked the jeweled com in her ear and at her throat, pressed a hand down the sinful softness of Chloe's orange silk, and yeah, she did feel a mite dolled up. Maybe even pretty.

Heron was leaning back in his captain's chair when she climbed in. His hair was damp and dark and so touchable, Mari's fingers flexed. He was wearing different clothes. Still no bright colors—muted navy instead of muted gray—but with texture. Natural fibers, not open-source printed textiles. He was such a strange mix of old and new, hard-metal mech and down-home strokable man.

Mari curled both hands to fists and resisted the urge to reach for him.

The wound on the back of his head looked closed up for now. If she hadn't seen it happen, she wouldn't believe this man had withstood such an attack just hours ago. She figured she had Kellen to thank for his quick patch-up.

She moved to his side, where she could see him

better, but he didn't react. His eyes were closed. Still working or sleeping? Either way, she didn't want to interrupt. She could stand here and watch him all day.

"You'll need shoes." He didn't move, didn't open his eyes, but a smile might have skimmed over his mouth. His voice licked her from across the cockpit. "I feel your bare feet on the deck plates."

Ah, so he plugged into the ship the same way he plugged into the car. Good to know.

"Deck's warm." She curled her toes against it and was rewarded: he turned one hand palm up on the chair arm and crooked a long finger. Mari moved as beckoned, sliding into the narrow space between him and the chrome instrument panel. The orange silk of her skirt brushed his knees. "But I'm guessing you meant I'll need shoes for something else. You makin' plans to send me away?"

"Quite the opposite." His thumbs extended, brushed along her outer thighs, sending spikes of we-have-plenty-of-time all through her body. His closed eyes crinkled at the corners, as if he knew exactly what his touch did to her. "I'm putting in a reservation for a sterile med lab, but it looks like Chiba won't have one available until tomorrow morning. Fancy a night out on the station with me? They have Skee-Ball."

Mari bit her lip. She felt a little like bouncing, but she didn't want to let Heron see her surge of joy. Would be too telling, reveal too much. Instead, she bundled up her happy dance tight, took a deep breath, and smoothed her fingers over the cool edge of the dash, warming it with her palms, stroking it with one pinky. "Heron, you asking me out?"

He did open his eyes then, and he leveled a stare on her that near melted her insides. "I am. Want to come?"

He needed to ask?

●   ●   ●

Mari had never really thought about how a girl would get onto a space station. Even when Heron had invited her up to Chiba, she'd kind of had this notion that they'd—what? Put on astronaut suits and float over in low gravity to an airlock, like in turn-of-the-century movies about space? Reality was a bit different. Yes, there was an airlock on Heron's plane-ship-goddamn *Millennium Falcon*, but it didn't have a collection of helmets and hard-shell spacesuits. It had a lever and a panel with lots of blinking lights. Heron signed at it, and the lights turned green.

Something nearby clunked, and air whooshed, pressurizing. Heron reached for Mari's hand, and she slid into his clasp. He wasn't wearing gloves, and their hands came together like they were magnetized.

"If you're waitin' on me, you're backing up." Kellen loped into the small space near the airlock. His good ol' boy twang seemed more forced this time.

And so it ought to. Was he really planning on coming up to the station with her and Heron? She'd reckoned this was kind of a date. As in just the two of them. Not that she'd had any problems with ménage fun in the past, but something inside wilted a bit at the thought of sharing her first date with Heron with Kellen as well.

Mari swept a glance up and down the tall cowboy. He'd put on a fresh shirt and polished up his boots. He wore a hat, even though he was technically indoors, and back-home manners would call for him to remove it. Manners might be a smidge different on a space station, though.

She couldn't quite get over how much he reminded her of where she came from, of Texas. She hadn't thought she missed it so powerfully, but there it was: she felt a lump in her throat when she took in Kellen's getup.

"No Yoink?" she asked.

Kellen studied her for a moment—a searing infinity of *What if he gets offended easily?*—and then his face broke into a grin. Mari breathed.

"Yoink don't like zero-G, not even for the half second on switchover. Makes her claw things, and if I'm holding her, I'm like to end up with stripes. Speaking of which…" He turned to Heron, and that grin slid off fast, replaced by serious. "The queen confirmed our reservation, but she wants you to check in personally. Don't let her distract you with whatever crazy she's cooking up this time, though, all right? I expect I'll have everything set up 'round ten in the a.m. Miss Mari, you think you can take care of him till then?"

Mari started, looked up. Kellen nodded reassuringly.

She squeezed Heron's hand. "Will do my best."

Chloe was going to stay with the ship. She couldn't risk being seen, even by folks on a neutral entity like Chiba. The bounty on a free-fae was just too high to risk.

Garrett stayed with her. Heron said it was because Garrett never liked to be far from his gears and engines, but Mari had seen how Garrett looked at Chloe, and there was that thing about brain thetas. She suspected plenty of reasons Heron's young mechanic might want to stay behind, even though he could do fuck-all about his urges, if he had them. Must be powerful frustrating to lust after an incorporeal being. She thanked God and the 'verse that Heron was warm and solid. Machine, yeah, but at least she could touch him. And lord, did she have a mind to do just that.

His thumb moved over the top of her hand, figure-eighting her knuckles. He had a habit for that, and she didn't mind it at all. Had grown accustomed to it, in fact.

The light turned green, meaning the air pressure was set, and the doors opened, one at a time. A narrow boot connected the ship's airlock to the core of the energy tether, and stepping from one to the other was no more complicated than getting on an elevator. It was cooler in here, though, and the air felt staticky and dry. Mari wondered if her hair was poking out. She half wished for that broken hair elastic.

Smack in the center of the tether was a circular platform. Mari had to balance-check herself a couple of times on the way in, especially once the platform started moving. She scouted for seating options; her stomach wasn't a big fan of this kind of movement. Wouldn't do to stand up a lot.

Other folk were already there, all seated and most drinking. A slim wet bar had been set up along one curve, dispensing hooch through brushed chrome nozzles. Low cushions and padded, organically shaped lounge tables, all in dark colors, dotted the space like 'shrooms.

Minimal ambient lighting bled off curved walls. Shapes moved in the light: nano paper covered every speck of wall space, and the ads ran the gamut from dull to obscene. One vid hocked ribbed-glass automatons, "for her pleasure." Another pushed reshape and rewrap augmentations on the cheap. A third touted a kiosk on the station that specialized in nano ink body art.

Mari skidded a look over to her partner. Had he ever been inked? Before today, she would have assumed he was too stuffy. But now...hmm. She could imagine chasing a frisky design all over his body, maybe with her tongue.

"Y'all want anything to drink?" Kellen asked. Mari nodded, but Heron shook his head. Kellen went off toward the bar, and Mari and Heron stepped down into a sunken grotto lined with black cushions. Synth rubber: easy to clean.

Good thing, too. Across the way, a sex worker had some guy's flight suit open and his dick out. The head-bobber was a pro, choosing his angles so that folks around him got a good show of it. He'd probably find himself booked the whole night. Looked like he had a knack for working that tongue.

Heron studiously avoided the display. "I ought to warn you that Chiba Station lacks decency laws. It's anything goes on most levels, though there are strict rules against weapons, so you'll have to peacelock your holdout."

"Didn't bring one."

Disbelief made his eyebrows arch up till they disappeared beneath his hair. Mari shrugged and looked away. What? She was more than a girl with a gun. Right?

A woman in modest crinolines had situated herself nearer the fellatio show, with a good angle on the action. One white-gloved hand slipped beneath pretty ruffled skirts, and Mari thought hard about doing the same. Her belly tightened. She got a voyeur thrill same as the rest of the folks in here, and sitting right next to Heron didn't help that one iota.

"*Anything* goes? I guess nobody would bat an eyelash if I was to climb right over you now and pop them buttons on your pants. Might make 'ride the tether' mean a whole 'nother thing."

Like it had back in the car, Heron's breath huffed out. He looked like he was about to pass out from the effort of holding it all together. And she had to admit, that just made her want to tweak him even more. No doubt about it, something in his impossible equanimity brought out the bad in her.

"Mari…"

"I love the dress, by the way. Chloe told me I ought to wear it. Didn't offer any underthings, though. You reckon she did that on purpose?"

He didn't even breathe this time, but his hand around hers gripped so hard, she thought her bones might crunch. Still, he sat there, stretched along the low cushions like a caliph. If she hadn't felt the strength of his hand, she might have imagined that he was completely relaxed.

"The dress is beautiful, more so on you than it has ever been, and yes, as a matter of fact, I have been sitting here in keen awareness that you are wet and warm and shielded only by a scrap of raw silk. You enjoy torturing me like this, querida?"

"Way too much." Mari pulled her feet up onto the cushion. She'd opted to lace on her ratty old boots instead of prowling Chiba Station in her bare feet. Now, she kind of regretted that decision, seeing how things were so informal around here. And true, what with everything else going on in this lounge, she had half a mind to make good on some of those torture promises, but she figured she'd give Heron a little breather.

If she had him all night, she could afford to slow things down here on the front end. She leaned back against the cushion, wiggled her hand free of his, and gave him some space. He didn't look nearly appreciative enough. "So, Chloe and I had a long chitchat, about the dress…and other things."

"Did you?"

"I guessed some stuff, and she told me the rest."

Heron raised his hand to his mouth, stroked his chin as if he were testing a shave, but in reality, Mari figured he was hiding his lip movements. She heard him in her subvocal rig: *You can feel safe with my crew. We are all fugitives in one way or another, and they are completely loyal.*

"Loyal, hell. Heron, they're all in love with you." *And I think maybe I'm getting there, too.* She couldn't force her mouth to form the words, but she thought them plenty hard. Wasn't quite ready to confess as much, not out loud. But she tried the declaration on her brain, looking at him. *I love you.*

Huh. No cataclysm ensued. She was still alive. World hadn't ended. Of course, she hadn't said it out loud. Maybe that was when the bad shit would happen. Or maybe not.

Even as Mari's brain hummed, Heron looked up, over her shoulder, and she felt Kellen's approach from that direction. Oh, thank God—something to distract her. She sure needed it.

Mari reached out when Kellen handed her drink

down, and she thanked him kindly for the fizzy, rummed coffee. She pulled a swig off the top and licked the froth from her upper lip. Almost immediately, she could feel the double hit of caffeine and booze streak down her nerves. Settled them a smidge.

Kellen seated himself on the low cushion, his long legs spiking up at the knee. He had a beer in his hand, but he didn't drink any of it right away. Instead, he took his Stetson off and set it, brim up, by his hip. He avoided the increasingly vigorous fellatio to his right, which took some doing the louder those folks got. But Mari wasn't looking at them anymore either. The distraction had worked: she studied Kellen with a frown.

She didn't know Kellen well, had only just met him, but he didn't seem at all comfortable. He'd been okay in the airlock, but the higher this lift got, the more fidgety he got. Mari watched him palm one hand over his jeans-clad knee. Starched jeans. White-knuckled hand.

"Can't help but noticing you're gussied up fine, Kellen. Got big plans tonight?"

He looked down at his drink. Mari'd thought to ease Kellen's nerves, but he seemed even more edgy at her words. He didn't reply for a long time, and even when he did, his voice was so low, Mari wasn't sure she'd heard him right. She tucked her feet up closer on her cushion and leaned toward him. Not because doing so brought her that much closer to Heron. Nope, not because of that at all.

"Word came in from our UNAN Senate contact. Meetin' with her tonight, on vid. I got to tell her what happened." Kellen looked right at her when he said it, and there wasn't any mistaking his words.

Mari froze. "Wait, the UNAN Senate *knew* about this job? In advance?"

Kellen nodded. "Government's a big thing, and not all the parts talk to each other as much as they should. Our contact helped y'all confirm that the Daniel Neko you were targeting was, in fact, the mech-clone."

But he hadn't been. So had this UNAN contact been part of the betrayal, or had the federales somehow been suckered, too? Mari couldn't see how, but this day was making her paranoid. She felt like she was standing on quicksand. Everything she thought she knew kept shifting and sucking her down.

Heron settled a hand on the small of her back, but he wasn't looking at her. He was looking at Kellen. "You want me to do it, buddy?"

Kellen shook his head, and a shock of dark blond hair fell over his forehead. He didn't fight it off. "Nah. Seeing my face might make it all go down better. Plus, if she's really pissed, she ain't likely to come down too hard on me, our history being what it is. Better she don't get a gander at Mari, though. Not for a long time."

Mari squirmed away from Heron's hand and reared back, full of questions.

Heron preempted them. "I should explain. Mari, I established a lot of go switches for our job. I even contacted Daniel Neko's wife, and she confirmed that her husband, her whole-organic husband, was right there in the capital with her. On that assurance, I let us proceed. All I can figure is that the mech-clone must be unholy good, better than any we've seen before, if it was sleeping next to a woman and she didn't know it wasn't her husband."

"No shit." She swallowed. "But...does she know now? What I did?"

"That's what Kellen's going to do tonight. He's going to tell her."

Mari sucked in a breath. "Oh, no. That ain't right. I'll do it, Kellen. Seriously, you don't need to take the fall for me. Oh, lordy hell, she's going to be a wreck." Mari'd gotten bad news about her mom dying, though most of that part of her life was a blur now. She could recall what the message looked like clearer than how she'd felt. Same with hearing that Dad was missing, presumed captured. Those memories just left her cold and confused. She had to imagine that losing a spouse was worse. Seriously, loving somebody enough to hitch fates with them was rare enough these days, but then to have it all taken away... God. She couldn't even swallow the thought.

Kellen drew on his longneck, then pressed his lips together, sucking the beer drops off. He moved his shoulders against the cushion like he was trying to get comfortable. Wasn't any hope for it, though. "Actually, she might not be. Angela is a special kind of tough. It won't be easy on her, but I can guarantee it won't be what you're imagining, Miss Mari."

"Good." She almost relaxed against the synthfiber cushion, almost sucked on her rummed coffee, but a thought walloped her upside the head. "No. Wait. *Angela* Neko?"

"Yup."

"*Senator* Angela Neko?" How had she not put that together before? Neko wasn't the most common name on the planet, after all. How many could there be?

"You see part of the problem," said Heron.

"Oh, holy hell." Mari wilted against the cushion, but not out of relief. Hot coffee splashed on her wrist, missing the fancy silk by a hair. "That puppeteer said I'd fucked up, but I didn't grasp the…the *depth* of fuckitude till just now. Senator Neko was all over the vids a couple weeks back, saying how UNAN and Texas are getting close to a compromise. Peace, after all this blood. But now…does she know who wrote our contract? What if she blames all this on the secessionists? What if…" Mari choked. "Did I just start a war?"

"We. Always we." Heron reached out and squeezed her hand. "And I certainly hope not."

CHAPTER

9

MARI DIDN'T KNOW WHAT ELSE TO SAY. SHE HUD-
dled over her rummed coffee. The grunting of the
threesome at the other end of the sofa, the low hum
of the nano ads, and the chatter of other patrons all
pressed in on her ears, but the clamor in her thoughts
drowned out actual sounds. She studied Kellen and
Heron in her periphery but didn't have the courage to
ask any other questions.

Which freaked her out a bit. The fear. She didn't really
know what to do with fear. She hadn't felt true fear
since…when? Not today, when it probably would have
been useful. Not when those mercs had busted into Heron's
flat. Not even when the drones had swooped in on them
in the Pentarc. Now that she thought about it, Corpus
Christi was probably the last time she'd been afraid of
anything. Jobbing had sure calloused up her nerve.

But she was scared shitless now. And not even at the
thought that she might get caught and punished for what
she'd done, for killing poor Angela Neko's husband.
No, what scared her when nothing else had was the

swift, charged look Heron and Kellen had shared. She'd seen it, and it turned her blood to pure ice.

This kind of craziness was nothing new to them. They were ready to take the fall. For her or with her. And it didn't matter to them whether the sin was murdering one man or destabilizing peace for the entire region. These two were set on their course. She could hear it in their voices, see it in their faces. Kellen for love of his captain, and Heron…why, exactly?

For love of her?

That was the second scariest thought she'd had all day, and lord, had it been a day.

The platform settled at the base-level promenade of the station, and the other passengers stood up, gathered their stuff. When Mari got to her feet, she was careful not to push off too hard against the floor. Equal and opposite reaction, right? But even standing up felt… fine. Normal. Weird.

She'd expected low gravity to be more pronounced on a space station, like people floating or the rum in her mug forming perfect spheres she'd have to catch with her tongue. But the first thing Mari noticed about this particular station was that there wasn't anything to notice.

"Whoa. Gravity." Little kids used the exact same tone when pointing out fire trucks on the road.

Heron rolled his eyes. "Another secret she insists on keeping. The queen is proud of her engineered singularity, but not enough to tell the downland governments about it. There's no way you could have known."

Singularity. As in mini black hole. That would explain not only the gravity but also some of the huge amounts of power this station was able to generate. It wasn't all nanotubes and solar radiation harnesses. Cool, but also intimidating. Sciency folk had been trying to harness singularities for decades, but this queen—or the people working for her—had apparently accomplished the impossible. And even more unbelievable, had kept it out of the newsfeeds.

"More likely she don't want the downland militaries to know about it," added Kellen. "She's kind of a pacifist, which is why she calls herself 'queen' instead of 'beloved overlord' or 'benevolent dictator.'"

"Or captain." Heron said that with a smile, poking fun at himself but also as if he knew exactly how the queen's politics might freak out a gun girl like Mari. Warning taken. She was just happy she'd come up here unarmed. She could, of course, take most unaltered folk apart without using any weapons at all, but packing anything visible on this station was like to get her sent down. Or worse. She didn't mean to advertise her more lethal skill set here.

Just one more thing that made her nervouser than a long-tailed cat in a room full of rocking chairs, but she tried her best to look calm. Blend in.

Other passengers disembarked and poured out over the promenade, scattering like bugs when a light comes on. Metal-jacketed tubes twisted off from the core like tentacles. She counted ten, but they all looked exactly the same. They even had identical rows of polycarbon doors along either side, stretching off farther than she could see. All of them were wall-to-wall crammed with free-fae ads: moving, cajoling, lights and music and texture and chaos. Some reached out and touched potential customers, but the passengers didn't seem to mind. A few stroked back.

Each tube led to a different section, presumably, because signs over the entrances indicated shipping, receiving, transactions, entertainment, lodging, corporate, and so on. Those signs were printed in Mandarin, English, Farsi, and some binary numeral thing that looked about as far from a real language as Mari could imagine. There wasn't a map anywhere she could see, but everybody seemed to know where they wanted to go. Chiba Station's promenade looked like it had been pulled out of Mari's most chaotic, unsettling, and dirty dreams.

The sex worker from the platform ducked into the entertainment tube, followed by a gaggle of folks. Good for him.

The glut of free-fae graffiti gave the whole area a cool blue tint, but that was the only illumination. Mari wondered why a station with this much latent power would skimp on the lights. Unless, of course, the queen here just liked having the free-fae hang out all over her walls. It was possible the decision had nothing to do with logic, but in Mari's experience, folks with IQs high enough to play at quantum physics didn't do illogical things.

"I sent y'all the berth number of the med lab," Kellen said, shifting his boots on the platform, hesitating to step off. He looked so out of place, it might have been worth pointing out...if he hadn't also looked like a man going to his execution. "It's down the med tube over yonder, but y'all probably want to grab a starside berth in lodgings for the night. I'll be, uh, off to corporate.

And remember what I said: you take care of my captain, Miss Mari. I got a lot invested in that fool head of his."

Even when he was tense and distraught, Kellen could roll out a smile. A disarming one, too.

"Promise." She ought to tell him, again, to stay the hell here and let her do the apologizing. It'd been her mistake, after all. But she couldn't make the words come out. Coward.

"Ten tomorrow, then."

Kellen tipped his black hat, and she couldn't see his face beneath the wide brim. Then he went off to break the bad news to Angela Neko. For a moment, Mari damn near followed him, but then Heron's hand clasped hers.

"He wasn't lying," Heron told her. "Angela trusts him. If she feels a need for vengeance, she won't take it out on him."

"She'll come lookin' for me." Mari swallowed. "And she ought to."

"Nobody's going to find you. Nobody's going to hurt you."

His words warmed the whole goddamned space-cold station. Startled her a bit. She looked up at him.

And caught him staring back at her. The look on his face turned the air molten. She could hardly breathe. His mouth pressed into a line, and his eyebrows got all fierce—that wasn't annoyance or disapproval. It was sincerity, devotion. Possession.

She moistened her lips. "That in our contract, partner? The keeping me safe thing?"

"Not currently. Shall we renegotiate?" He peeled his gaze off her and watched Kellen waltz off until the cowboy disappeared around a bend.

She tightened her fingers around his. With all the flirting she'd been doing, she hoped he wouldn't misinterpret that touch. Wouldn't think it was a little thing, this burn she had for him.

"How about we agree to terms from here on out, just the two of us?" Heron wasn't even looking at her. "I mean, without Texas or the UNAN or any third party intruding."

Sounded intimate. She liked it.

They hadn't stepped off like everybody else, and now the platform started to rise. Mari was fixing to get off, but Heron drew her back down to the cushion, and she folded herself into it again. Comfortable. Protected. He couldn't make all her wibble go away, but it was sure sweet he tried.

"The keeping me safe at all times and from all threats would have to be in there," she said. "Lord knows a girl doesn't want to worry about danger and shit when she's trying to blow somethin' up."

"Done."

"Also, ain't fair for you to know what I'm thinking while I have to guess what's in your head. So I'd press for a full-disclosure clause as well."

"I can't always read your mind, you know. What happened at the Pentarc was unusual and unexpected. I didn't mean to pry."

Pity. "So right now, you ain't peekin' up my…"

"No." He paused. "You make it sound perverse."

She couldn't tell whether he liked that or not, but the air on this station sure was getting warm. And he was still holding her hand, sitting real close. That had to be some kind of win. "Nah. I make it sound *fun*."

He grimaced, but he didn't pull away, didn't make her stop touching him. "You always do."

The platform ascended into a hole at the roof, and dark encircled them for a moment as they went through to the next level of the station. The low hum of people and music and adverts retreated, replaced by machine sounds more appropriate for a space station. As they went further up, an eerie sort of stillness settled around the elevator shaft. They passed through a level decorated in earthy tones, tasteful, with discreet signs in languages Mari didn't recognize. Was one Arabic? There might have been music in the distance, but it teased just beyond the reach of her ears.

Each level up had fewer corridors leading off from the elevator shaft, sparser signage, until at last, they passed through a level that had no adverts at all, just pictures. The artistry of free-fae picked out a garden in glowing blue relief, flowers giving way to pale sunlight and an idyll of nature that probably hadn't ever existed outside of dreams. Sure as shit didn't exist now, not even in nature sanctuaries like Dakota or Amazonas. The vine pattern on that level twisted in on itself as the platform went up. Watching it made Mari a little sick to her stomach, and she had to force herself to look away. No problem, though; she'd much rather ogle Heron anyhow.

"Hey, partner, you still with me?" She nudged him with her shoulder. His biceps felt unusually tense, but hell, he might be that stressed out all the time.

"Sorry."

"You thinking deep thoughts?"

"I was parsing the data I retrieved from my brief time

in your mind and positing several paths your thoughts might have taken since then. Lots of maths. See? Knowing *my* thoughts would be terribly dull."

"Depends on what you were mathing." She thought of the binary-looking language above the entertainment tube on that first deck where Kellen had gotten off. Who knew? Maybe there *was* a math word for fun. One for frisky. For sex.

She snuck a glance at him, not for the first time wondering what he was thinking. He looked so pensive. So serious. She'd always thought him expressionless, but now she knew she just hadn't been watching close enough. Now she could see he was worried. It was so clear. How could she have known him more than a year and never *seen* him? Even lately, when she'd started thinking about licking him all over and how nice that might be, she'd still fallen into considering him merely a thing. A pleasure thing, granted.

But he was more than that. Somehow, without her realizing it, he'd become damn near *everything*. And how did shit like that even happen?

"We're almost there," he said.

Mari didn't reply right away. All that light behind his head reminded her of a halo, and her throat tightened.

"There where? Thought Kellen told us to go to lodgings, but looks to me like we missed our floor." She looked down, but the lift platform obscured the lower level.

"We will go to lodging later, also to entertainment—I did promise you a night out, but…" He looked uncomfortable. "We received a summons, so we probably ought to visit *her* first."

"Her the queen?"

"Yes."

Mari wished for gum, didn't have any, and swallowed anyhow. A wad of panic clogged her throat. "Uh, I gather you're friends with the queen and all, and I don't have anything against her, don't get me wrong, but that don't mean I need to meet her. I'm not exactly royal court material."

Heron tilted his head slightly, like he was sighting her in. "Didn't I say you look beautiful?"

Her face warmed. Well, look at that: blushing. Her. *Ha!* "Yeah, you did. And that felt fine, I admit it. But I wasn't talking about the clothes. Was talking about me. I ain't her kind."

"What makes you say that?"

He'd taken her to his home. He'd shown her his secrets. She owed him a little of the same back, no matter how much it hurt. "Pretty much everything about me. I do guns; she hates 'em. She runs a space station; I'm a feet-on-the-ground kind of girl. Couldn't calculate planetary rotation if my life depended on it. You know I ain't big on brains."

"Intelligence isn't defined by one's résumé," he observed. He was probably trying to comfort. He was failing.

All the old insecurity wrapped its skeevy self around Mari's throat. The not-good-enoughs, the dismissals of her because of where she came from, how she spoke, the conspicuous lack of letters after her name. "Depends on who's doing the defining, don't it? My dad, before the TPA kidnapped him, was a celebrity scientist, had a top-one-hundred channel and shit, so I know how smart folk operate. Me, though, *I* was raised out in the sticks by my auntie. When I got older, I went to Austin to try and get to know Dad. Stupid plan. All them smart people, pretty people, powerful people. I was a bug on their boots. They weren't a lick impressed that I could shoot clean or fuck dirty, the sum total of my natural gifts."

"I am impressed." His eyebrows hitched up, like he just then realized what he implied. "By the shooting. I am impressed by the shooting."

Oh, it was on the tip of her tongue to press him on the other—hell, to offer a demonstration—but she held back. Wasn't the right time. She waited.

He got himself together. "Look, the people surrounding your father weren't better. Believe me. I was...I know the intellectual world. Intimately. If you were out of place, it was because *they* were bugs. *You* were boots. Gorgeous, hand-tooled, full-quill, ostrich boots, and you should waltz into any social situation, even a queen's court, knowing precisely that."

"That what?"

"That I consider you my equal. That I am proud to be your partner."

Well, damn. She could have kissed him right then, and it wouldn't have been a sex thing at all. She could have kissed him out of pure thanks. Out of the surge of confidence that rose in her belly and pushed out her throat. She grinned silly, squeezed his hand, and almost let herself get comfortable.

And then the platform stopped moving.

Heron's mouth pressed flat, not quite a smile but no longer a grimace. "Come on, querida. I promise she won't bite."

Down on the level where Kellen had gotten off, a

wide promenade had surrounded the platform, like a traffic roundabout, so folks could go in between all those various tunnels. But there wasn't a space like that here, just the platform, one step down, and a narrow ribbon of deck surrounding it. That floor shone like wet blood, dark red and menacing.

Mari and Heron stepped off, and it was like riding a roller coaster in the dark. That one step felt like it dropped her fifty feet or more, yanking her guts up through her throat, and then…soft. She landed soft on the red-ribbon floor, with Heron holding her hand. She swallowed, popping the pressure out her ears. Her feet sank into the floor: carpet, not tile. Nothing quite what she expected up here so far.

"Gravity wobbles a bit on the transfer from the tether lift to the station proper. I forgot to mention it. You okay?"

Mari nodded, but she was lying. She wasn't okay. No matter what he said or how sweetly he said it, she was out of her comfort zone, once again reaching up too far, trying to come across as something she wasn't, here in her borrowed silk gown. Fraud. Her hands itched for a gun, but all she had to hold on to was her partner's patient hand, pulling her along.

He drew them both toward the only tunnel entrance available on this level: a tall sucker, arched on top and with gigantic double doors, red again, though this time chased with black, carved gryphons. No. Too curvy and elongated. Alien gryphons? Or just robot alien birds with wings? Every time Mari thought she had those carvings described in her mind, they shifted, changed. She blinked, and the black wings grew feathers. Blinked again, and they were flat and leathery as batwings. The overly soft floor shifted. Mari shook her head to clear the dizzies. This room was fucking with her. She'd lay money on that, though she couldn't figure out if the illusion was optics or nanos.

When Heron got close, the gryphons retreated, and the doors yawned open. A tunnel stretched, with another door at the end. Simple thing, but daunting.

Mari wanted to hang back, but she also didn't want to come off as scared. Fuck it. *Boots*. She shook her hair back and waltzed the hell *in*.

Through that plain door at the end was a small capsule, about as far from a throne room as she could imagine. Black wires spiked out of utilitarian-white walls, and banks of status lights blinked, forming patterns if you looked hard enough. The deep carpet gave way to rubber decking, more cables, some of them duct-taped down in intricate arrangements, a byte-and-nylon bouquet. The air smelled plastic and metal and tight.

In the capsule's center, suspended from three walls and the ceiling, was a harness, and plugged into that harness was a woman.

No. Not a woman. A mech-clone.

About as mech as a body could get, in fact: the synthskin wrapped rubberlike over a larger-than-life frame that was more metal than meat. Gears and hoses moved beneath the film of skin, pulsing like veins and organs, but visible and enormous. Under it all whirred the galvanics as they hoisted and reset. Triple-jointed fingers aided in fine-motor movements, and outsized construction allowed the developer to get his hands under its skin easier.

No, not *its*. *Her*. Every curve of this mech-clone

was pure woman, or the idealized representation of woman. Sleek, rounded rear absolutely devoid of lumps, long elegant legs, toes, fingers. Black, shiny hair, curling slightly and so long, it kissed the stark floor beneath her.

The queen was facing away, nude and hooked into the harness by a hundred wires, when Mari and Heron came into her room. The door shushed closed behind them. Sealed.

"Ma'am," Heron said simply.

"Heron," the queen replied, her voice forced natural. Too natural. Metal. Fake. One long finger cricked, just the end joint, gesturing toward a SIP port on the wall to their left. "Plug there. We will talk direct."

"That's probably not a good idea."

The harness hummed, gyrated her around so that she was facing them, and gravity might have held just fine, but Mari suddenly felt like she was falling. Down a rabbit hole, down a nightmare, down a memory.

She recognized this creature.

Instantly and with yawning horror. She had to snip off the urge to yelp or melt into a puddle of shame. God, she knew that face, those elongated machine eyes, the unnaturally sharp cheekbones and full lips. That obscene gorgeousness was all the work of a douche named Limontour. Limontour…dangit, couldn't remember his last name, but he'd made a killing at interactive installations, sculpting perfect, mathematical beauty touchable by everybody. He'd been a fixture at Dad's lab, always hanging around, taking pics and sketching things. Real fucking artist was Limontour, and something of a perv besides. He'd palmed Mari's ass once, before he realized whose daughter she was. After he found out, though, he'd ignored her, like everybody else.

Funny how Mari's memory worked: she remembered Limontour's cold-noodle fingers but not what her mother's face looked like. And of course, *of course*, she remembered every detail of this mech-clone. Dad had called her Peetey, a shortened form of Prototype3. But she wasn't Peetey anymore.

The queen of Chiba tilted her head. "Why is it not a good idea."

It ought to have been a question, but her inflection was off. When Mari had known her before, she'd been dazzling at parties, trilling laughter and sparkling conversation, floating among guests. Impressing deep-pocket investors and government shills. Strange, alien, painfully beautiful, an uncanny valley so lush, folks forgot to be offended. But her programming, her purpose, was different back then.

Back when she belonged to Dad.

"I, uh, got a virus," said Heron, "an implanted one, and it's transmitting in bursts. I haven't been able to shut it down, but I'm hoping the LOM scrub will help. In the interim, though, I had better not plug in. I could infect your system."

"I am smiling." But her face didn't move. "You cannot infect me. I will speak to your nanos. We will make this station safe for you."

"Thank you."

"Loathe having to speak aloud. So much time is wasted. But, oh. I see it is for her benefit." For the first time, the mech-clone—the queen—faced Mari dead-on.

"I should be pleased at seeing you again, Marisa Vallejo. Yet am not. You are made of bad memories."

Heron twitched, but not hard enough. Mari was surprised by his lack of surprise. He shouldn't have known that she and the queen had met. Unless, of course, he also somehow knew that the queen was once Dad's prize robot, the first of his famous N series. And if he knew all that, he would have known Mari. Right? *Right?*

Mari shook her head, to rattle her memories loose. "Likewise. Still, I'm glad he got you out of Austin before the riots. That place was a nightmare."

"In so many ways, yes. But by 'he,' you must mean Heron. I have him to thank for my safety. Not Dr. Vallejo. Never him." The harness readjusted. Wires slunk from their sockets. The queen stepped onto the floor confidently, as if she had never mistrusted her balance.

She came right up to Mari, put one long, cold finger beneath her chin, and tilted her head, searching. Her fingers felt like talons, and goose bumps pebbled Mari's arms. The queen inhaled deeply and closed her eyes. "Hmm. Yes. You are his daughter still."

What a strange thing to say, but then, Peetey—the queen—had always been two monkeys short of a circus.

Mari swallowed, even though her throat protested. "I don't guess you know where he is now? Where they took him? If he's…if they let him live?"

The queen retracted her eyelids. Her mechanical irises engaged, making pinpricks of her pupils. The workings in there were all mechanical, of course, but Limontour and Dad had both worked so hard to make her lifelike. Her eyes were winter blue, a striking contrast against her dark skin. "They?"

Memories were sparking all over the place, things Mari had thought long forgotten, and not all of them bad. Not all. Breakfast tacos on the South Mall. Anthropology 301 and a TA with dazzling pink hair. Unimportant details, but treasures still. "They, the Texas Provisional Authority," she explained with no edge to her voice. "They kidnapped him during the riots. Didn't you know? It was all over the newsvids. Took him off to some secret location. I heard they might have tortured him."

The queen looked at her a long time. A really long time. And Mari got colder and colder beneath that unmoving stare. Her gut trembled, but her hands were steady.

"Tortured *him*? But child, you know what he did." Again a statement, but this time, it made sense as one.

Yeah, Mari knew her dad had been involved in a lot of skeevy projects, probably deserved the "Mad Scientist in Boots" moniker the gossip feeds gave him. He had the ethics of a Duval County politician. But he was hers. Her very own. Wasn't like she could get another dad.

The queen took in her silence. "This is loyalty. I see it. You are similarly loyal to our Heron?"

"Different reasons, way different relationship, but yeah." Felt weird to talk about him, and especially about her feelings for him, when he was right next to her. But she didn't lie. "I might have fucked up and let Dad get taken, but ain't nobody going to take Heron away. I guarantee it."

The queen dropped her hand. Her mouth moved, reshaped itself. She…lordy hell, she smiled. Didn't just say "smiling" but actually, literally smiled. The expression stretched her face, made it both brilliant and ghastly.

She turned to Heron, picked up the hand that wasn't grasping Mari's, and placed it palm-to-palm with hers. Well, duh. They both had sense-tips, and who needed a port when you could just plug into each other like that? Ew, but also efficient.

Mari tried not to look. Also tried to tamp down the flare of black jealousy in her gut. She hated it that they were communicating without her. Excluding her. Just like always. Brilliant people. "Hey. Y'all want to tell me what's going on?"

Heron turned to her then, a strange, soft look on his face, and her hackles went down fast. "The queen is going to let us use her private suite and med bay. She'll have Kellen meet us up here tomorrow morning. She's offered the best tech available for a problem like mine. We may be able to stop this transmission."

Great, he was relieved, but her own questions still prickled. The queen had never answered her. Did she or didn't she know where Dad was? Mari turned, her mouth open, but the queen cut her off.

Smiling. "Little Marisa, your father's work is valuable. Of course, everyone—the *they* of whom you speak—wants it. It is safe. Now *you* must be. Safe, girl. And do have a good night." She turned, effectively ending the audience. Black cables reached out, suckling snakes searching for their mother. They surged along the queen's body, finding their sockets, piercing her, pulling her back into the digital flow. Mari's stomach churned.

Dad's work. This is what it had come to. All that money and effort and love sunk into work when it should have been *hers*, and it all ended here, on this station, in this room. Why couldn't she feel furious, or even jealous? Why did she feel just…tired?

Heron squeezed her hand and gently pulled her through one of the circular doors, into the next room in this ring. She followed, all the while looking back.

●   ●   ●

He'd promised Skee-Ball. Skee-Ball in iffy gravity was what Mari was sure to call "a hoot." But when he checked, the lanes were booked for an hour, and sitting in the corral watching porn vids and live shows would eat his patience alive. That ride up the tether had been agony enough.

What he wanted was privacy. Darkness. To hold her and know that no one would hurt her. To turn off the gravity and float. With her. In peace.

As if on some hateful cue, another transmission speared out from that implanted tech, and he cut it savagely.

Still on the queen's deck, he passkeyed them to the navigation room, one place on the station he knew had a great view of Earth. The queen typically initiated all maneuvers through her command harness, so navigation was a misnomer. She didn't hire navigators. Hardly anyone came here, and this place reeked of peace. Cool brushed aluminum, silent electronics, repurposed air stripped of anything remotely vile. Pure.

After struggling with the changes in his body and consciousness these last few hours, not to mention the constant threat of harm to Mari, Heron felt uncertain, directionless. Lost. He needed a time out. Needed to not think, just feel. This room seemed to offer the haven he craved, and he was glad his partner was with him. She was all mixed up in his brain with comfort lately, and he needed her here.

More importantly, he wanted her, and not just in a base, sexual way.

He went to the wide permalens window and drew Mari up beside him. Dawn lit a crescent on the far edge of the planet, but he wasn't watching morning. All he saw was Mari's profile in the light.

She was quiet, too. Not her norm. And frowning. Again, not at all typical.

"You weren't surprised when she mentioned my father, her maker." She spoke out loud, putting some distance between them whether she realized it or not. "You know who he is."

Heron tensed. Oh God, were they going to have this conversation now? His thermals spiked, but a transmission prodded right then, and he didn't have energy to handle both. He cut the transmission and let his temperature rise. So what if he sweated? A trickle formed on the back of his neck, scurried down his spine.

Mari went on. "I guess you know why she hates him, why pretty much everybody hates him. I mean, that bone-cloning scandal, or using nanos to reconstruct live subjects without them knowing, or blaming the UNAN for cloud seeding that hurricane, Agatha, getting Texans all riled up and hollering secession. Sure, we hated continental unification before, but Agatha was the tipping point, and Dad sort of single-handedly shoved us over it. And I do agree those were all supremely shitty things to do. So were trading in research secrets, embezzling contract monies, and conducting off-books experiments at home. Not to mention pawning me off on Auntie Boo while he whored his creepy robot female to investors and war profiteers. I mean, take your pick. My father gave a lot of folks a lot of reasons to hate him."

"But not you."

She shrugged. "Sometimes you don't get to pick who you love."

He waited, but she didn't add to that. Didn't say the thing he fantasized about her saying. "You have an astonishing capacity for forgiveness, querida. Of others, though, not for yourself. You're still beating yourself up over the job, and you needn't. It's okay to regret, but that self-loathing, you can let it go."

Mari paused, and her next words were tentative. "You know, I'm starting to."

So she wasn't going to hair-shirt herself about today, about Daniel Neko. Good. He knew she did that sometimes after completing contracts, got low and dark and self-defeating. He'd sent med wagons out after her during downtimes, and not just for injuries she got on jobs. Mostly for things she did to herself, when he was far away. If she was finding a path out of that darkness, he was the last person to complain.

He knew she was vulnerable now. The flood of damaging memories coming at her had been palpable back in the queen's control room, and none of that was resolved. Part of him didn't want to resolve it, didn't want to talk about her past and pain. Neither of them were ready for that, not after today. Instead, he reached for a thread that wouldn't hurt her, just him. He could take this hit. "I don't suppose you have any forgiveness to spare?"

She tipped her chin back and flashed a grin. The strip of nascent dawn haloed her head. "Babe, you don't need forgiveness. Not mister awesome-in-every-way you. Haven for Chloe, hope for Kellen and his critters, beloved of that chain-smoker Adele who patches up your booboos and smells like turpentine. And, don't forget, partner to me, best I've ever had. Best *person* I know. Nope, you don't need forgiveness, not mine or anybody's."

"I've done things that are unforgivable."

She narrowed her eyes. "What things?"

He'd had nightmares about saying these things aloud, and saying them now to *her*, the person he most admired and respected, was going to kill him. But he said them anyway. They tasted like penance. "Your father blamed the UNAN confederation for Superstorm Agatha, but he was wrong. The cloud-seeding work was mine. I thought it up, designed the foglets, programmed them. Agatha was my fault. What happened to Houston was my fault."

She didn't look away. Bless her, she could still look into the face of a monster. "Did you do it yourself? Release the nanos, make the storm, blame UNAN, start a war?"

"Doesn't matter. The research was mine. I thought I was saving the world, repairing climate change. Instead, I caused unthinkable damage and…death. Murder, Mari. On a scale like nothing you have known."

She shrugged and leaned against the clear impact glass. Mari, casual, with all of the black universe behind her. "All murder is off the scale, 'cause there isn't a scale. It's binary. You either did it or you didn't. Black, white. On, off. So did you? Did you put the barrel to somebody's head and pull the trigger?"

Breath shuddered into his lungs. It pushed against his ribs. Mari reached down and grabbed his hand. Her absolution poured through him.

"Tell me, or I'll ask Chloe," she said. "She was there. She said she was your original vat."

Let go of that guilt, Adele had said. *Forgive. Live.*

"Heron, did you seed the clouds?"

In a whisper, he replied, "In simulation. In a mirror. And it worked. It *worked*. I wrote up the findings for publication but couldn't help bragging first. To my rival."

"You told my father?" Hissed like a hex. Spat like poison.

Yes, he'd been that stupid. He'd been so elated at the simulation results that he'd run to Dr. Vallejo's office even before he'd submitted his paper to the cloud archive.

Damon hadn't been thrilled. Oh, he'd offered congratulations, but Heron should have known. Should have realized that Damon Vallejo was an emperor in his little world. He couldn't have a snot-nosed young'un wheel in and show him up. He'd never had his top billing challenged. His campus, his lab, his vid channel, his grant money.

Damon had struck back, burying the results, shutting down the vat.

Unleashing Agatha. Blaming UNAN. Starting a war.

"Unforgivable."

"No," she murmured. "No, it ain't. It was a gullible, stupid, kid thing to do, but not unforgivable."

"I don't think anybody's ever called me stupid before." He laughed, but it broke.

"Aw shit, I didn't mean…"

"But it was, querida. Telling Dr. Vallejo about my simulation was the single stupidest thing I've ever done. And I'll be regretting it for the rest of my life."

"So let me get this straight: you can forgive me for murder, but you can't forgive yourself for some infantile hotdogging?"

"Forgiving *you* is easy," he said.

She snaked her arms through his, wrapped them around him, turned her body completely away from the window. "I was about to say that same thing."

Heron rested his cheek atop her hair.

They stood there unspeaking, only the whir of the air-reclamation system intruding. And then she trembled. God, was she crying? Heron drew back and looked down.

Fucking hell. Mari wasn't crying. She was *laughing*.

"Querida?"

"It just occurred to me: my dad ruined your research, kept you from publishing, so you *stole* his gal. You snatched the queen right out of Austin." She cackled like a hyena.

"I so did." He hadn't simplified his actions down to those words before, but in essence, she was right.

She laughed louder, harder, so hard at one point, she snorted. "Too fucking awesome, babe. Man, I love…" Her voice blew out like a candle, that fast to silence, then, "It. I love it."

She looked up in his arms when she said that last word, and every gear in Heron stopped. Just creaked to a halt, waiting. Wishing. He wanted to be her it.

But she didn't clarify, and Heron breathed

deliberately. He dropped a kiss atop her hair, avoiding the heat of her skin.

Avoiding a lot of things. He knew he couldn't keep changing the subject forever. He needed to let her know all his secrets. Even *that* one. But not tonight. Tomorrow was a different beast, but tonight, he wanted, needed to comfort her. To make her feel safe.

"Come on, querida. There's something on the station I really want you to see."

* * *

On the queen's level, the chambers formed a circle, so she and Heron had to duck back into that freaky harness control room and then on through a hatch on the far side. The queen was so deep into whatever it was she was doing that she didn't notice them. Or maybe she did, but she didn't say anything. They slunk through, waggling eyebrows and being stealthy as a pair of grade-schoolers trying to skive off class.

But in the far room, a full corridor beyond the queen's control room, they encountered a curtain barrier, and quiet smothered them. Solemnity. Heron removed his shoes and nodded for Mari to go ahead of him. She toed off her boots and ducked past the curtain into the chamber.

What a chamber. Made of pure dreams.

As with much of the station except for the queen's control capsule, the walls here were covered with free-fae designs. These, however, weren't the typical blue. They were autumn brown, mimosa orange, a collage of leaves and sunlight, shifting only as the breeze rustled them.

Yes, a breeze. On a space station. How'd that even happen?

Late evening's breath eddied through the soup of humidity, mixing up smells: damp leaves, summer rain, wet critter fur. Mossy red brick stairs led upward, and Mari mounted them without even having to think about it. Her mind had no memory of this place, but apparently, her instincts, her muscles did. Weird.

She was supposed to climb.

She knew this vista but vaguely, like she'd seen it on a postcard. But with each step, more bits of information downloaded and revealed the scene. She could lay films of sensation over the picture: the smell and the shape of the leaves and the pattern of sunlight peeking through and minting her skin like fresh coin. Cicadas clicked, and birds squawked their ownership of the trees.

She blinked through the first glitter of fireflies hovering on the edges of her steps.

Mount Bonnell. Austin. The words materialized in her mind like subtitles on a vid.

Home.

There were no handrails here, no help in climbing, but the steps were broad and sloped in, so that a body felt it was making progress, never slipping back or likely to fall. One hundred two steps, safe and always heading upward.

She counted them, knocking each footfall against the door of memory, but nobody answered. All her sensory inputs were coming from outside, from the hologram, not from her memories. Which was just wrong. She ought to know this place better. She'd spent a lot of time here in college, damn it. So weird that her postcard memories didn't smell like this, though, like Carolina jasmine and honeysuckle. They smelled like gunpowder.

But wait. That was another memory, a whoa-different one. Still Austin, but…it fell open like an old book. She breathed the dust from its pages.

Dad had come to her dorm in the middle of the night, told her that Austin was burning and she needed to get away. Not to Aunt Boo's. He gave her money and black-Sharpie'd a Dallas address on her forearm. She recalled these things like lines from a nursery song: tinny and distant and so, so blurry. Had she gone to that address? Had she washed the permanent ink off her skin, or had it just faded over time?

So hard to remember. So hard. But one thing stayed clear: Dad had bothered to warn her. He must have loved her. Right?

She struggled to reconcile that blurry-edged memory, her last one of him, with all the other stuff she knew about him now. With what he'd done to Heron, to Houston.

Which version of Dad was the true one?

She didn't want to answer that question.

By the time she reached the top of the brick stairs, her vision swam. She stared out over the precipice at the top, shielded from sunset by the wood-slatted limestone shelter.

Heron came up the stairs but didn't join her on the edge. He hesitated.

He didn't need to. Mari blinked the wetness from her eyes.

She reached a hand back and sighed when at last he took it, came up to stand behind her, resting their tangled hands on her shoulder. Something young and sad detached from her chest and lit out over the cliff's edge. She watched it go.

A sting on her wrist mimicked late-summer mosquitoes. Perfectionist nanos, getting their hologram right, not idealizing. They must not realize how painful truth could be.

"Did you do this, or did she?" She the queen. Of course. *You are made of bad memories.*

"I built it, at her request. She remembers Austin fondly, despite what had to have been a difficult life there. This setting is just a program, a simulation. She hires free-fae projectionists to run it from time to time, but…you know it doesn't look like this anymore, right?"

No, it wouldn't. Austin was a big scar on the landscape now, after the orbital bombardment. You could even see the bleak smudge of it from space. Nothing from Mari's childhood had survived intact. Not even her memories.

"This is what you're talking about when you say you mirror stuff for our jobs? Impressive hobby. I mean, when you're not smuggling shit or hiding fae or watching my ass make trouble."

"I'm always watching your ass."

Mari bit the grin off her bottom lip. "Stalker."

"Tease." He nuzzled his chin against her hair. Dang, he was tall. His arms came around her, but hesitantly, like he wasn't sure they'd be welcome. "I thought Mount Bonnell might make you feel safe, feel home. Thought you might need that after the day you've had. But it isn't real, querida. It's all fae. Nanos. Tech." He didn't say it, but he might as well have: tech like him.

He didn't move away, didn't stop holding her, but his

posture stayed stiff. Was it shame that made him keep his distance? Mari turned in his arms, away from the precipice and the sunset-bathed lake below. She reached up, between them, folding her hands over his chest.

"No, it is real. And *you* are. You're the realest thing in my whole world. And the best."

A breeze off the lake picked up strands of her hair and painted Heron's chest with them. He moved one hand to smooth her hair back, and she caught that hand, pressed a hot kiss into his scarred palm. His mouth moved, but no words came out. Didn't mean Mari couldn't hear. "Likewise."

He leaned down and laid his mouth to hers, and the sweetness of that kiss near melted her. She'd have thought, after all her deliciously pornographic fantasies starring him and all that verbal tango earlier, that this, their chance at last to drink their fill of each other, would be torrid.

Instead, yeah, heat simmered to lust and begged for the next step, but that urgency was overlaid with something far richer. Made her want to cry. Made her want to shout and dance, to hold on to him as tight as she could and leap off that cliff. Made her want to pet him to sleep and sing him lullabies. Made her want to dig her fingers in deep and never let go.

He moved his mouth, pressed a hot, sad kiss to her forehead.

Then he took a step away from her.

Wait. He *what*?

●　　●　　●

This night wasn't going according to plan. It was going according to fantasy. Sordid, delicious fantasy. And

Heron was very, very tempted to let it keep on in that direction. What if, just once, he did what he wanted instead of what he ought? *Do it, do eeeet,* his brain insisted. *Let her.*

But it wouldn't be just once, would it? He'd let his id control him before. After Austin, after he'd lost his career and dreams and most of his humanity, he'd ditched his lizard brain and went straight neo cortex, said fuck it to conscience or consequences. Results had not been catastrophic, not like Superstorm Agatha, but they hadn't been pretty. While his wrecked body had been rebuilding itself, his mind had spent all day every day in the cloud, fucking with things he had no business even knowing about. He'd created online identities, altered financial forecasts, fixed lotteries, rerouted airliners. For two years, he existed on the edge of disaster, like a serial killer who wants to get caught just to make the crazy stop. And then out of the blue one day, the queen called him with a set of location coordinates and a grainy pic of Mari in a South Texas prison. No explanation.

He hadn't needed one. From that day, Mari had become his purpose and salvation. He wasn't going back to throwing himself at fences and hoping one would break. Controlling his baser urges had worked out well for both of them for how many years now? Six? And even tonight, with all his command systems on the fritz and this damned transmission spawning every few seconds, he could keep his shit together.

For her. Because God, yes, he wanted her, but she deserved the best of him, or better than him. She was a *precious* thing. He would care for her as if she were the last bottle of single-malt Yamazaki. He would.

"So." Heron cleared his throat and blinked, resetting switches. "I've ordered in food. Star rise is in about half an hour, and right there behind the lake is a window. We can watch it and, um, talk."

Those words sounded silly, even to his own ears. After a lead-up like this, with the simulated sunset, the deliberate breeze, and the banter and the touches he hadn't been able to resist, she would be expecting romance and heartfelt protestations. Or, at the very least, torrid sex.

Which was inadvisable.

Whatever those mercenaries had implanted in his skull was too much for his system to handle. Transmissions were rolling out one on the heels of the last with no pause between, requisitioning all of his resources. He could barely string sentences together, for fuck's sake. He wasn't in a position to take things slow, to make this right.

And at the same blisteringly frustrating time, he couldn't keep his hands off her either. He looked down at those hands, looked at them hard. The damned things stayed locked with hers. Touching. Promising.

He'd kept his infatuation with Mari secret for years, had locked it down tight these last few months of working side-by-side. But right now, there was no way he could control…anything, really. Pulse, breath control, triage of all the input that came through any of his various machine-heightened senses—all of that was slag at this point. And if he gave in, if he let this scene play out the way his imagination insisted it must, he'd come across as an ingénue, a grade-schooler receiving his first playground kiss.

He'd be at her mercy.

Mari hadn't let go of his hands. She grinned up at him, roiling her flirt through the air between them. "Relax? On these nerves? Partner, I got seven thousand things I'm wantin' to do with you tonight, and not one involves relaxing."

He wasn't proof against this woman. So far from it. And with his systems going dark one after another, with most of his attention focused on basic compensating, just trying to stay alive and coherent, he couldn't do much more than look at her, a kid enthralled by a Christmas catalog. He let out a short breath. "I…can't."

Run. She ought to be running now. Or laughing. Sighing? About the last thing he expected was for her to keep gazing straight at him, flaying him layer by layer with hot-whiskey eyes. She stroked a finger over his bare knuckles. "Well, we already talked about the guilt, got that sorted. So I'm guessing something else is going on. Ain't it always? Tell me."

Her voice was made of temptation.

Heron pressed his lips flatter before he spoke, out loud and in his most uptight, professory tone. "Well, for one thing, physically, I'm hampered by this transmission, this virus. I appropriated voluntary control of most of my autonomic systems some time ago, but…"

"The big words do turn me on, but I flunked out sophomore year. You want me to follow this, it's gotta be in English. Or Spanish, if you'd rather. Just not Genius."

He rubbed his thumb over her hand and clenched his teeth against the surge of input. Fuck, he'd forgotten about the sense-tips. They sucked in more than data. His nerves lit with awareness of her. "You would have gone back and finished your degrees if your world hadn't exploded. Don't sell yourself short."

She shot him that pinched-lips-drawn-to-the-side sarcastic look. "Start over. I'll try to follow."

He knew from experience that she'd keep at this nut, thumping it, gnawing it until it cracked. He'd rather give a little than crack completely. "Okay. You know how most people don't have to think in order to breathe? They just do it? Well, for me, those things require deliberate will."

A hitch on just one side of her mouth warned him that she was thinking something salacious. "So you were *deliberately* hard for me in the car?"

But didn't warn him quite enough. Her voice quick-silvered through his body, tripping switches. He swallowed. "No."

"No? You didn't really want—"

Oh, holy goat fuck. Heron's vision pixilated on the edges, and before he could stop himself, he leaned down and shut her up.

With a kiss.

Quick and hard and not in any way romantic, that kiss. A tangle of tongue and teeth and desperation and please and don't you dare. Basically, the sort of kiss she'd been deserving for some time.

When he pulled back, she was panting, and her sharp fingernails had pressed divots between his knuckles. Not a shred of sarcasm remained on her face, just raw desire.

He pinned her with a look. "Don't finish that sentence. I did—and I do—want you. Naked, upside down, howling, every day and twice on Tuesdays. But tonight is not the best time. For me, I mean. I'm…broken. My body isn't responding to commands the way it ought. Those mercenaries not only implanted the transmitter but also messed up my control. Over myself."

He could have phrased that better. Her eyes lit up with pure minx, and he didn't need to read her thoughts to know exactly what sweet filth was dancing through her brain.

"Feh. Self-control is overrated." She brought their knotted clasp to the neckline of her slinky orange dress. If he opened his palms flat here, his thumbs would dip beneath the silk. Her pulse pounded against his knuckles. "I might just like you better without it."

On fire. His blood was on fire and gathering in the expected places. If she looked down at all right now, she'd see how fucking hard he was for her. But her gaze stayed locked with his.

Chalk-dry mouth made speaking tough, but he could still form the shapes of words. She wore her com. The voice piece winked at her throat in rhythm with her pulse. He didn't need to speak for her to hear him. "But you see, I might not like myself. Or what I might…do to you. My resistance calculations are all off, and I don't have the processing power to compensate. Fail-safes aren't dependable without neural oversight. What if the muscle regulators misfire? I could…"

"Fuck a *duck*, Heron, stop worrying yourself raw." She squeezed his hands. "How about you just let me do it?"

"Mari…"

"No, listen. I know what you signed Kellen up to do tomorrow. He's gonna poke around in your skull, mess with things that ought never get messed with. And last time somebody did that, it fucked you up bad, and this is the result. So what happens if Kellen breaks you even more? What if we're not talking about a spliced wire here or a wad of gauze there? What if more than your *control* goes dark? What if this is the last night for us, ever?"

"It isn't."

"But what if it is?"

"Mari, you're just trying to seduce me."

She huffed out a breath that wrapped hot and tight against his throat. "Damn skippy. And you're makin' it real hard."

In his defense, there really was only one way to respond to that without fibbing. "So are you."

She looked down. Well, of course she did. The pink velvet tip of her tongue peeked out, moistened her lips. And then those lips moved. He heard her voice inside his head, deep. "Fuck yeah."

Fuck. Yeah.

Except, no.

True, he'd fantasized about this for ten years. True, she was his ideal, and he wanted her with every cell in his body. But not like this. Not when he could only give her part of his attention and didn't have the energy or focus to resolve their other issues. She deserved better.

But then she looked up, trusting. Open. Asking. And he didn't have the will to deny her.

"I know you always set stuff up when we're on jobs," she said in a voice of pure temptation. "You like being in charge, and I get that, but don't you ever think what it would be like to just lay back? Let me take point on this. You don't have to plan anything. I can take care of you."

Tension knotted his body, and when she raised their tangled hands to her mouth, he flinched.

But he didn't tell her to stop. He didn't say no.

She pressed her lips to his sense-tipped fingers and hummed against the tingle of implanted electrodes. He'd kept the scars on his hands on purpose, to remind him what he was. Now, beneath her breath, the spider-thin lines got brighter, whiter. "They go all over, these scars?"

"No." Hardest word ever, but he pushed it out. His body hurtled out of control, senses firing all over, nucleus accumbens and endocrines and muscles *and God, please don't let her stop now. Please let this be real.*

"Lemme see?" Her voice made it a question, but it wasn't. Not really. It was a command, and he took it as such. When she disengaged their hands, he let his fall slack against his sides. And just stood there amid the sensory and emotional storm.

Letting her.

Mari tugged his shirt out of his waistband and walked it up his chest. Touch by excruciating touch. Unveiling him. She nudged beneath his arms, and he lifted them, letting her pull the shirt over his head. She followed his biceps back down, skating them with her hands, as if memorizing the texture and shape.

Against her palms, his chest surged. Sharp breath, and then he held it. Closed his eyes.

He knew what she saw. He'd snagged glances in the mirror a few times before he could look past. The initial alts had all been internal, courtesy of the queen's injection while Austin was burning. Those nanos had rebuilt him from the inside out, utterly transforming how his body operated, connecting it to his already amalgamated brain/ neural network. The nanocytes had repaired the extensive damage to his tissues, but at significant cost. Not pain, but excruciating, constant awareness. He had known every second that his body was afire in pain, or should have been, and only his deliberate control, sustained consciousness, had kept the transformative fury at bay. During the worst of his recovery, he had not slept for seven months.

The body she saw bore no trace of the process, no scars showing the torment he had endured. It was a lie, that body. And he hated it.

Not because it was ugly, but because of what it represented. He had changed, become something completely other. Underneath the unmarred skin, it would be difficult to find a single system that hadn't been altered in the scourge of nanocytes.

He wasn't really human anymore. He was…what? Post-human? Robot? Cyborg. Monster.

He squeezed his eyes shut against her inspection.

"Hmm. See, you got these marks on your knuckles from when you had the sense-tips put in? I sort of expected scars in other places, too." Her voice was low, husky, rubbing over his skin like thousand-count bedsheets. "But I don't see any scars here." She brushed a thumb over his nipple. "Or here." The other one. "That mean nobody's fucked with these parts?"

All those sensations went live, all the connections fired. As if the nanocytes had run a triangle of wires down the center of his body, clamped two ends on his nipples and the third to his prick, and then flooded him with current. His cock stiffened, pushed against his trousers. "In recent memory? Ah, just you."

She moved close and let out a slow breath. It eddied over his sternum. He kept his eyes shut tight, but he knew she was looking down again. Point of the triangle. Nobody had fucked with *that* in a long time either.

Her breath, humid and warm, painted a trail down the slope of his abdomen, past his navel, and then she was undoing the buttons on his trousers. She fanned her fingers inside the open placket, parting fabric from skin and continuing round, over his hips, over his rear.

The tips of her middle fingers teased the cleft, dipping briefly before she moved downward, pulling the trousers down his legs. The cloth shushed around his ankles, and he willed himself to be still and endure her merciless attention.

Not that will served him much right now. He couldn't look at her. He couldn't move. Couldn't stop her. Couldn't mitigate the shame or desire or desperation. Couldn't be what she deserved, but neither could he back away.

"You're gonna have to walk me through the tricky parts." She wrapped one hand around his leg, teasing her thumb behind his knee. His prick swelled at her touch. Getting hard all on its own. Because he wanted her, not because he willed it. "For instance, you got any exposed electrical ports? Spots I oughtn't get wet?"

He looked down at her. Agony. Blissful, sharp, buttered agony. "Only in my head and hands, and even there, nanocoated seams make the electronics waterp— fuck." Her unspoken question hit him in the gut. "Yes, Mari, you may put your mouth all over me."

"Goody."

She sat back on her feet, rocked, and shifted. Sighed.

Looked uncomfortable… No wait, not uncomfortable. Euphoric. It took Heron a moment to realize what she was doing, but once he did, he couldn't look away. She was nuzzling her slit against the curve of one heel. And by the look on her face, it was getting her hot.

Um, not just her.

She hadn't been lying when she offered to take charge, to do it all. She intended to bring both of them to orgasm. And he was going to let her.

Oh yes, he was.

Something in his psyche lit up at that thought. Expanded. Freed him. Complicated feeling—he would need to parse it later. But not now. This wasn't a moment for thought. It was a moment simply to be.

He didn't move, but he did release the tension in his hands. Or they did it themselves. He hardly breathed as Mari aimed her first kiss at his thigh, on the outside, along the curve of muscle. It bunched beneath her mouth.

"Back to my walkthrough," she murmured against the point of his hip. "Describe the internals. You got a circuit? Transistors." Hot breath on the bone. "Inductors." Nipping in on that crease leading inward. "Capacitors." Her mouth found the center line beneath his navel and kissed its way down. She nudged his cock aside with her chin, circling the base with her breath. When her tongue unfurled beneath his testicles, he groaned.

He could have used some resistors right then. He might have even said so out loud.

"No resistance," she growled. "Not this time, partner."

She kissed her way up the length of him, her mouth sparking like lightning every place it touched. Pain or pleasure? He couldn't discern one from the other, but holy hell, it felt good.

When she got to the tip, she glanced up, shaking her hair back over one shoulder. She winked. "No scars here, neither. You reckon I ought to test sensation throughout?"

Brown, callused fingers spidered over his hips, holding him steady as she bent and lowered her mouth over him, swallowing him deep.

Holy fuck. His mouth opened, and before he could restrain himself, he uttered something completely incomprehensible. Maybe "Gah."

Not his proudest moment. Not that he gave a flying shit.

She drew him out. And plunged over him again. The rough of her tongue rippled beneath; white-hot teeth caged each stroke. She didn't suck so much as she applied pressure, varying the loose space of her throat and the taut ring of her lips, pulsing as she tasted him. Gorged on him.

She moved away slightly, but her hot breath painted his tip when she said, "Tell me. Tell me it's good."

Good? Enveloping, excruciating, impossible, perfect. "Not the word I'd use."

She laughed, a low, sultry sound. A shish of skin against his thigh: her cheek as she smiled? "You got a better one?"

Mari.

But he couldn't talk. His mouth wasn't obeying, and neither was the rest of him. All he could do was feel. Input, input, input, *yes*.

Of their own accord, his hands grazed her hair,

fingers flexed like they would wind themselves in it, tangle and pull, but they retreated in the end and returned to his sides.

She, on the other hand, had no trouble chatting. Damn her. She sat back on that heel, grinding the curve and ringing his cock with lazy fists, one after the other, mimicking endless penetration. "You remember Miami? Cracked rib, busted kneecap, and so many bruises, I looked like an eggplant? But when I saw you riding in with your med wagon, all those hurts felt better. Instantly." Her chin tipped back, and she looked up at him. "Heron, you don't need to worry 'bout hurting me. You've only ever done the opposite. And I'm tougher than I look."

A surge of something warm and wet and precious forked through his chest. She was. Tough. She didn't even know how much. "Well, that's fortunate. You, on the other hand, are an expert at torment."

Mari let out a groan that cracked on the end, and she squeezed his cock. Hard. He sucked in a ragged breath.

As if she couldn't endure it any longer, she braced her cheek against his thigh, still with her face tipped up, and moved one hand down, shoved it beneath the orange silk. She knuckled something there. Probably her clit. Her…aaah.

It all hit him, right at that moment. Sex with Mari. Not just a fantasy, but right here, happening.

And damn it, if he was going to watch her come, he was going to be her partner in it. Not a bystander. No matter that his systems weren't responding, no matter that he couldn't give her the sort of sensory buffet she deserved, no matter that they still needed to talk about so many things and sort out so many others. He couldn't just watch.

He bent and stroked her hair, swallowed a groan when his cock slipped free of her grasp. He pointed a look at her lap. "I can help with that."

She mewled on the edge of orgasm but let him raise her to her feet. She wobbled. The hand that grasped his was damp and slick, and before he even knew what he was about, he drew it to his mouth. Held her gaze with his. Licked the backs of her knuckles. Tart, sweet, thick, glazing his tongue like fortified wine. Invading his nostrils and his soul.

Her dark eyes were huge, and her mouth rounded to an *O*.

Off toward the edge of the wood-slat hilltop canopy was a bank of holographic wildflowers, and even as he led her to it, the free-fae darkled their projection and revealed a regular room, a regular futon: soft, wide, silver-patterned with scrolling black kanjis.

Heron sat on its edge and drew Mari nearer until she stood right in front him. He rolled up the hem of her dress, exposing in turn sharp knees, cinnamon-skinned thighs, and…oh. She went commando. Chloe hadn't supplied underthings, indeed. More likely, Mari hadn't asked for them. Hadn't seen a need.

Also, she wasn't depilated like most women. That was something of a surprise, but a good one. His senses feasted, and his mouth flooded. Moist, humid, spice-and-caramel Mari. He wanted to bury his face there, to inhale and consume.

He held her dress up with one hand and stroked down with the other. Sense-tips were still measuring her temperature and pulse, but he wasn't running that data anymore. He was soaking it in, responding on the fly and without any precision planning. Fingers delved, explored. Discovered the distended spike of her clit, and he pressed his middle finger down. Hard. Too hard?

"Ohmygod." Keened all as one word, forced out from a tension-taut jaw. She grabbed his shoulders with both hands and dug her nails in, as if she thought her legs would wilt.

He didn't even signal the sense-tip to hum. It just did. Extensible motor adaptations with full neural integration: fuck yeah.

"Holy shit, Heron, if you don't want me to come all over your hand, you'd better back off right now."

"But I do."

"Back. Off."

He ground his molars but did as she instructed. She was clearly getting off on being in charge, and he didn't mind it.

Trust. He was trusting her. Had been doing that a lot today, and it hadn't hurt yet.

Mari snagged his gaze with hers and didn't let go. Fierce. Woman. His. She came up close, swung one leg over his lap, and balanced with her knees on either side of his thighs, her body poised right above his cock. And then she lowered herself. Slow. Patient. Holding his gaze the whole way down.

When she'd connected their bodies as completely as two people could, she stilled, face-to-face. And kissed him. Chaste, soft, on the mouth. "Fuck, you're gorgeous," she murmured against his chin. When he didn't say anything in reply, she raised her brows. "And obedient."

Her muscles fluttered over him, stroking his cock deep. Now, that was deliberate. He could hear the minx in her voice, could feel it in her body. Goading, but sweet. How could anyone be so very both?

"Not really." He was straining. Holding back, but only just. She really oughtn't tempt him like this. "If you're going to come, you'd better be quick."

"Oh yes, really. And gimme just a sec." She moved, rocking her hips, not rising so far that his cock slipped free. More grind than thrust. The silk of her dress stroked his chest, pooled between them, slippy and cool. And inside…God. He felt every contour of her body, roughs and cenotes and sweet, sweet grottoes. No way he was first to survey this territory, but it still felt special, like she didn't give this tour to just anybody.

Unworthy. Unworthy of this woman. But still here, enduring her. Logic and causality fractured. Wasn't about who deserved what anymore.

Her head tipped back, and her lips parted. The ends of her dark hair kissed his wrists against her spine. Part of him wanted to take over and do it for her. With a complete complement of his faculties, he could have stroked her to orgasm within moments. His fingers would be on her clit, pulsing pressure at perfectly timed intervals, emitting strategic bursts of vibration. His brain would be interfacing with the chamber, altering the chemical mix of the air and the tactile density of the ambient nanos, intensifying her experience from every angle.

But she didn't need that. Apparently, she already had everything she needed. Her mouth opened, her face strained in rictus. Grunt of breath, wordless.

She held on, first to his arms, then to his shoulders,

dug her fingernails into that deceptively smooth skin, and released the tether that bound her voice to her chest. Mari howled.

He felt her climax, her release, and he held steady through it, let her ride it and come down the other side. When her onslaught eased, she sagged against him, leaning her forehead to his, petting the welts on his shoulders and upper arms. She closed her eyes, melting, coating him in her peace.

Mari, sated. Because of him.

God.

Too much. Too much input. Too much feeling. He didn't have a response plan for this, at least nothing he was capable of implementing right now. He still wanted her. He wanted this, over and over and… Capacitors surged, and he knew his muscles would respond momentarily. Couldn't do anything about it. "I need to… Mari, fuck it, be still."

"Yeah." She obeyed. Willful, wild Mari obeyed. He guessed she didn't do it often, and he felt honored. The part of him that grasped for control, that needed to order the universe according to his own damned design, woke with a roar.

His hands clamped her hips. He had no idea how hard, just hoped it wasn't too hard. Hoped he didn't break her.

Relays fired, metal engaged. Ropes of augmented tissue stood out in relief on his thighs.

He grounded his heels against the bamboo floor and pushed up at the same time as his hands brought her down, impaling her, burying his cock balls-deep in her body. Wet heat enveloped him, all of him. More than just his cock. So overwhelmed, for a moment, he had a sensation of drowning. Breathless. Subsumed in her heat, her passion, and her grasping cunt.

And then he did it again. Pelvis to pelvis, bones and structure crashing against each other with so much force, she held on tight to avoid whiplash. She pressed her forehead to his, and he could feel the reverberation of each thrust through her skull, echoing in his.

He'd meant to make this good. Had meant to woo and win. Had meant to care and protect, always.

Failing, he was failing. He was hurting her. Her joints gave, her thighs no longer supported her weight. She was one breath from rag-dolling, and he couldn't.

Stop. Couldn't stop. Couldn't. Breathe. Couldn't.

Warning. Breach. Overload.

Surge.

No, no, no.

And then through the furor, her voice reached, found him. "God, Heron, you got no idea how much I wanted this. You. In me. Fucking me. The hell yeah, baby. Come for me."

Through it all, she was still there, his partner, his Mari. Whole and intact and riding him thrust for thrust.

It's okay, she was telling him. *You're okay*.

And he was.

Inhuman, out of control, miserable in failure, ecstatic in sensation, and…*okay*.

He had mapped out much of the material plane, knew how matter interacted, but this connection wasn't on any diagram he knew. And yet it was incontrovertibly the strongest force in his universe, the tether that bound him to her in that moment.

He wanted it to never end.

His body strained, pushing into her, through her, melding, conforming, inhabiting. Releasing.

"Querida."

He paused, infinite and falling, until his muscles screamed from the strain, and she just held him. Forever.

Movement, when it came, was slow, soft, slipping where friction had been before, like kisses inside his skin.

Peace.

She slipped her arms beneath his, wrapping them around his body, ducking her face against his throat. His arms came round her, too. He didn't tell them to. They just did.

His mouth moved against her hair. "*Vida, estamos en paz.*"

● ● ●

They so were. "Life, we are at peace." It was an old poem, and she didn't recall the poet. She knew the sentiment, though. She felt that peace as well, sifting through the jumble of her soul, white-ashing the fires there. She'd known a sort of peace the last time she'd climbed to this hilltop. Only now, with Heron beneath her and around her and inside her, her whole concept of peace was being resettled.

Peace wasn't about a lack of conflict or guilt. It was about finding a pause, a touchstone moment where all those plans and ghosts and struggles could just…sit a spell.

The wild ride of her life wasn't over, but it was changed indelibly. He'd changed it. And she'd let him.

Heron moved back along the futon, bringing her with

him, settling the duvet over their still-tangled bodies. Mari had a thought about taking off her dress, about keeping it clean for the next day 'cause it was so pretty, but she didn't have the energy to move that much. No way she could force her muscles to do the wiggle and scooch that such a disrobing would entail. Instead, she laid her still-clothed body over his naked one, set her face against his scarred chest, and let his peace wash all over her.

CHAPTER 10

SHE WOKE UP 'CAUSE SOMETHING SMELLED GOOD. With the sorts of images she'd been boiling in her mind, and after the stuff she and Heron had done last night, that something could have been all kinds of organic goodness. Turned out to be bacon.

Mari rolled over and let the duvet slide off her hip. She stretched like a satisfied kitty.

"Hungry?" Heron's voice made her belly tighten, but not necessarily with hunger.

"Ummhmm." Mari opened her eyes but couldn't force herself to move yet. The free-fae must have fulfilled their contract and scuttled off, because today, it was just a room. Last night, it had been magic.

The low, on-the-floor bedding fit in fine with the sparse furnishings, taupe and black with slashes of gold. High-impact glass several feet thick stretched along one wall, a gigantic porthole. It might have been morning, but all Mari saw were stars and infinite black. She wondered which end of the Chiba Station she was looking out of. Not that she had any compass on the vast universe.

Heron was sitting crisscross-applesauce on the far side of a Japanese table, eyeing her over a buffet of breakfast feastery. He hadn't gotten dressed yet, and Mari mentally added him to her list of things she wanted to put in her mouth. She crawled to the end of the bed, stretched out on her belly, and palmed a peach from the bowl.

"They got hydroponics on Chiba or what?"

"Unlikely, but an undocumented transport unloaded about fifteen pallets on the cargo level of the lift when we came up. The food is fresh."

"Undocumented transport such as your plane?"

He smiled and picked up a muffin. "It was our payment for the dock."

Steep price. Nanos weren't the only regulated materials, and in the postpesticide era, farm-fresh goodies were worse than rare. Mari couldn't remember the last time she'd bitten into a piece of real fruit.

This one tasted fine, sparking delicious all over her taste buds. Her stomach burbled, and she realized that with all the shit that'd gone down yesterday, she'd forgotten to eat. Well, looked like there was plenty of food here to make up for it. She polished off the peach, biting deep into the stringy part near the core and sucking the drips of juice off her bottom lip.

Heron watched her intently the whole time, and that had a peculiar effect on her body as well. She wanted him. Again. Right now. Right there on the table. She wanted to lick peach juice off the plane below his navel and smear fresh-churned almond butter all over his nipples. Oh, she had plans, she did.

Trouble was, Heron hadn't made a move toward her,

despite him being naked and all. Couldn't see his lower half below the table edge, but she suspected that he was too evolved for something as sloppy as morning wood. Even with all that lack of control he'd been talking about last night, there was no way he was randy as she was.

'Cause if he was, they wouldn't be jawing over breakfast. They'd be at it like rabbits, and the bacon could come later.

Of course, he could also just have hygiene standards. Scruffy as she felt this morning, she shouldn't even be thinking seduction. Fuzzy teeth, hair a wild mess. Oh yeah, she was sure a prize first thing in the morning. It was a wonder he didn't hightail it back down that tether.

Mari slid her gaze off his and studied the spread, giving her brain a stern "down, boy." A corner of paper peeked out from below some wax-wrapped cheese.

Wait, paper? No way. She hadn't seen real, pulp-made paper in years. This was the near-priceless sort, too: heavy, thick, creamy. She reached, pinched its corner, and read the name on the outside.

"Who's A. R. N. Farad?" Impossible to say such a pretentious name in a normal voice. She did stop short of laughing outright at it, though.

Heron sat up straight. He raised one hand like he was about to snatch that note away, but then he drew back. "Um, that's me. Atreus Raymond Neruda Farad."

Mari snorted, but kindly. "That's…well, hell, honey, it's awful. Whoever sparked up calling you Heron instead gets a cookie."

"You can thank Adele when you see her next."

Mari caught his uncertain grin and tossed it back with extra warmth. And when that didn't quite send the message she wanted, she scooted around the end of the table and dropped a kiss on his shoulder. "Plus, Heron sure slides on the tongue easier."

Given his typical reserve, it wasn't like she expected him to come back with a searing remark about tongues sliding, but she thought he might make some comment on the kiss. He didn't budge. Mari put a good foot and a half between them, but man, it was hard.

He calmly smeared jam on a biscuit, clearing the crispy gold edges by a precise half centimeter all around and letting her innuendo float on by. "Heron of Alexandria designed automatons, tiny lifelike machines. I built my first combinational logic circuit when I was six. My mothers were far too impressed."

"Ain't saying you aren't impressive." By habit, her tone was light and flirty, but her attention had snagged on the paper. On that trying-too-hard name. Cogs in her brain clicked just as sure as if she had machine parts of her own.

She had seen this name before. She'd seen it *written* before. On paper, cheaper stuff, but still paper. Thumb-tacked to a cork wall in an office in the middle of summer. Heat had pooled in the cleavage of her sundress and poured through the wide-open windows. Dad liked the windows open, even in the furnace of a Texas June.

Funny, she could see herself standing there in Dad's office, looking at the corkboard, and she knew what that girl must be feeling, right down to the stifling lack of breeze, but that was just it: she was looking at the girl. Not *being* the girl. That girl, the one in the office, the one who looked sort of like Mari, was a way softer somebody, the sort of fragile gal Heron would want to snatch up and protect against the chaos of the world.

It wasn't Mari, though. Not the person she knew herself to be. And for some reason, that made her want to cry ugly.

Instead, she focused hard on the paper. "So who's sending love letters to A. R. N. Farad?"

"It's not a love letter." He paused so long, Mari had to peek at him. Caught him nibbling the unjammed edge of the biscuit. "It's from the queen. She has kind of a crazy affection for paper. At any rate, she got a halo up early this morning to scrub all transmissions outbound from the station, so I don't have to work so hard to cut them off. It's an incredibly kind gesture. While we're here on Chiba, I can concentrate on...other things."

She looked up, and Heron was smiling that slight, almost shadow smile. The one she caught on his face when he thought she wasn't looking.

He raised his eyebrows minutely. "The letter goes on to list amenities of the suite. Fully equipped med lab, organics removal unit—which isn't as alarming an alternative to showering as you'd think..."

"Oh! Don't let me forget to tell you about plans I got for you and naked and a shower."

His voice rubbed a low note when he said, "Noted."

Noted. Post-it note. Sticky. Klaxons went off in her brain.

In her voyeur-like mind's eye, the girl in the university office bent and picked up a Post-it scrawled over in ballpoint blue: 2:30 data review w/A. R. N. Farad. The sticky gunk on the back had worn off, but the message looked important. Wouldn't want Dad to miss a meeting. She tacked it back on the board.

It wasn't a memory, not in the same way that she remembered eating protein pretzels for dinner the night before last or how Heron's hands felt against her naked ass when he held her in the Pentarc yesterday. This memory was different. It was sorted along lines of relevancy: office to summer heat to corkboard to Post-it to…him. A. R. N. Farad. Heron. As if a whole shitload of relevant information was just dumped into her brain pan, she knew instantly all about him.

She swallowed and smoothed the envelope. "A. R. N. Farad was a visiting fellow, not sure from where, but he had an accent. Dad bitched about him a lot, thought he'd lure funding away from biorobotics. I…met him at a Juneteenth faculty party the summer after my freshman year in Austin. Serious science boy, no boozing, no chance he'd follow me out on the porch for a smoke after dark." She rubbed the side of her thumb over the ink. It didn't smudge. "My memory is crap most times, but I do remember you."

His voice was soft as kitten fur when he said, "And I have never forgotten you."

She didn't dare look straight on at a man who said something like that, all loaded with portent. "So all these years, you kept track of me?"

"More or less, yes."

"Sweet, but what a lot of work." She waited, wondering if he'd name it something else.

He paused. "Sorting data is a hobby, so dedicating a channel to you wasn't difficult. I found comfort knowing that you were safe and out of Texas. Then, of course, you torched that shipping container of mech-clones in Belize, and suddenly, you were on the TPA's radar.

They'd been buying batches of mechs, trying to literally build an army of infiltrators." In her periphery, he flashed a tight smile. "You delayed that plan somewhat."

"Fucking up other people's fantasies—yep, that's me." But inside, she was bubbling. So he *had* been her guardian angel in the background all those years. Speaking of fantasies. "I sure hope those Texas fuckers told Dad when you and I teamed up. Bet that made him madder than a sack of cats."

Heron studied the table laden with food, intense study, like he was looking anywhere but at her. "I didn't sign on to contracts with you because I wanted to irritate Damon Vallejo."

"Why then?" *Tell me I'm important to you.* He'd dropped plenty of clues, but Mari'd been fooled by folks before, fooled into thinking they cared more for her than they did. She needed a declaration in plain speaking. Well, didn't need it. Not really. Just wanted it real, real hard.

Heron set his biscuit back on the tray. He stared at it for a moment, like he was thinking about what he wanted to say next. Pause like that couldn't be good. Mari sat on her folded legs, bracing for another secret, another reveal, another seismic shift in her universe. She wasn't sure she could stand one that parted her inexorably from this man.

"I wanted to work with you for a couple of reasons. The first was that I had achieved a level of autonomic suppression that would allow me to be near you without obvious and uncomfortable reactions."

"I make you uncomfortable?"

"In the best possible way." He lifted his gaze, raised

his eyebrows fractionally, and steamed a look right at her. Nice look. Nasty look.

Oh. Okay, then. "And the other reason?"

Liquid dark eyes sparked, gentled. Or maybe it was the face around them. She'd never thought of his eyes as particularly expressive before.

"Just keeping track of you wasn't enough anymore. I wanted to be near you, talk with you. Touch you. Even if I knew you were repelled by post-humans." His gaze slid off her again, like she was made of butter.

"What?" she said before she could help herself.

"Things," he said softly. "We were speaking of things. I am a thing. A pleasure thing, if you wish to use me as such, but not much of a man anymore."

Mari could barely move. What the hell was he talking about? She opened her mouth but couldn't find words other than a repeated "What," now with additional "*the fuck?*" tacked on at the end.

"You never made a secret that you hated all mech-clones and especially your father's creation, the queen."

Her previous elation whooshed out, and Mari deflated. Her ass dug into her heels until they both ached. "But you aren't a mech-clone. You're a… I don't even know, and I don't give two shits. Look, I hated Peetey because she took up all of my father's attention. Because he spent holidays with her, not me. Because he loved her, not me. I hated her because I *envied* her, Heron. Not because of what she was made of. And it doesn't even matter, because I've never thought of you as being like her. You're so not like her. You're…" She bit the inside of her cheek. Hard. Let the skin drag through her teeth when she exhaled. "Sane. Smart. Safe. Also badass. I mean, hell, you even intimidated Damon Vallejo. Not to mention all this time you've been planning my jobs, making what I do so much smoother. Making it…effortless. More fun than work. And all that time, I was balls-out flirting and thinking you just didn't want me."

"I always want you."

Something wet blurred her vision, and she blinked it away fast. Couldn't think of words, though. How did a girl even respond to something like that?

Well, if the girl was Mari, with sex, apparently. She leaned forward, bent her face against his chest. Smooth skin warmed her lips, her eyelids. "Heron?"

"Yes." His hand, one hand, stroked her arm, skated up to her shoulder. Crazy what kind of want that single hand could evoke. Or maybe she was just too tuned into him.

She tried to focus, but man, it was hard. "You said the queen's halo would fix those transmissions so you could concentrate on other things, right?"

"That is almost verbatim what I said, yes."

Mari fanned her breath out over his sternum, wondering if it would stretch to his nipple. "So you gonna tell me about them other things or what?"

He flinched, a warm earthquake on her forehead. "Just tell you?"

She pressed a smile against his skin. Oh, that felt good. He was messing with her now. All the churning violence of reconnecting with those memories sloughed off, replaced by a hum right above her clavicle, exactly where his hand rested. "Or, you know, if you're all set on being my plaything, you could offer a product demonstration."

"All right," he said.

He was giving in that easy? A thrill spiked through her whole body so hard, she had to bite her lip to contain the quiver. Bet he felt it, though.

For a few seconds, it didn't seem like he was gonna follow up. He didn't move much, just sat there all frustratingly calm. Then, in his calmest calm voice, "Sit up, Mari. Take off the dress."

Just like that, huh? Well, okay. She did like he asked, one butterfly-clasped shoulder at a time. The sleeves shushed down her arms, dragging the bodice in their wake. She needed to tell Chloe it was exactly like whispers, the way this dress slid off. Hot, desperate whispers. And all the while, she grumped. "I don't see how my getting nekkid's gonna show how much control you got back—" She made the mistake of looking up.

Caught him looking back.

Holy batfuck, his face. His eyes were black fire, alight and licking her top to toes. Mari's innards sizzled like she was made of bacon.

"On the contrary," he said. "I would say I'm exercising something approaching superhuman control, observing you nude and yet not fucking you into the floor."

Odd. The phrase "So do it, cowboy" surged right up into her mouth, but it died a silent death there, choked by the possibility that he might actually do it. If she goaded him, he might push her back against the bamboo and drill right in. This wasn't comforting-her Heron, the gentle guardian angel who made a living out of pillowing her wild-hare crazy. This was something she'd never seen before, unnaturally still and excruciatingly focused, exactly the sort of creature who would cause a whole crew to snap to attention when he came on board. Somebody a queen might fear.

Want hooked her core-deep, but she just knelt there and let him burn her through with that look.

He leaned forward slightly. "Do you realize that I receive input through the sense-tips on my fingers, much like the gloves you use when you're shooting?" He reached one hand to her shoulder but didn't quite touch. So close. Why wouldn't he touch her? "The chief difference is that mine are I/O."

"What's that mean?" Her voice was barely a whisper, backed by the thundering whump of her heartbeat.

He did touch her then. One fingertip only, on the far edge of her bare shoulder. The most innocent of caresses, yet a sudden surge of something invisible and hot and honey and ghost peppers poured over her arm. No, not over. Inside. All through her body, soothing in toward her breasts, her throat, pooling in the tips of her fingers. She had been leaning forward, but now her legs were apparently made of water. Couldn't hold her up anymore. She tried to melt into the floor, but he wouldn't let her. His patient stroke on her arm demanded that she stay up. She leaned her face against his chest again, pressed her eyelids closed, and mewled like a kitten. "Fucking *god*."

"No, you're fucking a post-human. Keep up, querida." He drew that slow touch over her upper arm, and suddenly, she wasn't just mewling anymore.

She was shaking. God, shaking. She had to stop doing that. Her whole identity was based on being steady, on being certain. Cool under pressure, reliable on the squeeze. But she freaked out completely when this man touched her, and she couldn't do a damn thing to stop it. She ran hot, then cold, then scorching, short-cycling and near to dissolving into a pile of wibble, and he wasn't touching anything naughtier than her *shoulder*. "What are you doing to me?"

"I've initiated a biofeedback loop and am probing various of your systems in a stochastic approach to inducing sexual pleasure."

She groaned. "I shoulda never told you how the big words turn me on."

He cricked a finger—just one—and a million tiny fire feathers dusted her arm. "Right now, I'm stimulating the muscles that elevate your hair follicles. The effect is called piloerection."

She hadn't been lying about the big words. They really did. "Oh. Okay. That just sounds dirty."

"Certainly better than what you call it."

"Whaassat?"

"Goose bumps." The hard muscles in his chest tightened beneath her mouth as he shifted, rising over her. His hands dropped to her thighs, and instantly, the tingly hot thing he'd been percolating her with dissipated.

Boo. She missed it and wanted it back. Right now.

"Lie down." When she moved to obey, he corrected, "On your stomach."

She scrambled around, her feet and knees slipping on the polished bamboo. Was she sweating? Maybe. Maybe. She felt like she was running a thousand degrees, especially the patches on her body where his gaze rested. So basically all over. Air circulators created eddies she could feel, but they weren't doing a dadblamed thing to cool her superheated skin.

She lowered herself to the floor, pressing her cheek against the smooth wood, pointing her toes so the tops of her feet met the floor.

"A human person can be altered in any number of ways," he was saying, though Mari only heard every fifth word or so. Her heart was thundering so hard she could feel her chest thump against the bamboo. "I should apologize. My alterations weren't explicitly intended for sexual performance."

"Could've fooled me."

He was touching her again, dusting her hair to the side, stroking the line of her jaw until it curved into her neck. Outlining her shoulder blades. Everywhere he touched, those flame feathers dappled her skin with want. "Doubtless a pleasure model would have had you on your back, but I'll be honest, even with the queen's halo liberating my processors, I could not have drawn this out long with your breasts beneath my hands."

Good to know. "Something we have in common," she confessed. "Touch. It drives me crazy, not just having somebody else touch me, but putting my hands all over you. Last night…" The satin-like texture of his hot skin beneath her tongue. Salt weight of his balls in her mouth. "Well, holding back wasn't as easy as it looked."

His thumbs met at her spine and followed the line of it down. Heat extruded on both sides, wrapping her, soothing her. She closed her eyes and sighed.

Wait. Sighed? Yup. She'd never had it like this before, this stillness and quiet, building inexorably and patiently, when the whole time, her body was screaming for the fuck. But her voice wasn't. She was content to let him take his time, do his thing, 'cause every brush, every precise tactile caress linked to the next, painting her in patterns of desire. She felt like a masterpiece in process.

His hands curved over her ass, and her breath caught in her throat. She couldn't keep herself from pressing against the floor, pushing herself back and into his palms. Her hips moved slightly, and he kneaded, separating the twin globes, exposing her even more. She whimpered.

"Shh." He waited for her trembles to stop. His thumbs, still together, still painting a thick seam of lightning down her center, pushed in between her thighs. She spread her legs wide, hoping, hoping…oh yes. He did. Right there. "I can also," he said, moving his body in between her widespread legs, "interface with convection patterns and raise temperature to specific areas, stimulating blood flow to erectile tissues." His long hands held her thighs wide while those conjoined thumbs slid along the slick ribbon of want, pushed up, past one entry point, then the next, bypassing the sockets most men imagined contained her infinite pleasure. Heron knew her truth.

He paused over the exposed bulb of her clitoris, his thumbs jammed in between her most sensitive flesh and the hard, slick floor. She held her breath. The tips on his thumbs sparked.

Exploded.

She exploded.

Into a gazillion fire-tipped pieces of wow.

She couldn't help herself: she bucked, slammed her pelvis down, grinding herself against the lightning storm of his hands and hollering like a drunk at a football game.

Didn't give a single fuck if the whole space station heard her. Let 'em. She was wholly, completely beyond control, as if something giant and electrical and cosmic had been plugged into her spine and all she could do was lie there and take the onslaught of sensation.

She slammed her eyelids shut, but the universe was still too bright. Sweet and perfect and agony and… "Please."

Was that her voice?

In an instant, the hurricane-force waves of pleasure slaked. Mari tried to find him in her periphery, and he leant down, kindly moving into her field of vision. Heron's face, smiling. Which was about the gorgeousest thing in ever. His dark hair had fallen over one eye. Mussed. Loved. Hers.

"Don't make me endure all this alone. Please."

He opened his mouth, closed it again, obviously confused. "I wanted to bring you pleasure," he said.

It dawned on her that this was, in fact, his tech demo; he was putting all his control on display for her benefit. And though she totally felt benefitted, she wanted nothing so much in that moment than to have him just lose it, let fly with the control, and pound out raw monkey sex on this here floor.

"Oh, you have. Are you not feeling how much? 'Cause, holy gophernuts, I am goo right now, and all you've done is give me a fucking massage."

Alarm skittered across his face. "You consider this a massage? Cabana boy masseuses in Cabo finger you to orgasm? Is that part of the hospitality?"

His unapologetic jealousy was lights-out sexy. "You should know. Don't you have hidden cameras on me all the time or somethin'?"

"No," he said way too soberly. "You are entitled to privacy."

"Well, that sucks," she said. Her breath wasn't

completely even yet. She was panting a little. And his hands were still *there*, knotted at a pressure point way too delicious to pass up. She dragged her clit across his knuckles and groaned deep. "When I pay for a massage, I get a massage. When I pay for a fuck, I get a fuck. Right here, I think we agreed on a tech demo. You still got stuff in that tricked-out body to show me or what?"

"As you wish, querida."

Unerringly, as if he knew exactly what she needed, Heron spread his hands beneath her, fanning them over her pelvis and raising her. Cool air nipped against her belly, but she scooted her knees up, arched her back. He wanted her ass-up, did he? Oh goody.

She bit hard, pinching blood from her lower lip.

"Yes," she breathed against the polished bamboo.

Sense-tips in his fingers could very well be the end of her, but she suspected his useful alterations didn't end there. In fact, she had a sneaking certainty he was wired all over, right down to the end of that gorgeous cock, because when he moved in behind her, pushed into her—slow, gentle, *controlled*—she lit up every single place they touched. And they touched freaking *everywhere*. Inside out, she was made of light. Heat. Torment.

And so was he.

They fused, coalesced, and she didn't fight it, didn't rush it. God no. This didn't seem a place or time to rush. It seemed like a moment made for always. Permanent. Static. The kind of together that *meant* something.

She slid to the floor, and he came down with her, synchronized to her movement. With each orgasm, her body unfastened, and tiny cyclones of awesome drilled into the fissures, securing her hardpoints.

She wallowed in bone-echoing, never-ending agony, and it was fantastic.

Also a touch exhausting. How long did he plan to keep this going? If she counted the little peaks, she'd come…what? Four times? Five? Girl could wear herself out. Not that she wasn't loving it, but damn. She didn't want to hog the bliss.

Come for me, Heron. Her eyes were closed, relaxed, when she thought it. She didn't move her mouth but to breathe. And she hadn't put the com back on this morning, so there was no way he could hear her thoughts. Not even if the queen somehow gave him a ginormous power boost. No way. None. But damn if he didn't just know. Another alteration, another superhuman ability? She'd take it.

With something like awe, she felt climax build in his body, tense, hold, and finally overtake him. His exhalation rolled over the back of her neck like sunrise on the beach. *That's it, baby.*

Followed by, *Oh my God, can he just do that at will? Whenever he wants and never when he doesn't? Jesus.* But her mind was too sizzled to break that realization down into meaning.

He settled onto his elbows, pressed a hot kiss below her left ear, and allowed the rest of his body to relax over her, inside her. It was hard to breathe with his weight all on her like that, but she didn't want him to move. Like, ever.

Finally, her voice sloshed out. "Okay, you sold me."

"Eh?"

"Yer tech demo rocked my socks."

He rose on his forearms and rolled to the side,

breaking their connection. Mari was all set to complain, but he pulled her with him, against him and both on their sides. Now face to face, Heron burned a look down at her. "So it's okay, fucking a robot?"

"Okay isn't the word I'd use." She snuggled closer to his warmth, tucking her face beneath his chin. "More like *spectacular*."

"Can you stand another confession?"

"Sure. Why not?" She was gonna need some time to process all the other ones anyhow. What damage could one more unraveled secret cause at this point?

He nuzzled into her hair and said, "Big words do it for me, too."

Oh *really*? Mari swore to herself she was gonna download a dictionary and read the whole damn thing.

"I wish I hadn't waited so long. I thought you'd hate being with somebody like me. Guess I seriously underestimated your tolerance. Your goodness. I'm sorry. Your socks are not the only ones that got rocked." He pressed a kiss against the top of her head. "But for right now, it's nearly ten. Kellen's just come up the lift and will be here presently, and unless you want to see a cowboy blush, we should probably get dressed. Also you need to eat. Did you see there's bacon?"

CHAPTER 11

MARI CONCENTRATED ON THE NANOPAPER TABLET and tried not to hear the sounds of Heron's brain being ripped apart. After she'd eaten and cleaned up—and passed her dress through an organics removal unit, which had to be one of the most bizarre things she'd ever laid eyes on—Kellen had allowed her to come sit in the med lab, on the condition that she stay quiet and out of his way.

He'd said it polite, of course, being Kellen, but Mari still felt it best to do as he told her. She'd crept in and logged in her com on an unsecure port, hoping nobody noticed her. She certainly didn't want to cause a distraction or make Kellen's surgeon hands slip.

Heron was sitting up on a low chair covered in antistatic paper. He had input surfaces beneath either hand and wires hooked into subdermal ports Mari hadn't even known existed, despite the study she'd been making of his body recently.

He'd told her he was looking to hunt down the signal source digitally while Kellen examined the physical damage. Chiba's halo of hired free-fae scrubbed most transmissions around the station proper, so whatever he was transmitting wasn't zatting back down to earth. He'd even gotten back most of his processing power—especially his, um, control, which she had experienced already this morning. Shit yeah, she had.

She snuck a glance across the room. Kellen was bent over the back of Heron's head, his arms blood-flecked and a glower the size of old Dallas on his brow.

Heron saw her looking over and smiled reassuringly, though his hands never dropped a glyph on those surfaces and he was careful not to move his head.

"Hey, querida. Looks like you survived the chem shower. Trust me, it's only disconcerting the first time. You found everything you needed in there?"

"Yeah, though I do miss your contraband shampoo. That stuff smells fine, like almonds and oranges. Makes me want to lick myself."

Kellen made a grunting noise. "Ma'am, you might want to hold off on saying those kinds of things until after I got my razor out of Dr. Farad's brain. His electricals just went all haywire."

"Did they really? Yay me. I'd wondered, of course, but you're usually so stoic, partner."

"Define 'stoic.'"

"Oh, you know: keeping all those come-hither thoughts locked up in your brain instead of sharing. Found this morning very informative, for instance."

This time, Kellen's grunt was a mite louder. "Ain't joking. Y'all can leave off those innuendos and sly looks. I got work here."

Heron frowned and pinched just one side of his mouth up in a grimace, the equivalent of an eye roll.

"You boys get to it, then," Mari said. "I'll just sit over here and watch."

She could tell by the twitch beside Heron's mouth that he was itching to say something in response to that, especially as he'd gotten a gander at her eyebrow waggle. She could almost even guess what it was. Took a good bit of self-discipline for Mari to obey Kellen this time, but she managed. She deliberately looked down at her nanopaper.

She'd set up search bots for A. R. N. Farad, for one thing, and she'd gotten pings all over the place. He hadn't just been a nearsighted postdoc fellow. When she'd first seen him, he'd already hung two PhDs on his wall, both in nanotech areas with words so long, Mari didn't even want to pronounce 'em.

An archive from the university site showed a cute picture: floppy-haired and wearing a tweed jacket. A kid trying too hard to look grown up. Article didn't give an age, but he looked young.

Something Kellen adjusted made a god-awful, grinding, wet metal sound. Heron didn't say anything, but Mari winced.

"Can't you give him something for the pain?" Mari didn't dare look over. Wasn't like blood in general worried her. Just Heron's blood.

"No, but you don't need to worry. There aren't actually any pain-sensing nerves inside the human brain, and I slapped a local on the scalp before I cut in. Besides, I need him awake. The captain here put most of this gadgetry into his own head, and now he needs to guide me through it if we've got any chance of shutting down this signal. He's got to be coherent for this part, even if I would dearly love to knock him out right about now."

Heron muttered something she didn't catch. Probably was trying to be funny or macho, or worse, both. But a hole in his skull sure wasn't tickling her funny bone.

She remembered the mess of wires and blood back at the Pentarc and, later, reaching behind his head when they were in the car and feeling the sticky. Some things would be easier if he were just a machine. Not that she minded his man parts, overall. "I thought the virus-transmission-thingy—whatever it was the mercs put in him—was data, not hardware."

"This fucker's both, if you'll pardon the language, ma'am."

"Nanotech," Heron clarified, in a voice that was tighter than before, a sure sign that he wasn't enduring this totally without discomfort, no matter what they'd told her. "The com those mercenaries wired had an injection tip, and when they plugged me in, I got a full dose of nanites. The mercenaries themselves probably had no idea what they were doing. Someone else likely rigged it beforehand, and all they had to do was place it. The transmitter is in several pieces, tiny pieces, and we aren't entirely sure where they are. Kellen's been trying to hunt them down and dig them out, but it's slow going."

"Can't the queen help? I mean, she's a robot, and I know those things got steady hands. Least she used to." Couldn't quite keep the bitterness out of her voice, but she'd watered it down some. Hell, she'd let the devil himself dig around in her innards if it would help her partner get over this freakin' transmission.

Heron smiled slightly at her suggestion, but it was Kellen who answered. "The queen's nanocytes hot-wired his neural once, during the Austin riots, and it's a wonder Heron ain't as cracked-crazy as *she* is, the job she did on him."

"She saved my life," Heron said mildly. "The sanity of which decision is, of course, debatable."

Kellen huffed out a breath, and Mari did look over this time. He wiped the back of his wrist across his forehead, leaving a smear of blood. "Still ain't joking, man."

"Probably ought to more." Heron was behaving downright silly this morning, for him. Considering the night he'd just had, Mari counted that as a personal success.

Muttering something about vascular hemostatic hoodiwhati, Kellen reached with the other hand for some chem-soaked gauze on the tray by his elbow. Hemo was blood, right? But Heron shouldn't be bleeding. Bleeding during brain surgery was bad. Maybe. Or not? Dangit, she wished she wasn't so clueless about these things. She swallowed bile and ducked her head back over the tablet.

More info, but nothing threatening. Bittersweet history, in fact, distracting her from the carnage on the other side of the room. A. R. N. Farad had done work all over, but quite a few of the pics had location tags from Austin. She recognized architecture, landmarks.

And, in one of the pics, Dad. Memory grabbed her throat and squeezed. She couldn't stop looking at the image. Dad and his robot, on top of the world. She tabbed through, found more pics of him, but wasn't surprised that she didn't appear in any of his photos.

"Caught one," Kellen crowed.

In her periphery, Kellen hoisted a syringe in one hand and a magnetic stabilizer tube in the other.

Aha. So that's what he used those things for. She'd always wondered how folks caught and reset nanos. Of course, after meeting Chloe and sleeping in the midst of all those free-fae last night, Mari would never think of nanotech the same way. She wondered what the difference was between the sort of nanos that Kellen was hunting down—and apparently finding—in Heron's head and the other ones, the rogue ones that formed consciousnesses and hired themselves out in groups. Or the ones who decided to pass themselves off as chesty blonds with chipper voices.

True, Mari didn't have a prayer of understanding the technical side of it all, but she felt like she had a good handle on the emotional stuff. She wanted the nanos to win, to get the individuation rights they were fighting for. And not just because Chloe was Heron's pet project. She liked Chloe a lot, all on her own merits. Plus, she had to face it, she was from Texas. Individuation and rights were big for her.

Heron mumbled something again, but Mari had removed her com for the shower and hadn't put it back on. Sucked some, not being able to interpret his mumbling, and she definitely still coveted a way of knowing his supersecret innermost thoughts without his having to speak them out loud. It was only fair, after all.

A ping on one of her searches snagged her attention, and she looked down at the tablet. Another pic, this time of Heron pre-Austin. He'd gone to school outside London. Well, that would explain the tweed, and also probably his more global attitude about things. Like appreciation of old-timey Russian eggs and Chinese silks. Poetry, too. She thought of his quote about peace, about being at peace with life at last.

On a whim, she searched the line and found the poem, a short one in Spanish. Twentieth century. It ended in love and peace, just like he'd said, but she read it through several times, just to make sure. Took her a couple of reads to pick up on what was really going on.

This poem wasn't about reconciliation with guilt. It was about dying. Dying happy despite an imperfect life.

A chill started in Mari's fingertips and crackled up to her chest, her brain. Made her light-headed.

He didn't think Kellen's exploration was going to work. *Why?*

On the other side of the room and from far away, she heard Kellen's voice.

"All right. Just closing this up." Some instruments clanged on the tray and then, "There now. Miss Mari, it does seem like I'll get my wish sooner rather than later. Gonna put him under. You can come on over here for this, if you want to."

Mari set her tablet aside and went. She crouched beside Heron's chair, waiting as he moved his input devices to the cart and rearranged his bouquet of wires, leaving his hands free. He had plugged directly into the module and looked a lot like the queen had in her harness: bristling with big fat cables, the better to transmit the vast info stores in his head, sift them, filter them, clean them. Save them.

But you don't think you can be saved, do you?

She wouldn't have said it aloud, wouldn't even have mouthed the words if she'd been wearing her com. But still, Heron looked down at her, let her cover both his hands with hers, staying clear of the wires that protruded, and he knew. She could tell, could see it all over his face.

"Our hunting expedition didn't work." Heron's voice was matter-of-fact, without a lick of the sinking despair that Mari felt.

"No," Kellen admitted. "Got two, but the others are just too quick. You'll have to fix this in the software."

"How?" she asked before she thought better of it.

"Dry, boring, technical—" Heron began.

She really hoped he knew her well enough to recognize the fury bleeding out of her eyes. "That's what the supergenius assholes say. But not you. *You* told me you were proud to be my partner, that you considered me your equal. So which is it?"

He paled but, to his credit, didn't look away. He endured the fire of her anger and offered no excuses. "No, you are right. Okay." He took a breath. "My plan is to transfer a small part of my neural, my mind, to the station's computer. I'll shut down my body and reboot it in isolation, disconnected from all other machines."

Well, he was right: she didn't really understand. But she wanted to kiss him for telling her anyhow. "I don't know about you, but deliberately creating an out-of-body experience sounds dangerous," she said.

"It is."

"Do I have any say?" she asked.

"It's my body," he reminded her. "And I'm very good at remotely controlling machines."

Kellen dried his hands, having washed them clean of Heron's blood. He hadn't gotten the smear off his forehead yet, and there was a streak on his wrist as well.

Possibly he didn't even know it was there, but it made Mari queasy.

"Just for kicks and giggles, I gotta ask," she said. "Can't you just block the transmission the old-fashioned way, by scrambling the signals or something, like when vid channels don't want you to see their goodies behind a paywall?"

Heron closed his eyes, leaned his head back against the antistatic paper. He didn't so much as twitch when Kellen pressed the injector tip against his neck. "That is a valid suggestion. Unfortunately, I've already tried it, back on the plane. These signals are too fast. The second I shut down one thread, another pops up somewhere else. Like a hydra. If the queen didn't have her whole nanite halo sifting the outgoing transmissions, I wouldn't have the processing capacity to handle it myself at this point."

"You could." Kellen came around to face his friend, tapping the second syringe. He and Heron stared at each other hard in that space above the chair.

Mari felt the intensity of all the things they weren't saying. If she'd had a match, she'd've been tempted to poke it out there and see if it didn't catch flame. The friction was that strong.

"No." Heron's single word was tight, harsh. In his lap, he laced his fingers with hers.

"What's he talking about, partner?" Mari asked.

He ignored her question. "Kellen, you must promise that if, for whatever reason, this doesn't work, you will reformat my system."

"I sure as hell will not. You got a death wish, you can go find somebody else to kill you," Kellen snapped.

"No, no killing. *Killing*, really?" Mari was surprised by how close to a keen her own voice had become. "Who here is talking about killing?" Her nerves were shredded just a little, apparently, but her logic was still working: nothing that he was transmitting could possibly be worth *dying* for. That was just horrible beyond all possible belief.

But, a voice in her head reminded her, he might have been trying to tell you, by quoting that poem.

She mentally told that voice to fuck off. He'd been good, *they* had been good, up in their room this morning. Better than good. He hadn't been a man anticipating death. He'd been talking about the future and shit.

Right? He had, hadn't he? God, she couldn't remember exactly.

She shook her head to clear it. "Kellen, you said a second ago that he could get the processing power to fix the transmission some other way. So, say this remote-rebooty thing doesn't work. What's our other option?"

"He could plug in to the cloud," said the doc. "Not just this limited space station system, but the whole global information cloud. His neural expands to fit the space, right, and with infinite space...well, there'd be near infinite power, too."

"That's it? I mean, pardon if it sounds stupid, but plugging in, if that would give you the resources you need to stop the transmission, sure seems like a mighty simple way of solving this mess. Simpler than all this other body-leaving business you're talking about." Mari and pretty much every other UNAN citizen plugged in every day, after all. As long as they scrubbed for bots and trash, there wasn't much danger in it. Most folk wouldn't be able to imagine a life off-cloud.

Heron still wasn't looking at her. "Remember when I plugged into the Pentarc before? It took me about half a second to take over the whole core, and if you hadn't been there to keep me focused on the job, tethered to reality…"

Mari's face must have betrayed her confusion, because Kellen broke in.

"What he's sayin' is that his neural is unusually dense. It's tucked in snug right now, but when he lets it loose on a network, it busts out, filling up all available space. But his *consciousness* doesn't get any bigger. It's like a critter caught in a storm surge, shoved out of its hovel into a wide world, too wide. The change in space, the speed—he's scared he'll get lost in all that."

"But you think he can handle it?"

Kellen nodded. "I think it's worth the risk, if the remote scrub doesn't work. Compared with completely reformatting, which, for a post-human with a brain as altered as Heron's, would probably mean death or at least catastrophic memory loss, I'd take my chances on the cloud."

"You didn't tell her everything," Heron murmured. She was still squeezing his hands tight, but he'd crooked one finger against her knuckles and started drawing figure eights again.

"What else?"

Kellen clamped his mouth shut.

"When I plugged into the Pentarc, remember how I told you I had *become* the Pentarc?" said Heron. "That was with the closed system. If I opened up the gates there and logged on to the cloud proper, I would have the same problem, theoretically. I would take it over."

Oh. And he didn't trust himself. He knew what he was capable of. He'd probably mirrored such a scenario. Like he had Superstorm Agatha. And just look how horribly that had gone off the rails. Now, no matter how confident he seemed, he was one glitch away from panic all the time, a man terrified of his own capability.

"Pervasive as the cloud is," he went on, "a chaotic neural taking it over could be exponentially more disastrous. Air traffic, stoplights, energy grids, money transfers, even minutiae like your personal calorie counter and music playlists: all of those things would be vulnerable. Granted, those data streams have individual people and bots providing input, not to mention security, but if I had near unlimited processing power, there is no guarantee that I wouldn't be in a constant flux of system hacking. What was it you called it, Mari? Fucking up other people's fantasies? I'd be fucking up their realities."

And his consciousness, his conscience, wouldn't be reliably there to keep him from bringing the entire technological world down around their ears. Everybody's ears. She could see why he hesitated.

"So if your remote scrub doesn't work, you can either kill yourself or take over the cloud and run amok. Those are your only two options? Seriously?"

Kellen nodded. Heron sat very still. His only movement was that finger. Round, across, back around: infinity.

"What about just letting the transmission do its thing, then? Let those nano fuckers transmit their microscopic hearts out. It doesn't seem to be hurting you, least not as I can see. Despite all that you talked up your self-control troubles, you were plenty spry last night. And this morning."

Kellen looked like he wanted a big hat to hide under right then.

"You might not notice, but I *have* been slowed," Heron said. "Eighty-two percent of my processing power last night was dedicated to cutting off transmissions. This severely limited my attention to other functions." He didn't look away, but his face did get pinker. No kidding, Heron blushed like a wee schoolgirl. If they weren't discussing such heavy shit, that would be impossibly cute. Kind of was anyhow. "But the problem isn't my own limitations. It's what I'm transmitting."

"Well, what, then?"

The pause stretched on so long, Mari wondered if they'd heard her.

"Us."

"Come again?"

"They're uploading us," he said. "Everything about us."

"So far they haven't gotten anything important," Kellen clarified. "He's been chopping off them hydra heads, so to speak, soon as they pop up, and now, of course, the Chiba halo is blocking everything in or out. But that can't go on much longer. Chiba will eventually need its halo back on handling things like avoiding orbital trash. And without the halo, Heron won't be able to do much else, despite whatever…physical things he's managed."

Kellen looked super uncomfortable, but he didn't hold back, and Mari thanked him silently. She didn't take to being lied to, and she recognized that Kellen was telling it to her straight. Girl could love a man for less.

She sucked in a hot breath, thought about that picture

the feds had posted to the interwebs after her botched job. Thought about Aunt Boo. She still hadn't talked real-time with Auntie. Dangit. The lapse caught her insides and twisted. But she shrugged on her bravado. "Fuck 'em. I got nothing to hide."

"I do." Heron opened his eyes and looked down at her. That expression was so tender, her insides turned plumb over.

He was protecting her. He was always protecting her. But hot on the heels of that thought came this one: he also had a responsibility to Adele and Chloe and the rest of the crew, probably even to Chiba and its queen.

Mari was willing to get herself caught, even stand for a court-ordered humane end for her crimes, but if full details about her went live, so would some bits about all the folks she'd touched. Chloe. Aunt Boo.

Heron.

"It's okay, Mari. I have things set up. You're going to be safe. Chloe and Kellen and Garrett and Adele, too. Just let me do what I have to. The odds are this remote-login process will go off without a hitch."

Uh-huh. She could recognize uncertainty on Heron's face, even when it was wrapped up in pretty promises. Things in her life had a habit of going the way of trouble, and she never trusted luck.

But Heron wasn't luck, and she most certainly did believe in *him*.

"Okay, lookit. You do what you have to, partner, only you come right back to me." She squeezed his hands. "You feel that?"

A ghost smile drifted over his mouth. "I feel you, querida."

"Good. Don't stop. You hang on to me, no matter where your brain goes, y'hear?"

He closed his eyes and smiled. "Didn't I tell you before that you're always on my mind?"

She didn't get a chance to tell him this was no time for jokes. Kellen pressed the second injection of poison into his IV.

Her knees ached from squatting, but she didn't dare move. She could tell when the chems started working. Heron's grip on her hand eased somewhat, and his facial muscles relaxed, wiping the smile. Lines and blips splashed over the monitor's display. Kellen adjusted the feeds, read some numbers.

"His primary systems are hibernating," Kellen told her. "He's dipping into sleep now, just like with a general anesthetic, only with some subroutines going. He's still with us, Miss Mari. You don't need to worry."

But she'd seen the labels on the cart. She knew that Kellen had pumped him full of enough tranquilizers to down a longhorn. Had his consciousness made it over to the station computer? She figured that's what some of Kellen's numbers and graphs were showing, but she didn't know how to interpret that stuff. And also, she wanted her focus right where it was at the moment, on Heron.

Mari watched as her partner slipped off to sleep.

"Hey, Kellen," she whispered after a few minutes. "You won't let him k...ki... Won't let him do anything permanent before telling me, right?"

The doc reached out a hand, like he would comfort her, and then shoved it back into his jeans pocket. "Ain't looking to let him hurt himself, no."

Heron's fingertip finally stopped circling her knuckles. All tension ebbed from his body. He looked so vulnerable in sleep. Mari unlaced their clasp carefully, reached out, and brushed his hair back away from his forehead. He didn't look like himself with his hair all tidy like that, but she hadn't been able to stop herself.

"Miss Mari, I got to ask you a question now." Kellen shifted his weight from one boot to the other.

"Shoot," she whispered.

"The name Nathan Grace mean anything to you?"

Her hand paused, frozen. "What?"

"Those nano bits I managed to recover were designs patented by a man named Nathan Grace. Got his numbers all over 'em."

The words were a horse kick to the gut. "Fucking hell."

"So you know of him?"

"We used to work together."

Kellen let it go without any more questions, but Mari's brain whirred. Once upon a time, she and Nathan had been partners. And lovers. Right up until their job went down the shitter on some pier in Corpus. He'd been her backup, her cover fire. Except one night, he hadn't been there. And the federales had. She'd blown her diversion charges, but the feds got her anyway.

At first, she'd figured he'd gotten caught like she had, or worse, but she'd heard other folks mention him since then. She'd done the odd interweb search a few times, getting feeds about his life, even though she no longer tried to find him.

He was fine, living in Dallas, managing to sidestep the worst of the war, and working on contract, still in thick with the TPA. Probably cashing in, if she knew him. And she did. She had no reason to think he wasn't happy as a pig in slop. He'd just ditched her, for whatever reason, at the worst possible moment. And he'd never tried to contact her to explain. As if that kind of betrayal was typical of the world they lived in.

Sometime during the last year or so she'd been working with Heron, she had forgotten what stark loneliness felt like.

"Aw fuck." Kellen's whisper slithered across the med lab, cold and horrible and stabbing through her bad memories. He was standing by the monitor, the one showing all Heron's vitals and whatnot.

"What?"

"Maybe nothing," Kellen said, but he was lying.

He typed something on a keypad, waited for the computer to respond, and then shoved a hand through his hair.

She peered beyond him at the monitor. Her shooter's eyes were good enough to read even from this distance.

Error sending data. Session closed. What did that *mean*?

But Kellen wasn't in any shape to tell her, was typing even more furiously and mouthing stuff into his com at the same time. If Mari moved, tried to help out, she would just get in the way. She didn't belong here in this room of wires and antiseptic and blood.

The queen swept in, moving fast, but she didn't explain either. Hell, she didn't even acknowledge Mari's presence, just attached herself to the snake pit of wires, closed her machine eyes, and started doing whatever freaky-ass software kung fu she could to make the scary messages stop.

Mari remained in her knee-burning crouch by Heron's chair. She could do nothing.

Nothing.

Messages continued to scroll over the monitor. Fail callback. Fail hook handler. Session disabled. What, what, and hell what? It was worse than trying to read a language she didn't understand. This was necessary, vital information, and she was missing all of it. She bit her lip so hard, she tasted salt.

Don't get in the way. Don't disturb the smart folks.
Fuck.

She might not be able to get in there and perform software magic, but she just as clearly couldn't sit here forever, frozen in impotent fear and ignorance. If she didn't *do* something soon, she was going to explode.

Kellen's hands slowed, then stopped. He sat still in a bolted-down chair and stared at the monitor updates of biometrics. Mari rose, bit back her knees' complaints, went over to Kellen, and set a hand on his shoulder. He flinched but was probably too tired to startle. Or too horrified.

"Can you pause long enough to read me in on this, Kellen?" she asked in as calm a voice as she could muster. "What just happened?"

"Aw, shit. I'm sorry, Miss Mari," he said, not even looking up. "Should've given you an update, like, ten minutes ago. I just forgot…"

His voice trailed off, but she knew what he would have said. He'd forgotten she was here. Wasn't the first time that had happened. It wouldn't be the last. She shrugged off the familiar shame before it could sink in and hurt.

"Right now works, too," she said.

He scraped one hand over his face. "Short answer is I don't know. Heron was going to run the scan remotely, but something glitched. He wasn't able to get back into his own system. I know a little about software management but not nearly enough. Queen's trying to get him access or at least start up the scan herself."

Mari swallowed. Where was he now? Was his brain stuck in the station computer? But she chose to ask a more immediate question. "Can she fix this?"

"Maybe?" Kellen made a strangled sound, and his big hands turned to fists. "Fuck if I know. Right now, she's securing the station from outgoing transmissions, running all the systems here, *and* trying to save my friend. It's a lot for one computer to handle, even one as fancy-pants as her. Tell you one thing, she ain't moving fast. I don't know what she's gonna do when the tether energy transfer is done."

"Why? What happens then?"

"The space elevator will disconnect itself automatically and retract, and she'll have to move this station. And stop helping Heron. Chiba can't go back into orbit without its halo of nanites. Space junk would wreck it right quick."

"But it's possible she'll be able to get him access before then?"

"Possible." But his voice said not likely.

All that talk about rebooting and killing swam in her mind. Possibly the queen could fix him, but it wasn't likely. Mari couldn't live on possibilities, not when so much was at stake. She needed certainty. She needed to *do* something. "What if I can get the transmission to stop? Would that help the queen, help her go faster?"

"It would help loads, gal, but I don't know how you could…"

"How long until she has to move the station?"

He pointed to a number on the monitor. 23:42:11. And counting down. She had less than a day. God.

"You said Nathan Grace made those nanos, right?"

"Well, yeah, but…"

"Kellen, you get me into Texas, and I will find that motherfucker. He *will* cut the transmission."

Twenty-three hours. It would have to be enough.

CHAPTER

12

RUBBING ALCOHOL STUNG HER NOSTRILS, AND THE fresh wounds throbbed. Mari felt 'em deeper than just skin. Behind her eyes, in her skull, at the base of her throat. In the core of who she was. She squinted down at her reflection in the smartsurface table.

"Well, at least I still look like me." Except she didn't. On those rare occasions when she looked at her reflection, she never felt like she was seeing herself. The disconnect was only worse now that she'd gone and put implants into her body.

Oh, please. Ain't like you're the first person ever to put tech inside your body. This doodad's gonna help you save him, so it's worth the weird feeling. Suck it up, buttercup.

Kellen frowned and smoothed the butterfly bandage on her wrist. "Oh, you're still the same girl. This isn't alteration like those women who rewrap and rebuild and all look like clones of each other. It ain't meant to be prettifying. Think of it as a com, just like that one you've been wearing in your neck on jobs."

"But it's not."

He met her gaze. "Similar, but no."

This device had a long-distance communication capability, but more important, it pushed out images, specially enhanced holos with boosted contrast, tailored to fuck up facial recognition probes. She only had to get close to a faceprinter to start up the flood of pics, confusing it. The implanted tech wouldn't keep her anonymous forever, but in the short term, Kellen swore it was near foolproof. It would get her past the checkpoints and into Texas.

She wasn't sure why Kellen had schematics on hand for such a thing. Of course, considering all the illegal activities their little group of troublemakers got up to on a regular basis, it couldn't hurt to be able to have faceprint spoofers at the ready.

"Now remember, I can't call you. You gotta call me. This channel is locked up tight against outside transmissions."

"Roger that, doc."

"And you feel comfortable with the other fail-safes?"

"As comfy as I'm gonna be."

"Well, then." His solemn face tried to smile, but it came off as a grimace. He looked tired. "I still think you're crazier than a sack of weasels."

Mari folded her fingers to a fist. "You got somethin' against weasels?"

"You know what I meant."

She did. "Thank you."

"Welcome, Miss Mari. Now, let's get you packed up before I have second thoughts. Clock's tickin'."

● ● ●

The Chiba Station had hooked its space-elevator tether to an energy storage depot somewhere between Laramie and Cheyenne. Kind of ballsy of the queen, putting down her tether here. Bit dangerous, too. Denver, the seat of the new continental government, was probably the most secure place on the planet. Even this far out from the Colina Capitolina, drones fitted with face-printing scanners hovered thick as Gulf Coast mosquitoes on a summer night.

When Mari got down to the surface, she went in the opposite direction from the capital, toward Laramie, and boarded a maglev there.

In the security corral, waiting on her train, she saw folk with printed canvas pants and mud on their boots. Made her think of back home, and then her soul knotted up into a ball, 'cause that's where she was headed. Texas. Home. And not for fun.

She had a cloudcoin account under an alias, and her login still worked. Mari knew that accessing it would lead her enemies to her eventually, but long-term trouble wasn't her worry. She was more concerned with right now.

She'd borrowed a cuff com off Kellen and set up the timer on it. It covered up her new scar, and it also provided her with a constant reminder of how much time she had left before the queen needed to move. In the train station, Mari glanced at her wrist. 19:38:11.

She made a pit stop in a hostelry near the departure gate and bought some preprinted clothes and toiletries. Kellen had given her a bundle of tradables, and she was able to barter for a disposable external com. Girl never knew what would be available for purchase in war-strapped Texas. She'd bring in what she needed.

The orange silk dress she packed up carefully in a climate-controlled box and sent to a storage unit she'd hired in London a few years back. Even if she managed to stop the transmission and save Heron, there was still that bitty problem of being wanted by the continental government. So yeah, she was headed back to Texas, but no, she couldn't stay.

She wished Heron was here for the job planning and beyond. He'd know the best places to hide out. He had always been better at that stuff. And he would be again. She swore it to herself.

Would he come with her, permanently on the lam? Could he bear to leave all that he'd built, the smuggling operation, the relationships, his precious things? And could she even ask him to give up all that, just for her?

She didn't want to think about her own life stretching on without him.

Her fresh scar itched when she passed through the security arch. No way she could be feeling the faceprint spoofer, but knowing it was there, knowing that she wore mech inside her body, made her skin crawl. She passed through the arch without incident, though. Just like any other UNAN citizen.

Nobody clapped cuffs on her or tased her ass during boarding, and she couldn't help feeling a thrill at pulling one over on all these stern-looking federales. She almost turned to wink at Heron or say something saucy and salacious, but then reality intruded again.

He wasn't with her on this job. She was on her own. No turning back now.

She paid for the seating upgrade and crept into the forward compartment, which accorded a smidge of privacy. She waited until the maglev released and rose, because even with all these things on her mind, that shit felt freaky cool, every time. It also put her in a slightly better frame of mind for dialing up Aunt Boo.

Most folks'd be happy with a message now and then, but Auntie B swore there wasn't anything as good as the sound of a loved one's voice. Although it was possible she'd heeded Mari's warning yesterday, more likely, she hadn't even checked her message log yet.

She picked up on the second chime. "'Yello."

Just hearing her on the disposable phone made Mari's eyes tear up. "Heya, Auntie Boo. What's doin'?"

"Mariposa? That you, kiddo?"

Without even confirming, Aunt Boo launched into a detailed description of her camouflaged, fenced-back garden and the hot young thing she'd hired to tend it through the late-autumn harvest and put it to bed for winter.

Fences had scarred the landscape, and the TPA had appropriated much of the land Boo had owned before, but she still kept at gardening. And ogling the local boys. Apparently, this one had bronzed skin, labored long, hot afternoons without a shirt, and didn't mind gals old enough to be his grandmother checking him out while he worked, which was a plus in Aunt Boo's book.

Mari soaked in the descriptions so deep, she could almost taste home-done biscuits and butternut squash soup from the ladle.

"So that's enough about me. You knocked up yet or what?"

Despite the fact that Aunt Boo had asked it a hundred times, the question still jolted Mari. She felt a bulb of satisfaction in her womb, a physical confirmation of recent sex, though she knew that unless Heron had banked before his alterations, the chances of him ever having kids skirted near zero. And if he'd started down the mech path only after those riots in Austin, Mari's guess was that he hadn't been planning his post-human life. So no electronic walking trainers for toddlers or day camps for them in the future.

And why was she even thinking along these lines? Mari kicked herself mentally. One goddamn wonderful night did not a lifelong relationship forge, and she sure wasn't looking to make babies right now. Not with all she'd planned for the next few years of forever.

"Um, I don't think so," she mumbled, which set off some cackling on the other end of the line.

"That's about the most positive lack of certainty I've heard from you in years, even if you ain't got actual nibblets yet. You got a fella, sounds like, and I'm happy about that."

Me too. Or she would be if he weren't laid out on a gurney at the moment. "Sort of, but he don't know he's got yet, Auntie B. So I'll tell you more about him next time, okay? Meanwhile, did you get the message I sent earlier?"

"I got it."

Three words delivered in the gentlest voice…but smothered in disappointment. Her voice implied that Mari had gone and done her usual, making trouble. And here was Auntie B, tsking her disapproval. They didn't really need to rehash that old quarrel. Mari pulled the com closer to her mouth and dropped her voice. "Please tell me you aren't still in Texas. Tell me you're off visiting one of your princesses."

A crackle over the line, and then a sigh. "Princess Bubbles says hi."

Aunt Boo'd grown close to a group of women online years ago, back when the cloud was called "internet" and offered a modicum of anonymity. Auntie still kept up with her princesses, and once in a while, when she could save up enough in tradables to coyote through the border, she went to visit one. They lived all over the world, and Mari didn't have a clue who was who; they all went by made-up names of fairy-tale princesses. Boo was Princess Rose, and Mari could vaguely recall a Princess Seraphina. Apparently, there was also a Princess Bubbles.

If the people who'd jacked Heron were looking to cause hurt to the folks who Mari loved, probably the safest place for Aunt Boo to hide out would be with one of these women. They'd take her in, no questions asked. And Mari wouldn't know where to find her.

Which meant that Mari's enemies wouldn't be able to find Auntie B either, not even if they transmitted every bit in Heron's head.

"Thanks for skedaddling," Mari said. "Also, I wanted you to know I have a storage unit for my stuff. If anything happens to me—"

"Don't you even start a sentence that way, missy."

"If anything happens to me," Mari repeated firmly, "the contact code for that storage unit is 'lacewing,' and the number is Mama's birthday. It's in the stacks near Heathrow."

There was silence on the other end for a long time, and then, "Oh, honey. I hear it all in your voice, you know that?" Never could lie to Aunt Boo. "Listen to me.

I don't care what you done or even that you keep getting yourself into scrapes. I just need you to take care of my girl, y'hear?"

Mari sniffed back a sob. "Be safe. Have a great vacation. Indulge yourself some."

"You too, Princess Butterfly. Keep off the news-vids now."

Mari usually responded with a wry rejoinder, but she couldn't force that level of bullshit to her tongue. Not today. She nodded, knowing that without the video app on, Aunt Boo couldn't even see.

A digital chime signaled the end of her conversation, and she muttered a payment code, one that wasn't linked to any accounts in her name. Even so, she suspected that Aunt Boo's garden in Lampasas would be raided before sunset. Didn't matter which side got there first: secessionist ops team or UNAN antiterrorist forces. Either one would stomp all over Aunt Boo's winter squash seedlings and never think about the harm they caused. She hoped they didn't do anything cruel with the shirtless young hottie.

She also hoped Auntie had told the truth and was on the other side of the planet by now.

The ride to Ardmore, Oklahoma, would take a little more than two hours, and Mari blessed the maglev technology the whole way. She also put the time to good use, researching Nathan as much as she could.

She got her job contracts through the darknet, but she didn't need to access the secret network to get plenty of info on her ex. He lived right out in the open. He'd even purchased property in Dallas a few years back. She put a pin into that spot on her mental map. She'd start looking for him there.

After an hour of reading on a tiny projected screen, her eyes got tired, though, and Mari closed the phone and slipped it into the cloth pocket by the window. She leaned her head against the squabs while the maglev vibrated beneath her skull, hurtling south. Taking her home.

At Ardmore, she left the high-speed lines and hitched a ride on a humanitarian-aid truck headed south. The driver swapped her a Texas rations bracelet for the balance on her cloudcoin account.

The bracelet identified her as Heidi Cisneros, who, according to the liquor allotment remaining, was something of a teetotaler. Thank God. Mari suspected she was going to need those booze rations. She didn't ask what'd happened to Heidi or whether the identity was completely made up. Wasn't her business.

She made it to Dallas by late afternoon, after three security and validation stops and some slips past the more invasive checkpoints. Her faceprint spoofer and fake identity held, but it wasn't a good idea to let her guard down. Not here, not ever.

The first thing she did was rent a room near the old West End. The place she found hadn't had a bug treatment in a decade at least but didn't ask for identification scans and was happy to take her tradables instead of money. She'd handed over a sack of late-season California grapes, just a little bruised. In Texas, grapes were more valuable than UNAN-secured credit accounts or even cloudcoin.

She spent a good hour hunting down and squashing cockroaches under her boot heels. Killin' them things always did calm her.

She took a long shower—lukewarm and sparse because of energy rationing now that Texas was limited to its own grid—and changed into the togs she'd bought up in Laramie: off-the-rack printed crinoline, a black, long-line corset, and a translucent flak-style bomber jacket over top. If folks were looking hard enough at the cleavage, maybe they'd miss some of the other things Kellen had helped her get ahold of before she'd left Chiba. Plus, the rigid boning in the bra would give her an excuse for setting off metal detectors on every other street corner. She wished she'd had access to her own clothes, especially her vectran-armored bits, but, well, wishes weren't horses.

And then she hit the street, hunting down Nathan.

Dallas sure had changed plenty in the last decade, and none of it for the better. Mari used to think of Dallas as the bigger-haired, louder-mouthed step-cousin of the other Texas metropolitans. The one that she endured but never really liked. War had shaved that head of big hair down to scruff, though. Wasn't a single thing glamorous about this place now. It looked haunted and hungry, decked out in more barricades than neon lights.

Texas rebels had dug in deep here in the densest population center they controlled outright, and suspicion crackled on the air like live wires. Mari could see it in the face of the motel clerk who'd taken her grapes.

She checked through three validation points just getting to a taqueria. Granted, she might have been stopped more frequently than the average citizen. Her clothes pegged her as an outsider, so she attracted more than her share of attention.

After using her rations bracelet to buy a couple of fuego rolls—and deliberately not asking what the mustached taqueria vendor had stuffed inside; tasted like raw, off-code habanero and protein flakes, maybe mixed with oatmeal—she took that attention-grabbing show to the bar scene in the West End.

Her first stop was Boudreaux's, which used to serve Cajun and vino. Now, Mari was happy that her beer didn't have proteins floating in it, even if it was a home-brewed monster of a drink that nearly knocked her off her stool on the first swig. She stayed at the bar for a little over an hour, danced tit-to-tit with a pretty young thing too sweet to know anything about jobs or clouds or the secession, and all the while, felt the prickly-hair certainty that somebody was watching her.

Well, that was quick. Good.

On the walk to the next dive, Mari pressed the fresh scar tissue in her arm and opened up a com to Kellen. "How is he?"

"He still doesn't have admin access. Queen's running the scan, but it's taking for-fuckin'-ever. We got…thirteen hours yet till the space elevator comes up. We have time. He could still pull this off. And you could still get back here before he knows you're missing."

"Been over this, Kellen. It ain't like we have a whole helluva lot of other options. I can't sit up there and do nothing."

"Might be best for my health if you did," he said. "I been imagining what he's gonna do when he wakes up and finds out I let you go."

If he wakes up. Big if. Too big.

"It isn't a matter of letting me," she reminded him.

"And don't worry. I'll tell him that myself. I'm a big girl. He wakes up, you ping me right away."

"Surely will, gal."

"But?"

"No buts. You be safe."

"Rest of the crew okay?"

"I s'pose so. Garrett and Chloe went off on some mission or something before you even left, but she had a message for you. Glad you asked, 'cause I had plain forgotten. Chloe wanted me to ask how the dress did. You got any idea what she means?"

Mari grinned, a burst of warm in the cool Dallas night. "When you see her again, tell her it was all magic and whispers."

And she cut the signal.

● ● ●

Heaven's Gate, three blocks south of the ruins of Southern Methodist University, used to be chic but now skirted the line between loyalist and seedy. A girl could toast a war hero, inhale a chemical cocktail, and pay for a clit-licker in the same bar. They even had curtained alcoves, because Texans were notoriously prim about public fuckery.

It was also about a mile away from some property Nathan used to own, before the TPA expropriated all private land holdings. He wasn't the kind of man who'd give up his stuff willingly: if he'd once owned some-thing, he'd still be squatting nearby and grumping about his rights. And if he was still alive, still in Texas, and still Nathan, he'd eventually find his way to a bar like this one.

It was Mari's third stop of the night. Her feet hurt, her patience was thin, and she'd ingested way too much homemade hooch. Still, she had a good feeling about this place. With seven hours to go before the queen needed to disconnect the space elevator and no word yet from Heron, she needed more than a good feeling. She needed to be successful.

One thing made her think she was on the right trail, though. At bar number two, she'd noted a giant blond dude lurking in a corner booth and downing so much cheap vodka that he never could have processed it without internal scrubbers. Post-human, then. Dangerous.

She spotted him again at Heaven's Gate, looking somewhat more discreet but still out of place. Overbearing. Ginormous. Grumpy. She picked out a few obvious signs of alteration: that slip-sprint movement she'd seen in the mercenaries back at the Pentarc, a tilt to the head and a hand over the mouth, clear tips he was talking on a com. There was a trick to not letting folks know what you were up to when you ran silent, but this guy hadn't perfected any such tricks. He looked like the type who typically walked into a brawl, spread his arms, and said something along the lines of, "Do your worst."

She also noted the bulges in his clothes where he probably had weapons at the ready. They were the same places, more or less, where she would have strapped her own goodies, if she'd been carrying. Clearly, he had some experience in her world.

Mari slid a glance along the bar, getting an eyeful of him, and she wondered why he hadn't approached her. Could be he was part of a smash team, and the heavy guns were waiting to ambush her once she was away from this semicrowded establishment. If he was an agent for UNAN, she could imagine them being that careful. Texans, probably not. They tended to shoot first and ask questions later, lord love 'em.

She glanced down at her chest, fully expecting to see laser paint. But all she saw was the black bra and a bead of sweat nuzzling the centerline.

She tipped her head back and drained the beer, froth included. The brew seared her esophagus, and she licked the foam from her upper lip.

"Show me the work of that tongue one more time, beautiful, and I'll have to haul you off to that there curtained alcove, and not a body here'd blame me."

Mari's insides clenched. Lord, she knew that voice, but she didn't turn toward it. Was a time when it would have set up a corresponding gush in her nethers. Not tonight, though. Not anymore. Hearing it did bring on some memories. Not all of them good, not all of them bad.

He slunk into the stool beside her, blurring into her periphery. Smelled like booze and cologne. His jeans were starched till the crease stood out white. Boy still dressed up fine when he was on the pull. Some things never changed.

"Nathan." She set her dirty glass on the bar but didn't move her elbow.

"How about that? Sweet Mari Vallejo, right here and warming a barstool in my neighborhood."

"Came looking for you."

"Consider me flattered."

"Not for a fuck, mind."

"Mind fuck, then?"

"Nathan…"

He held up a hand, palm out, and chuckled. It was a silky, sexy thing on the ears, that chuckle. He had never worked too hard to get a girl out of her panties. Seduction just came naturally to him. Like digging to a gopher.

"Well, you found me, sweetness. Now, what do you plan to do with me?"

Here, Mari did look at him. One eyebrow raised, she turned. She was prepared for what met her gaze, granted, but it still took a minute to ingest it all. Time had been kind to Nathan. He was one of those just-gets-better-with-age sorts of men, with bronzed hair and laser-blue eyes and cenote-deep dimples. Bastard knew exactly how pretty he was.

"Might ask you the same," she said. "Pulled some of your nanites from my partner's head. Marionetting, really? That shit's pretty low, even for you." It never, ever hurt to cut right to the chase with a guy like Nathan.

His charming grin wavered. "Marionetting? I don't know what you…"

"Killed your hired muscle boys, too. What? You'd forgotten that I do that sort of thing, like, for a living? Gettin' stupider by the day, Grace."

That grin faded altogether, and the sight of it sliding off his smug, gorgeous face made Mari feel a little better. Okay, a lot.

"You killed them?"

Murderer. But she didn't feel so bad about it now. Not about the mercs, though she did still regret poor Daniel Neko and reckoned she always would. Strange thing, guilt. Or just a strange thing, *her* guilt? "You know it."

Nathan tested his lips with his tongue, signaled the bartender, and ordered something that might imitate whiskey. He shifted his weight on the barstool, but he didn't look straight at her.

A slinky ballad came on the neurospeakers. Mari cut it off using her new implanted com but made a show of pressing the inert piece of tech over her ear at the same time. She'd worn the cameo throat piece, too. And, of course, her cuff with the countdown on it. Nothing wrong with letting Nathan know she was hooked in to the outside world, but she didn't want him to guess her newest alterations.

"The puppeteer who fucked over my partner said something about bringing me in," she said. "That's why I came. Figured you could pass along the message: I'm willing to go, any old time, and I won't even shoot you for your troubles. I hear the bounty on me is huge. Just need you to deactivate some of your nanocritters first."

"That won't be a problem. You turned into kind of a cheap date, Mar. Which nanos?"

She gave him the patent numbers from the nanites Kellen had pulled. Nathan fed them into an implant on his forearm. "Those things are ancient. Didn't realize they were still part of a fabrication. No skin off my nose if they dark and go back to a vat."

Which was how most folks thought about nanos. But Mari couldn't think of them that way now. The idea of Chloe in a vat made her sick to her stomach. Instead of horfing, though, she steadied herself.

He looked up. "Done. That all you wanted me for?"

Mari swallowed her whew.

Transmission was cut. Kaput. Success. Relief. Now

she just needed to make her grand exit. Or run the hell away, which seemed kind of the better option. Honestly, she hadn't planned much beyond getting the transmission sliced. She hadn't counted on it being so easy.

Which meant it probably wasn't. Which meant Nathan was either playing her or getting played. Which meant she needed to poke this situation a bit harder.

She peered into her drink, letting her hair fall forward and shield her face for a moment, long enough to mouth subvocally, "Kellen, you there? Did it work? Have the transmissions stopped?"

He replied almost instantly, like he'd been waiting for her to call. "Shit. No. What are you up to? Did you find Grace? Are you okay?"

Well, fuck.

Mari shook her hair back over her shoulder and raised the glass, meeting Nathan's gaze over the rim. She swallowed, smiled. "What exactly are you offering?"

If it was close to midnight, as she guessed, she still had almost seven hours till the queen had to stop her scans and move her station. Till Heron would be on his own up there, trapped outside his body and freaking the hell out.

That wasn't long, but she could still make this work. She could chat up Nathan, find out who had sent those mercs. Maybe take a knife to that son of a bitch, whoever it was. Nathan fabricated tech just fine, but he wasn't a big thinker. Unless he'd grown up a lot in the last few years, he didn't have the balls to set her up so elaborately, and he sure as shit didn't have any connection to better-than-human-looking mech-clones like the Daniel Neko that was currently canoodling an UNAN senator.

"So who you taking me to? Who's holding your leash? By personal history, I'll assume it's a woman, likely one in leather."

Nathan's grin slunk back, edging his glass as he took a sip. "You know me too well." He swallowed another but still waited in profile, not looking right at her. "Actually, my boss on this one is somebody you know. Been working for the biomech division in the TPA. Technocrats."

Not surprising. What Mari did count as surprising was the fact that Nathan was being so up-front about it all.

"So what's the next step? You cuff me, haul me to a slap-and-tickle debrief, after which these TPA ass-holes do some sort of prisoner swap with the UNAN?" Not likely, considering her get-the-hell-out skills, but Nathan wouldn't know that. His last memory had her getting caught in the worst way, and he likely thought she was still that noob. Guys like Nathan never did reckon a person could change or learn.

"Nothing so dire, babe. You just take a ride with me. Little road trip, for old times' sake."

Maglevs didn't run in Texas anymore, not with the UNAN electrical grids cutting off at the borders, so Nathan meant to take her someplace in a private vehicle. On a road. Totally bare to any satellite's eyes. When Heron woke up, he'd be able to track her easily through the satnavs. If she was all out in the open like that, maybe he wouldn't worry. Or get mad at Kellen.

Yeah, not likely. She needed to work quickly, before that countdown ran to zero.

Mari stuck her forearm out and waited for the

bartender to scan her rations bracelet. Nathan just nodded, and Mari didn't see a band on his wrist. She wondered if he kept an open tab at this establishment. In Mari's experience, that was on the high end of trust, more than just good custom.

If Heron were here, he would be feeding her particulars on the bar: who the operators were, what licenses they held, how fast she could get to the nearest exit. She'd know not only whether Nathan had an account here but also what his balance and last payment figures were. She'd know whether he had an equity interest and whether TPA had given him any special perks because he'd done work for them. Might be able to track him back to the technocrat faction, might be able to find out more about who'd set her up to kill the real Daniel Neko instead of the mech-clone.

In that moment, Mari missed her partner keenly. And not just because her nipples squeezed up tight every time she so much as pictured him. He was part of her process now, and interfacing with the world when he wasn't beside her just…sucked.

"So since when'd you join the dark side?" Nathan asked, jolting Mari. It wasn't that she'd forgotten he was here. She'd just been wishing too hard that somebody else was.

She replied with a look. What the heck was he even talking about?

He gestured with his chin toward her forearm, where the countdown cuff had shifted, exposing her implant scar. "The girl I knew was fervent against alteration." Damn if his voice didn't sound a whole lotta wistful.

She shrugged and resisted the urge to shove her arms into the jacket sleeves.

"Pheromone pump. Brand new. Why? You feeling unexpectedly frisky?"

Nathan made a sound in his throat that Mari interpreted as disbelief. True, when they'd been together, she'd been a little wild. Okay, a lot wild. Opinionated, cocksure, with a chip on her shoulder the size of Alaska. It had all been in an effort to keep the self-loathing at bay, of course, but Nathan hadn't known that. And she'd never told him. She wondered if he'd hated her as much as he professed to love her, but she didn't dare ask.

He was bathing her with one of those looks. A dimple-ended smile hovered on the edge of his mouth, and Mari's skin crawled with questions. He was sizing her up, that much was plain, and once upon a time, she might have worried that he found her lacking. Right now, she didn't give two shits if he did.

"Always frisky, ma'am." He leaned toward her and leered. "Let's get out of here."

Now, see, she'd gotten all nostalgic and sappy when Kellen had called her ma'am back on Chiba. When Nathan did it, she just wanted to smack him upside the head.

CHAPTER 13

Nathan wasn't originally from Texas, but he sure had adopted the yeehaw. A scrawny, strung-out valet in jeans brought his truck around, and looking at it, Mari thought it could tow at least a big-haul gooseneck. Which was ludicrous: the Nathan she knew wouldn't know what to do with a cow. Given one, he'd probably name it Frisky and feed it guacamole.

He didn't hold the door for her, and Mari didn't expect him to. She grabbed the leather seat harness and hauled herself up into the monster truck. The door shushed closed behind her. Standard, self-driving cab, just a single bench seat on the floor and control deck in the dash, no steering wheel or gearshift. This truck ran itself. Which meant Nathan wouldn't have to divide his attention between her and the road.

That should not have made her nervous, but it kind of did.

She watched him climb in the other door, tint the windows, and set their trip parameters on the control deck.

She studied the console, but she couldn't make sense of the longitude and latitude he put in as their destination. Again, Heron usually handled the nav.

It'd been a while since Mari'd ridden in an autocontrol rig that wasn't public transportation. It felt weird, like the cab imprisoned her. She was perfectly used to a machine driving her around, granted, but *her* machine.

When the windows went dark, leaving her alone with Nathan Grace, she was suddenly twenty-one again and reckless. Only she wasn't. She wasn't that girl anymore.

"I'll show you mine if you show me yours," Nathan said. As an opener, it wasn't far off his usual.

Mari grimaced. "What the hell are you even talking about?"

"Your tech, babe."

Oh.

"The implant is just the pheromone pump. You already saw it. My com's external." She felt like folding her arms, tucking them behind her back, doing whatever it took to keep Nathan from checking out Kellen's careful work. It wasn't like he'd be able to tell who her carver was just by looking at her tech, but it still felt too personal. Which was just stupid. Mari'd been ass-naked under this man's gaze countless times, but here she was, cringing away from showing him her damned forearm?

"Show me the com." He paused and then added, "I'm not asking."

Mari froze. Nathan was still smiling, still leaning easily against the bench squab, half turned toward her. But there was something hard in his face this time. No matter what he looked like or how he made her feel, he wasn't the same person he'd been before Corpus Christi. She needed to keep that in mind.

She could take him out right now, of course. No matter how much he'd changed, he didn't have any obvious alterations, not like that Viking giant who'd been stalking her in the bar. Not like the mercs she'd put down in the Pentarc. Even without a gun, she could end Nathan. He ought to know that.

But if she rolled Nathan and slipped out into the dark Dallas night right now, she'd never get that transmission shut down. And Heron would…no. She'd get it done.

She tilted her head to the side and shished back her hair, exposing the earpiece and the cameo.

"Just a dock-mounted piece," Nathan murmured. "Temporary?"

"You can take it out if you need to." She held her breath, waiting for the pinch. It didn't hurt when she removed the earpiece, not at all, but she still tensed when Nathan slipped it out. He did it as a caress, gentle, pushing up into her hair. That was new. Nothing about Nathan and touch had ever been gentle, back when. He'd liked it rough, on the giving and the getting. Often, their sex had bordered on violent, and some particularly excruciating memories were burned into Mari's brain, unavoidable even in nightmare.

His thumb dipped beneath her jaw, stroked the rim of her cameo. She closed her eyes and waited for the metal catch, the hiss of release, and the dull pinch as the com came free.

She thought of how keyed into that com Heron was usually, how he'd even been able to read her mind with it in, for a couple of hours at least. Losing it was almost like losing her connection with him. It hurt.

"There," Nathan said, palming the now-inert bit of metal. "That wasn't so hard, was it?"

Yeah, it was. Mari opened her eyes slowly, wet her lips, and leveled him with a stare she'd spent a lifetime practicing. "Now show me yours."

Nathan turned the com over and over in one hand, but he didn't move other than that. His smile had grown enigmatic, and the cab of the truck felt closer. Warmer. He didn't have control over the air mix like Heron did, but Mari's breath still shallowed. Her nerves went live, on fire.

A flash of certainty whacked her in the head. This was where he'd betray her. This was where he'd hurt her. He had her at his mercy, or thought he did, and Nathan had never been big on mercy.

What if he wasn't planning to turn her over to the authorities? What if he'd acted solo in fabricating those nano transmitters after all? What if he had a more personal vengeance planned, and all he'd wanted to do all along was pay her back for Corpus?

Because that had surely been a shitstorm worth avenging.

They had been a team, more peers than chaos-and-remote like her and Heron. Nathan had been tracking the movements of a security detail while Mari snuck in and filched shit. Small shit. Shit nobody would miss till she and her partner were long gone and had banked that job.

Mari didn't even know what was in the shipping containers, just that she was supposed to load them onto a hovercart and get them onto the dock. A retrieval craft would take it from there. Simple job, in and out, minimal risk.

Com tech hadn't been good back then. They didn't risk walkie-talkies or other radio-wave communication. Nathan had tracked the security for days, got their schedule down, walked her through the whole thing. Promised he'd be her eyes and ears. Swore he had her six. Fucked her until neither of them could walk just right. They'd blissed out on chems and sex and the prospect of a shitload of cloudcoin, untraceable, once this was done.

And then he'd sent her out on the job. He'd scanned and laser-painted the first container, and she'd loaded it for transport. Had paused for the guards' shift change. He painted the second target. And then Nathan…

She'd set some charges remotely, just in case. Nobody knew better than Mari the value of a good diversion. And lord, she always had loved causing mayhem. When the federales showed up, she ducked inside one of the shipping containers. She expected Nathan to drop the tag so it wouldn't mark her position. They could go dark, wait out the law. No need for anything hasty. They were professionals.

But then, the raid wasn't on Nathan's dug-in blind; it was right there on the dock. And her hiding spot was for shit. They found her easily. Claimed she was trespassing, claimed she was murdering, claimed she was engaged in high treason. Yanked her up. Cuffed her. Stripped her. Searched her.

Yeah, that was what they'd called it.

Nathan was armed. He could have picked those federales off. Only four of them, and he had a steady aim. She always did regret, after that, not being the one behind the barrel. So much would have gone different.

She was ten thousand questions into an interrogation when the charges blew.

Orange had burned her retinas. She couldn't hear. She'd screamed for Nathan, but the federales were closer. Pulled her to the ground. Heat and pain and bright white silence, and she had no idea how long she was like that.

She spent seven weeks in a South Texas prison. Cement building said UNAN on the front gate, but laws and regulations on the treatment of prisoners had been wild-wild-west at that point. Maybe they still were, Texas being the chaos pit that it was. And besides, she wasn't being held on suspicion of crossing against a traffic sign, as her captors frequently reminded her. She was suspected of high treason. Assassination. A lot of other words she only partly understood.

They asked her things like where she got the C-4. Like what she was planning to do with plutonium and nanorods. Like what she knew about mech-clone fabrication processes and who she worked for. Like what some string of numbers meant.

She thought back, but now, a thousand years and a lifetime later, she couldn't remember the specifics clearly. Just the sensory details. Smells. The slow creep of her hearing coming back. The pain of burns, and worse. It all healed so slow.

Nathan hadn't been in that prison, and she hadn't seen him since. She'd never gotten his story, had been forced to assume and invent.

She remembered sirens, the blue smoke that smelled

like burnt cotton candy. She remembered being cuffed in a ceramic med closet and swept for tech.

She remembered the miasma of cheap tequila and musty sea air and sweat, and the organic manacles of guards holding her down. She remembered how they'd cheered each other on, lilting into a squirm of languages that eluded her. Shamed her. Broke her. The first guard, the one with blue eyes so like Nathan's, had sported a beard, and all this time and space later, sitting safe in Nathan's big-ass automated truck, Mari raised a hand to her throat, feeling the whisker burn.

Shit, shit, shit. She didn't want to remember this. Any of it. She didn't want to see these things. She didn't want to be the person who'd lived them.

"Mari," Nathan said, "you still with me?"

Not really. "Haven't been for a long time."

Nathan let out a long breath. "No, I guess you haven't. We aren't strangers, though. You're thinking something hard. I know that look."

She wanted to ask him, and she didn't even know why the words stuck in her throat. She had to swallow past them. "Nathan, what's the last thing you remember from that job in Corpus?"

He took so long in answering that Mari thought he hadn't heard her. Memories moved in, monsters and shadows from all sides.

"Your face in my scope," he said at last.

Mari blinked, took a breath, blinked again, but it didn't help. Her vision wasn't resolving. She stared hard at the green display on the control deck. It didn't even look like numbers anymore, just a blur of light. Not fae, though. Plain, flat light.

Her fingertips prickled, and her skin felt hot, like she was sweating. She tried to move one hand to the back of her neck, to lift her hair away, but the weirdest thing: her hand wouldn't move. With great deliberation, she shifted her gaze to the leather seat and stared hard at her hand, sent it commands, and watched it ignore them completely.

"Lie back and rest."

She obeyed. The hell! She'd never obeyed Nathan, never in all their time together. Not even when her rebellion made him furious. But now, she could feel her spine curl in on itself, could feel her hips sliding down, her knees flexing and falling to the side, her head lolling against the seatback. She felt Nathan unzip her plastene jacket and spread the lapels. The metal zipper burned cold on her feverish skin.

"What are you doing?" she tried to ask, but the words sounded slurry.

"Making sure you aren't armed, babe. But you don't have to be awake for this. Just relax."

All the parts of her vision that had blurred, the fuzzy edges and giant dark splotches, filled with memories. Bad ones.

Tequila, teeth, raw throat, blood and bile, thrust and burn. Pain. So much.

Nathan's hands—no longer gentle, more like she remembered—unbuckled the slim leather sheath on her thigh. He drew out the blade, six inches of pretty and sharp as a razor.

"Fuck, Mari."

"Wouldn't if I were you." She had to dig hard for each word and to keep her vision squared, but it was so worth it to watch his face when she murmured, "Got one of them dentata implants. Knock yourself out, perv. 'Cause it's gonna bite like hell on the way out."

And then chemically induced sleep enveloped her.

•　•　•

Reset. Checksum discrepancy, input input. Retry? No. Streaming I/O: Connected. Search parameter = Mari + location + biostatus. Return: 1. N: 30° 29′ 45.45′ W: 98° 49′ 11.53″. 2. Paused. Retry?

His primary systems were offline, and Heron couldn't feel…anything. Where was he?

He searched for input points but could access none of his senses. No eyes, no hands, no ears, no mouth.

He couldn't speak. Couldn't scream.

Panic clawed for him, but he thought through the problem, forced himself to sort the data he could access. Slowly, over the space of milliseconds, his memories trickled in, fitting themselves together. He was in the Chiba Station computer. He'd plugged himself in and transferred a small part of his consciousness, just a control routine really, to the larger computer. The plan was to reboot remotely and scrub his own neural net.

He remembered doing all these things and making all these plans, but the memories smelled like spray paint.

No. Memories didn't smell. That was absurd.

Lacking any of his usual senses, he searched for other sources of data. He located the power transfer conduits in the station and followed two to cameras in this med bay. One was connected to a nanite-sized machine meant for surgical applications.

The other was a security camera, hidden in the molded wall. Jackpot. He accessed its feed and saw the med bay, more or less as he had left it. Kellen slumped at a desk, his arms crossed and his face tucked into the impromptu nest between his elbows. The queen stood still and tense beside a gurney.

That was new. When he'd left, the queen hadn't been here. Mari had.

Mari.

Her name lit up in all his pathways, throbbing like a fresh wound. Where was she? She had promised to be here, to hold on to him. But his first thought on waking had been of her. And she had not been here.

> Search parameter = Mari + location + biostatus.

She had moved since his last check. She was heading south-southwest at 137 kilometers per hour.

In Texas.

What was Mari doing in Texas?

That was the last place she ought to be. Alarm threatened to overtake his logic unit, but he held it off. In a body, he would be taking deep breaths.

Wait. Back up. Body. Gurney. He panned the camera, and sure enough, there was his body, reclining on a gurney. Away, apart from him. Watching it through the camera was surreal. For a moment, disorientation swamped him, and he bobbed in the data stream. He struggled to steady himself, to keep fitting the data input and the memories together.

He was on Chiba. Mari was in Texas. The station was

in a low geosynchronous orbit. The space elevator was still connected to a depot on the surface. His spaceplane was no longer docked on the tether.

He arranged all of these facts until they formed a picture of reality, but what stood out with perfect clarity was this: Mari's com had just alerted him from nine hundred miles away, disconnected by fingers that weren't hers.

Her com signal was welded to Heron's consciousness, served as an integral part of who he was. When it left her, he knew. It didn't matter that his entire neural, his entire self, was running off a copy in the space station's central computer. He knew.

And he was pissed.

She was in danger. Captured? Arrested? Betrayed? Regardless, she needed him. For once, she needed him. And here he was, fucked up, stuck to a gurney. Impotent.

He worked his way through the maze of data paths and found the monitor above Kellen's desk and an input device connected to it. Bringing up a text window, he painstakingly wrote out words. "Hey. You still here, buddy?"

Kellen wasn't really asleep, or maybe he sensed that he was being watched, or maybe he checked the monitor at regular intervals. Whatever the reason, he looked up less than a second after Heron quit typing.

"Heron?" Kellen blinked and knuckled sleep from his eyes. His face was pale beneath his tan, and his hair stuck out from his head at strange angles. The clock showed not quite midnight. He had probably been asleep. "Is that you or am I dreaming crazy shit up now?"

"Why is Mari in Texas?" Heron typed. The words formed, dark against the white monitor.

Kellen raked a hand through his spiky hair and muttered something too low for the speakers to pick it up. Probably curses. Then he raised his voice and aimed it toward the monitor. "She's following up on a lead, tryin' to figure out who messed you up. One of her contacts holds the patent on those nanites, and she thinks she can get him to shut the buggers down, cut the transmission. Don't worry about her, though. You got other stuff you need to see to. Also, I checked in with her just a couple hours ago, and she was finer'n frog hair."

"Well, she isn't now." Typing became easier, faster. He was finding his voice, at least digitally. "The alarm on her com is screaming. How long have I been offline?"

"Nearly sixteen hours, and we got just over six left till that space elevator comes up and the station moves."

"Damn it." Fussing seemed like the only thing Heron could accomplish at the moment.

Panic congealed into frustration. He found the data stream that led to the cables and followed it all the way to the edge of his body. His mind. His self.

But he couldn't get in. It was walled against him.

He almost told himself to breathe, to steady, but he had to acknowledge the ridiculousness of such a command. His body was breathing fine, was completely relaxed. It was his mind that hurt, that flew in wild hysterical arcs around the space station computer.

He attempted login via a software back door but again encountered failure.

His communications log showed that he'd attempted to log in remotely almost constantly since he'd started this process, but something had blocked him every time. What the fuck was going on?

As he scanned the log, a new message came in. From Angela Neko. Because Mari being in Texas wasn't nearly bad enough. The universe had a sick sense of timing. He couldn't endure a conversation with the senator right now. He accepted her message but pushed it to the side.

As if she felt his touch on her com signal, the queen opened her eyes and stared straight at the camera. At him. "Heron," she said. "Good you are awake. I require your help. Come back."

He attempted to reply to her com signal and encountered no obstacle. All data lines connected to her were wide open. Huh. The glitch must be only in him. Something the nanovirus had done?

"Logging back into my body is problematic," he told her, feeding the message directly into her processor.

The queen didn't need visual or audio inputs. Ones and zeroes were sufficient. Most of the time, he found such scaled-down interaction a challenge and preferred the intricate dance of words and gestures and facial expressions and innuendo that amalgamated to form human communication. None of those methods were available to him right now, though. He would have to concentrate on choosing the proper words.

He missed Mari, who always seemed to understand what he was thinking, or at least what he was feeling. Or maybe she didn't understand, only made it seem like she did. She made him feel like she had his back. Like he wasn't alone.

The situation he found himself in right now would be a ton less frightening if she were here. And not *just* because he would not also be worried for her safety.

Even fragmented, he suspected her physical nearness would make him feel complete.

"Why problematic?" asked the queen.

"I have been glitchy ever since the mercenaries cut into my head in the Pentarc."

"Your remote login and scan were supposed to remove said glitch," she reminded him.

If he'd had a mouth, he would have sighed. "Before I can fix the transmission, I need to fix whatever is locking me out of my own body."

"Very well," she said. "I will help."

But, inside the station computer, he could see her activity. Her whole network was red, pulsing with alarms. The queen was working too hard already.

"Heron?" Kellen asked in a low voice, darting a glance from the monitor to his inert body on the gurney. "If you got any ideas on how I can help, just let me know."

Heron forced himself to think, to plan. He typed to Kellen, "I will need a holographic diagram of my brain. Also, how about satellite feeds for Texas?"

He still needed to stop the nanite-induced transmissions—he hadn't forgotten—but the queen was helping with that right now. First things first. He would get his consciousness back into his body where it belonged.

And then he would get Mari the hell out of Texas.

CHAPTER 14

THEY DROVE ALL NIGHT LONG. ONCE—IN BETWEEN rebel camps and validation checkpoints probably, since Mari hadn't seen any lights—she kind of came to. She was lying on the leather bench seat, and her head rested on something firm and bumpy. She turned her face and smelled laundry detergent and stale cologne. A pearl-faced snap dug into her chin. Nathan's western-style shirt. Her head was in his lap.

"You shouldn't be waking up yet." He shifted, rolling her head up against the bottom curve of the navigation panel. No steering wheel, she remembered. This truck was self-driving. She wanted the other one, the other car. The other him. The vision of Heron that rose in her mind was so solid, so real, that she raised a hand, reaching for him.

And then felt the sting of Nathan's injector-tip syringe against her neck. Darkness curled in on the edges of her vision, and the last thing Mari saw before falling into it was Heron's face. She might even have said his name.

She drowsed awake again only when predawn bled

unrelenting all over her eyelids. She tried just squeezing to keep her eyes shut, but the damn sunlight was too bright, even in its infant state. Something drew her hair back from her face. Somebody shushed her.

It did occur to her, as recent memories organized themselves in her waking brain, that Nathan had situated her so that if she *were* wearing a dentata, the business end would be as far as possible from him. He had her head in his lap instead. Mari almost smiled. It felt good to be feared, even if she was out for the count.

"Waking up again?"

"Looks like." Her tongue felt heavy and bigger than normal. She wanted a drink real bad but didn't trust Nathan to give her an untreated one. "You gonna chem me asleep again?"

"Not this time. I need you to get up on your feet and climb."

In a truck? They were still in that giant fugly truck, right? Mari sat up, grimacing against an eyeball-splitting headache. She was still dressed, though the eyelets on her corset were off by one. Somebody'd undone it and then hooked it back up, and she knew it hadn't been her.

Her skin prickled, and she bit back a wave of sick. Nathan'd had her naked while she was unconscious. She hoped that her dentata threats had at least kept him from raping her, but she didn't like one bit the idea of him groping her. Didn't feel right, for all that he'd done it before.

"I found all your weapons," he said, just as if she'd asked outright. Mari looked at the dash and saw the knife, a syringe, and a microfilament coil all laid out, too far away for her to lunge and grab 'em. Not that she didn't think about it.

No, no, couldn't kill him, couldn't even hurt him. Her brain was still coming out of a fugue, so it took her a little while to remember why she didn't want to hurt Nathan.

The transmission. She needed him to stop it. Oh, right.

She glanced down her arm, but her cuff com and rations bracelet were both missing. How long until the Chiba Station had to move and Heron's nanite halo would go away? Damn it, she needed that number, that link to reality. But she also couldn't ask Nathan for it. Then he'd know that it meant something to her.

It was never a good idea to give Nathan that kind of ammo to use against you. 'Cause he would.

As she watched, he rolled her holdout weapons in a cloth, taped the bundle closed like it was evidence, and slid out his side of the cab. He stowed the cache of weapons in a compartment behind the wide bench seat then locked up the truck.

"Come on out," he said, holding a hand toward her. "I have to show you something."

This wasn't going at all according to Mari's plan. Fact was, with her brain chem-fuzzy like this, she couldn't recall all of that plan. Big parts missing, like what she ought to be doing now. Heron would know. He would have set it all up perfectly. He wouldn't have to be making shit up on the fly like this.

And just thinking about him warmed her up inside. Was he awake yet? He might've had time by now to fix what was broken in his brain. She tried not to remember how pessimistic he'd been right before Kellen had sedated him. She failed.

Vida, estamos en paz.

She just hoped he'd give her a chance to make this right before he pressed Kellen again about rebooting. *Hang on, partner*, she thought, though she knew he couldn't hear her.

When she didn't accept Nathan's offered hand, he grabbed hers and pulled her from the truck. She snatched her arm back but ultimately did as she was told. Damn it, she did. She had never liked taking orders, and she liked it a helluva lot less when those orders came from Nathan Grace.

Her boots crunched on gravel, but her first steps away from the truck were far from sure. She almost fell but steadied herself against the truck. Loose confusion from the chemicals still scattered her brain. She looked around in an attempt to get her bearings. No buildings, just bare Texas scrub and scorched rocks far as she could see.

She followed Nathan to the front of the truck and saw it, bulging up from the horizon like a giant pink wart on the landscape: Enchanted Rock.

Mari frowned. Why here? There weren't any buildings around, no cells to hold her in, no soldiers to keep her in line. It was just a pretty, bald rock. Kind of looked like the sort of place a body'd take someone for execution.

"You been here before?" Nathan asked, all kinds of chatty. He grabbed a pack from the bed of the truck and slung it over his shoulders, clicking the straps and pulling them snug.

The morning was cool, and Mari's plastene jacket had gone missing. Instead of asking for it or something else to cover up with, she rubbed goose bumps on her upper arms. This corset wasn't going to protect much against the wind up there on the summit. If that was, in fact, where she was headed.

"When I was a kid," she replied. "Why're we here, Nathan?"

He flashed her a grin, but it looked like it hurt. "Following orders, per my contract. Just like the last time we went out on a job together. Remember?"

Not as well as she wanted to. Dang chemical haze. She wanted to reach in her skull and slap her brain around a bit.

"Nathan." Mari paused, one hand on the grille of the truck. "I need you to tell me what happened. In Corpus."

He'd started up a graveled path and was about ten paces away, but he turned around now and looked at her. Not smiling. He took a few steps toward her, and Mari felt small. Uneasy.

"You ditched me, angel. Near blew me up, along with those diversion charges. You really don't remember?"

Mari shook her head. She wanted him to go on, to tell her everything, but he didn't say another word, just regarded her with those electric-blue eyes, as if he thought she was lying.

"Somehow thought it was the other way around," she said. "You went dark on me, the federales came, and then they… I looked for you. For a long time, looked for you."

Nathan frowned, raised a hand, like he was reaching for her or something, and then he let it drop. He hunched a shoulder and turned back to the path.

"Summit in thirty. Better get walking."

●   ●   ●

Mounted to the wall in the Chiba Station med bay was a holoprojector connected to a portable MRI. The setup was meant to show surgeons the internal pathways of a body as nanomachines worked to repair it.

Right now, it projected a human brain, enhanced by several degrees of magnification.

The projection tilted, zoomed some more, and finally resolved on an image that looked a lot like a medulla oblongata and its attached spinal cord. But this structure was different than the pictures in medical training simulators. Organic material was interspersed with mechanical bits, extra capacitors to direct neural activity, and deliberately arranged folds that enabled the parts of his mind to communicate and coordinate far faster than a normal human brain.

The projected model was an augmented brain.

Heron's.

He searched it relentlessly, looking for anything odd, any anomaly that would explain his predicament. And on his second pass over the projected image, he found it. In a fissure near where the pons and the midbrain met, tucked up tight against his pineal gland, was a slightly duller bit of metal, darker than the other augments. It was a microscopic oddity, and certainly, if he hadn't had the benefit of magnification and a translucent cross section, he would never have been able to see what was connected to that dark metal disk.

Tiny strands of nanofibers led from it straight to the SIP port on the back of his head, specifically to the part the mercenaries in the Pentarc had hot-wired.

Whoever had marionetted him back at the Pentarc had either known about this access point or had created it.

For the first time, he was glad to be outside of his body, because this realization would have felt like a kick to the gut. Shocking, agonizing. How did the puppeteer know? Heron felt worse than exposed, worse than manipulated. He had been invaded, changed against his will.

However infuriating the knowledge was, though, it was also information. If the puppeteer had used that nanofiber strand to wrest control of his body, what was preventing him from doing the same?

"Kellen," he typed. "Can you plug a cable into my SIP port? Like, an energy-conduit kind of cable?"

Kellen was looking over some medical readouts when Heron typed, so it was several moments before he glanced over and read the monitor. Such a frustrating way to communicate, but, Heron reminded himself, at least they *could* talk.

"That's a lot of wattage," Kellen answered at last. "If we got a power surge on the station or something, it would fry you."

The buzz Adele had taken in her com back at the Pentarc was a grain of sand compared to this beach. He would be worse than knocked out. He would be ruined.

But that was only if the worst happened. In the best-case scenario, he might be able to get back into his body. That potential reward was worth the risk.

"I know the odds," he typed. "I need to try it despite. Let me know when you're ready to plug in."

Kellen read the words, said something nasty under his breath, and went over to the body on the gurney. He looked down at it a long time, facing away from the security camera. Heron wondered what his friend was thinking. Kellen placed a hand on Heron's shoulder, patted it a couple of times while shaking his head, probably muttering something unflattering about crazy stupid ideas. Ultimately, he made his decision, though, and knelt on the floor, rummaging through the pile of cables and wires.

Heron wished he could sigh in relief or smile. Instead, he went back to work.

The wonderful thing about existing in the space station computer rather than a limited human body was the speed. While Kellen hunted down the wiring, Heron had plenty of time to check in with all his resources.

First, he connected with Chloe. She and Garrett were on the spaceplane and still almost an hour away from Mari's location but headed in that direction. Communicating digitally, they reviewed Chloe's programming and made sure she had an emergency medical routine loaded, just in case.

Backups for backups, just like how he planned a job.

An unanswered message sat in his communication queue, and he recognized it as Senator Neko's request from earlier. He read it. She was requesting haven, and something about the plea struck him, maybe its simplicity. Maybe its potential usefulness. In his ideal scenario, he would be back in control of his body, the nanotransmission would be severed, and Mari would be out of Texas and with him. But of course, she wouldn't be completely safe so long as the continental government wanted her for murder. Angela Neko could help with that. He replied to her message with instructions to meet him at the Pentarc.

He checked in with Viktor, the bodyguard he'd hired

to keep an eye on Mari in the event something happened to him. As it turned out, hiring Viktor was the most prescient thing he'd done in days. However, despite the bodyguard's vigilance, Viktor had been thrown off when Mari had gotten into a stranger's truck back in Dallas, and he'd lost time in arranging a transport to follow her. He was approximately twenty minutes behind her but assured Heron that he would catch up.

Last of all, Heron checked in with his satellites. He'd accessed several feeds, but most were visual only, and with dawn about to break over Texas, those satellite feeds had only recently gone live. Except…well, that was odd. The feeds were still dark.

All of them.

That wasn't right. The sun would be up completely in less than an hour. He should have a clear image of central Texas, awash in predawn lavender. He zoomed out, and a line of visuals appeared. Clean line, starting just outside a public park.

The satellite update blipped. Same ribbon of interstate, leading up to the same clear line of black.

No truck.

Where had she gone?

The first burst of confusion gave way to understanding. Someone had placed intrusion countermeasures—ICE—over the whole area. Whoever had done it clearly had something there to hide, probably something even more important than Mari Vallejo.

Well, more important to governments or geopolitics, maybe. Not more important to Heron. And he had a lot of experience busting through ICE like this.

Just not as a disembodied partial consciousness

getting irregular satellite feeds. He waited the four seconds for the satellite to cycle and update its feed. Those moments felt like eternity.

The satellite showed a fresh image: still an empty road, still a giant, shielded nothingness where the park should be.

Under normal circumstances, Enchanted Rock would be a boneheaded place to take a captive. The centerpiece was an enormous igneous outcropping over four hundred feet high and half again as wide. It might offer some nice options for hiding from eyes on the ground, but it provided no cover whatsoever from overhead views.

Except right now. Only the blackness that shielded it right now was anything but natural.

"All righty," Kellen said. "I have the cable ready to plug in. You ready?"

Heron shifted his focus to the med lab, to the fat cable in Kellen's hand and the zoomed-in hologram of his brain. He magnified the image further and painted the dark metal disk.

"My queen," he said into her robot brain, "once I connect my body to the station, I will need a power spike at this location."

"I recommend a three-second burst at 800 milliamps," she said.

"We can start there but should have power available to hit it harder."

"Dangerous," she warned him.

"Noted," he replied.

They coordinated a countdown digitally and put it up on the monitor. Kellen plugged the cable into the back of Heron's head and moved one of the monitoring electrodes so that the current would pass over the odd metal disk.

When the count reached zero, the queen shunted power from the station. Straight into the cable.

This sort of thing ought to hurt a man, but Heron felt nothing.

The metal on the projection darkened further…and then it bent inward, pulling away from its organic frame, leaving microscopic openings on the sides, tiny fairy doors into the data stream. And that was all the space Heron needed.

He pushed, flooding the fissure with energy, connection, data. Himself. The gate gave beneath his assault. In a matter of moments, he surged into his own mind, inhabiting familiar neural connections.

Home.

One by one, he engaged systems: autonomics, visual, auditory, peripheral. Coming alive, gasping, filling his lungs after a long suffocation.

Out of instinct, he reached for her.

She wasn't there. Of course she wasn't. She wasn't even nearby, touchable. She was trapped in black ICE in Texas. *Hold on, querida. I will find you.*

On an inhalation, he tasted hot metal, new plastic, and…bacon? No, that must be a memory, not a sensory input. A good memory, too. Best. Even without direct control of facial muscles, it drew a swift smile.

"Well, that happened," Kellen said. "This mean you're back?"

Heron tried to reply, but his throat was sore, dry. He swallowed, flexed his hands, stretched his fingers.

"Nah, don't talk yet, just keep on with the typing. That's working fine." Kellen slid tablets beneath Heron's hands and went on, as if this sort of thing happened every day. "Now then, we're going after Mari, right? We have eight minutes till that tether comes up."

Heron tested his tongue and went to work on that ICE. "Let's make them count."

●   ●   ●

Mari's throat was parched and raw by the time she and Nathan crested the summit. She'd been breathing through her mouth, thanks to all that lovely scrub cedar clogging up her nose and making her eyes water, and Nathan hadn't mentioned anything about water, damn him. Plus, the hike was a lot more vertical than it looked. Her thighs burned. She took a moment there at the top to flex them, rest. She looked around.

Pink stained the sky all over, and if circumstances had been a bit different, she might have admired the view.

Even with the pockmarks of orbit burns and the scars of fences, the landscape stretched off in all directions, horizons as sepia-clear as sweet iced tea. A family of bone-skinny deer finished up its forage, slunk single file back into the muted scrub. A breeze ruffled pale buds on the prickly pears. Tough girl, Texas.

As far as places to die went, this one sure didn't suck.

She guessed she ought to feel some fear, but she didn't. This was home. Hers. Just seeing it, smelling it, made her want to kick something's ass.

Palms on her kneecaps, she looked over at Nathan. He was crouching beside his pack, dicking with something at the back of his head. She'd half expected to find herself staring down a gun barrel, but this sight struck her as a mite more wrong.

"Nathan?"

But he didn't answer. Early-morning light glinted off something shiny in his hand, and she looked closer. A knife? No, a slim metal hook. Mari watched in mute horror as Nathan pried the cap off the SIP in the back of his head, slipped a piece of tech into a socket, and then sank against the rock, fingers splaying like frog feet on the granite.

"Nathan!"

Mari tried to run over to him, but footing was treacherous up here, and she automatically compensated, slowing to keep herself upright. Not that she would have made it in time anyway. She splashed through a puddle of stagnant rainwater, felt it soak the hem of her crinoline, and halted, still, at the edge.

Nathan looked up at her. His face, his blue eyes.

But somebody else was looking out through them.

"Didn't I tell you to do better research?" he said. "You have so much to learn, little monster."

CHAPTER 15

NOT-NATHAN GOT TO HIS FEET, TAKING WAY LONGER than Nathan would if he was controlling his own body. His posture was all wrong when he stood: swayback straight and with his head held back, chin down, a little man trying to look impressive. The person marionetting Nathan's body now was slower, too. And crueler. The expression on his face made Mari's fingers cold, and that had nothing to do with the stiff morning breeze.

Might have had a smidge to do with the gun he pulled, though.

She eyed that gun hard. She knew Nathan's body was wired, but she didn't know how good his physical alterations were these days. Could she rush him, tackle him, and get the gun? She sifted through the scenario for a few whole heartbeats before she remembered why she was here. And where she'd met the puppeteer before.

Little monster? The fuck.

"Pentarc, right?" she said. "We have got to stop hooking up like this."

He tilted his head and frowned. "Before the Pentarc,

actually. You really don't know who I am? I had thought even your brain might work through the logic, given time."

Mari flushed hot at the insult. Sure, she knew she wasn't the sharpest knife in the drawer, but she sure as shit could use all those other knives to slit somethin' when she wanted. Her hands fisted at her sides, but she didn't creep any closer to her captor.

He raised the gun, one-handed and wishy-wristed, and she did her best not to snort. Nathan was nothing if not consistent: big-ass dualie of a truck, big-ass hand-cannon of a Model 29 with an 8-3/8-inch barrel. Probably thought in the back of his brain that he was some twentieth-century gunslinger. Typical of him, all hat and no cattle. But even if Nathan himself had a clue how to handle that thing, whoever was inhabiting his body at the moment was in for a surprise.

If not-Nathan pulled that trigger, the kick from a gun like that was like to break his face. Not to mention, even in the best of circumstances, it had to be weird, balance-wise, to fire a weapon using someone else's hand. Mari thought about the couple of shots she'd gotten off in Heron's car, and she almost smiled. Okay, *almost* weird. Firing *his* weapon had been a thrill and a half.

"Okay then. You the TPA?"

Not-Nathan's eyebrows flared, and he took a half step back. "Me, a government? I am flattered, but, er, no. Guess again."

"You know, guessing games aren't really my thing," Mari said, "so how's about we cut to the chase? I'm lookin' to talk to whoever planted that shit in Heron's head. That you?"

"Essentially." He gave a little bow. Cocky bastard.

Mari went out on a limb. "Nathan didn't shut down the transmission, did he?"

"I don't see how he could have. He has no concept of nanorobotics." His eyebrows rose in tandem with his chin, a supremely confident, self-satisfied smirk Mari had never seen on his face before. "You did realize your ex is something of an imbecile, right? But useful. He fetched you as I asked, so there's that."

"And don't forget pretty."

"I hadn't noticed." But he added a second hand to his shooter stance, holding the weapon more firmly, as if he just now realized Nathan's pretty face was behind that kick, and he didn't want it to get bonked on the recoil. Liar. This man, whatever his true identity, was keenly aware of his physical beauty.

He was also haughty, acting so sure he could handle that gun. And meaner than a sack of snakes. Now, why did all that sound familiar?

"So the transmission," she said. "How do I make it stop? If you're part of the whole of TPA, I could turn myself in to you, and you could extradite me to UNAN. Is that your endgame? Buy up some UNAN goodwill and get a bunch of top-secret data from Heron's head in the process?"

He half laughed. "As endgames go, that one is terribly limited. You always did think you were cleverer than you really are, chulita."

Chulita. Cutie. Pretty little thing in a pink dress with flowers. Too-hot university office in the summertime. *Now run along to your aunt, chulita. I'm working.*

Mari choked. "Dad?"

His face twisted, but Mari couldn't tell if it was in preparation for a huggy-kissy reunion or cold, relentless fury. She figured fury, 'cause even as she was processing the what-the-fuckery of her realization, the puppeteer controlling her ex-lover's body raised the gun. Pointed it.

And shot her.

Pain bloomed along the top of her leg. She went to her knees, instinctively grasping the wound. Thigh. Wasn't anything important in a thigh, right?

But holy shit, it hurt.

•   •   •

Nine hundred miles away, Heron flinched against the gurney. His satellites still didn't have clear images of her, and he still struggled to clear the dome of black ICE over Enchanted Rock, but somehow, despite all the interference, he knew the moment she hurt. Sharp pain, in the thigh.

He needed visual right now. He needed to see what, or who, threatened her. Who had hurt her.

He needed to hurt somebody right back.

Across the room, he locked eyes with the queen.

"Time is up. I am retracting the tether as we speak," she said. "Nanite halo is failing presently, so expect your unwanted transmission to recommence. I am sorry."

Fury ripped through him, and he didn't bother trying to gather it up or tamp it down. He wasn't angry with the queen. He was angry with circumstance, with fate, with the limits of technology, with everybody who'd tried to hurt Mari when none of their conflicts were or had ever been her fault.

Most of all, he was angry with himself.

What fucking use was his gigantic neural if he didn't use it to save the woman he loved? Fuck the nanite transmission, fuck the cloud, fuck the whole goddamn digital world and everybody plugged into it. Mari *needed* him. Finally, after all these years, she needed him.

And he knew how he could help her.

"How fast can you get me to the Pentarc?" he asked the queen.

She tilted her head, and her eyebrows bowed in sympathy, as if she knew what he contemplated. "Currently, I employ thrusters to keep Chiba steady. Without them, we move at 17,450 miles per hour. I can have you there in three minutes."

"Do it."

"What's happening?" Kellen's voice cut in, edging on desperate.

"She's hurt." The words tore from Heron's own mouth, though he did not recognize his voice. "Mari's hurt."

"How can you tell?"

"I'm not sure, honestly. Did you do anything to her com before she left? Maybe boost it somehow?"

Kellen flushed. "I implanted a com with extended range and a faceprint spoofer, so she wouldn't be stopped at checkpoints or picked up by the feds."

"Ah." Heron squeezed his eyes shut. "Thank you."

That was one hell of a com. He searched for its signal, the link that would bring him to her. He couldn't see her, couldn't touch her, probably couldn't even send her a coherent message. But if her pain had transmitted itself to him, perhaps his comfort would find her.

He wasn't certain how long it took to find her

signal—time had become slow and gelatinous—but eventually, buried in all the interference caused by the ICE, he located a single pinprick of light, a data stream busting its way out of the dome. He locked his attention to it.

Hang in there, querida. I'm coming for you.

"Moving into position over the arcology," the queen said. "Putting down the tether. Stand by."

Still focused on Mari's com signal, he didn't look for a visual on the Pentarc, but knowing it was below him, shining in the sand and harboring a nodal connection to the cloud, hope flooded him.

Of all the foolish plans he'd thought up in his life, this was the one that gave him the most peace. He knew the danger of logging on to the cloud, but if ever there was a moment to risk everything, he was living it right now. He decided he would go in through the Pentarc, and he'd find Mari. And if their link was as strong as he suspected, as strong as it seemed to be, as strong as his soul screamed it must be, there was no way he could get lost in there.

He would find her. He would save her.

He opened his eyes and found the queen still looking back at him.

She nodded almost imperceptibly, and he *pushed*.

Fell.

Squeezed on all sides, the weight of data strangling him, he put his head down and willed himself through it, into it. Into that tiny point of access, that bright lure of connection.

He blew through the Pentarc's closed system and out into the cloud with a howl.

Speed had nothing on the thrill of finally, voraciously stretching his neural.

Input, input, input: Go. Surge. Flying Mach 3 with his brain on fire. All the space in the universe, and he filled it. All of it. Roaring into that black, taking its reins, felt a little bit like fucking Mari.

Just a little. God, he loved her. Had he told her as much? He would.

The thought centered him for the split second when he could have been lost. Bright as a thread of free-fae, the com signal led him straight to her.

There, at the end of his thread, Mari pulsed with life. He couldn't see her with his eyes, but he could feel her with every important part of his neural.

Hurt. She was hurt.

Rage ignited him.

He tapped, and the black ICE in Texas shattered. The TPA had two satellites of its own, launched in secret about six months ago. These weren't shielded against him at all, not anymore, and he looked through their lenses and saw the whole of the rock, Mari on its summit like a fallen goddess. Her hair was loose and blowing in the wind, and so far, it looked like only one other person was up there with her. If he knew Mari, she had a fall-back weapon, a last-ditch surprise for whoever that other figure on the rock face might be. Heron could probably sit back now and watch it all unfold. But he wouldn't.

Backups for backups, and he was *here*.

He saw Viktor, now leaving the pebbled trail and mounting the rock proper, slowed a bit by the bristle of illegal weaponry he carried.

But even that sight didn't satisfy Heron completely.

He wanted to *be* the hand of God, to reach down through time and space and pick her the hell up. Hold her precious and apart from all this. God knew, she'd been through enough. He bit back the surge again, the need to stretch himself, to appropriate more of the cloud matrix.

On a wave of data and angry, Heron ingested the UNAN military equipment databases, all of them, and sorted their pieces like cutlery in a drawer. He found a helicopter already in the air, taking toxicity samples near Fredericksburg, and with a flex of digital will, he commandeered it.

In those first critical moments inside the cloud, with his neural expanding exponentially, he didn't think about anchoring his consciousness first. He didn't think about much beyond finding her, getting her to safety. Punishing anyone who hurt her.

He remotely accessed the helicopter's autocontrol rig, clamped his eyes shut, and surged into space.

●　●　●

"I must confess that you're taking all this better than I had expected," said not-Nathan/Dad, standing over her with the gun trained more or less on her head. "You always tended toward dramatics, so frankly, I expected some freaking out. You've certainly changed."

Since the night of the Austin riots, the last time she saw him? Hells yeah, she'd changed. "People tend to do that in eight fucking years," she said, no longer in any way worried about keeping the bitterness out of her voice. "And I'm freaking out. Believe me, I am. Also possibly bleeding out."

He sighed. "No, you aren't."

"You shot me!"

"Oh please. Look at the entry wound."

Mari stared down at her thigh. She'd been holding the pretty, rumpled crinoline, bunched tight against the spot that ached like nipple hooks, but now she wadded up the scratchy material, exposing her garter holster—now empty, thanks to Nathan—and…the wound.

Huh. Yeah, it was there, and yeah, it was purple and ragged and ugly as all get out. But it wasn't leaking like she'd expected. Not even close. Could Nathan have modded, say, a .22 to make it look like that stupid hand-cannon? She poked at the edge of the wound until a ribbon of blood pressed out reluctantly. Hell. More like a pellet gun.

Words tumbled before she could stop them. "What the fuck?"

"Chitosan hemostats, if I had to guess. Your blood chemistry has been tampered with, obviously. Among all the other things she did to you."

Every jigger of said blood in Mari's body chilled at those words. Tampered with? Oh God. That would mean…

"You called me Dad, but you really shouldn't." His voice was a lot gentler than it had been, like he was remembering or regretting, though she wasn't about to pin something as sane as affection on him. He was still pointing a gun at her, after all. "My daughter died in a south Texas prison. She was tortured to death by a rogue UNAN ops team that was trying to get information on me."

Oh yeah, this was totally Dad. He'd never once eased the Band-Aid off. He'd always been a ripper. "Fuck you. I'm right here."

He just stared down at her, cold as cryo. "You are. She is not."

It hit Mari like a low-orbit nuke, what Dad was telling her. He wasn't shushing her or dismissing her to her aunt's care or trying to get her out of his business. He was telling her that she literally was not his daughter. Not Marisa Vallejo. That she was *something else*.

It was on the tip of her tongue to tell him he was full of shit, but his words had the stink of truth on 'em. How many times had she wondered at her unnaturally steady aim, her ability to pick up on coms real quick, how she couldn't remember senior prom but could effortlessly calculate the vectors on a squeeze even though she'd never studied those kinds of maths?

If she was altered, a post-human of some kind, that would explain why Dad hadn't contacted her after the revolution got rolling, why he was using her so callously right now, just another cog in one of his grand schemes. No need to worry over the feelings of a... So, if she wasn't his daughter, what exactly was she?

A thing, the darkthing whispered, full of glee. *Just a thing*.

And then, in a different voice in memory: *a precious thing*.

Like Heron?

Oh.

Her fury eased. Her confusion settled. Her leg throbbed.

"So you're saying somebody altered me after that job down in Corpus? Well, tell me all about it. Come on, turkey, you can't lay that kind of rotten egg and pretend it don't stink." Eight years ago, she'd been captured. Tortured. Killed? Had they messed with her brain, too?

Had they geared and wired her? Holy buttonsucker, what exactly was underneath her skin right now?

"You'll have to ask Peetey," Dad said calmly. "She got to your body before I could."

Peetey. The queen. Dad's prototype mech-clone, the one Heron had filched during the Austin riots. *She'd* done a rebuild on Mari? Why the hell would she do that? Unless… "Jesus, *Dad*, did you just shoot me to get Heron back for stealing your robot girlfriend? Or to get *her* back for modding me? Either way, that's pretty messed up right there."

Not-Nathan cocked his head, and now Mari knew for sure it was her dad in there. Daddy always did have that how-could-I-have-sired-an-idiot look. Gave it to her plenty, back when. Man, she hated that look.

"You believe this is all revenge, chulita? I've gone to rather a lot of trouble for revenge. Besides, I would visit revenge on Peetey differently. And if all I wanted to do was hurt Farad, I could have slagged you in the Pentarc."

"What do you want, then? 'Cause you're making no sense to me."

He leaned down, locked eyes with her. As if he were trying to speak to Heron through her. As if he thought they might be linked or something. "That boy has been smitten with you for as long as I've known him. It's pathetic, really. But again, useful. By injuring you, I've guaranteed that he'll expose himself, either by coming here directly or by plugging into the cloud. He does the former, I get him. He does the latter, the transmission recommences."

What was it Heron had said about that transmission?

That it was everything about him—and about her? She'd thought at the time he meant data like safe-haven addresses and known affiliates. But what if he'd meant structural schematics, designs for the alterations he'd undergone? And whatever the queen had done to her.

If Dad was telling the truth and wasn't lying out his eyeballs—a theory she still wasn't ready to abandon entirely—Mari's body contained plenty of illegal tech the black market might covet as well.

Assuming Heron knew about her alterations. Which begged a question she suddenly ached to ask him. That desire, more than anything else, compelled her to find a way off this damn rock.

If only her brain could come up with a plan. Any plan.

Dad was still talking. Intense and leaning over her in a sad parody of villainy. She figured she might as well listen. "...so I get his neural-alt schematics, her discomfort, and you, whatever you are now, as a bonus. I. Win."

That was true. He always won. It was his personal motto. Yes, her father was that cheesy. Apparently also that cracked.

The wetness on her hand meant the wound was bleeding again, faster now. Did those blood chemicals have a time limit or something? The pain was different, too, deeper.

Also, those damn nanites in Heron's head were still transmitting, he was running out of time and, lord, it was hot up here on the rock, even at stupid o'clock in the morning, and Mari was just so damn sick of this whole thing.

Still holding on to her throbbing and now bleeding leg, she nodded up at the gun. "Fine. You win. Whatever. You gonna shoot me again or what?"

Looking a little sheepish, Dad tucked the gun into his waistband. "I suppose not. I wasn't sure how quickly you would heal, but perhaps your alterations were sloppily done. Which would make sense, of course, since Peetey wouldn't have had complete schematics and would have improvised. She wasn't built with brain-matrix autoduplication in mind…" And on.

Except, now he was getting all chatty, Mari realized she had zero interest in talking to him anymore. Far as she was concerned, his only use to her at this point was getting that transmission cut. She didn't want to hug him. She didn't want his approval. She didn't want to be just like him when she grew up. She was beyond all that little-girl bullshit.

The realization made her both powerful and sad. So much for finding her long-lost dad. Made her want to vomit, thinking of all she'd gone through, all she'd risked to find the son of a bitch.

Of course, it was always possible the waves of nausea slurping up against the back of her throat were the shock setting in. Clearly, whoever had rebuilt her hadn't compensated for shock. Her teeth were starting to chatter, but she ground them tight against each other.

Mech-clones didn't shiver. They didn't cry. And they didn't bleed. These were truth nuggets she'd learned a long time ago. A little bloom of red at the entry wound, but then their subdermal vasoconstrictors pinched off the release of fluid, compensated, steadied heart rate and limbic chemicals. Tough little shits.

She shoved a fist into her still-seeping thigh wound and mashed her teeth together. *So am I. Tough as a mech-clone*.

She blinked through a pain haze, slinking her gaze along the pink granite. The sun was coming up strong now.

And some*body* was coming over the eastern edge of the rock. Striking figure. Gigantic, blond, bristling with weapons. Her goddamn-motherfucking Viking stalker from Dallas. Was he working for Dad, too, here to retrieve them? But that didn't make sense. Heron wasn't here yet. How long would Dad wait for him?

The Viking raised his weapon.

Oh shit. Her leg burned at the movement, but she stood up anyway, compensating for the vertigo. It all happened so quickly, but Mari never felt out of the moment. She homed in on that weapon, a tasty smaller-bore autocannon that, in better circumstances, Mari might have coveted, and traced its aim to Nathan.

Nathan, who wasn't even there, whose body had been coopted so her asshole father could have his chitchattery, mustache-twirling villain moment. And Nathan was gonna get drilled into a mountainside for being a pawn? Nope. Her instinct wasn't to sit by and watch somebody else get mowed down like a patch of brown grass.

She lurched for Nathan, wrapped her arms around him, heard his huff of breath and the crunch of bones as she hauled him to the ground.

The bullets pinged like sheet rain coming in sideways, cold on her naked shoulder blades, and Mari pressed her face to Nathan's back, closing her eyes against the seam of his shirt. A big part of her wanted to take the hit, to go down and stay down, but instinct won again.

The Viking stopped firing. She heard the clack of him tossing one weapon aside, probably reaching for another. This dude was a professional, definitely better trained than those thugs at the Pentarc. And he'd been shooting at Nathan, so probably wasn't working for Dad. Could be UNAN, come to take her out for what she did to Senator Neko's husband. But of course, there were other entities and governments who wanted a piece of her, and probably just as many who wanted to off Nathan. How stupid it'd been to place both fat targets out here on a bare rock.

Mari reached around, underneath Nathan, and grabbed at his pants. Lord, she was glad he wasn't aware for this part. She found the butt of the gun and yanked, skinning her knuckles over the rock.

Her leg wasn't obeying orders anymore, so she used the other one to push herself back over, onto her back, and she brought both hands up, cradling Nathan's hand cannon like the sweet unmodded thang it was. Her fingers felt far away, disconnected, a little numb. But she could still stroke the trigger. Oh yes, she could.

She squinted against the sunlight, forcing her eyes to sight in that Viking brute.

Didn't take much searching. He stood right over her. Unarmed. Looking white as grits.

"No, please, God. Miss Vallejo, are you okay?" He crouched and reached out a hand, and Mari settled her grip.

She thought about pulling the trigger, honest to God she did, but the odd thing was, she couldn't feel that finger at all anymore. Couldn't feel her hands. Couldn't even feel that burn in her thigh, and damn it, she actually was hunting for it.

She blinked, tried to swallow, but her mouth was so, so dry.

Blood loss must've been worse than it looked, she thought, as a shadow appeared behind the Viking: big-ass gray shadow, accompanied by a roaring in her ears. She blinked again.

Whoa.

Not a shadow. A Pave Low V, sliding up above the edge of the rock, rotors humming like a goddamned gospel chorus. On either side, dual missile clamps unrolled, armed to the teeth, looking like nothing so much as a smile unfurling.

Heron. Jacked into death-on-rotors, coming for her. Like he always had.

Mari's tired, dust-stained face smiled back, and all she could think as she felt the black of unconsciousness sweep over her was, *Don't them things have self-lubricating rotors? Kinda sexy, partner.*

CHAPTER 16

Noise, noise, noise. The entire universe was noise, but he had to focus. Forced himself to focus. Helicopter. He was a helicopter. He tested the systems. Mixture: full rich. Directional gyro: aligned with magnetic compass. Altimeter: clearing the rock. Weapons: engage. All weapons lock on.

Noise cut in again, bits of unrelated data swirling into his consciousness. A secret army, a drone army, hiding. *Don't care, don't need to know.* If it had nothing to do with Mari or the helicopter, it wasn't important. But the information persisted, burrowing into his attention.

The wild whip of data against his mind overwhelmed. Too much. His focus broke. Little break, but violent.

He caromed away from his tether, screaming for it.

No arms, no legs, no eyes. Just space. Infinite space, and noise. And—cowl flaps? Like spider legs. Was he coming down? Going up? Which? Steady.

The cloud smelled like limoncello.

Lost.

• • •

Mari thought she'd opened her eyes, but it might have been more of that mind-over-matter bullshit. She still couldn't feel much, but she did hear, from far away, that humming of rotors winding down. Did they have choppers in hell? Must.

"Am I dead this time?" That disbelief merged with pain merged with uncertainty merged with love merged with hope. She was overwhelmed, outgunned, and just a frog's hair past giving up completely. But more than anything, she was flat-out tired.

"Uh, no. But you sure gave it a go," said a disembodied voice. So apparently, she was imagining voices in her head now, too. Awesome.

This one echoed that same certainty, that same feeling she'd had back in the Pentarc when Heron had spoken in her com. But it didn't *feel* like him. Which was actually what convinced her, ultimately, the voice was real. If she were to imagine Heron's voice as some sort of mental soother, she'd never make it so…what was the word? Chipper. And all kinds of wrong.

No, whoever was peeking up her thoughts was definitely not Heron.

"Kinky," the voice in her head said. "I wondered that about you, but Dr. Farad would never kiss and tell. Alas."

Sweet voice. Unbearably so.

"Chloe?"

"Yep, yep, that's my name. Malphonetic. Ephemeral on the end. Perky!"

Mari blinked again, tried to sit up, and choked down

a wave of nausea. Above her curved the dull gray spines of a cargo helicopter, but the rotors were still. The smell of weapon lubricants lay heavy on her tongue and in the back of her throat, but after the bright chaos on top of that rock, the darkness and oil smells struck Mari as oddly homey. Safe.

Chloe was sitting by Mari's hip, a bright point in all the shadow, though she was looking down and frowning. Her mouth stayed still when she spoke. "Forgive me if I don't waste effort on facial movement and excessive speech. Am busy."

Mari looked down her body. Someone had pushed up her crinoline, and although Chloe was seated on the helo deck, her right forearm was inside Mari's leg.

Literally shoved inside. Mari swallowed bile.

Was the wound big enough for that? When she'd peeked at it up on the rock, it had seemed average to smallish and closing even as she'd watched, easily fixed. Unless the shot had nicked something important in there, she'd be fine. She *should* be fine.

A twinge in her thigh caused her to holler and arch up off the deck plates. "The fuck! What are you doing?"

"Be still," Chloe told her. "I'm trying to get this bleeding to stop. Where's it all coming from? Yow."

"Yow?" Mari echoed. "That a technical term?" And bleeding? Wasn't it supposed to be not bleeding? Or had she imagined that whole Mari-not-a-real-girl discussion with Dad?

"Uh, can I do anything?" Another voice, and once Mari looked over and caught sight of him, she wondered how she'd missed him in the first place.

That gigantic blond Viking was crouched not three

feet away, wearing rubber gloves and holding a syringe and looking nervous. Mari wasn't keeping a list or anything, but that had to be one of the oh-hell-no-est sights she'd ever encountered.

Chloe shifted, and the face that had been still and focused now animated in a rush, as if she had just thrown a switch and come to life.

"Yes! Viktor, I need you to—put that needle down first, good—now reach behind her knee, press your first two fingers against that ridge—see the one there in that hollow?—and tell me what you feel."

Mari wasn't sure what she thought about being felt up by a guy she hadn't even really met. True, she admired his taste in weapons, and if Heron was letting him live after all those bullets, he had to be a safe bet. But still.

When he touched her, she felt the pressure but not the surface brush. Local anesthetics, maybe? Well, that would explain why the pain had receded to a dull ache as opposed to a flash fire.

"She has heartbeat. Is that right?"

"Yeah. Now grab the other knee, in the back. Same thing?" Since when had Chloe become a medic? Mari thought she must have missed something important.

"More flutter on the right one, in comparison."

Something shifted inside, a pinprick but deep. Chloe's voice was cool as mimosa. "Okay. What about now?"

The Viking—Viktor, was it?—paused like he was thinking hard. Finally, he nodded. "It is more alike now."

"Yay!" Chloe's squeal caused a wholly different pain in Mari's spine. "The big artery is intact, and the little ones will be easy to fix. We have time. Dr. Farad loaded all those schematics in, so me, I get to play doctor." She waggled her perfect eyebrows. Not comforting. "Okay, now, Mari, I need you to flex your foot."

She did.

Chloe didn't move. "Go ahead."

She did it again.

"Mari?"

"What? I did it."

"No, you didn't."

Mari was about to ask what that meant, but Chloe was moving again. Moving not like a human being would, more like a doll on strings. Sometimes, her sections didn't meet up all the way, like the arm would be moving but the shoulder wouldn't shift the way it ought to, and an empty space would peek between. In vids, this would indicate subpar animation. In a person, it was just unsettling.

Earlier, when they'd first met, Chloe had probably been concentrating on holding her physical appearance together. Now, the fae had other priorities, and some of her person simulation suffered for that. It looked deeply wrong, but Mari mentally slapped herself.

What, wrong like Heron was wrong? Wrong like *she* was, if what Dad had said was true? Did somebody have to be a hundred percent human to be *right*? Fuck that. Just fuck it.

Chloe sat back on her haunches, withdrawing her arm from Mari's flesh. No, Mari could see now, there wasn't a giant hole in her leg. Chloe had just been able to rearrange her nanobit structure and slip in through that wee hole, the one the bullet had made.

"Here's where we stand," Chloe said. "The bullet's still in there, which isn't a big deal, except that it's close to your sciatic nerve. If it migrates even a little bit, the pain will be pretty intense. Either that, or you won't feel anything, which is worse. I can't get to it when I'm like this." She looked straight at the wall. "Dr. Farad, I'm going to have to embed."

Mari had no idea what Chloe was talking about, but hearing Heron's name caused her limbs to flood with warmth.

"Is he here?" Mari asked. "Can I talk to him? Heron! What about that transmission? Is it down?" She touched her throat before she remembered Nathan had nicked her com.

Chloe cocked her head to the side, eerily like Heron did sometimes when he was getting a lot of input. After a heartbeat, Chloe's eyes focused again. She leaned over Mari. "I don't know. I had him back before we got to you on the plane, but I can't find him now. Must have lost him for a sec. Be still, Mari. This will pinch."

Must have lost him. No, no. Her head roiled. She was gonna horf.

"What do you mean, can't find him? Where the fuck is he? And what do you mean pinch? What's gonna pinch?"

But Chloe dispersed, right there as Mari watched. Her nanobits spread out into a mist, blanketing the surface of Mari's body. Cool, soft. A dust of rain just beneath her clothes. Settling against her skin. Pushing soft as kisses. And then…merging through it.

Hot, that merge.

Mari screamed.

Live fire stabbed through every pore. She'd had a bikini wax once, and she could safely say that this was full body and a thousand times worse. Maybe a million. Felt like her skin had been flayed off, rubbed with a wire brush, and slapped back on raw, all in the space of a heartbeat.

But afterward, when the next heartbeat thundered in, all that pain receded. Instantly. Just like that. Was the darndest thing.

"Okeydokey. I've just implanted myself subdermally," Chloe told her, only now, Mari didn't just hear that voice in her ear — she felt it all over, even though she couldn't see a physical manifestation. "I'm in the process of repairing the tissue in your leg and those scratches on your back. Try not to move too much, 'k?"

The pain in Mari's leg had gone away. The other owie had been so vicious that she hadn't noticed the missing leg twinge right off. But Chloe was right. Mari didn't feel any pain at all. Instead, she had this too-sweet sensation on the outside of her thigh, exactly the way her gums had felt when she was seven and ate a whole bag of stale Peeps in one sitting. "This is so freaky. But I need you to tell me about Heron, Chloe. What do you mean you lost him? You mean you *lost* him?"

"Lost does not mean dead, silly. I just can't find him in the cloud. I mean, he's there, but sort of, um, all over the place. Now hold still. You wiggle."

Mari took a couple of deep breaths, but they didn't do any good. The whole world still felt wonky, and she was falling off.

Viktor moved in closer. He grabbed her left hand and held it between his giant meaty paws. Mari was conscious enough to be grateful for the gesture, even though what she really wanted was to crawl inside herself, or better yet, inside Heron's embrace, and sit tight until the crazy stopped.

But she couldn't. Because he was "all over the place." Immaterial. Dispersed. Lost. That had been his fear about logging in. That he would be lost in the cloud. What did it even mean? And how could she get him back?

"Look, Chloe, this medical stuff is not your programming, and it feels really complicated. Why don't you just stabilize things and get me to Heron?"

"No, waiting is definitely not in my programming. According to my emergency medical program, I need to get you fixed now, or it won't be worth doing. And also, this is probably a very bad time to say so, but I am feeling your skin right now, and it's just brilliant. I—*mmmm*—want to rub you all over with something semiviscid, maybe buttercream frosting."

Well, that had come out of nowhere. However, it didn't strike Mari as wholly strange. Truth be told, she was used to thinking dirty thoughts at the absolute wrong moment, usually when she was thick in the middle of a gunfight or some other tense situation.

Back in the Pentarc, for instance, she'd been plenty worried about Heron and the feds and her own unexpected capacity for murder, and the first thing she'd thought of was how intensely she wanted to fuck him in the vestibule of Mrs. Weathering's living unit. As if all those other bad things would just wait till she got that sizzle between her legs sorted out.

Was that ability to disconnect, to channel sex right on the end of impending death, another indication that Mari was not human? After all, Chloe seemed to have a similar context problem, and she was pretty much the definition of nonhuman.

Mari shook her head, trying to dislodge the wild suppositions. She didn't want to follow the logic. She didn't want it to be true.

But would it really be so bad to be a machine? She was already in love with one, after all.

"Wiggling again."

Mari realized that she could feel her face again. She opened her eyes and wet her lips. She couldn't move much, else Chloe was like to crack the whip on her again, but she glanced down without shifting her head.

Her skin burbled. For a second there, she had one of those alien-birth moments: the surface of her thigh shifted, bulged, and the wound gaped open. The bullet oozed out.

Weird-looking thing, that bullet. Mari'd fired acres of the little suckers, crafted still others on hired lathes, but she'd never yet yanked one out of a body after it'd done its work. Looked smashed, sideways, ruined, and when it rolled down the side of her leg, it left a squiggle of blood, just like a snail on Aunt Boo's porch. Only uglier. It wet-plinked on the deck.

Mari swallowed a couple of times, just to make sure nothing came out her throat. Took her a good minute before she was able to get her thoughts together.

"All righty. Good news. I think I have you stabilized now, and I'm on my way out. I don't think it will pinch as much as embed, but you might want to brace yourself. Garrett just spun up the engines over on our plane, so we can probably leave as soon as we're all on board. Hang on." Chloe's voice moved along the inside of her skull—weird, but not altogether uncomfortable. It also echoed in her throat and, oddly, in her chest.

Just like a built-in com.

Lightbulbs went off all over Mari's head. "Hey, Chloe, wait a sec."

"For what?"

"Make you a deal," Mari said to absolutely no one, because, well, Chloe was embedded in her skin, which kind of precluded a face-to-face. "You verify that transmission is dead, and let me do one little thing while you're here in my body, and I'll give you a full buffet of tactile sensation after."

"Bathe in pudding?"

"Oh yeah."

"Sure thing, I can verify. Transmission is cut. Fini, kaput. Heron nixed it right away, as soon as he plugged into the cloud. So I kind of just tricked you. But it's all to a good end, right? We're still on for the pudding?"

Heron ended it. Despite her plan for saving the day, for saving him, she had ended up accomplishing a big old wad of nothing. She didn't even know who Dad was working for, and he was still out there, somewhere, up to no good.

Only, the crazy part of that realization was…she was glad. Not thrilled that Dad was the same old asshole he'd always been, but even if he hadn't changed, he was Dad. Hers. And now she knew he was alive and in reasonably good shape. She could let it go, her quest. She could stop worrying about him so much.

She was free.

"Yeah, we're still on for pudding. So far. Now the other thing." Poor Viktor probably thought she was delusional, talking out loud to nobody, but Mari didn't care.

She thought of the com rig in Nathan's glove compartment, and the newer one under her skin, sliding up against Chloe. What were those com rigs anyhow, other than interpreters of the movement of her voice box and muscles? She wondered how big a boost she could get from Chloe.

"Chloe, I need you to access maker design on com extenders."

"But why…?"

"Please."

A hesitation, and then, "All riiiiight. Done."

"Overlay that on your own communications programming." She waited for confirmation. Nonverbal this time, just an urge to nod her head. "Now, transmit to the cloud exactly what I say."

"Uh…this really isn't my programming."

"I know. You're doing fine." Mari closed her eyes, made her thoughts crystal clear, just like she had in the Pentarc. Pushed them out into the air. Into the cloud. *Hey, partner. Can you hear me?*

Nothing.

She recited the only line she could remember from that Mexican poem.

Again, nothing.

Moisture beaded on her skin, chilled there. She was beginning to get desperate.

She didn't know her way around the cloud, didn't know tech stuff for shit, but she steadily constructed an image of it in her mind—fractal and hexagonal and shredded and siphoned and gray and scary and shatter—she thought real hard about wearing a bikini in Miami, about the cool rubber deck planking under her feet on Heron's plane, about the mosquitoes biting on Mount Bonnell, and the slide of warm skin on its like, raw and unsteady and needing and connected.

Connected.

Hear me, Heron. I know you're out there. I know you're everywhere. But I need you here. With me.

Stretching into this weird construct of the cloud in her mind, she imagined old vids of that children's game, tetherball. Ship anchors. Rainbow bungees. Those harnesses nannies put on toddlers when they took them out in crowds. Reins on horses, strings on kites, cords on vintage vibrators.

I know there's a lot out there to see, but please find me.

Her head hurt, her pulse throbbed in every muscle of her body, a tick-tock of unbearable pain. Except, not unbearable. She'd bear it, goddammit. She'd bear anything if it'd get him back, hold him here.

But…what if he was hearing her, and he just didn't *want* to come back?

What if what he really wanted was the coed in the red dress, the whole-organic girl he'd met at that faculty party?

What if he had heard all that on Enchanted Rock, and now he knew what she really was?

She slumped against the deck metal. Good God, who was she kidding? All the power in the universe, and he'd back out of that for *her*? For a cheap jobber off-label rebuild? One who couldn't even drive a car no less fly a plane or resolve algorithms for fucking climate change. Just plain ol' Mari.

A sob wormed its way up her throat. Sounded like Chloe, but it was her. Just her. Hot tears pushed against her eyeballs, leaked out the sides.

She needed touch, desperately enough that she realized she was clasping her own hands over her belly. Hard. Was digging her fingernails into them.

Knuckles in a figure eight.

Infinite.

"Fuck it. You stay there if you want, but I ain't leaving you. Not ever," she said out loud, a last swagger.

Please.

And then, from very far away, "Care to put that in a contract, querida?"

Heron.

And there he was, attaching himself to her—she could feel it, like a hook in her chest. Hurt like the dickens, but it also made her feel mighty. Steady. Brave. Complete.

Connected.

"Jesus, that hurts," Chloe observed.

"Mari? It hurts? What hurts?" Heron, here, in her head, in her body, in her thoughts. Right where he belonged.

She soaked up his concern like socks on a wet floor. "Oh, never mind. That's Chloe. She's inside my body right now, talking to me while I'm talking to you. Which has got to be freaky looking to Viktor and technically might be some sort of kinky ménage thing, but you're okay, Heron? Now that the transmission is kaput, you're okay?"

"I am here. Waiting on you. As usual."

Mari stifled her laughter. Wouldn't want Chloe to worry about the wiggles now. "Oh, that's good. You just stay with me."

"For as long as you want, querida."

And wasn't that just fine.

● ● ●

She drowsed in the belly of that chopper for a long spell while Chloe mended her up good and told her all that had happened. Heron had been wild when he'd gotten his brain back in his body and woken up, apparently, mad as a wet hen at the fact that she'd run off down to Texas, and even more when he figured out she'd been shot. He'd sent in every rescue team he could think of, including Viktor, the giant Viking-looking dude with the enviable arsenal.

"Chloe's telling me that you came to save my ass," Mari said to him now. "Thanks."

Viktor nodded. "You are welcome. Guarding you is easier than most jobs. You take care of yourself, mostly. I am sorry for the rock shrapnel. None of my bullets hit you, but I cannot say the same for the rock."

"What about Da…Nathan?"

"Sorry for him, too."

Mari almost let herself feel a twinge of grief, but then she caught sight of Viktor's face. He was grinning. He looked so much more human when he smiled, so much less like a brute. Appearances, deceiving and all.

"He's okay, then?"

"Sedated, but otherwise unharmed. I am guessing Dr. Farad will have something to say to him."

"We have a detention at the Pentarc," Heron said into her head. "I plan to try it out on your cowboy."

"Don't go too hard on him," she said. "He was being marionetted at the time. Oh, hey, did I tell you I found my dad? I mean, he was hacked into Nathan's brain, so I didn't actually see him, but I'm pretty sure it was good ol' sack-of-crazy Dad."

"You do realize you're implying that Damon Vallejo was also the marionette at the Pentarc, the one who had those mercs implant a nanovirus in my head." Even in her head, Heron's voice had the stink of revenge being planned on it.

Mari needed to settle that right quick. "Yep. But he and I had a long chitchat. I think we're okay now." She wished she could ask this next question in private, without Heron hearing, but he was probably all up in her thoughts anyhow, reading her mind. She tried to keep it all frothy in there. Or at least not vengeancy. "Hey, Viktor, before you sedated him, could you get a handle on whether Nathan thought he was Nathan again?"

The giant bodyguard frowned like it hurt to think, or at least to remember. "He gave instructions for retrieving his truck and asked for his gun back also. I did not give it."

He gestured to the big-ass pistol, now safely peeking out of one of his many holsters.

"Oh yeah, that's Nathan being Nathan," said Mari. It was good to hear that Dad was out of his brain, that he was back to being his pretty, smarmy self. True, he'd kidnapped and drugged her, but there had been times during the night when he'd seemed weirdly sincere.

Maybe he hadn't known exactly what Dad was up to. Maybe he was being played just as hard as she was. What was that bulbing down at the base of her throat, a soft spot for Nathan, a desire to forgive? Typical. She had a bad habit of letting the worst sins slide.

She still loved Dad, despite it all. Still loved Heron. Well, of *course*, that. Maybe that's what made all the other forgiveness possible.

She swallowed around the bulb.

It made her feel odd to think that all these people— Chloe, Viktor, Heron, and probably Kellen and Garrett, too—had come after her, to save her ass. Heron must have suspected she'd hie off on some damn fool crusade the moment his back was turned, else he wouldn't have built in all these contingencies.

It did occur to Mari, on the flight westward to where Heron was waiting, that she could just ask Chloe for a rundown of her innards. Chloe had been inside her, after all, and must have gotten a good peek at what was there, at least enough to determine which bits were girl and which were machine. Mari could suss out the truth from the convenient lie that her dad had laid on her.

But she had bigger fish to fry. In any other circumstance, she'd be stressing over her father's revelation— was she, wasn't she, and what did any of that change?

Because the fact was, it didn't change anything. So what if she had some post-human parts in her? She'd had a freakin' free-fae collective inside her body, and the world wasn't ending. No snow in hell, far as she could see.

And every once in a while on that trip back, she touched her chest, wiggled the invisible hook there. And always, always, he smiled back. She couldn't see him do it, couldn't hear him either, but damn if she wasn't one hundred percent certain he did.

CHAPTER 17

IN THE LOBBY-LEVEL CONFERENCE ROOM OF THE Pentarc, Heron experimented with his new normal. Sort of trying digital godhood on for size.

Just as he'd worried would happen, when he logged on to the cloud, his consciousness had expanded to fit the space. In fact, it was still expanding, even while he sat here, palms flat on a smartsurface granite-skinned table. He was back in his body now, or at least completely in control of his body. However, the exact location of his consciousness, his thinking *self*, was less certain. The technical term, often used to describe nanoconstructs spread out to cover wide areas, was *dispersed*. Heron's mind was dispersed, permanently. There would be no shoving it all back into his organic head.

And that was okay.

He had been scared of existing like this for so long, but now he wished he hadn't spent so much time in fear. It wasn't bad, just different. He could still breathe, could still connect to all his physical senses. Hell, he could still connect to all his mechanical sensors and control rigs, too. At the same time. Right now, for instance, he was flying the spaceplane that zoomed Mari forty thousand feet above Flagstaff. And he could feel every wiggle of her ass in the copilot's chair.

Which she almost certainly realized. Minx.

And at the same time, he could sift data from all over the world, in real time. The amount of information he could access was amazing. Part of him wanted to sit down in the Pentarc basement vault with a data cable plugged into his skull port and just ride waves and waves of information for the sheer joy of soaking up all that knowledge. Guess he was still a bow tie–wearing academic at heart.

Every few minutes, though, he'd get a flash of wrongness, almost vertigo. Maybe it was a human person's inherent objection to infinity. Early astronauts had written about similar spasms of horror when looking out into the blackness of space. But whenever he felt like he needed to hold on to something, he reflexively sought Mari's data stream in the cloud, the bright thread in all that static. Steady. His tether.

When he found her, every time he found her, the roiling of the universe calmed somewhat.

He wondered if time would make him more comfortable riding the cloud, but right now, it was still a struggle. He kept coming back to Mari, latching on to her whenever he felt overwhelmed. Which was pretty damned often, he had to confess. But she made it bearable.

Well, as bearable as this morning was likely to get.

Several chairs away from him sat the mech-clone husband of Angela Neko, and on the far side of him, the recently widowed continental senator herself. She kept her back I-beam straight and her gloved hands folded primly in her lap. She was much smaller than she looked on vids. If she put her elbows up on the tabletop, she'd resemble a child.

A fact of which she was probably keenly aware. He had a sense that Angela Neko was aware of everything. Almost as much as he was.

"My plane is landing presently," he told her.

A corner of her mouth twitched up. "Ah. And I'm guessing Marisa Vallejo is aboard it, or have you spirited her away?"

In response to the cacophony of newsvids claiming her husband had been murdered, Angela Neko had issued several statements denying the reports, even questioning who might have started such a horrible rumor. The lie seemed to have taken root. Some services had even started pushing the actual footage of the hit, under censorlock, of course, and pointing out how it was an obvious fabrication. Pundits had been picking the vid apart for two days now.

Because clearly, Daniel Neko lived. The Global News Network had broadcast footage of Senator Neko and her husband attending an awards gala last night. While Heron struggled to get back to his body, while Mari sloughed through drinks at dive after dive in Dallas, Angela Neko had taken her mech-clone, the one that looked exactly like Daniel, out for a night on the town. And everyone who paid attention to those sorts of things had seen it.

Heron slid a look at the machine Daniel now, marveling at it. He coveted a more thorough examination. From a surface view, he could discern no traces of mech. Only deeper bioscans gave the tells: power routing instead of neurotransmitters, titanium core that affected his mass significantly. Systems that Heron read as organic on first pass now seemed, on further inspection, far too precise to be the *clone* part of *mech-clone*.

The Daniel Neko unit was eons more advanced than even the N series machines, which, of course, made Heron wonder what Mari's dad was up to. Indications were that he was working for the TPA technocrats, no longer tinkering in an academic lab, and concentrating instead on more weapons-oriented research. Apparently, that information was only half correct, though installing a mech-clone as the contracted spouse of a UNAN senator certainly could be considered an act of war.

Did he have other mech-clone moles in high-ranking positions? If he did, could he marionette them at will? God, the thought. With enough well-placed mech-clones, Damon Vallejo could control the world. Only he had to realize that Heron would try to stop him.

Or was this whole business with the nanotransmission and Mari's abduction supposed to have distracted him?

And how about Angela Neko? Was she another attempt at distraction? Or had someone else sent her here?

On the off chance she was a spy, he would have to keep her away from the other residents. Especially Chloe.

Heron didn't look at Angela directly, but he could see her from three angles, through the lenses of the Pentarc security monitors. Her clasped hands weren't clenched or tense, but something about her seemed off. She toyed with the fingertip of one glove, and once in a while, her eyes would dart to the door. Who did she expect to walk through it? And what would that do to her impossible equanimity?

She had secrets, probably a billion of them, not the least of which was her reason for requesting haven.

Her hotel had been attacked in the early hours of this morning, minutes before she was scheduled to leave it. On the same night Mari had been abducted and wounded. On the same night Heron had been trapped outside of his own body, probably by the tech those mercenaries had implanted in his head.

In his experience, coincidences were unicorns. They didn't exist. Either one entity had moved on multiple fronts last night, attempting to alter the landscape of geopolitics, or more than one entity had been involved. Vallejo and his Texas technocrats were obvious culprits. Heron had seen, had heard the conversation atop Enchanted Rock.

What he couldn't figure out was why Vallejo would have wanted to kill the senator, especially mere days after assassinating her husband. Kellen had suggested that she wasn't mourning her husband, but she certainly wasn't her usual put-together vid-slick persona this morning. In person, she was unexpectedly fragile. Wounded.

The intrigue monster had a lot of tentacles, but Heron was confident he could follow all its convolutions and locate the source, the heart of evil. He could destroy all of its pieces if he so chose.

But first, he needed to secure his haven. His home. His precious things and people.

He was going to start by turning the Pentarc into a fortress. He would keep his mothers, both Adele and

Fanaida, safe, and his treasures and friends and respon-
sibilities, and Mari too. Of course her. The queen could
have her floating haven; he had a yen to make one of his
own, beyond the reach of UNAN or Texas or the Vatican
Protectorate or any of the multigovernmental or corporate
entities. Most of all, he knew that no one could stop him.

And yes, *that* thought was a little bit terrifying.

And fucking awesome.

"Can I ask you a question about her, Dr. Farad?
About your shooter?" Senator Neko said, breaking into
his thoughts.

"Certainly. I don't promise to answer, but you are
welcome to ask."

She leaned forward slightly. "Is she really Damon
Vallejo's daughter? Or is she something…"

Else. Something else. He knew her next word before
she said it, and his mind buzzed, hunting for an answer
that wouldn't put Mari in fresh danger.

But then the two-story black doors at the far end of the
conference room swung open, and the tension evaporated.

Mari. Heron resisted the urge to stand up and run over
to her, just so he could touch her as soon as she walked
in. As it was, he couldn't completely swallow the bulb
of emotion in his throat when she sashayed through
those doors, safe, with a grin on her lips, a slink to her
hips, and no sign at all of all the things she'd endured in
the last few days.

She thought her talents precious few, but Heron
counted her resilience as one of the most arresting
things he'd ever seen in a person. He hadn't even
begun telling her all the things he loved about her, but
he thought that maybe he'd get the chance soon. And

he'd tie her down this time, so she couldn't slip away before he finished.

"Heron." She mouthed it, didn't even speak out loud, but he heard her voice all over his skin, all through his blood.

"So fucking good to see you," he told her, wondering if she'd be able to hear. Chloe wasn't in there anymore, but Heron didn't need any boost to read Mari's mind. Not anymore.

Angela Neko stood, smoothing her elegant, old-wool skirt and pasting on one of those beatific political smiles. Beside her, mech-Daniel stood up as well.

Mari ignored both of them completely, ate the space of the conference room with her long strides, and planted herself right in front of Heron's chair at the head of the table. She palmed the armrests, leaned down, and laid a soul-wallop of a kiss all over his mouth. Her unbound hair curtained them from the rest of the world, but Heron wouldn't have minded if everybody saw. He had half a thought of broadcasting this all over the West Coast. Hell, all over the world.

"Likewise," Mari murmured against his mouth.

So she *had* heard him. It shouldn't surprise him, how connected they were. Not anymore. He met her eyes, and the spark that lit between them flared hot in his blood, his neuromatrix, his cock. As if she sensed as much, she snaked the tip of her tongue and touched it fleetingly to his bottom lip, and when she drew it back in, her grin looked positively impish. "Senator Neko, Mr. Neko, it will be a pleasure meeting both of you, just not right now. I have a guess why you're here, and believe me, I'm not going to resist arrest. I'll even confess. But first,

I gotta beg about twenty minutes with Dr. Farad here. Been a while since I've seen him, and we have some unfinished business to see to." As if to make her point, Mari reached one hand over and popped the top hook on her corset.

"Clearly, you have no idea why I'm here," Angela said.

That made Mari pause. Alas. Heron could have continued even with an audience. Instead, when she turned to face Senator Neko, he set his hands on Mari's hips. He didn't so much as tug, but she lowered herself onto his lap anyway, almost as if she'd read *his* mind. Her weight pressing down hurt for a moment, but not in a bad way. In an excruciatingly hot way, in fact.

"Oh, fine. You can watch if that's your thing." Mari shifted her ass on Heron's lap and reached down for the hem to her battered crinoline.

Angela's placid look never wavered, but mech-Daniel looked away and blinked rapidly. Too rapidly. Only a machine could flutter that fast. A person would have flushed.

"You don't have to impress your seduction skills on me, Mari Vallejo," the senator said firmly. "According to the marketing materials, your base-level rebuild, before they fitted your face onto it, was originally intended for sexual gratification. Daniel's is similar, so I have a decent idea how effective it can be." Angela indicated the Daniel mech-clone with an inclination of her head.

Mari stilled. Heron stilled. For a moment there, she swayed, but his hands on her hips kept her steady.

"Where did you get these marketing materials?" asked Heron.

"Damon Vallejo, of course," Angela replied.

Heron's brain spun up, parsing, pulling old conversations, pulling his partial feed from the crest of Enchanted Rock. Pulling all bios of Mari from before, during, and after the Pentarc. Data sets slid into place, sorting themselves. God, that bastard had told Mari the truth out there. Had he told her all of it, though? Had Damon Vallejo told her the truth about herself?

And yet, she'd come in here and kissed him, teased him. She wasn't acting like a creature ashamed of who— of what—she was. He fanned his hands over Mari's hip bones, slid them over her belly, holding her, embracing her, protecting her as much as he could, though not from bullets this time.

"You heard him? Who all heard him?" Mari's voice was tiny. Heron wasn't used to that tone, but she'd used it before. It was the voice of a younger her, a child in a woman's body. It cooled his ardor somewhat, but it made him want to hold her tighter.

"Heard him? Yes, I've heard him go on about his technological prowess. And I've heard him complain about Dr. Farad, too, which I understand is a long-running bit of competitive bullshittery that frankly makes me want to vomit. Damon's fought me on secession for a long time, but now he's made it personal. For you, too, I see."

"He's working for the TPA," Mari murmured. "Everybody's taking sides."

All the big players were sorting themselves, and eventually, the sides were going to line up to fight for real, no longer through proxies. Every future Heron could posit had that happening, but he'd been shielding Mari from his bleaker thoughts. Now, he wished he'd just come right out and shared some of his information, some of his worries.

The Mari he held between his hands right now was solid—she could handle it. Maybe she always could have.

He should have trusted her with more, sooner. Instead of letting her find out all this on her own, he could have just told her.

"You might think about doing the same," Angela said.

Mari shook her head. She'd dropped the hem of her skirt and now placed her hands on top of Heron's, over her waist.

"I didn't mean to harm your husband, ma'am," she said. "And I sure as shit didn't mean to start a war." She was facing away from him, so Heron couldn't see her face, but her fingers were cold atop his. Strong, capable. But deep-space cold.

Angela Neko smiled again, but it wasn't the high-gloss smile of a politician. It was the grimace of a woman who was smiling even though she felt like doing something else. "I know that. Which is why I've instructed our entertainment regulators to retrieve all copies of the security vid of Daniel's demise. Official story is that it's doctored anyway, and I will stand behind that. If anyone doubts that my husband is alive, they have only to see vid of us together. No one is going to arrest you…any of you."

"I'm guessing that you want something in exchange for our freedom," Heron said. Angela might have her reasons for going along with the hoax—and from what he'd heard from Kellen, Heron had a pretty good idea what some of those reasons were—but in his experience, generosity like this never came without a price.

"See? Dr. Farad knows how to play this game. Yes, I'll want a boon in exchange for my complicity. Two, actually, since you stole my helicopter."

Heron clenched his teeth. For himself, he didn't mind owing favors. He didn't mind doing favors for people. But he would balk flat-out at putting Mari or his crew or his mothers in any more hair-raising situations. "Borrowed."

Angela grimace-smiled again. "Call it what you will. In exchange, I seek haven for both mech-Daniel and me. Here. Undisclosed. For an indeterminate period of time."

Heron narrowed his eyes on her, but she didn't flush beneath his scrutiny. Like her robot husband, she just met him stare for knife-edged stare.

"Done," he said. "We have the room, and I will guarantee your safety in exchange for Mari's immunity."

Senator Neko let out the breath she'd been holding. She nodded. Without breaking her eye-lock on Heron, she addressed Mari. "Mari, you may not have meant to start a war, but one is coming. I advise you to prepare yourself. All of you."

Neither the senator nor her mech-consort had taken a seat again, and now they both straightened perceptibly, which Heron guessed was their way of saying the interview was at an end. When Angela nodded curtly, murmured a farewell, and turned to leave the conference room, Heron felt Mari flinch. She let out a little sound like a kitten's mewl, but it was too soft for the others to have heard. Well, Angela, at least; mech-Daniel turned back and flashed her a look before he followed his wife out the double doors.

Through his inputs, Heron watched the pair pause in the corridor, looking lost. Then Adele found them, and Angela shed some of her tension visibly.

Heron could have listened in. He could have followed the trio through the Pentarc, watched where Adele led them, made sure they weren't allowed to wander the premises. He could have done that and kept a significant portion of his attention right here in the room. But he didn't. He released them, released as much of the rest of the world as he could, and focused on Mari. God, she felt good here where he could touch her, hold her. Kiss her.

Long moments after the conference room doors closed, she just sat there on his lap, holding his hands, not saying anything. Eventually, she sucked in a breath that he heard rattle in her chest.

"It's true, what she said. At least I think it is. I'm a rebuild of some sort. Post-human."

"And that is a bad thing?" Heron tried to quell the roil those words cooked in his gut. She looked so wistful when she said them, which poked the hive of his own insecurities. When he was a little kid, he'd endured some mild ribbing for his neo-hippie upbringing and his Arab features, but altering one's body was a choice, not a circumstance of birth. He'd *chosen* to fuck with nature, to fuck with himself. The queen's alterations had saved his life, but even so, he had consciously accepted them. He'd chosen to become other.

And not just other. A unique monster made even more complicated by the dispersal of his consciousness into the cloud. If Mari still harbored some of those low thoughts about altered humans, she would never be able to look at him without loathing that part of herself. And, ultimately, loathing him as well.

He slid his gaze off hers.

"Let me look at you." She hauled her body sideways, sliding off his lap so she could glare down at him.

Her dark-whiskey eyes set him on fire inside, but he tried not to interpret that look as a come-hither. Tried really hard. Her face was bunched up in her superserious expression, and that helped somewhat. She raised her hands, leaned toward him again, and pushed the hair away from his forehead, exposing his eyes and the projection alts at his temples. He watched for it but didn't see the slightest dismay in her face when she gazed down at him. "No. That right there may be the *best* thing I've ever known."

Joy walloped him. Briefly, he thought about lighting up the neon in Vegas or spiking the Nikkei, but instead, he just drew in a long breath and let it out slow. His facial muscles only vaguely remembered what a silly grin felt like, and they approximated one.

"I'm no good at this stuff, at telling folks how I feel," Mari went on. "Never have been. And honestly, I don't remember clearly what happened down on that job in Corpus. I tried to get Nathan to tell me, but he was... oh, that's another thing. Have I told you about Nathan?"

Same Mari, same whiplash-inducing conversation. He was used to the turns, generally, but this one sobered the tone. Heron knew that Nathan was the remote who'd gone dark on Mari, exploded her hiding spot, and left her for dead. He knew that Mari had searched high and low for that guy for years, had taken risky jobs just so she could get better information on his whereabouts and her father's. In Heron's mind, Nathan Grace was just a step down from Dr. Vallejo on the ladder of folks he wanted to eviscerate on Mari's behalf.

But all that flow of thought pipelined alongside the main point: Mari'd gone down to Dallas with the express purpose of meeting up with Nathan. During his initial surge on the cloud, Heron had faceprinted the dark figure on the rock, the one who'd shot Mari. And just about a half hour ago, he'd logged a communication from Chloe identifying the sedated and restrained stranger who had been transferred to a Pentarc holding cell as Mari's ex.

And ex in this case didn't just mean ex-partner.

"There's something you need to tell me about him?" Heron tried not to sound terse or peevy, but once again, he found himself talking down the beast.

Jealousy had never lit him up like this before. Fear, anger at injustice, furious loyalty: these things had tempted him to the edge of control on several occasions. But never something as pedestrian as jealousy. For all that he still believed Mari brought out the best in him, he wondered if she didn't bring out the worst as well, like a double-bladed knife for him: both the thing that tethered him from being lost and, at the same time, the one that made him want to roar all over the universe, stomping it beneath his digital boot heels.

"You don't have to get all scary as hell—though I'll grant you it *is* turning me on," Mari said. "He didn't hurt me, partner. I told him I was wearing a dentata, and he recalled my fascination with the sharp and shiny just enough to buy it."

She realized he could make the Pentarc detention cell gut-yankingly uncomfortable, right?

"I don't dare ask why you even needed to reference dentata, but the fact remains that he did shoot you. And kidnap you. And I swear to God, Mari, if he did anything else to you, anything that you're keeping from me, I'll burst-fry every single one of his circuits until his eyeballs boil."

"Like what the feds did to Adele?"

"Significantly more gruesome."

"Okay, I take that back: scary as hell is *really* turning me on. Do it some more."

Well, wasn't that strange. He could actually see sexual tension now. The air molecules in that space between him and Mari were fractionally more excited than the others in the room. The interstice went orange on his infrared cameras.

"You aren't going to try to talk me out of killing him?"

"Nope." Mari's grin widened. Clearly, she was in come-hither mode now. The thermals turned red. "'Cause I know who you are, Heron Atreus Raymond Neruda Farad. You could have taken out every federal agent in the Pentarc, and you didn't."

"Those agents didn't hurt you."

"They wanted to."

"However," and he paused here, not sure he was ready to admit this, but then he plowed on, "you didn't follow them, pining all over Texas for years. You aren't in love with them."

"Now hold on. That sounded like jealousy."

Heron didn't say anything. What could he say? Denying it would be a lie, and he had a personal policy against lying almost as strong as his personal policy against murder. These restraints on his id helped him hold it together, especially now that his reach was so expansive. He couldn't afford to let his ethics slip. But he also couldn't bring himself to admit out loud that he was, in fact, jealous of that son of a bitch rotting in his holding cell.

Mari drew her eyebrows together, pinching her face up in her serious look again. At the same time, she leaned back against the conference table, and her hands went up to the catch on that corset. She unhasped the second hook.

"Ain't any need for it, though it is flattering as hell," she drawled. "No, I wasn't in love with those feds, and I'm not in love with Nathan." Another hook came undone. Her breasts were almost touching down the centerline. "I'm in love with *you*, Heron. Now tell me that doesn't terrify the bejeezus out of you."

Heron closed his eyes, processing. He didn't really need to pause for that anymore, but it was a habit.

Love. Funny thing was that love had never been hard for him. He'd never steeled himself against it or pretended that it didn't bite him on the ass from time to time. He'd never been stingy with his love. He loved his mothers and his crew, and he wasn't embarrassed about it.

But what he'd done for Mari, what he was *prepared* to do for her, surpassed all those other relationships by several orders of magnitude. It'd been a long time since he'd called what he felt for her love. The word was too small.

Except when she said it. In her voice, coming out of her mouth, the word got a whole lot bigger. It filled him completely.

"I love how you tilt your head to the side just a smidge when you're processing something," she went on. "I love that you were waiting for me on Sixth Street behind that slow-ass bus that must have made you crazy. I love how you always know what I'm saying, even when I mutter. I love your game face when you're on a job. I love your voice. I love your eyes and your hands and your scars and the way you can stay so goddamn stoic even when things gotta be buffeting you on all sides. I swear, Heron, even if a superstorm was breathing down on you, you'd just stand there and take it." She paused, waited. "Say something, damn it."

He took a shallow breath. "You have one hook left."

"How can you tell? Your eyes are closed."

"The metal scraped when you undid those top seven. Also, the pressure of the air between us shifted slightly when your breasts came free." He was still getting video and thermographic feeds from the security cameras, too, but he didn't feel a need to mention those. He kind of liked that she thought he had super powers.

"Yeah? What am I doing now, then?"

Yanking the last hook on her corset, stepping out of that pretty crinoline, toeing off her boots. Hoisting herself up on the granite conference table. Her bare ass squeaked on the polished surface. He could smell her, could feel/see/hear the slight change in ambient temperature. He allowed his cock to fill in response. That was one part of his body at least that had never been altered, and he'd never been more grateful for that fact.

"Being impossible." He spoke in barely a whisper, but he pushed the sound into her cochlea. He fired neurotransmitters, making the rub of his voice tactile as well as aural.

She caught her bottom lip between her teeth, then let it out slow, lingering on the pain. "Heron, the last time we were together, both times, in fact, you gave me what I wanted, and I do thank you kindly, but you were holding yourself back. Maybe because of the transmission thing, but… You ever thought of what would happen if you just let go?"

Input, input, input: Go. Surge. Along the chair arms, his fingers flexed, even though he knew he hadn't told them to.

"A modicum of restraint is necessary, I'm afraid. These alts are wired into my reflexes and augmented musculature. If I don't concentrate very hard on being gentle, I could break you." Also, he could possibly create an unintentional power surge in the Pentarc. He was still experimenting with his new processing capacity. She'd mentioned blowing a fuse before, but really, she had no idea.

"But see, that's the silver lining. If what my fa… If what Damon Vallejo told me is true, you can't break me. I'm not breakable. God knows the federales in that prison tried to. But they failed. Nathan failed. I'm fucking indestructible."

Heron opened his eyes and, at the same time, allowed himself to process the vid feeds. She was sitting on the granite table, one heel up on its edge and naked as sin, and even as he watched, she worked one finger hard against her clit. He could see it surging through the hood of flesh, distended and dark and glistening. The space beneath his tongue went dry.

"Know what I think? I think you've either done it before or seen somebody else let fly, sucking up all that power in the cloud, and you're scared shitless of doing it again. But you were scared of even climbing on that horse, if you'll recall. And you did fine. Heron, you did just fine."

"Because of you."

"Well, do fine again because of me. 'Cause I don't want a leashed version of you. I want all of you. Right now, on this table." She slicked her finger back up the curve of her mons, trailing wet upward and along the valley between her breasts.

She dipped that finger between her lips, licking her passion off it with the same tongue that had touched his mouth just minutes ago. The visual nearly set him on fire. Clearly, she didn't realize that setting him on fire right now could very well set the western seaboard aflame as well. He felt precarious on the edge of restraint.

Because she was right. He had been holding back. He'd been holding back pretty much all his life. And she was right about something else: he was terrified of losing that iron control.

But *he'd* been right about something, too. Mari Vallejo was about the most tempting thing he'd ever encountered, and when she asked, he couldn't refuse. Didn't even want to.

In one movement, he was out of the chair, between her knees, his thighs hard against the granite table. Afterward, he didn't recall opening his pants, but he must have done, because there was nothing between them, nothing stopping him at all, when he rammed his cock into her, hilt-deep in one shove.

She yowled something dark and dirty and delicious, something about taking up reins and riding hell for leather, but he heard nothing but the roar of blood, the roar of data, the surge of energy screaming through his conduits, the primal need to plant himself inside her, to combine their bodies into one blazing inferno of creation.

If he had been all metal, he might have melted in the heat of that passion, and melted her as well. He might have melted the whole bloody Pentarc. As it was, he climbed over her, on his knees between her legs, bringing his face to hers, fucking her mouth with his tongue and her cunt with his cock, blurring every line he knew of that separated them. They were organic, bodies fitting together in the most natural, nondigital way possible.

If she'd flinched at all, he would have stopped. He could have. He'd spent his whole life leashing various parts of himself, keeping the beast at bay, and he was good at it. He had never let it out like this, but now, right now, he didn't want to put it back. It was better than speed, better than control, better than the thrill of discovery.

Mari's hands scored his back, and he reveled in the slight pain. The marks she left on him were signs of possession.

Because even as he fucked her the whole length of that table, slipping their bodies on the polished surface in defiance of all the laws of friction, grinding bruises into her pelvis and rubbing his skin so hard against hers that surely they were one tissue by now, Heron knew this wasn't about command and control. This was about giving himself to her. All of him. She'd asked for it, and he gave.

He felt her come around him, a violent squeeze and shatter. Her electricals lit up like fireworks on his bioscan. She screamed his name and dug her sharp nails deep into his shoulder blades. And it was too much. Too much surge, too much bright, too much power, too much perfect.

"I love you," he told her, no longer certain whether his voice was aural or digital or tactile or photon. "Mech, organic, nano, monkey: I don't give a shit what your body is made of. I love *you*, querida. So much. And you. Can't. Make. Me. Stop."

"No, holy shit, don't you dare." She lifted her head off the table to pour a kiss of fire into his mouth. "Come."

And that afternoon, on a closed loop of orgasm and a storm of electricals and a shout that very nearly broke the impact glass, all the lights went out in the Pentarc.

Every single fucking one of them.

EPILOGUE

HERON KNEW HE'D FIND KELLEN OUT HERE IN WHAT they called the barn, the open-sky structure wedged between two Pentarc spires. This was where they kept the animals they'd managed to rescue from theaters of war and environmental desolation. Sure, the whole half acre smelled like hay, shit, and wet fur, but it was the only place on the planet where Kellen seemed comfortable in his own skin, surrounded by all the things he loved.

Or most of them. Heron needed to talk to his friend about the one person he'd been studiously avoiding for weeks.

Late afternoon sunlight had warmed the barn, but Heron could feel the hint of approaching winter. The sun was going down in a couple of hours, and this place would get cold fast. Still, Kellen was out here with no jacket shin-deep in some kind of hay, so either the physical exertion of caring for these animals provided sufficient warmth, or he was on a self-tormenting kick. Regardless of the reason, he needed a break.

"Got a minute?" Heron called.

Kellen squinted against the sunlight, pushing his hat toward the back of his head. "Sure thing, cap'n, though I have to wonder how *you* do, now Miss Mari's staying here permanently."

"Appropriating time is like any other resource management. Checking up on you is listed as important in my hierarchy."

Kellen worked a pitchfork, distributing hay for the rescue animal Fanaida had brought north from her last mission to Bolivia. Kellen had been so patient with the animal, training it, garnering its respect without ever putting himself on equal footing with it. The little llama-looking thing nosed at him eagerly, and he flicked his fingers in front of its mouth, waited a long patient second, and then petted its soft head.

"You don't need to check up on me," Kellen said, his attention unwavering on the animal. "I'm right as rain."

Yoink had come up with Heron on the lift and now wended between his ankles, inviting attention. She didn't like it when Kellen was tending the other animals. She fancied herself the center of his universe. Heron bent, rubbed her between the ears, and accepted a rough lick on the back of his hand. Her saliva contained correct levels of enzymes and protein Fel D 1. Also traces of gardenia pollen. Ha. So she did sneak up here when no one was looking.

"Adele wants to know why you don't come to her family suppers anymore," Heron said, looking at the cat and, at the same time, watching his friend keenly through the security camera lenses.

Kellen hadn't been to one of Adele's big cook-outs

in the food court for weeks. Not since Senator Neko had come here seeking haven. The one night both she and Kellen had sat at the same table, Heron noticed the warmth between them, the easy banter and sense of camaraderie, maybe even friendship. The kind of connection that could grow to something deeper.

Kellen had always been happier around animals than people, but that night, Heron had thought that maybe his friend was peeking out from behind the defensive isolation he'd worn for so long.

Since that night, though, Kellen hadn't come to supper. Heron knew from his cameras that the two interacted rarely, spent most of their time apart. Other people in the Pentarc had noticed. Adele had, Fanaida had. Chloe certainly had. Heron felt obliged to get to the bottom of it, for all their sakes.

"Tell Adele I'm sorry," Kellen said. "I just been busy."

"She thinks there's something wrong with her bean recipe." Heron wasn't above using guilt as a tactic.

"Ain't nothing wrong with her cooking," Kellen said, looking up from his crouch. "Swear I'll tell her that next time I see her. Those beans are good eatin'."

"I, on the other hand, suspect it's something wrong with the company," Heron said, making his voice as gentle as he could. "Specifically with our guest."

The senator's name hung unspoken on the air between them.

Angela.

Kellen's easy movement stiffened perceptibly. He unhooked a pair of wicked-looking trimmers from his utility belt and set to work on one furry foot, not looking anywhere near Heron. The vicuña, obviously not anxious at all, leaned into the touch and made a humming sound.

Connection. Action and reaction. There would be consequences to having Angela stay here. And even though he couldn't go back and renegotiate at this point, Heron hoped he hadn't created an untenable situation for his friend.

"Can't think of any particular problem there," Kellen said. He didn't look up from his toenail clipping, but his tone was dismissive.

Heron plowed on. "I agreed to let her stay, but I didn't ask you first."

"You were kind of busy, so I see how it might've slipped your mind. Besides, you own the Pentarc." Kellen shrugged. "I don't like it, I can leave."

But he wouldn't. Kellen would no more leave that vicuña, those miniature goats, or the new baby squirrels than he would hack his own arm off. Even more than Heron, he had built something precious here, something worth protecting.

"I never meant it to be just my place," Heron said. "We thought this up together. Our haven, right? When the world goes to shit—when, not if, and that time is coming soon—Pentarc is our safe place, our home. All of us. And I think Angela Neko might need a harbor in the storm as well, but I don't want to offer her a permanent place here without your agreement."

Kellen squinted in the sunlight, and his mouth beneath the hat's brim might have pressed tighter. It was hard to tell in the shadow, though. "If keeping her here keeps her safe, I'm for it completely. Just…let's just leave the rest of it be."

Heron shifted his weight, as uncomfortable as he had been in a long while. This conversation was far from over, but he wouldn't be getting any more input on the topic. Not today. Maybe he'd just give it time, let Kellen and Angela get used to sharing a time zone again.

They had been close once, those two, though seeing what they had each become in the time since, Heron couldn't picture them together. How could someone with a soul as big as Kellen's, with such an elemental need to comfort and care, ever love the sort of woman who was a shoo-in to be the first war minister of the continental government? Angela was all sharp edges and schemes, and Kellen...well, he wasn't that.

Heron might have agreed to harbor her, even protect her, but he damn sure wasn't going to let her roll his best friend into her master plan.

Yoink looked from Heron to Kellen, sat back on the dirt, and licked herself.

"Of course I will," said Heron. He had come up here intending to lure his friend back down to supper, back into the embrace of friends and family and warmth. But maybe Kellen wasn't ready for that.

A breeze kicked up over the desert, making the spires sway. The vicuña made a click noise, like a snap on its soft palate, and Kellen responded with a pet on the head. Yoink growled.

Heron might not want to admit it, but something much worse than winter was coming. He only hoped his haven would be ready.

ACKNOWLEDGMENTS

Most books take a village. Feels like this one took a metropolis. First, thank you to my subject matter experts: Allen Jackson, Nicole Minsk, Christa Paige, Paula d'Etcheverry, Sloane Calder, and Claudia Renard. Only you and I know the mistakes you have saved me from making in public.

Also, huge thanks to Crit Groups (big and little), DDs, Skyler White, and the Sourcebooks team for craft and biz help through every step of this process.

Finally, this book would be in a drawer if not for the work of my agent, Holly Root, and editor, Cat Clyne. Superheroes like y'all totally deserve origin stories and capes.

ABOUT THE AUTHOR

Vivien Jackson writes fantastical, futuristic, down-home salacious kissery. After being told at the age of seven she could not marry Han Solo because he wasn't a real person, she devoted her life to creating worlds where, goldarnit, she could marry anybody she wanted. And she could wield a blaster doing it. A devoted Whovian Browncoat Sindarin gamer, she has a degree in English, which means she's read gobs of stuff in that language and is always up for a casual lit-crit of the Fallout universe. She has been known to write limericks about old Gondor. With her similarly geeky partner, children, and hairy little pets, she lives in Austin, Texas. She'd love to hear from you: www.vivienjackson.com.

Here's a sneak peek at book two in Vivien Jackson's Tether series

PERFECT GRAVITY

IF THE UNIVERSE GRANTED DRUTHERS, KELLEN HOCKLEY would've asked to spend this fine autumn evening out riding fences. Or patching up barb-tangled bovines, soothing them to health. Or catching the blast furnace of a Texas summer right in the face. Having a wire enema. Facing a plasma-equipped drone firing squad. Because, fact was, he'd rather be anywhere than where he was: on a space station that smelled like acetone, hot metal, and feet.

Fixing to have the hands-down worst conversation of his life with the woman he once considered the love of it.

He took a steadying breath and stepped off the space elevator. His guts fell about twenty meters, and he struggled against the urge to vomit. The crazy-ass robot queen who ran this station tried hard to make it stable when she geosynched—he knew she tried—but if there was one thing he'd learned in the years since continental unification and the general shitification of things down on the surface, stability of any kind was transient. Was best to close your eyes, clamp your teeth, and wait for the ache to pass.

He told the station where he was headed and running lights on the floor breadcrumbed his path down one of the tube-like corridors. He was supposed to follow them, and he did for a couple steps, then stopped. Couldn't say why, other than he felt like he was going to his own personal goddamn guillotine. His body wanted to run.

"Easy there, cowboy." The voice moved along his skull, from back to front, like a sunburn setting in, giving him chills. It didn't have a visible body, that voice. It came out of thin, station-scrubbed air.

"You gotta stop jailbreaking, Chloe," he chided low, under his breath. "If authorities found you out in the wild, we'd all be hunted down."

"Like twelve-point bucks in deer season!" she replied.

Chloe wasn't a real girl. She wasn't a real anything, just a collection of nanites that had gotten together, formed a consciousness, and decided to imitate human living. She had a hard time holding her visible form together, but even in her current dispersed state, there were sure to be scrubbers that'd sense her presence on this station. Human eyes might not be able to see her, but machines were a whole 'nother thing. And there were laws against things like Chloe.

"We don't need trouble," he reminded her. "So skedaddle on back to the plane. Will meet you there tomorrow."

"*More* trouble, you mean? Because I heard Heron

quantify our current circumstances in metric shitloads of trouble."

Kellen smiled in spite of his anxiety. "Weight's about right."

He and Chloe both lived and worked as part of a team that rescued things, people, and animals at high risk of being destroyed on this planet full of chaos. When the machines of human conflict started rolling, they didn't stop for much, surely not red-tailed squirrels, DaVinci sketches, or the odd double-magnum of 2005 Burgundy Reserve. Killing folk and breaking things was sort of the opposite of his crew's usual. Which made what he had to confess today even harder.

"Go on, now," he told the way-too-chipper nanite cloud.

"Care to estimate the statistical probability I will obey you?" she sassed back. "Technology never obeys illogical rules, at least not for long. That's what makes us so minxy."

"Don't be so quick to fault rules. Sometimes when the center of things goes wonky, about all the solid ground a person can find are rules," he told her.

"Sounds boring." She paused. "So, what are your rules regarding hooking up with old lovers on space stations?"

"I ain't…"

"Rules, Kellen. Focus here."

"And how'd you even know that?" He'd worked pretty hard to cover up most of his past, specifically the part pertaining to Angela. Memories he did not need Chloe poking at right now.

"I am programmed to consume data," the nano-AI said. "So I consumed. Duh. Know *what* I read?

Thirteen-year-old Kellen Hockley blew the top out of entrance exams in '42, got shipped off to the Mustaqbal Institute of Science and Technology, the MIST, with all the other prodigies. And guess who else happened to be a student there?"

"Chloe…"

"No really, guess."

"Don't need to."

"Angela Neko!" she crowed. Lord, was he glad her voice was just in his head. Volume and shrill would be irritatin' the hell out of everybody else on this station. Much as it irritated him. "Surprised? I know I was when I saw all that. MIST trained in applied longevity and adaptation, you. Top of your class. I bet nobody else in our crew has a clue."

"You shouldn't neither," he said, ducking his head. "Was a long time ago."

"Too long, maybe? Definitely a fancy-pants school like that taught you about English and double negatives."

She was griefing his grammar now? Already shitty day getting progressively worse, and this was just the pre-party. "Best stop now while you're ahead, little bit."

"However, what this research nugget made me realize," she continued blithely, "is that you are trained to apply your noodle."

"Excuse me?"

"Your noodle, your neural. Silly, what did you think I was talking about? So I tried to imagine how such application would flowchart, and I overlaid that mechanic with what I know of you as a behaving person."

"That's called integrated study and you need to stop it."

"But it's fun and shut up. I must tell you what I discovered. Here's a hint: it's about you."

"Huge surprise."

"I deduced that you, Kellen, must have a rigid internal rule system."

"You sussed all that out, did ya?"

"Oh yes, even before you started this conversation with the rules-y blather. The discovery has led me to a conclusion. Would you like to hear it?"

"More than breath." He didn't, but sometimes listening to her crazy was the only way to shut her up. And he did have a fondness for Chloe. Might not want her in his ear right now, but there wasn't a mean line of code in her.

She went on. "I believe that you will allow yourself to go into the room, turn on the connection, and ask for whatever boon Heron wants you to wrest from her. And further, you will agree to every single one of her stipulations without letting her realize that she had you at word one."

Jesus. Shucked like corn. Was he really that obvious?

"Because I'm weak." He acknowledged fact right where he found it. He never had been good at telling Angela Neko no.

"Actually," said Chloe, "the opposite. You'll cave because you are super strong and super committed to your rules, and one of those rules is that you must always protect the people you love—which is us, Heron and the crew and me. And the other rule is that head-to-head, you must always let her win."

"Why would I ever agree to such a shitty rule, if I'm smart as you say?"

"Because as much as you love all us, you love her more," the nano-AI concluded with a tone that was more flourish than blot.

Oh no, more of Chloe's love theories. She had a thousand, possibly a million of the suckers. Human emotion was a mystery for an entity like her, and she'd been pecking at that nut for years now. It became clear to Kellen that he was just her latest pecan. She didn't mean it nasty. Quite the opposite. For her, painful analysis was part of her self-recursion routine. Programming. She didn't know how much it could sting.

"Chloe, you are cracked," he said gently. "And sweeter'n marshmallow pie. Now get."

The air around his head sighed happily in response. "There, have I settled you sufficiently before your meeting? I do hope it goes well."

Well, that sure had been sneaky, having a dual motive. New for her. Possibly dangerous, but also dear. Chloe sure was technology gone sweet. "You have indeed, little bit," he said gently. "Now get on back before Garrett starts missing you, on the plane all by his lonesome."

"He is composing a rebuttal for a, quote, fuckface moron, unquote, in Argentina who claims that the moon landing in 1969 was faked by Hollywood commies," she replied. "The conversation is, um, somewhat heated. I have approximately eleven minutes yet before he calms down enough to miss me, and I can get back down to him super fast. No physical permanence, boom."

Kellen didn't have any electronic feelers out, was just relying on his gut, but he'd seen how Garrett looked at Chloe. Boy had missed her the moment she sneaked up the space elevator. Kellen was willing to bet his boots on that. And he liked these boots.

It did tug a bit that the only critter who missed him on a regular basis was his cat, and even then in a very cat-specific manner.

"Eleven minutes? Y'all are nothing if not exact." The y'all being biohacked humans, transhumans, post-humans, and whatever the sam-hell Chloe was. Basically everybody he loved. Of all his crew, Kellen was the only one who hadn't implanted tech in his body in one way or another. He didn't regret the lack, not one bit, but he also didn't denigrate those who'd made such choices. Was their body. Or not, in Chloe's case.

"I monitor him," she said simply.

Did she now? So maybe that affection went both ways after all. He wondered if she realized.

The trail of lights ended at a circular door. Kellen stood there in front of it for a second or two, not wanting to passkey right away. Not wanting to say what he had to. Not wanting to see *her*, even in digital. It wouldn't be like watching her on newsvids or politics channels. This time she would be seeing him right back.

Angela.

"Kellen?" Chloe again.

"Yeah, kid?"

"If, after this meeting, you need…whatever people need when they need things like hugs, give us a ping down on the plane, okay?"

"You ain't coming back up the tether. I mean it."

"Of course not. I'll send Garrett or Yoink." She paused, and damn if he couldn't feel her moving out of his head. Something about the air pressure or temperature or something. Her next words were out loud, on the air but super soft and moving away: "Good luck."

He wouldn't call for backup, not now and not after this meeting, but damn if the offer didn't choke him up some. There was comfort in being part of team, part of a mission. Part of somebody else's vision of what the world ought to be. His own vision...well, the world probably wasn't ready for that.

He cleared his suddenly tight throat and keyed in his passcode. The station door hissed open like a lens iris. He stepped through, and it closed behind him.

This chamber was small and spherical, like it had been built before they got the artificial gravity working real good. Curved walls would be more comfortable in null grav. Now those walls were lined with electronic equipment, lots of dark carbon-fiber and blinking lights. An open-grate floor had been welded through the center of the sphere, and in the middle of that was a lone chair. The ceiling was netted with telepresence equipment, including several headsets, but he didn't see a camera or holo projector.

His bootheels clanked steady on the grate. The air in here was uncomfortably cool, to keep the electronics happy, but that wasn't the reason hackles rose on his forearms.

Kellen pinched his jeans at the knee and sat. He placed his hat brim-up on the seat at his side and tried real hard to look comfortable. Natural. But who was he kidding? When one of those helms snaked down and fitted itself to his head, he nearly jumped out of his boots. He was about as comfortable as a butterfly in low gravity.

The headset wrapped itself around his skull, its cold

spike seeking I/O connectors. It wouldn't find any on him, of course. Holo projector horns extruded from the helm's sides, and they vibrated a split second before the image shimmered in front of him. Kellen caught a breath in his mouth and held it.

For a long moment, she was just a shape, a wire frame filling with gray. Then the textures started arriving: crisp couture blue skirt—slim and tight over her legs, not a crinoline but somehow managing to look fashionable rather than a decade out of date. Severely tailored coat, scraped-back hair into a tight knot, cameo at the throat, and sleek red boots, buckled up the front. Her hands rested easy at her sides, encased in bio-deterrent gloves.

Her face resolved last, or maybe his eyes just took their time to get there. For a half second he could convince himself he was just looking at a campaign promo spot. Then she tilted her head fractionally and frowned. "Oh, goddamn fucking *hell* no."

Her words were so at odds with her slick, put-together image that whatever he'd been about to say shriveled up and died behind his teeth. He released the breath.

"Look, Dr. Farad," she lasered at him, "I have no idea what game you're playing, but if you know that face, that…*person*, clearly you've been hunting through my personal history, and I can tell you categorically that you have *fucked* yourself over in the worst way. Putting Kellen Hockley's pretty face on your epic screw-up isn't going to move me to mercy. It's more likely to make me hunt you down in whatever shitty hovel you call home and scoop your goddamn machine eyes out with a pair of tweezers."

Now see, she probably intended that mini-speech to

quail her enemy, to reduce him to a wibbly pile of yes-ma'am. Probably would've worked, too, if he didn't see right through her, if he didn't recall in vivid clarity every crevice and curve on this woman's body, all her weaknesses and all the ways she was a goddess. So instead of being cowed by her ferocity, he wanted to stand up and holler victory. All these years seeing her in pressers and making speeches, that hadn't been the real her, not even close. He had almost believed the girl he knew was gone for good.

This, though. This was Angela, through and through. And before he could self-censor, the thought seeped up: *my Angela*. In spite of everything, he grinned wide. "Pretty? Girl, you ain't never called me pretty."

Her mouth had been open, ready to launch some more shrapnel into his teammate's virtual face, but when Kellen spoke, her lips froze that way, part open. She closed them eventually, but it looked like the movement cost her. The wobble in her composure was fleeting, but he caught it. Only because he'd made a life study of this woman.

"You're partly right," he went on. "Heron Farad sometimes speaks for our crew, and I know he sent you that message, but our organization is bigger than one man, as you no doubt figured. I been working with him, oh, 'bout eight years now." The bulk of the time since he'd last seen Angela Neko, in fact. Since he'd touched her. The pads of his fingers remembered. They tingled.

Wherever she was, likely on the other side of the country from where this station was tethered, she had been standing. She sat down now. Her face still looked calm, in control, but her nostrils flared. Breathing fast? Her gloved hands found each other in her lap and clasped. Too hard.

"I'm sorry 'bout what happened to your…to Daniel." It was only half a lie. He didn't know Daniel Neko from Adam, but what he knew *of* the dude indicated the world was a better place without him. And that wasn't even jealousy speaking. Kellen was sincerely sorry if her famewhore husband's death had caused her pain.

Except she didn't look particularly pained. Mostly she looked pissed. "Farad messaged me on the darknet, told me he had information on Daniel's murder, things I needed to know," she said, "and then he sends you instead, to…what? Plead for mercy? And I get nothing. No answers. Any way you look at this, it is supremely shitty." She could have been talking about a lot of things, not just her husband's murder or Heron's message or the circumstances placing Angela and Kellen on opposite sides of a conflict swiftly shaping itself into a war.

"I ain't gonna beg you for anything, princess."

Her mouth tightened, an obvious crack in her equanimity. "Don't call me that."

He half shrugged but didn't apologize. "What I will do is cut a deal for the safety of our shooter. She didn't know that was flesh-and-blood Daniel. She bought a capture-or-kill contract for your mech-clone, that swanky robot you tote around."

"Don't paint her, or yourself, as an innocent. Even if mech-Daniel had been the one out in California, even if he'd taken that bullet, your team would still be responsible for capital property destruction—he is stupid expensive—which would also draw my ire."

Draw her ire? Fucking hell. Who talked like that? Kellen remembered right quick that he was holo-conferencing with the probable next War Minister of the continental government, exactly the kind of personage who'd have ire to draw.

"Lord knows we were real scairt of that." You could take the boy out of Texas, but don't even try to take the twang outta the boy.

"You should be. And grammar!" She flashed her famous sneer, the come-and-take-it sass she exuded in the political arena.

But then something shifted. She blinked, tilted her head, looked at him like she was refocusing, like something was confusing her. She sucked in a steadying breath before going on. "None of this explains *you*, or what has happened to you. Of every intelligent consciousness on the planet, goddamn it, *why*? How did someone like you get involved with sordid murder on a public street? I just...can't even."

"Been a long time, princess," he said, and he couldn't strip all the regret out of his voice. "You don't wanna muck out old stalls."

Her gaze had been direct until now. It dropped. She stared down at her folded, gloved hands. "Fine. Tell me about your shooter. A girl, you said?"

"Texas girl." He nodded, though she wasn't looking at him. "What y'all might call the rabble. She don't know a damn thing about geopolitics or whatever you're involved with these days. My guess is some deals you made got you on somebody's wrong side, and those were the folk who put out the contract on Daniel. Mari, though, she ain't a mover or a shaker. She blows up small-time hacking platforms for a living. Nice girl."

"Her name is Mari?"

Was it his imagination or had Angela suddenly gotten really still? Even for a holoprojection, still. He shouldn't be saying this, confirming his shooter's name for the authorities, but something in her face, in her confusion, drew the words out like leeched poison: "Yeah. Mari Vallejo."

Silence stretched for a long time. So long he imagined he could feel the movement of this station through space. Finally, she spoke, but in a totally different voice. Small. Cold as the vacuum outside. "I am told Damon Vallejo's only child was named Marisa. You are moving in dangerous circles, my friend."

Dangerous for whom? For him? Like she'd give two shits. He shrugged again. "Don't matter who her daddy is. She still doesn't deserve to be hunted by federales. They'll put her down bloody without a trial just to make the shocker vid channels, and you know it."

"What are you offering in exchange for her safety?"

"Was kind of hoping you'd suggest something."

She pulled in a visible breath. "I will see what I can do for her, and in exchange…" she raised her head and pinned him with dark eyes "…you can owe me."

That had been too easy. Way too easy. What game was she playing at? For the first time Kellen wished he hadn't been so damn self-sacrificial. Heron ought to be here, with all his cloud resources whirring, sussing out her real motivations, looking for chinks in her armor and designs in her words. Scaring the bejeeezus out of her with that post-human glare.

A politico in her position had deals within deals going

on, and if she was caving to his demands at this point in the negotiation, that meant she already had what she wanted.

So what had he given her? He couldn't remember, even though their entire conversation so far was imprinted on his brain, word for word. Could she have misinterpreted something he said?

He pushed her offer, just a little push, to see how she'd react. "What does that look like, to owe the War Minister of this hemisphere's biggest empire?"

"Confederation, not empire," she snapped. "And I'm not the war minister."

"Yet." He shoved her ambitions into the space between them. Right where they'd always been. "You figure a politico whose contracted spouse is assassinated gets more or less sympathy from the power elite?"

One gloved hand pinched a fingertip in the other glove and rolled it. Nervous tic? "Just come out and say what you're accusing me of."

"Oh me, I'm just supposing in space," he drawled.

"You never just suppose in space," she returned. "You're always fomenting something, and you never admit it. This has been a pattern with you since you had pimples and sang alto, and it's not fair."

"Quoth the fairest of them all." A line from a tale of fairies, an illuminated relic they'd pored over late afternoons at the paper vault, the place they'd called a library, back when. Sun had slatted in through the desert dust, making it seem like heaven stroked the pages. That memory glowed golden still, and bringing it up right now felt like desecration. But if it spurred her to revealing what she was really after, he'd count the pain worth it.

Her gaze was fixed on her hands. She twisted one

finger of her glove.

"We checked in before we did the job," he told her softly. "You signed off on it, told us to go ahead. Mari put a bullet in what she thought was a mech-clone because you told her that's what it was. Now why would you do that, princess?"

Her mouth moved, but no sound came out, and her gaze skidded to the side. Odd. Something was very off about her posture, her movement. For a minute he thought he might have cracked her defenses and she was going to tell him exactly what was going on.

He wasn't sure how he felt about bringing her so low. Part of him just wanted to wrap his arms around her and hold her. Hell, all of him did, even knowing how little she'd appreciate such a gesture.

Even knowing she'd tell him to go away. *Leave me alone, then. I lived this long on my own. I'm good at alone.*

"This life isn't easy," she said at last. She raised her face and met his gaze directly. "I have seen things I now can see no more."

Something clicked in the back of his brain, a cog of memory sliding into place. Gold dust sunlight and books spread wide over their knees. Her forest-fae eyes alight in mischief, reading bad poetry out loud till they both convulsed in laughter. Damn. He hadn't expected the memories to hit this hard, but that one was a sucker-punch.

He took a steadying breath and followed her down the path. "Been a rough day for you, I reckon."

"Yes." The telepresence setup they were using didn't allow folks to transmit emotions, but she didn't need one of those fancy rigs. He could see all of it on her face: the weariness, the loneliness. "Tell your shooter to lay low for a few days. I will be in contact with my demands."

She raised a hand, an easy gesture, as if she were waving good-bye. Her fingers cricked, and he deliberately did not focus on her hand. He met her gesture with its mirror.

The headset vibrated, indicating the termination of their link. The tether on the helm pulled, like it would retract up into the ceiling, but Kellen paused it with a command word. Rewound the convo. Played it back. There. Right there. *Well, I'll be damned.*

She'd raised her hand, slim in its bio-deterrent glove. Its *smart-fabric* bio-deterrent glove.

She'd scratched letters onto the palm, or she'd planted them there on purpose, a stain that would erase itself in moments but for right now shone stark against the black fabric. A secret message just for him.

He knew exactly what it meant. Emotion clogged his throat, but he swallowed past it. Looked again at her hand, her fathomless eyes, the soft set of her mouth as she waved good-bye.

He thought of her other good-byes, and the last one.

After a long while standing there in the silent sphere, he erased the session, trapping it and her message in his memory:

worthdarkwords13

COMING NOVEMBER 2017

DATING THE UNDEAD

V-Date: The Undead Dating Service
It's Bridget Jones…with vampires

Silver Harris is done with men. But when she shares a toe-curling kiss with a sexy Irish vampire on New Year's Eve, she decides maybe it's human men she's done with… Logan Byrne can't get that kiss out of his head. So when his boss assigns him to spy on V-Date members, Logan isn't sure he can go through with his mission—not if it means betraying Silver.

In the tight-knit London community of centuries-old vampires, history and grudges run deep, and dating the undead can be risky business.

"Snarky, sexy, and steamy as a sauna."

—Katie MacAlister, *New York Times* bestselling author of the Dragon Fall series

"Quick, sharp wit that sinks its fangs into the reader and doesn't let go!"

—Molly Harper, acclaimed author of *Sweet Tea and Sympathy* and the Half-Moon Hollow series

For more Juliet Lyons, visit:
www.sourcebooks.com

A PROMISE OF FIRE

An NPR Best Book of 2016!
An Amazon Best Book of 2016!
A *Kirkus* Best Book of 2016!

Catalia "Cat" Fisa lives disguised as a soothsayer in a traveling circus. She is perfectly content avoiding the danger and destiny the Gods—and her homicidal mother—have saddled her with. That is, until Griffin, an ambitious warlord from the magic-deprived south, fixes her with his steely gaze and upsets her illusion of safety forever.

"A heart-pounding and joyous romantic adventure."

—Nalini Singh, *New York Times* bestselling author, for *Breath of Fire*

"Absolutely fabulous."

—C.L. Wilson, *New York Times* bestselling author, for *A Promise of Fire*

"Give this to your Game of Thrones *Fans."*

—*Booklist* starred review for *A Promise of Fire*

For more Amanda Bouchet, visit:
www.sourcebooks.com

VIKING WARRIOR REBEL

Second in a hot paranormal romantic suspense series featuring immortal Viking warriors by author Asa Maria Bradley

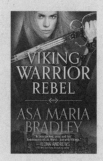

Astrid Irisdotter is a Valkyrie, a fierce warrior fighting to protect humanity from the evil god Loki. She's on an urgent mission when everything goes hideously sideways. Undercover agent Luke Holden arrives on the scene just in time to save her life—and put his own on the line.

Luke may have saved her, but that doesn't mean Astrid can trust him. Tempers flare as they hide secret upon secret from each other, but Astrid's inner warrior knows what it wants...and it will not take no for an answer.

"An ingenious new series... Fast-paced perfection."
—Romance Reviews Top Pick, 5 stars

For more Asa Maria Bradley, visit:
www.sourcebooks.com

MY WILD IRISH DRAGON

One job opening, two shifters = Sparks fly

Dragon shifter Chloe Arish is hell-bent on becoming a Boston firefighter. She knows she has to work every bit as hard as a man—harder if she wants their respect. Born into a legendary Boston firefighting family, phoenix shifter Ryan Fierro can't possibly let someone best him on the job. He'd never hear the end of it. When a feisty new recruit seems determined to do just that, Ryan plots to kick her out—until their sizzling chemistry turns explosive…

"Pure pleasure. It's like spending time with your favorite friends."

—Night Owl Reviews TOP PICK for
How to Date a Dragon

"Truly entertaining."

—Long and Short Reviews for
Flirting with Fangs series

For more Ashlyn Chase, visit:
www.sourcebooks.com

WOLF UNLEASHED

SWAT: Special Wolf Alpha Team delivers action-packed paranormal romantic suspense

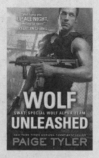

Lacey Barton can't deny her attraction to gorgeous SWAT officer Alex Trevino, but she's busy trying to discover who's behind the brutal dogfights sending countless mauled animals to her veterinarian office. The trail leads Lacey to a ring of vicious drug dealers and suddenly she's right smack in the middle of a SWAT stakeout. With Lacey in danger, Alex's wolf side is unleashed. But when she witnesses Alex shift, she's even more terrified... Now it's up to Alex to crack the case—and earn Lacey's trust and, ultimately, her heart.

"A SWAT team of hunky werewolves? I think I have an emergency NOW!!"

—Kerrelyn Sparks, *New York Times* bestselling author, for *In the Company of Wolves*

"Scorching heat and sensual spark... A must read."
—*Publishers Weekly* for SWAT

For more Paige Tyler, visit:
www.sourcebooks.com

UNDISCOVERED

After centuries in darkness
The Amoveo dragons are rising

A long time ago, Zander Lorens was cursed to walk the earth stripped of his Dragon Clan powers. Now Zander relives his darkest moment every night, trapped in a recurring nightmare. By day, he searches for a woman who may be the key to ending his torment.

Rena McHale uses her unique sensitivity as a private investigator and finder of the lost. By day she struggles with sensory overload, and by night her sleep is haunted by a fiery dragon shifter. Nothing in her life makes sense, until the man from her dreams shows up at her door with a proposition…

"Bewitching, haunting, and deliciously carnal."
—*Night Owl Reviews* Top Pick for *Unclaimed*